I0686079

HUMAN

A NOVEL
BY ROBERT G. BERKE

Human

© 2011, by Robert G. Berke
and MultiModoMedia, Inc.
Los Angeles, California,
All rights reserved

ISBN: 978-0-9849507-0-6
Library of Congress Control Number: 2011963329

Printed in the U.S.A.

DEDICATION

This book is dedicated to the loving memory of all the those who passed during its writing: my father-in-law, Roberto Espinoza, my mother-in-law, Victoria Espinoza-Tejada, my dear friend, Bob Yannetti, and our beloved pet Riley.

The spirits of the departed will always remain connected to those of us who remember them with love. To the extent they have all become a part of me, this book was as much written by them as by anyone else.

ACKNOWLEDGMENTS

There were many, many people whose ideas influenced this story, but special acknowledgment must be made for the cutting edge thinking of Raymond Kurzweil and Jaron Lanier whose ideas about mankind's relationships with technology inspired the ultimate theme of this book.

I must also acknowledge the patience of my beautiful wife and daughters. My wife, the love of my life, Lorena, spent many hours alone without complaint while I was ferreted away in my little office typing sometimes until the early hours of morning.

I have always tried to impress upon my daughters that they should do what they love without exception, and they had to teach that back to me. For that I am forever indebted.

Finally, I must acknowledge my father, Sidney Berke He was the first one to read it and his suggestions made this book much, much better than it was when I first declared it done.

HUMAN

I.

Elijah Smith's overcoat was open and flapping in the wind as he climbed the stairs up to the platform that had been erected in front of the building that bore his name. The sun was bright, but the air was cold. Smith, however, was warmed by the pride he felt that day. This building that he had sketched on a napkin at a bar so many years ago now defined the very skyline of downtown Schenectady. Smith himself was hardy and robust, his cheeks almost as red as the ribbon across the door to the building behind him. The little aches and pains he felt in his arms and legs were still easy for him to dismiss as natural consequences of aging.

His staff had assembled to hear him dedicate the building and representatives from SmithCorp facilities across the globe had flown in to be present for the inauguration of their new flagship building. The Mayor and the City Council were in attendance. Members of the general press were present and he could see the froth of flashes from the cameras that were documenting his every move. Reporters and photographers from the more specialized media outlets -- technology shows, medical journals, science magazines -- had been offered preferential placements nearest to the stage. Placing these lesser known journalists in the most desirable spots from which to document the event was an unveiled nod to those that he considered his brethren in the pursuit of knowledge for the benefit of men. Smith was well known for symbolic gestures of this sort.

The tired looking reporter from the Schenectady Gazette had no photographer, just a notepad. He was not offended at having been placed toward the back of the press area. He really just didn't want to be there at all. He cursed his life and wished he was dead instead of standing in the cold among a crowd of sycophants who all seemed so certain that with wealth came wisdom. Julian Waterstone was too old to believe that anymore. He just wanted to go home.

As Smith approached the podium, he could hear the applause of the spectators. Taking his place at the podium and looking out at the gathered crowd humbled him. All these people had gathered to hear his words, but his passion was not words, it was science. The fact that this passion had ultimately rewarded him with material success meant little to him. He had no children, no wife, no one to leave his vast fortune to. There would be no legacy. The value of his work- the reward that satisfied him- was the recognition that his company was making people's lives better. The fact that the assemblage had greeted his approach to the podium with applause was the only proof he needed that his efforts were appreciated.

He reached into his coat pocket and felt some stiffness

in his elbow as he pulled out his notecards. He blamed it on the cold and on the fact that he hadn't buttoned his coat. He cleared his throat and began.

"Ladies and gentlemen," he started in the only way he knew how, "thank you all for coming. I promise that my remarks will be brief and then we can all go inside and have some hot chocolate. But before we do, I just want to express my gratitude to all of you for being here. I have dedicated my life to science and technology, not for my own self enrichment, but in order to better the lives of people the world over." He paused to let the audience applaud politely before continuing. "As most of you know, in the last 20 years or so, SmithCorp has led the way in technologies to assist doctors in the treatment of serious illnesses, rehabilitative technologies, bio-engineering, genetics, security, and home comfort systems for the critically impaired and much, much more. We have the world's best minds at SmithCorp, engineers, designers, programmers. We now hold more patents than any other company in the U.S., and quite possibly in the world."

There was applause from the audience again, and Smith let the applause run its course before continuing.

"This building," he said, pointing at the highrise behind him, "though it bears my name, is not intended to be a legacy for me. It is a legacy to all of the amazing, creative, and talented people who made SmithCorp what it is today. And so to everyone in the SmithCorp family, I dedicate this gorgeous building to you."

He paused again to allow the applause to pass.

"Let it forever be a beacon for all those who put their faith in technology," he continued, "an altar for all those who know that the ultimate salvation of mankind lies in the pursuit of knowledge. And though its spires point upward, the answers lie right here; not in the unknowable mysteries of the heavens, but in the measurable and quantifiable elements and forces of nature.

"So as I cut this ribbon, do not consider this to be a dedication to cement and glass and steel, but a dedication to what this building represents to me, what all of SmithCorp represents to me: the limitless capacity of men to learn and study and experiment and ultimately bring forth a glorious future for mankind."

As soon us he uttered the last word of that last sentence he reached under the podium and drew out an oversized remote control to cheers and enthusiastic applause. "Mayor?" he asked, looking for a particular face in the crowd. He quickly spotted the familiar face he was seeking and motioned to the Mayor to join him on the stage. "Come on up and join me in the honors!"

The Mayor was all too happy to jump on the stage and wave to the cheering crowd. The Mayor walked to the podium and gave Smith a warm and genuine hug. After all, the construction of this building had already brought hundreds of new jobs to the city and the promise of thousands more.

"On the count of three!" Smith shouted.

The assembled crowd began to count off, "One, Two, Three," and at three the mayor and Mr. Smith, with exaggerated sweeps of their arms, pushed the button on the giant remote control.

A loud crack and a puff of smoke came from the big red ribbon which had been set across the door to the brand new building. The ends of the ribbon blew apart and the doors to the building opened releasing hundreds of balloons into the sky. Mr. Smith and the Mayor turned to leave the stage and lead the crowd inside. Smith stumbled a little on the way down the stairs because his leg had stiffened in mid-stride. *I'll have to get that checked out,* he noted to himself as he quickly regained his balance.

Julian Waterstone also noted the nearly imperceptible stumble and noted on his pad: *Smith looks stiff.*

That day, though many years had passed since then, was the proudest day of Elijah Smith's life. And on that day, he had no doubt in the truth of the words he had spoken. But that was before the number of days yet before him had been quantified. That was before he became trapped in the hospital bed in which he would ultimately die. It was before the wheelchair, and before the walker. It was even before the cane.

As the number of days measuring his life became fewer and fewer, the words he had spoken that day became his own devout petition. He recognized the irony in the fact that his declaration of the supremacy of science was indistinguishable from a prayer. It was a desperate prayer that somewhere, within technology's reach, a procedure or mechanism could be devised that would keep him tethered to the world of the living. It was a prayer that the number of his days did not end at zero.

A desperate mind is capable of superhuman achievement, and Smith's achievements, even before he became desperate, had been exceptional. There are endeavors of such incredible complexity that most people dismiss them as being impossible. Smith was not one of those people. He had spent his entire life dissecting complex endeavors into small component parts and in doing so had repeatedly done what most had believed could not be done. It also made him very, very wealthy.

Smith had the discipline to view his desire to stay alive, even as his body withered, as nothing more than another such complex endeavor. And as he did with any complex endeavor, he had started it on a spreadsheet.

Smith saw the blank sheet before him the way a painter sees a blank canvas. He could envision what the page would look like when he was done. He just had to translate the idea in his head into the columns on the chart. First it would be a sketch with broad concepts and many entries that just wouldn't look right. Finally, it would present a complete picture that made perfectly clear exactly what he wanted.

Just looking at the empty spreadsheet excited him, as it always did. But this time, the excitement had an electricity to it. A spark. A spark that made his whole deteriorating body shake. Six years ago, he wouldn't have noticed that spark, but, as his body began to do nothing but disappoint him, he became more and more fascinated by his consciousness. He had no problem abandoning his body, but he could not bear the thought that his thoughts and feelings would be buried with it.

Smith brushed his hands across the laptop's keyboard, delighting in both the sound and the sensation of his fingers on the keys. Even though his fingers were stiffened from his disease and the pain punctuated his every move, he smiled as the word "MODEL" appeared in the first column of the first row of the spreadsheet, bold and capitalized just as he had envisioned it.

The more he typed the less aware he was of the pain. For a time, he even forgot he was dying. Under the word "MODEL" he watched long lists of words appear on the screen as his fingers translated his ideas into words. Brain, hemispheres, lobes, cells, neurons, nerves, blood vessels. Some of the words became column headings in the spreadsheet and some of the words were grouped together under other words. Finally, his fingers would not move anymore and the pain blurred all of his thoughts. He stopped typing and let his mind wander. *In the beginning there was the word*, he thought, vaguely remembering something he had heard in church as a child.

He had always hated church. He was a man of science and faith seemed antithetical to science. Once you accept something as a matter of faith, that is the end of inquiry. Smith was never satisfied with the "just because" answer he heard so often from religious men. "Take it apart," was what he perceived to by the answer to every problem he encountered. "Take it apart more. Keep breaking it down," he often told his staff when they came to him for advice.

He had never failed to find a needed answer when he had the patience and resources to strip things down to their bare essentials. Even as a child he would disassemble his toys until he understood exactly how they worked. Once he knew how they worked, he could easily put them back together and sometimes even make them better. As he grew, he learned that the same principles that applied to his toys also applied to plastic models, fast cars, powerful computers, and ultimately even to the acquisition of wealth.

He had often proved the theory that once it could be understood how the smallest elements of any system work together, even the most complex system becomes simple. He attributed his success in all of his business and scientific endeavors to this belief.

As he rested his hands and contemplated the words and columns on the computer screen before him, he remembered the first project that had earned him international attention. When he was in graduate school, the stumbling block in robotics was to program a robot to go into the woods and build a simple structure, a bird's nest was the usual example, from the available materials. The task was seemingly impossible since the robot would have to recognize random items not for what they were, but for what they could be.

Two schools of thought prevailed and the answer seemed to be in some combination of the two. The "bottom-up" approach involved programming the robot with as much factual information as possible so that the robot could "look" at an item, compare it to a database of information, define the item according its qualities, and use the item in a manner consistent with its definition. This thing is brown, slender, porous, and has such and such a density. Therefore, it is an oak branch. An oak branch can be used for this or that defined set of tasks.

The second school of thought defined itself as the "top-down" approach. Rather than creating a database comprising a virtually infinite set of definitions, the "top-down" programmers created algorithms by which the robot could learn by experience and observation, in effect building its own database of knowledge as it gathered information about its environment.

Smith was not a student of robotics. He was a student of biology. He figured that the task required thought rather than programming. At the time neuroscience could not explain "thought", but biology could see all of the different elements of a brain capable of thought. His insight was to build the brain from scratch. Not a physical brain, but a virtual one. He used the brain of a European Quail. Each cell in the Quail's brain was already mapped and described in everything from chemical composition to electrical discharge. Smith took the existing data and created a computer simulation of each cell. He then began situating the simulated cells according to their arrangement in the biological brain. He simulated blood flow, oxygen use, electricity, protein bonding, and everything else that was observed to happen in a quail's brain. His theory was that by copying all of the measurable parts of the quail's brain he would have a machine that displayed quail behaviors-- including nest building.

The university could not fund the project to completion, but the theory itself put Smith in the spotlight for a while and he knew that one day he would try again.

Now the word "model" had replaced the word "simulation" in his thinking and the word "model" glowed in bold type in the upper left hand corner of his computer screen. He rubbed his aching hands. "Model" was the better word, he thought. His project was about an artificial brain. A working model of a human brain. The word "model" explained the difference between his project and an artificial intelligence project far better than the word "simulation".

Artificial intelligence is about programming a computer to do what a human brain does. It is about creating an instruction set which can emulate a brain. Smith had more respect for the brain than that. He reasoned that a computer could not be "programmed" to do what a human brain does, because a human brain can react to seemingly infinite inputs and process a seemingly infinite number of variables. Given an eternity and all the programmer's in the world, no computer could be ever programmed to process so much information among so many criteria as the human brain does in a nano-second. Infinity, even if only just an illusion, was an obvious problem.

But, although measuring in the billions, or even trillions, modeling each measurable component of the brain and ascribing a set of values and functions to each part certainly fell within the realm of human capacity. Creating a model of the human brain was a finite endeavor. In theory, by replicating the human brain, the mind too would be replicated.

He knew that he would have to map out his strategy before he would lose his ability to communicate just as he had already lost his ability to walk.

When his body started to fail, his home was transformed into a medical facility. When he first stopped walking on his own, he could still wheel himself to the elevator to reach the upper stories of his mansion. When he became confined to bed, his entire world shrunk to the size of his living room. Though his living room was huge by any standard, he hated living so confined to such a small space. He found it ironic that he was already formulating a plan to make his entire universe smaller than this one room. The furniture was replaced with two beds and numerous medical machines. One of the beds was Smith's electric hospital bed. The second was a bed for his live-in nurse, Hermelinda Posada, who treated him gently and never left his side.

The sicker he got the fewer people came to visit. Rather than resent those who did not come, he grew more and more attached to and dependent on those who still did come. He had long ago decided that he was madly in love with Hermelinda, and he correctly read her devotion to him as a reciprocation of that love.

Myra Shiltz was another frequent visitor. She had been his personal assistant for nearly ten years. He had barely noticed her until he became less and less able to conduct his affairs on his own. Now he recognized and genuinely appreciated her ability to anticipate his needs and carry out his instructions-- the same qualities which had made her virtually unnoticeable to him in the past. Now, she was truly just an extension of himself. His staff saw her as an extension of him too. Because of that Myra was able to control office affairs even with Smith gone. Smith once quipped that because of Myra he could be dead for five years before anyone at the office would notice. He trusted her completely notwithstanding the fact that he had no other choice.

Alice, his night nurse, kept watch over Smith when Hermelinda couldn't. Even though Hermelinda was there most of the time, she had to watch the monitors while Hermelinda slept. She was a cheerful, middle-aged Filipina.

She habitually updated Smith with the latest celebrity gossip. Though he had no interest in news of the latest Hollywood breakup, her lightheartedness gave Smith a special cheer and he always listened to her stories intently. Almost every week she would bring fresh fruits and vegetables from her own garden for Hermelinda to enjoy or to juice for Smith.

After Alice, his most frequent visitor was Dr. Bayron, his co-conspirator in the artificial brain project. Smith particularly enjoyed Dr. Bayron's visits. He felt they spoke a language that no one else quite understood. Not just the language of science, but another language known only to them that grew out of their still-secret project.

He also got occasional visits from Sam Takahashi, an old childhood friend and Smith's personal lawyer. Sam's visits began to taper off when Smith could no longer raise a glass and enjoy a drink. Sam was a famous alcoholic whose benders were legendary. Smith did not fault him for not wanting to spend good drinking hours entertaining a dying man. Smith once explained to Hermelinda, when he was still strong enough to hold full conversations, that in life a man will have very few friends he can call to pick him up in a strange city in the middle of the night with no questions asked, and that Takahashi was that friend to him. "We know each other for over 50 years," Smith assured her, "he'll be here when I need him, and no one will be able to keep him away".

The two beds in what had been the living room were close together. They had not started that way though. Smith had instructed the furniture movers to place the beds on opposite sides of the room so that Hermelinda could have some sense of privacy and personal space even though she had to be in sight of her patient. After just a few weeks of sleeping on opposite sides of the room, Hermelinda pushed her bed across the room right next to Smith's bed. She said she was tired of having to walk across the room every time Smith or one of his machines needed attention, but Smith thought, correctly, that she just liked being near him. Sometimes, when it didn't hurt too much, he would reach over to her bed and stroke her hair. She seemed to make a purring noise whenever he did so.

She did not make an excuse when she stopped sleeping in her own bed altogether and began climbing into his.

Smith liked having her close at night. He could smell her and she smelled nice, a little like roses, a little like jasmine, and a little like ... coconut? The smell made him feel safe. He wished that his body still worked well enough to be able to make love to her, but that function was one of the first to fail on his now almost completely useless body.

On a bright Monday morning Myra arrived, promptly, as usual, at 9 a.m. "Good morning, Mr. Smith," Myra said as she pulled a chair up close to his bed.

"Okay, okay everything hurts today, so let's just move the ball forward as much as possible before Hermelinda drugs me up and puts me out."

"Alright. We actually got a lot accomplished," she said. "With the additional staff and processing capacity, Dr. Bayron has changed his time estimate to one more year."

"Doesn't that son-of-a-bitch know I'm dying *now*? What the hell else does he need?'" Smith began to move his arms as he said this in an effort to emphasize his point, but the pain that showed in his face as he tried to move his arms made the point for him.

"Relax, relax, relax..." Myra said looking to Hermelinda to see if she was at all concerned by Smith's outburst. And in fact, when she looked at Hermelinda she saw Hermelinda looking at the monitor near Smith's bed. The two women smiled at each other, each recognizing that they shared the same concern for the man in the bed. Smith relaxed, so Myra continued, "There's more."

Smith had noticed the glance between the only two women in his life and forgot what had angered him in the first place. "Dr. Bayron has been in contact with a Russian research team at the St. Petersberg Neurological Institute who are also modeling a human brain," Myra continued. "They want to collaborate. Dr. Bayron told me to tell you that these guys already have a complete model of a hypothalamus and are well underway with the hippocampus. He said that combined with what he's gotten done, we could have a complete model in just about six weeks."

"That was not my plan. I am very concerned about that," said Smith.

"I'll get him on the web-cam right now." She said as she pulled her laptop from her bag. She pressed a few buttons on her computer and the lights in the room went dim as a large display mounted to the wall lit up with an image of Myra's desktop wallpaper of a sunset over the ocean. Myra adjusted a small webcam on Smith's notebook computer until his image appeared in the upper right hand corner of the screen. Moments later another image filled the remainder of the screen: the image of Dr. Bayron, a frayed, black spiral notebook on his desk in front of him.

Every time she saw him, Myra noticed new details about Dr. Bayron's transformation since he first began working with Smith. When she first met him, he was tall, dark, and handsome. A quiet and mysterious stranger of the sort she would have liked to have swept her off her feet. But under Smith's crushing demands, he had largely stopped taking care of himself. His face had begun to sag for lack of sleep. His movements became listless due to lack of exercise, his hair unruly for want of a haircut, and his posture stooped from too many hours hunched over a microscope.

No one in their right mind would sacrifice so much of his own life for his employer, not even someone paid as handsomely as Dr. Bayron. But Myra knew that Dr. Bayron shared her employer's obsession.

Smith spoke first. "Can you hear me?"

"Yeah. You got the news?"

"I did."

"Well, what do you think?" Bayron asked.

"Russians, my friend?" Smith asked incredulously. "I'm definitely going to want more facts."

"Like what?"

"Don't play dumb with me Bayron. You know I'm not giving you these obscene amounts of money to model any old brain. I want a model of *my* brain."

"I know that, but I also know time is running out. Look, I don't even know if their code is useful. It could be complete crap for all I know. Just authorize the information sharing for now. It costs you nothing and we may be able to speed our process by studying theirs. I think you need to give me a little latitude on this. Trust me, if I don't need it, I won't use it."

"It's your code, Doc. If you want to share it, that's your prerogative. Just don't go mixing up my brain with someone else's. You don't want to go creating a Frankenstein. But if I were you, I'd speak with legal before letting anything out of that lab. Between your time and my money, it's got to be worth an awful lot."

"If I thought the way you did I'd be richer than you." Bayron quipped. "I'll call legal in the morning."

Myra piped in, "Should he call in-house legal, or should he call Takahashi?"

"Nah," Smith said, "Keep this in house. Takahashi hates paperwork. I'll tell Takahashi in my own way. Bob Hanover in legal handles the intellectual property and patents. Give Bayron Hanover's extension. Someone in-house should know what we're doing anyway."

A short but clear silence followed as Bayron and Myra contemplated the fact that the project had been kept strictly need-to-know until this time.

Smith broke the silence himself, "...and don't forget to upload your progress to me." The instruction was completely unnecessary.

"Don't micromanage me Smith." Bayron said with a smile.

"Hey, remember, I'm the rich one. Don't tell me how to do my job." They both laughed. But the pain from the laughter cut Smith's chuckle short. He winced and lost his breath. Hermelinda came rushing to the bedside. Bayron opened the notebook on his desk and wrote some shorthand notes.

"I'll call you later with that number," Myra said into the webcam and then abruptly terminated the conference to give Hermelinda space to tend to her patient.

It was evident to both Myra and Hermelinda that Smith always enjoyed his conversations with Bayron. Bayron was smart, personable, and driven. But he especially liked talking to Bayron about the project. They had their own language for discussing the things which just a few months ago had been nameless and virtually unimaginable. That lexicon was a natural part of many of their conversations. Sometimes, when talking to Bayron, Smith felt like a visitor in a foreign country who finally hears his native tongue and at once feels -- even if just for a moment -- home.

"Hermelinda," Smith called out her name as loud as he could, even though she was right next to him, "be a dear and give me some morphine. My neck hurts."

In another part of the world, another man was also in pain, and he cursed his pain. He had suffered a life of ugly and difficult work and, in his own opinion, he had earned his pain and had also earned the right to curse it. He was not the unfortunate recipient of some unfortunate disease that chose its victims, like Smith, at random. He had pain in his hands and fingers and he accepted that he deserved that pain for having used his hands in horrible ways. He could not remember how many times he splinted his own broken fingers or dressed his own wounds when proper medical care was not an option.

He rubbed a medicated menthol gel into his twisted, arthritic, and abused fingers and as he did so, each irregularity that he could feel in his bones brought back memories of a time when he was young and an intolerance for pain seemed to be a luxury afforded only to the old and the weak. A dent below the second knuckle on his left hand reminded him that some doors are made out of steel and cannot be punched through. The lump that had never fully healed on his right hand taught him that sometimes the person holding the gun is at a disadvantage in close combat. That lesson had nearly cost him his trigger finger, which snapped back and practically broke off when an American tried to kick the gun out of his hand. His scars, both internal and external, were the only medals one could earn in his line of work, and he cherished them, even as he cursed them.

The fingers on his left hand still moved reasonably well, but the fingers on his right hand hardly moved at all anymore. This made it difficult for him to open the child-proof lid on his extra-strength Tylenol. He poured four Tylenol into his huge but barely functioning right hand and tossed all four into his mouth, washing them down with a large belt of Imperia Vodka straight from the bottle.

Vladimir Vakhrusheva had successfully adapted the skills that he had learned and perfected for the benefit of a now-defunct government to the new free-market economy which now dominated northern Asia. He had learned quickly that those skills were exceedingly valuable to his new, powerful, entrepreneurial benefactors. But still, the only mark of his success in Russia's post-perestroika free-for-all, was his rather quick transition from cheap Polish potato vodka to the finest quartz-filtered, Imperia Vodka made from the rarest wheat according to Mendeleev's original formula.

II.

Dr. Douglas Bayron was also a fan of Mendeleev. In fact, he kept a large poster of the periodic table hanging in his lab. It was something of a totem for him--a source to trace all of his understandings of the world back to. It was a daily reminder that all things, no matter how complex, were merely amalgamations of simpler things. It reminded him that there is simply no limit to the number of simple things there are in the world. It inspired his belief that all things in nature had orders and values and properties waiting to be discovered.

Myra had noticed that Dr. Bayron had changed since starting the project, but she did not realize that he had grown to look something like Mendeleev too. To her, it seemed that he had become a caricature of sorts-- a mad-scientist whose drive and intensity blinded him to even the face he saw in the mirror.

His lab, however, was meticulously maintained and orderly. It consisted of ten thousand square feet of highrise office space. One thousand square feet was fully occupied by the processors, servers, and RISC arrays that had already modeled billions of human brain cells in three dimensions. Another one thousand square feet was dedicated to high-speed, high density, data storage which long ago had exceeded one thousand petabytes making Bayron and his staff part of a very small group of people throughout the world to use the word "exabyte" on a daily basis.

Another three-thousand square feet was inartfully referred to as the sausage factory. It was in this portion of the lab, divided into twenty-five grey cubicles, that some of the most skilled renderers in the country sat, day in and day out, assigning attributes to each identifiable component on the detailed, three-dimensional MRI of Smith's brain.

The remainder of the space included conferencing facilities, Bayron's personal office, an engineering and fabricating lab, and a combination examination, operating, and recovery room, which was nicknamed, "the infirmary". On Smith's instruction, Myra had relocated all of the other offices that had been on the same floor as the lab to other floors so that the lab could be quickly and easily expanded as necessary.

Dr. Bayron, applying the theories of co-relational/oppositional holographic memory and processing which had won him a doctorate many years ago, spent most of his time assigning attributes to the empty spaces in between the cells which his assistants had successfully rendered. Those empty spaces used to be called "nothing" until science gave lie to that description.

As a research scientist at MIT, a young Dr. Bayron, barely 24 years old, had posited the theory that the higher functions of the mind, emotions, abstract reasoning, synesthetic sensory convergence (the ability to "taste" a steak immediately upon hearing it sizzle on a grill, for instance), all occurred in the empty spaces of the brain in which the invisible forces of nature like relative gravity and micromagnetic pulls operated to process non-linear, non-binary information instantaneously.

When the scientists operating the Large Hadron Collider at CERN discovered that empty space actually has some measurable mass, Bayron postulated that those empty spaces suddenly had to be considered as a part of the substance of the brain itself. Overnight, Bayron's theory had become a genuine hypothesis.

To test his hypothesis, Bayron wanted to model the brain of a European Quail, the least complex full brain in the animal kingdom. He wrote a grant proposal asking for a huge sum of money to fund his research. He was surprised when he received a call from the research director at SmithCorp. SmithCorp would fund the research, but not at the amount requested. It wouldn't be necessary, the director said, because the brain of the European quail had been thoroughly mapped and modeled, by none other than Elijah Smith himself. Smith had a very personal interest in this project, the director said, as years of research had been expended unsuccessfully trying to get the Smith model to work. As perfect as the model was, the computer never became a Quail. Not only couldn't the computer build a nest, it didn't even produce patterned data. But Smith himself personally believed that Bayron's theory was the key. And so, with the financial support of his unexpected benefactor, Bayron started assigning properties to the empty spaces. Everything he could learn about the properties of nothingness were added to the model. When the CERN scientists discovered there were actually many different kinds of nothingness, each with their own properties, Bayron's model became more complex. The more the CERN scientists learned about the nature of empty space, the larger Bayron's model grew.

One day, like magic, the model spewed out a pattern. It was definitely a pattern. When the data was plotted, there was the clear image of an oscilloscopic wave. Dr. Bayron, like Archimedes bolting from his legendary tub, ran to the audio lab waving his printout at the technicians. "Produce this sound for me!" he yelled at the first technician he saw. "Do it, do it!"

The technician scanned the wave diagram into his computer, pressed a few keys and turned up the volume on a speaker. A moment later, they all heard a clear sound:

"Chirp".

"What the hell is that?" The technician asked.

"It's a god damn European Quail!" Bayron shouted.

In retrospect, he wished he had just said, "Eureka."

After celebrating the almost magical chirp with his research team, Bayron made a phone call to the research director at SmithCorp. After explaining his result, the research director put him on hold. He was barely on hold for 10 seconds when a louder, different voice, came from the phone.

"Douglas Bayron?" The voice said. "Elly Smith."

Bayron, by virtue of some unknown instinct, stood up when he realized who he was speaking with. "Yes sir. I trust you've heard we got affirmative results?"

"I had no doubt, Bayron," Smith said, "I am not in the habit of betting on losers. But this is just proof of concept, you understand. Let me tell you what I really want."

When Smith offered Bayron the opportunity to model a human brain, Bayron jumped. The promise of unlimited resources and huge pay were appreciated, but were hardly necessary.

And so it was the European Quail that brought these

two men together.

Bayron protected his empty spaces. They were his. He didn't let anyone else at SmithCorp work on the empty spaces. He guarded them jealously; that's where the magic lay. He filled most of his black spiral notebook with the properties of the various types of nothingness that he identified in the model he was creating of Smith's brain. The pipes and tubes, neurons and arteries and the chemicals that drive the apparatus - all the quantifiable aspects: that work could be done by his assistants most of whom were really just highly educated technicians and mechanics. Myra called them the trained monkeys. But the magic he kept for himself in the bound pages of his spiral book.

Bayron did not think of his rendering staff quite as contemptuously as Myra, but he never let them near the empty spaces. Those were all his.

Besides the fact that they were intellectual blood brothers connected through the European Quail, another major reason that Bayron had signed on with Smith was because Smith was adamant about modeling the brain from scratch. Smith wanted the project started from scratch because he only cared to have a model made of his own brain. Bayron, on the other hand, wanted to start from scratch because no other human brain modeling project had been commenced with a data system that permitted the assignation of attributes to his beloved empty spaces. That is, no other human brain modeling project other than his and that of a particular team in Russia that had let him know they were modeling according to his own theories.

At first Bayron justified his decision to share his data with the Russians by telling himself he just wanted to see their data. He wanted to observe their processes to perhaps help him improve his. He hadn't intended to cheat his friend by using the forbidden Russian hypothalamus. But just to look would be no harm.

The arrival of the Russian model made a memorable impression when Bayron signed for it just a few days later. Few people in the world have ever had to consider how much physical storage media all of the specifications of a single human brain would take up when translated in into bits and bytes. At well over 100 petabytes, electronically sending the data for the hypothalamus alone would take days or even weeks. And so, the Russian model was burned onto plain old consumer grade blu-rays (thousands of them), put in boxes, and mailed. The number of boxes in which the disks arrived was a testament to the incredible efficiency of the biological brain.

When he was very young, Bayron had read the story of Flat Stanley, a little boy who was able to fold himself up and mail himself in an envelope.

Opening the first box made Bayron remember that story. Here he was opening a box containing, at least in concept, an actual person, with all of that person's loves and hates and desires and idiosyncrasies. Was it any more farfetched to think that the essence of self could be contained within a gooey mass of brain than in a cheap, Russian, cardboard box?

Atop the thousands of disks was a letter addressed to Dr. Bayron from Dr. Vadi Petrovsky of the St. Petersberg Neurological Institute, the large SPNI emblem splayed across the top.

"Dear Dr. Bayron," the letter began in excellent English which soon deteriorated into not-too-bad English-as-a-second-language. "It is with great pleasure that we look forward to beginning our great collaboration. Unlike your subject, we modeled according to the brain of healthy, 30 year old subject. You will find detail in attachments. Subject was also predeceased of our study so invasive technique was possible and employed. We have set up collaboration website secure server at SPNI.RU/Petrovsky/collaborations/us/3dmodeling where you will find all technical and esoteric information as well as anecdotal and narrative."

The letter was signed, in a friendly scrawl, "Dr. Vadi."

Bayron made a mental note to try to find out what Russian-to-English dictionary Dr. Petrovsky was using as words like esoteric and anecdotal were clearly not of the meanings Bayron believed Petrovsky to have intended.

Petrovsky gave no name for the "healthy" but "predeceased" 30 year old Russian subject, so Bayron decided to name him Stanley after Flat Stanley from the story. If Stanley was healthy, he wondered, why was he dead? He considered, of course, the possibility that Stanley had died from corporeal trauma or penal execution. In any event, as long as the brain was healthy, it didn't really matter. At least not to Bayron.

Bayron removed the disk which was marked 1/6575 and put it in his optical drive. A message box appeared on Bayron's computer screen: "This disk contains compressed data in tarball.gzip format. Please confirm unarchiving mode."

A few keystrokes later Bayron was looking at a page of data. He would have to read the documentation to make the data meaningful. He would assign that task to a team member. Someone who spoke Russian would probably be a good choice. He made a note in his notebook.

Over the years that the disease progressed, Smith had ultimately grown so weak that he could hardly be heard. Often he typed his thoughts into the computer and communicated through instant messages even with people just a few feet away from him.

Hermelinda tried to give him a little exercise everyday, but the weaker he grew the less it helped. She would stretch him, turn him, and massage him. She diligently did everything she possibly could to keep his blood flowing, prevent muscle attrition, and prevent bedsores. Every morning she would clean him head to toe and dress him neatly. As time went on and he was less able to control his limbs it felt to her as if she were dressing a doll. But she kept him clean and well groomed so that he could retain some small level of dignity. It was a battle she had been losing.

Myra eventually stopped coming to receive Smith's instructions in person. The last time she had come his voice was so weak that Myra needed Hermelinda's help to hear what he was saying. With the IV feeding units, a vital signs monitor, and a breathing machine surrounding his bed, Myra couldn't get close enough to hear. Hermelinda, on the other hand, climbed right into his bed and put her ear up to his lips.

Hermelinda, lying in bed next to the emaciated, almost-corpse, of Elijah Smith, repeated his words to Myra, "If I do not survive, or if a Court declares me dead, or if anything of that sort happens, you will receive an envelope from Takahashi transferring all of the stock in the Smith companies to a charitable trust. The salaried trustees of that trust are to be you, Hermelinda, Dr. Bayron and Takahashi." Smith stopped talking and Hermelinda began to get out of the bed. As she started to rise, he began speaking again. "I tried to move my finger to type," he said, "but I couldn't. My central nervous system is shutting down. I need Bayron here." Smith's eyes closed and he was asleep, exhausted from the few moments of speaking.

As Myra left the mansion and walked into the sunlight, she realized she had tears in her eyes. She reassured herself that it was okay to cry. Mr. Smith was her employer, but she had worked for him for so long that at some point he had graduated from being a mentor and teacher to something of a surrogate father. She knew she wasn't going to be able to hold back her tears. He was dying. Were she, his nurse, his doctor and his lawyer the only people on the planet he cared about? Were they really his only inner circle, she wondered. She dialed Dr. Bayron from her cellphone as she walked to her car.

It had been several weeks since Bayron had last visited Smith's home. The last time he was there it was to get new images of Smith's prefrontal cortex at various cognitive states. "Think about bunnies." Snap. "What's two plus two?" Snap. The prefrontal cortex was where the left brain's empiricism reconciled with the right brain's desire for uncertainty to create what laymen call a personality. The questions he asked varied from complex to absurd. Smith understood that the more questions he asked, the better Bayron could model this mysterious part of the brain. The more empirical data he could gather, the better he could formulate an algorithm to interpolate functions that he was unable to observe. But that had begun month's ago, when Smith's voice was still loud enough to be heard. Hermelinda remembered the two men, doctor and patient, sitting together for hours, laughing and chatting, and she remembered how gentle and charming Smith's smile was.

In the months since that data gathering mission (during which Bayron came to know more about Smith than one man should ever know about another), Bayron had completed an almost cell by cell perfect model of Smith's prefontal cortex and assigned attributes to all of them and his beloved empty spaces in between.

He could never have completed the task had it not been for Stanley, the Russian model. Because Stanley was "predeceased", the Russians were able to cut away the cells to view them in three dimensions. Thus they were able to measure things that could not be measured in living tissue. Bayron had kept his promise to Smith and didn't use the Russian model for anything he was able to glean from the images of Smith's own brain. He only used it for those things that were missing. It saved him what could have been years of guesswork, trial, and error.

Bayron arrived at the mansion less than an hour after receiving Myra's call.

Now, on this visit to Smith's house, Bayron had something no one else in the world had: a detailed, and quite possibly functional, model of a human prefrontal cortex. If the model was perfect, it would contain Smith's entire personality. Other parts of the brain, are largely about data storage and data processing, but who a person *is* takes place in the prefontal cortex, Bayron explained.

Smith barely looked alive to Bayron. He was neither moving nor speaking. Bayron skipped the usual niceties and started the meeting with a series of tests and measurements. Smith's prefontal cortex was still functioning perfectly well. Even though barely able to move or speak, Smith still managed to make clear when he was happy, sad, agitated and so on.

His memory, however, was not faring quite so well and this concerned him. Everything he could remember of his life, his childhood, his experiences, likes, loves and annoyances-had already been recorded. Even the progress of his disease. This is why he asked Myra to send for Dr. Bayron.

"He looks terrible." Bayron whispered to Hermelinda, cognizant of the fact that Smith ears were probably functioning fine and the human being was still present, even if stuck in a useless body.

"Everything is starting to shut down," said Hermelinda. "He still tries to work...but..."

"I've been monitoring his charts and vital signs from the lab, Hermelinda. I know it's not good. So does he."

"I read him the Wall Street Journal every day. Cover to cover..." Hermelinda said. Bayron knew that she had grown very close to Smith and that Smith had grown very close to her-- after all, he had modeled Smith's prefrontal cortex. There were no secrets he didn't know. He actually knew a little bit more about Elijah Smith than Elijah Smith knew about himself. He knew Hermelinda loved him and that he loved her–just the kind of information an outside observer might know long before the participants. After all, what else could she have possibly meant by, "I read him the Wall Street Journal every day"?

She could have cried if she wanted, Bayron thought. There was no need to hold back. Soon Smith would be a living, but purely technological entity. His body, though, would actually die. In a few years the world would know that the death of the flesh does not equal the death of a person. Until people could accept that fact (or soon to be fact) the death of the body was still as good a time for tears as any. He tried to remember the last time he had cried. And he did. It was when he threw a shovelful of dirt over a tiny coffin and he never cried again.

Hermelinda led Dr. Bayron to Smith's bedside and gently wiped a little spit off of Smith's chin with a soft cloth. Smith grunted when he saw Bayron. Bayron bent down close to Smith's mouth to hear. Smith struggled to speak and all that came out was a grunting whisper. "It's time," was all Bayron needed to hear.

In a matter of hours Smith's living room had become a beehive of activity. Hermelinda sat on the edge of Smith's bed and propped Smith's head on her lap so he could watch all the goings-on. She knew he wanted to see. She had developed a special sense for his needs and wants.

Several boxes of Smith's personal belongings were being carted out of his room under Dr. Bayron's watchful eye. Medical equipment, monitors, machinery, books, clothes, and records. Smith saw his laptop computer placed in a box by a beef-handed stranger and for the first time in his life he felt helpless.

He wanted to say, "Hey! Careful with that!" But he couldn't. He knew he had no power to exert control over what was going on. Everything was in Bayron's hands now. *This*, he thought, *is trust*.

As if reading his thoughts, Hermelinda squeezed his hand in hers, raised it to her lips, and gave it a reassuring kiss. Smith had never married. He regretted that. If he were still young and healthy, he would want a wife just like Hermelinda. When she was near, he knew everything was going to be okay.

Dr. Bayron came to the bedside and sat on a small stool so that he was eye-to-eye with Smith.

Bayron leaned in close and spoke softly. "I'm going to sedate you for the move," he said, "but you will need to be conscious for the surgery."

Smith smiled the best that he could. He hoped Bayron understood that the smile meant: "I trust you my friend. I trust you not to let anything bad happen to me."

Bayron nodded, and Smith felt confident that Bayron had understood.

Bayron continued, "The first surgery will have the artificial brain take over your involuntary muscle functions. Your breathing, reflexes, and heartbeat will all be controlled from the brain we modeled from your brain.

"To do this I will be physically removing a small piece of your biological brain. As you know this procedure is irreversible, but, should the artificial brain fail to work or fail to work immediately, these functions can be accomplished mechanically with a pacemaker and a respirator. If the model functions properly... well... we'd be the first..." Bayron looked for some reassurance from Smith, but all he could read on Smith's face was pain. He and Smith had reviewed the plans, the contingency plans, and the contingency-contingency plans over and over and over. Neither he nor Smith needed any reassurances. They were both men of science, after all. They knew the risks.

By replacing one small discreet piece of Smith's brain at a time with technology and letting those technological parts get used to performing their functions in conjunction with the remaining biological brain, they would have the best chance of ensuring Smith's survival during the transition.

"So let's just do it already," Bayron said as he injected the sedative into Smith's arm.

Smith awoke, he did not know how much later, in strange surroundings. It had been so long since he had been out of his home, that he could barely believe his eyes.

But soon he recognized some familiar things about his new location. The narrow, slightly grey windows, the unusually thick floor moldings, a particular scent in the air- like a caricature of pine- which at once brought on a flood of memories which he believed had been lost forever. He knew he was in the SmithCorp Building. Naming the building for himself was his first effort at immortality. Even if he would not be remembered for his accomplishments in science and industry, he would be remembered by this building for sure. The building would always be big, strong, warm, and confident.

He could no longer turn his head to inspect the details of his surroundings, but being able to move his eyes was sufficient for him to ascertain that he was in a makeshift hospital room. He could hear the familiar bleeps and blips of the vitals signs monitor that had been like a conjoined twin for at least a year and it gave him comfort. It was a constant, objective assurance to him that he had not, in fact, passed away.

He had barely oriented himself to this new, yet familiar, place when Hermelinda walked in. She said, not asked, but said, "How are you today, sleepyhead?" She knew he couldn't answer, yet somehow she could tell he was happy. That made her feel good too. "Welcome to the infirmary," she said. "We tried to make it nice, but we also had to bring in a lot of equipment. This place is as well equipped as the best hospitals in the world. This is our home for the next few months, I guess."

Smith was having trouble understanding everything he heard. Somewhere between his ears and his mind, little bits of information were getting lost. But he heard her say, "our home," and that sounded nice to him.

"Takahashi came by, but Dr. Bayron won't let him in. He said he just wanted you to know he was here for you." Hermelinda whispered in Smith's ear as she leaned over to adjust his pillow. "He and Myra are waiting in your old office. They both said they won't leave until they know your alright." She touched his freshly shaved scalp. "I already have you prepped," she continued. "Dr. Bayron doesn't want to waste any time. He's going to give you the local anesthetic in just a minute."

She noticed a far away look on Smith's face. "Mr. Smith? Are you in there?" It was the first time that Hermelinda had felt that, maybe, just maybe, Smith wasn't completely present. He seemed far away. Maybe lost. She brushed the feeling aside. After all the man was just moments away from having a piece of his brain replaced by an unproven technology.

Dr. Bayron came in wearing surgical scrubs. Hermelinda realized that she had never seen Dr. Bayron in surgical scrubs. Seeing Dr. Bayron looking like a real surgeon signaled to Hermelinda that it was time to start acting like a real nurse. She quickly, and without personality or fanfare, recited Smith's vital sign measurements to Bayron. Bayron's response, "Thank you, nurse," clarified that their long, cordial acquaintanceship would not be permitted to interfere with the consummate professionalism demanded by the circumstances.

Bayron then addressed Smith. Hermelinda noticed that Smith appeared to have come back from wherever his mind had taken him and that he seemed to be fully engaged in listening to Bayron. "I'm going to apply a topical anesthetic to your scalp. Then, once the skin is desensitized, I'll inject a local anesthetic beneath the skin. Once the anesthetic has the opportunity to start working, I'm going to drill six holes in your skull. This won't hurt, but the sound of the drill is likely to alarm you, so I'll be getting you high as a kite without letting you fall asleep. Blink rapidly if you feel any pain." Bayron continued to recite, as if it were a mantra, the order of operations.

"Now the only thing we're doing today," Bayron continued unnecessarily, "is turning over your involuntary muscle movements to the new brain so we can keep your body functioning until we move you out of it."

Smith could tell that Bayron had been over the procedure, both mentally and in simulations, hundreds, maybe thousands of times. This made him feel secure.

The entire surgery barely took two hours. Throughout the procedure, Smith had waking dreams about butterflies, rainbows, and flowers. He only felt pain once and began blinking his eyes. Bayron noticed the activity and explained that the pain was because his heart had stopped momentarily as he switched control of it from Smith's damaged brain to the new, artificial one.

Bayron reassured him that the pain was a good sign since it meant that his involuntary nervous system was already being controlled by the model brain instead of the biological one.

When the surgery was over, Smith felt very tired, but he knew from his conversations with Bayron that he could not sleep yet. He knew he would be given a stimulant to prevent him from falling asleep.

Other than being tired though, he felt no different. He wasn't sure how he expected to feel, but at least he expected to feel different. After all, by some definitions he had just died.

Hermelinda had raised the head of Smith's bed so that he was in a seated position. She sat on the edge of his bed near his knees. "You okay, baby?" She asked. He smiled a weak smile and Hermelinda knew he was going to be fine.

"Dr. Bayron asked me to keep you company for a few hours while he tries to get a little rest. He said not to let you fall asleep. He wanted me to let you know that all of your involuntary muscle functions are now being controlled by the model. He said that some of your circulatory system may have suffered some atrophy and he's worried about blood clots, so I'm going to give you a little massage now to keep your blood circulating and prevent clotting in your legs, okay?"

Hermelinda knew how to read Smith's eyes. It was a skill she had picked up when he was no longer able to speak. His eyes said yes, but they said it very emphatically. What was she noticing, she wondered? It was his pupils. They seemed somehow shinier or blacker or, maybe, bigger.

"Your vital signs are great," she said. Your heart rate is steady as a metronome, your pulse is strong. Your lungs are working at full capacity. Now that involuntary muscle systems are being driven by the model, you've got the vites of a 30 year old. Even your eyes look sparklier. Dr. Bayron must be opening a bottle of Champagne with his crew right now watching these vitals."

She began massaging his toes, then his feet, his ankles and calves, and then she noticed something she hadn't seen in many, many months. Smith had become visibly aroused. This was all the proof that either Smith or Hermelinda needed to accept that the computer running his involuntary muscle functions was doing a damn good job. She knew that, as a professional, she would have to report this event to Dr. Bayron.

For the many months she had shared a bed with him, neither had been able to act on their feelings for each other. Even though she had lovingly cared for him and even as he had gently stroked her hair, the idea that they could be intimate, physical lovers, had always seemed impossible. She wondered if it would cause any harm if she just...

She had wished for this for a long, long, time and knew that he also longed to make love to her. For years now they had been the main fixtures in each other's lives. His eyes said "please" and they said it with a burning intensity. They said it with desire.

Hermelinda's face went flush when she paused to consider what she had just been thinking. In fact, it gave her a chill. She couldn't believe that the thought of making love to him in this condition had even crossed her mind. But something else in her, something less rational and more instinctive repeated over and over in her subconscience: *this will be your last chance.*

After taking a furtive glance around, she climbed into Smith's hospital bed. Though he had no control over his voluntary muscle movements, his involuntary muscles did everything they were supposed to do.

She saw Smith blush. She couldn't recall the last time she had seen color in his face. It was a machine calling the shots for his involuntary muscles now, but between the arousal, the consummation, and the blush on his face, it certainly seemed to be working like a healthy human brain. Fortunately, Smith had been pumped full of stimulants, so he couldn't just fall asleep like the last man she had been with. She chuckled to herself a little bit: *Now that would have been the TRUE test of whether he was man or machine*, she thought.

She cleaned Smith quickly. She wished she could change the sheets.

Up in the lab, after the initial celebration for the success of the operation, Bayron had stolen away to his private office to shut his eyes. He had not quite dozed off yet when he heard a knock at the door. "What is it?" He asked, expecting the worst.

The voice on the other side of the door, marked with a hint of an Eastern accent, said, in cool clinical terms, "Dr. Bayron, there is an anomaly on the readings." Dr. Bayron was on his feet instantly and ran to the lab to look at the monitors. His team had gathered to look over his shoulder waiting for Bayron's reaction.

"My God!" He said, turning to address his team. "It looks like our patient just had an orgasm!"

A loud cheer filled the lab, punctuated by the pop from the cork of another bottle of Champagne. Bayron made a quick shorthand note in his black spiral notebook.

The young man with the slight accent shook Dr. Bayron's hand and said, "We did good, Doc."

"We did great, Sharky," Dr. Bayron replied, clapping the young man on his back. He was glad he was able to share this moment of success with his protégée.

Sharky had a unique talent for engineering and an

imagination which made it possible for him to fabricate tools that had never before had reason to exist. So many of this young man's ideas had been incorporated into the overall design that Bayron had been forced to acknowledge that he couldn't have accomplished what he had already accomplished without him.

III.

In a hospital room in St. Petersburg in Eastern Russia, a doctor walked into a hospital room with an x-ray and gave his patient unpleasant, but not unexpected, news. The stiffness and pain in his hands would not get better, it would get worse and it would spread throughout his body. Vakhrusheva accepted this diagnosis as he had long ago made it for himself and knew it to be true.

Smith's doctor had something more interesting to show to his patient than a mere x-ray. Bayron entered the hospital room carrying a jar. On the jar was a printed label: "JAR ONE., Smith, E., Ref. 1.1.0-1.1.964."

In the jar was a clear liquid which had just a suggestion of a yellow hue. Floating in the jar was a greyish lump. It looked spongy and fragile. Smith marveled at the fact that this tiny little mass had successfully controlled all of his involuntary muscle functions for nearly his entire life--His entire life with the exception of the last 24 hours or so. He also marveled at the fact that he didn't seem to miss it at all.

Bayron placed the jar in Smith's line of sight. "This is the first part of your brain that has been replaced with technology. You no longer control your involuntary muscles. But the model of you does. If the model is accurate, as I am certain it is, you shouldn't feel any different at all because the model is working the exact same way this little grey lump did when it was in your head." Bayron picked up the jar and held it up to the light marvel at both its complexity and its simplicity.

"I wanted you to see it before I dissected it," Bayron continued. "It's a dubious distinction, but you are part of a very small club of people who have seen their own brain and lived to tell about it." Bayron looked at Smith's eyes hoping to read a reaction to his remark. Like Hermelinda, Bayron had become skillful at reading Smith's eyes and, like Hermelinda had the previous evening, he noticed something new in them.

Bayron took a small penlight from his labcoat and shone it into Smith's eyes. His pupils: normal, his tracking: normal. Bayron took a small rubber hammer from his coat and began tapping Smith's knee. Reflexes: normal.

It had been so long since Smith's body had reacted normally that the "normal" readings were, in fact, remarkable.

Bayron looked at Hermelinda. Hermelinda wondered if she should tell him just how normal his body was acting. "Normal." She said smiling. "Very, very normal." Hermelinda saw a faint blush form over Bayron's face. The blush on his face wordlessly communicated the fact that he knew about Smith's orgasm. She was glad he blushed. She would have been embarrassed to have to tell him in words.

"Okay, there are just a few things I want to review with

both of you before I go to sleep for the next three days to recover and prepare for the next surgery."

"First, Hermelinda, I put shunts in his skull where I opened it for the catheters so the holes would not close. That way I won't have to drill again for future surgeries. The shunts are sealed, but you have to keep the skin around the shunts very, very clean.

"The shunts are glued in place for now, but eventually they will start to fuse with the bone. This could cause spurs, so be on the lookout for any discomfort in that area.

"The wires coming from here," he said holding up two thick cables that were coming out of Smith's shaved head behind his ear, "carry the impulses from the artificial brain to his central nervous system. Because those impulses are electrical, these wires are shielded in lead as is this entire room, but you cannot let anyone in here with any kind of radio or cell phone. Keep everything electrical as far away as possible. Okay?

"Now, the model brain is stored on the computer array in the next room which is also lead lined. If anything should compromise these walls or the wires, he's in all probability going to have a heart attack. Minimally an arrhythmia, lung spasms, god only knows. If that should happen, god forbid, we have all of the traditional life support systems right here, including a breathing machine, and an artificial heart. There is an alarm system to warn of problems. If you hear this.... don't even think, just get him on the life support.

"On a similar note, there is no substitute for vigilance and common sense. Do not rely solely on the alarm system. If you even just feel like something's wrong, just start the life support and call me immediately.

"Also, Hermelinda, as soon as Alice gets here to keep watch and you've gotten her fully briefed, I want you to get some sleep. Smith," he said to the corpse like body on the hospital bed, "you should get some sleep now too. You've had a busy day."

Hermelinda yawned. "Aye, aye Captain." Bayron chuckled. She was human. He wanted to say something to prove to her that he was human too, but he couldn't think of anything to say. He hoped the chuckle would suffice.

As Bayron walked out, Alice walked in. Even though she was nearing fifty Smith had always looked forward to her coming for her schoolgirl-like cheerfulness. He admired her for her easy smile, good disposition, and thorough competence. He didn't care about her daily adventures or the latest news about the latest Hollywood divorce, but she had such a charm and enthusiasm in the telling of her stories, that they always kept him entertained, even if he sometimes had to struggle to understand her thickly accented English.

That, in addition to the fact that she wasn't much to look at, made her a good choice as a night nurse.

Before she left, Hermelinda kissed Smith tenderly on the forehead. "Good night, lover," she said so only Smith could hear.

Six weeks went by, and the artificial brain was keeping the real one alive flawlessly. Bayron had often said that the only thing one could expect was the unexpected. Everything working perfectly was truly unexpected.

Smith's body had continued to decay. When he ceased to be able to swallow, he was switched to an intravenous diet. The lack of solid food coupled with the atrophying of his muscles made him look like a living skeleton.

The MRIs and EKGs showed normal brain function, but with Smith unable to communicate even with the smallest gestures, it was hard to be certain. Even if his mind was functioning normally, who could say how much longer it would do so?

Bayron spoke to Smith as Hermelinda sat on the bed and listened quietly.

"Over the next few days, we're going to get you talking again.

"I'm going to do this in two phases. First, I'm going to wire the speech emulator to your real brain. The emulator is just a mechanical replacement for your vocal chords. But I need to adjust it so that it converts the electrical impulses in your brain- that is, the things you want to say- into comprehensible speech.

"Once we are successful at translating the speech-related brain activity into words, then we can remove that part of your biological brain and replace it with the computer model. That will be phase two.

"If you can even hear me, I know you understand why I can't do this all at once. Hopefully, we'll be able to make the decision together as to when to start phase two."

Smith lay completely motionless except for his chest which was moving ever so slightly as the artificial brain controlled his breathing in a perfect emulation of the part of his brain that had already been removed.

It had become harder and harder for Bayron to read Smith's eyes. To him they looked hollow and dead. But Hermelinda still seemed to know what Smith was thinking and feeling. It was as if they were connected, which, because of the baby growing inside her, was more true than Bayron knew.

"Okay, Smith, old pal, you know the procedure. I'll give you a topical anesthetic followed by a local under your scalp. The only real difference this time is that there won't be any drilling. I just have to uncap the shunts and, if you'll forgive the humor, 'tap your brain.'" Bayron tapped Smith's forehead gently. He knew that Smith would have appreciated the humor and he smiled at his own joke.

He became serious again as he addressed Hermelinda. "Get the drip started. Just because he can't show it, doesn't mean he can't feel pain. Let's make sure he's as stoned as a hippie before I go in there."

Hermelinda opened a tiny valve on one of the intravenous tubes. Though nothing about his appearance changed, Smith's still functioning mind was awake. As the sedative seeped into his bloodstream, his thoughts were replaced with streaming images of meadows, tulips, and bunnies. He let his mind become absorbed in the images. He had been a prisoner of his conscious thoughts for weeks and he welcomed this waltz with his subconscious.

Smith was unaware that he had fallen asleep and was surprised when he woke up. He knew that Bayron would not have let him fall asleep until the operation was complete. So, he figured, the operation must be over. I'm alive and self-aware, he thought, so it must have went well. He wished he could see clearly but his brain had been slowly losing its ability to decode the information it was receiving from his eyes. If this phase of the operation had been successful as he suspected, then there would be another thick white cable coming out of one of the shunt holes on his head leading to a rack of computers. Smith could clearly recall the sketch Bayron had made for him when they were planning this phase. He wondered how Hermelinda was taking all of this. He felt fully alert and he heard voices. First Bayron and then Hermelinda. Did they know he could hear them, he wondered.

Ever since Smith's body stopped moving and he became unable to communicate, both Bayron and Hermelinda found it increasingly difficult to remember that he was actually still conscious and still human. His body had become a completely useless thing, emaciated and lifeless. With the plastic shunts around his skull, the wire connecting him to the speech computer, and the other wire disappearing through the wall to the array in the next room, he looked more like an object than a person.

Smith felt like the invisible man when they spoke. There he was, hearing everything they said while they conversed as if there was no one else in the room. He listened intently.

"Curious?" Bayron asked Hermelinda.

"It all looks so complicated," Hermelinda replied.

"It's not that complicated really. Let me show you. I'd like you to know how some of these things work anyway."

"If you have the time, Doctor, I'd like that. It's been lonely here without him."

"I'm not eager to get back to the lab, either. I have to keep things so serious there."

Smith was amused by what he heard. Was this flirting? It sounded so silly when other people did it. Was he ... jealous? Could he actually smell her, or was that just the memory of her scent? He pulled his concentration back to their conversation.

Bayron had become the scientist again. Was he afraid to flirt or just terrible at it? "This box here is what we've been calling the speech emulator," Bayron said. "Its not really a speech emulator though. When people think of a speech emulator, they are really thinking about text-readers. A text reader simply assigns different phonemes – letter sounds - to specific groups of letters. So if I input the letters 'c-h' into a text-reader, it outputs the sound 'ch'. Compared to what we have here, that's baby stuff.

"This machine, on the other hand receives a combination of non-binary electrical impulses and brain wave activity and assigns a digital value to them."

Smith could picture the confusion Hermelinda's face would have displayed when she tried to decipher that science-babble. Smith was relieved for Hermelinda when he heard Bayron continue.

"So, if I show Smith an apple, and he uses the speech center of his brain to associate the idea of an apple with the word apple we can assign a digital signature, sort of a fingerprint, to the concept of apple. Then that fingerprint can be associated with the word. Now what will be really cool to see is whether the artificial brain will throw off the same fingerprints as the natural brain. If it doesn't, our Mr. Smith will have to learn to speak all over again.

"When he was still communicative, Smith and I were able to get a vocabulary of about a hundred words working just off his brainwave activity. Now that he's hardwired, we should be able to achieve a conversational vocabulary over a matter of just a few days."

Smith heard typing and assumed that Bayron was pulling up the vocabulary list that he and Bayron had practiced many times before. He imaged Hermelinda standing behind him, peering over his shoulder at the monitor. Bayron would smell her very clearly if he was right and her smell would have made his heart soft. How could Bayron continue to lecture her about the technology? If I still had a body, Smith thought, *I would have her in my arms and I'd be kissing her neck.*

But Bayron continued, "When he was still conversant, Smith and I chose two words that have completely different and very unique brainwave fingerprints: 'spaceship' and 'blue'. He will think the word 'spaceship' to convey a positive value and 'blue' for a negative value and hopefully, even if we can't recognize any other words, as long as the emulator recognizes those two fingerprints, we will still be able have conversations. In fact, because he knows binary code, we could literally have full conversation using just those two words with 'spaceship' standing in for one's and "blue" standing in for zeroes.

"Of course, if he has any kind of damage that effects the speech fingerprints, I guess he's just going to be stuck in there all by himself." Bayron said with concern.

"I said I was lonely without him," Hermelinda said, "imagine how lonely he must be." She looked at Smith's seemingly lifeless body and wondered how horrible it would be to be stuck in a body that could not die, but also could not communicate. The thought made her shudder. Smith sensed the shudder.

"Here," Bayron continued, "let me show you how it works. Turn on that monitor there."

Hermelinda turned on a video monitor which had been installed over Smith's bed.

"Now watch. Look...you see all those numerical strings? That's actually his brainwave activity. Not all of it is speech though. If we filter out some of the known patterns and focus in on the speech center of the brain...there, look. Those are the digital fingerprints I was talking about. The computer is analyzing all of the strings to match them to patterns that we already have in there. When it matches a pattern, a word or concept should appear on the screen."

Smith was suddenly excited. He was going to be able to speak again. They were waiting for him, listening for a word. Any word. What should my first word be? He though fast.

Bayron and Hermelinda watched numbers unfold across the screen and then suddenly a word flashed across the screen: "Mama."

Bayron and Hermelinda stared at the word in stunned silence. A moment later, to Hermelinda's surprise, Bayron began to chuckle. "Look Hermelinda, he's said his first word!"

Hermelinda, now understanding Smith's joke, laughed

through her tears.

A new word flashed on the screen.

"Spaceship."

Another six weeks passed and Smith was holding full conversations. Phase Two, which involved removing the biological speech center of Smith's brain was accomplished without incident, and it too now resided in a jar. Bayron, Hermelinda, Alice, and even Myra had become comfortable with Smith's new "voice" which sounded no different than a low-tech screen reader for the visually impaired, despite the vast difference in the technology. Occasionally Smith used a word that the emulator did not recognize. However, even when the machine got the precise word wrong, everyone in the inner circle had become skilled at interpreting Smith's meaning from the general concepts that the machine displayed.

When this would happen they would quickly tweak the machine to add the correct word.

Smith's biological brain would think the words, the emulator would translate the fingerprints into written text, and the screen reader would pronounce the words.

Even though there were no inflections or subtle intonations, or even facial expressions to assist his staff in interpreting shades of meaning, they were all able to recognize Smith's personality, wit, and intelligence.

There was no doubt that it was Smith.

"Good morning, boss. Are you up?" Hermelinda whispered.

"Yes, I'm here, lover."

"I need Myra here (whirlwind, express, racecar, clock)." Hermelinda knew that the list of seemingly unrelated words signified that Smith had articulated a fingerprint that the emulator did not recognize. But the concept was clear.

Each of these words was related by the concept of speed. Hermelinda had gotten very good at this game.

"ASAP?" She asked already knowing she was right and already entering the word into the machine.

"Spaceship." Smith replied.

The words "spaceship" and "yes" still sometimes got mixed up, but it was generally easy enough to glean the meaning from the context.

"I'll call her for you."

Hermelinda picked up the phone on the wall to make the call. While she was on the phone, Bayron entered the room, his black spiral notebook tucked under his arm.

"Morning Smith," he said as he began checking his patient's monitors, intravenous tubes, and vital signs. "How do you feel?"

"I still have a headache" the computerized voice chirped.

"Better...worse?"

"Getting worse."

"Well they should go away after the next operation."

"I certainly hope so."

"As you know, I'm going to port all of your sensory input functions to the model. We'll be replacing your vision and hearing with mechanical replacements and processing the input with the model brain. That way, you'll be able to see again, and we won't have to worry about the fact that your ears are dropping so much information already.

"I'm still a little reluctant to take this step since your ears are technically still working. Weak, but working. The camera and microphone will feed data directly into the virtual brain thus completely bypassing your biological eyes and ears. The visual and aural data will be processed by the virtual brain. The risk here is that if the virtual brain processes this input any different than your flesh and blood brain, your flesh and blood brain may not be able to sort it back into images and sounds. You would effectively be deaf and blind."

"I'm already blind and I'm going to be deaf soon anyway," Smith said, "so your reluctance is uncalled for."

"Okay then, Smith, you know the routine. I need informed consent which means I have to tell you what you already know. Most importantly, we do not have sensors for tactile stimuli or for taste at this time. So once you are using the artificial brain to process your sensory input, you will no longer be able to feel or taste anything."

"Bayron, if you're trying to scare me, it's not working. I haven't tasted anything but the rot on my teeth or felt anything other than pain in months."

Hermelinda shot Smith a dirty look from behind Bayron's back which of course he could not see. Had he forgotten?

Smith corrected himself, "Actually, Doc, that's not entirely true. But that's none of your damn business. I may no longer have the ability to feel what I have felt, but I can't stand the thought of losing the memory of it, Herme."

"Alright," Bayron said administering the sedative to Smith, "Here we go."

This procedure also involved two steps. In theory, Bayron could have replaced Smith's god-given eyes and ears with the mechanical ones without porting them directly to the artificial brain. Alternatively, he could have ported the natural eyes and ears to the artificial brain and added the camera and microphone in a separate step.

After much debate, the decision was made to do both at once so as to avoid any additional trauma to that region of Smith's brain. One surgery instead of two and using one shunt instead of two mathematically decreased the odds of failure by a significant margin. Furthermore, by limiting the intrusions into the tissue in this part of Smith's brain, the odds of being able to restore at least some hearing were much greater if for any reason the operation failed. For these reasons, the two-in-one operation was actually the more conservative way to go.

The entire operation took less than two hours to complete. When it was over another one of the holes on Smith's head had been tapped and another thick cord extended out of it, went up through a hook on the wall down across the floor and terminated at the computer station near Smith's bed.

"Now you can go to sleep, Mr. Smith," Bayron said into a microphone near the computer terminal.

Hermelinda was taken aback by the fact that Dr. Bayron had addressed Mr. Smith by speaking into the microphone and looking into the camera instead of at Mr. Smith.

They both reacted when they heard Smith's computerized voice. "Spaceship."

Bayron smiled. "Looks like its working, Hermelinda. Get some sleep. We'll do tests in the morning."

"I'll leave for a while as soon as Alice gets here," she said to Dr. Bayron while looking into the camera that was now Smith's eyes. She couldn't read these eyes. That made her shudder. She looked at Smith's face: motionless, atrophied, lifeless.

Alice walked into the room and said, "Hi, Honey," even though she was addressing Hermelinda's back.

Hermelinda yelped. Her heart skipped a beat before she realized that Alice had come in.

"Oh, Alice, you scared me," Hermelinda said. Hermelinda was gathering some personal belongings to take home with her. She didn't really want to go home. She never did. She kept a small flat, though she had been living in Smith's mansion for the better part of the past year. She kept a couple of keepsakes there. Some books, a television set. She didn't like to be alone. She took her time gathering her things and then she changed her mind. Who would care if she didn't go home. There was no one there anyway. "If you don't mind, I think I'd like to sleep on the cot here tonight. I'm just too tired to drive."

"I promise to be quiet as a mouse." Alice said in a whisper, and making a mouse face to emphasize the point.

Hermelinda unfolded the cot and took some bedding from the cabinet. She made the cot as comfortable as possible and climbed in. She was asleep before her eyes were fully closed. The microphone attached to Smith's brain picked up the gentle noise of her slow rhythmic breathing and he wished he could see her. But she was not in view of the camera and he was falling asleep quickly too.

Only Alice remained awake in the room. She inspected her patient and decided he might be cold. She put another blanket on him. She reviewed all of the monitors and inspected the new set of cables coming from Smith's head. It only took her a moment to recognize the camera was Smith's new eyes and that the microphone was his new ears.

From the monitors she could tell Smith was asleep. She turned the camera to face the sleeping Hermelinda. "He might as well wake up to something pretty," she said quietly to herself, "not fat old Alice."

Morning came fast for Smith who was excited to try his new eyes and ears. The first thing he saw when he awoke was an empty cot. Someone had moved his camera during the night. Then he heard Alice's voice: "You okay in there, Hermelinda?" From this he surmised that Hermelinda was in the bathroom.

"I'm okay Alice, just a little nauseous that's all."

"Good morning troops," Smith's computerized voice buzzed out mechanically obviating all the friendliness he had intended to convey in this greeting.

"Morning, boss," Alice said to Smith's face. Then she bent down to whisper in his ear. She had forgotten that his eyes and ears were on the table behind her.

"Boss, I tell you a secret."

"Alice, you have to speak into the microphone for me to hear you now."

"Right, right." She said. She turned to the microphone and bent so her lips were very close to it. "Hermelinda," she whispered into the machine, "I think she pregnant. That seem like morning sickness."

"Can you find out?" Smith asked.

"Ooooh, he like the gossip. I bet I know who the Daddy is! I'll find out. You'll see, I'm very resourceful."

IV.

A light snow was falling near St. Petersberg, even though the bright sun created a sense of warmth. Sergei Kovaretsky did not like to wait for anything. He was generally an impatient man, but he was actually enjoying a moment of peace on this crisp and clear day in the park. He even felt a little disappointed when he saw Vakhrusheva walking slowly across the footbridge.

Kovartesky immediately steeled his demeanor. He could not let anyone think he was enjoying the day or was even capable of being happy. It was hard work to maintain a reputation as a dangerous man.

As Vakhrusheva approached, the two men exchanged nods. Vakhrusheva spoke with no further greeting. "I have just received a communication from our point of contact at SmithCorp. They already have speech, vision, and hearing done and working, Sergei. It looks very promising."

"It's, not time to celebrate yet my friend. These are just parlor tricks. The artificial brain is handling power management, input devices and output devices. Mechanics, that's all. I need the *memories* recovered. The rest is of no value to me. If I cannot recover the third code from Ashkot's brain, the entire arsenal is nothing more than... doorstops. Get me the codes, Vladi. I refuse to accept that they are gone forever."

"I will get the codes, Mr. Secretary." Vakhrusheva replied addressing Kovaretsky by the title he held when he was in the Politburo.

"I know you will, Vladi. Who else could I trust with something like this?" Kovaretsky added.

His question needed no answer, nor did Kovaretsky expect one. The two men looked over the river Volga. The snow sparkled in the sunlight.

"But are you well, Vladi?" Kovaretsky asked, this time knowing there would be an answer to the question and also already knowing that the answer would be a lie. "Soon you will need to go to America."

Vakhrusheva spat over the edge of the bridge into the river below them. He was offended by the question. "Yes. I am well and I miss being in the field, Mr. Secretary. I am looking forward to my trip."

"Nonetheless," Kovaretsky said, "I have arranged for you to be assisted in New York. Upstate is not like the city. You will need someone who knows his way around. I have a man there, he can be trusted. He already knows we have someone on the inside. They have worked together before. It will be better for you."

"I work alone." Vakhrusheva said with a hint of insistence.

Kovaretsky laughed at the river. "You are not 20 any more, Vladi. I count on you for your mind now, for your instincts. But even I can see that you move slowly now. Accept this fact with dignity."

"The winter has come early this year." Vakhrusheva said, unwilling to accept Kovaretsky's assessment, but also unable to deny it."

Both men nodded and watched the snow fall on the river as it flowed under the bridge before they wordlessly parted ways.

V.

"Smith, your body is becoming a liability." Bayron said into the microphone. "Even with the involuntary muscle systems being controlled by the machine, your body is atrophying. We just can't keep it alive much longer. I want to get you online as soon as possible. Let me show you something." Bayron turned the camera that was Smith's eye toward his computer monitor. "Can you see that?"

"Remarkably well, Doc."

"Good. Okay, you see this activity here?" Bayron pointed to a kaleidoscope of red dots glowing and blinking on the screen. "What you're seeing is new memories being written to the artificial brain in real time. Look..." he said pointing to active parts of the screen, "encoding... short term... long term... You are writing this conversation to both your real brain and the artificial brain at the same time. I've been watching this ever since we started doing the audial and visual processing on the model. Every memory you've had since the second surgery is both here...," he tapped Smith's forehead, "...and here," he tapped the monitor.

Smith interrupted, "So let me understand here. You've got all my memories as of the date of my last MRI which was before the first surgery because that's what the model was built from, right?

"Hopefully."

Smith continued, "And you've got all my memories from after the second surgery when the computer took over?"

"Exactly."

"So what about my memories from in between the first and second surgery?"

"They're not in there," Bayron said.

"Gone forever?" Smith asked.

"Well, I guess to the extent you have a conscious memory of some event in that time period and your mind has translated that memory into a visual image after the second surgery then you would have a memory of having the memory which I guess is similar to having the memory. Otherwise, I would assume, it'd be gone."

"I've got a memory in that time frame that I would prefer not to lose, Bayron."

"It would take months to create a new model of your brain incorporating the memories from that period of time and we just don't have that kind of time. Your going to have to try to journal the memory by creating a memory of the memory right now."

Smith could still create a picture in his mind. But would the picture in his mind be picked up by the image decoder that was now part of his machine? He did his best to remember the smell of Hermelinda's skin, the sound of her breath, the feel of her hands. He did his best to remember the sensation of his release, the pleasant dizziness, the feeling of his body merging with Hermelinda's body and the feeling of his soul merging with Hermelinda's soul. He tried to journal every second, every detail of Hermelinda's strange deed for his new brain. As he did so, he saw the red blips and bleeps flash and move on the screen.

Smith was surprised by an intruding thought. It was his first moment of doubt in this whole enterprise. Was it worth risking this memory? Would he rather die with the memory of this loving act or live forever without it? He began to drift off to asleep with this thought in his mind.

Bayron woke Smith abruptly by shaking his shoulder. "Sorry," Bayron said, "I just can't have you sleeping right now. I'm going to have get an electrode into your head so I can get you started on accessing your memories from the model and as you know, I can't have you sleeping while I'm poking around in your brain. "

"You're doing that right now?" Smith asked.

"That was the plan." Bayron replied.

Smith knew that it was silly to even consider gambling away his entire lifetime full of memories in favor of just one beautiful one. He quieted that part of his mind that disagreed. "Poke away my friend," he said.

Bayron thought he sensed some hesitation in Smith's answer. That must be some memory, Bayron thought. It took him just a moment to realize what that memory must have been and he smiled outside of the camera's view. He had no desire to disrespect his friend's privacy or the privacy of Hermelinda who was standing close by. He quickly got back to the task at hand.

"Okay, look, we've been over this many times" he stated, "but...Well you know the drill. Could lose your memories, blah, blah, try to keep the physical portion of the brain intact so that you can gradually start drawing memories from the artificial one, blah, blah, blah, first man in history to have two brains, completely unprecedented, unknowable and unquantifiable risks, blah, blah, blah. Any questions?"

"I don't have any questions, doc. I'm ready for the twilight."

"Hermelinda, I want you to keep him engaged while I'm placing the electrode."

Hermelinda pulled a stool up near Smith's bed and took his hand in hers. She kissed it gently then pressed it to her chest. She didn't care that Dr. Bayron was in the room. Everyone would know soon enough. She was certain that Dr. Bayron already knew what she had done and was enough of a gentleman not to say it. *He probably knows I'm pregnant with Smith's baby too*, she thought. *He always seems to know everything.*

"I can't feel anything, you know," said the cold, computer-generated voice.

"Nothing?" Asked Hermelinda.

"Not with my hands."

"How about with your heart," she whispered into the microphone.

"My heart is dead many months already. But I feel with my soul."

"What do you feel, Mr. Smith?"

"Joy and pain, fear and hope, love. And something else."

"What is it?"

"There is a sensation of becoming eternal. I feel the sadness of outliving my children, including those not yet born. I feel the sadness of not ever being able to feel the warmth of another human being again. I feel the absence of time."

Hermelinda was confused by his answer. At first she thought it was just the mindless babble of a highly anesthetized person whose brain was being manipulated even as they spoke. But then, Smith had always been lucid during the other surgeries. She wanted to know...

"The absence of time?" She asked.

"I can't die. Once my brain is completely virtualized, I really can't die. Of course, that is, unless you count me as dead already, I suppose. But I know I still have a soul and that I feel love. But every thought, feeling, sensation: everything you hear, see, say, touch, is timebound. The more irrelevant death becomes, the more time loses its meaning. Eventually time will cease to measure any aspect of my life and no moment in time will exist, including this one, Hermelinda." Smith paused. "I guess that's what death is. I guess I haven't cheated the reaper after all, have I?"

Hermelinda replied quickly, "Your not dead as long as you have memories."

"But over an eternity, each memory must be accorded a smaller and smaller incremental value solely by virtue of the continually increasing number of memories, until no memory has any significance."

"The important ones will always have significance, Elly."

"I guess that's where mathematicians and poets disagree." Smith's computer generated voice said. "They say that life is really just a string of special moments, Hermelinda, I hope I don't lose any of the special moments."

To Hermelinda the words sounded far too sweet to have come from a machine. Hermelinda began to tear up. She gazed deep into his camera but there was nothing for her to read in the glass lens as there would have been from his eyes. She felt that his soul was still in there. Only the window into it was now closed.

The moment was interrupted by Bayron. "Aaaaaand...Done."

"That was fast." Smith said.

"For this step, the surgery was the easiest part. We already have all your sensory input feeding the model of your memory center. But now we have to train your prefrontal cortex to access your memories-- which, by the way, includes all of your knowledge -- from the virtualized brain. I don't think this will be as simple as getting you to see through the camera or hear through the microphone. So, get some sleep and we'll start some exercises tomorrow."

No sooner had he spoken than Smith fell asleep. Hermelinda kissed him on the cheek and realized that he had no way of knowing that she had done so. The kiss was for herself anyway.

Bayron addressed Hermelinda. "I couldn't help overhearing. If you ever want to talk."

Hermelinda looked at Bayron's eyes. They were honest and kind. "Dr. Bayron, is it true what he was saying, that once the project is complete his memories will be insignificant?"

"There's no precedent for this, but, unfortunately it makes sense. Memories are temporal. They exist in time. In the absence of time there would be no memory since a moment within eternity is indistinguishable from eternity itself. This is the god paradox." Bayron stopped talking abruptly and his face went momentarily blank. He giggled nervously.

"What do you mean?" Hermelinda asked trying to read Bayron's face.

"Well, god, if you believe in god, is eternal. But He – or She if you prefer – frequently dabbles in the temporal. That wouldn't be scientifically possible. You can't be both time bound and above time at the same time."

"Do *you* believe in god, Doctor?" She asked.

"Of course. But we've been mortal enemies for a very long time," he replied.

As Smith slept, he dreamed. On this, his first night of

processing information through his new virtual cerebral cortex, his dreams were unusually vivid. Usually in his dreams, on those rare occasions that he remembered them, he saw people and places that he knew. Often out of context and character, but at least familiar and recognizable. His dreams this night seemed, somehow, not his own.

One dream in particular scared him more than the others. He didn't know why, after all it was just a dream. In this dream he was standing at the edge of a river. He had never been to Russia, but he "knew" the river was the Volga. In the dream he was in grave danger. He was scared. He was afraid of men he did not know. Then he was on a plane. He saw two leathery hands. They were reaching for his throat. He had never seen such wrinkled hands, nor such strong hands. The hands were dark and smelled of coffee. Then, as dreams often do, this dream trailed into another dream. This one was pleasant and becoming familiar. He was a child, playing in a field of starflowers at night. The starflowers were all Hermelinda.

Smith awoke refreshed. He felt sharp, and alert. He remembered his dream of the Volga clearly. His logical mind told him that it was just the kind of nonsense that the mind entertains itself with at night. His other mind, the illogical one knew that the dream was significant, but didn't know why. Russia. Bayron had spoken about consulting with Russians. Distrust of Bayron was the last thing he wanted to feel now that he was only half human and his life was in Bayron's hands.

Bayron was in the room moments later. "How do you feel?" He asked.

"Better than I have in a long, long time. No headache. I feel pretty sharp, and, I know this is going to sound weird, but, I feel strong."

"Well, you were in pretty good shape when we took the scans that we made the model from. I wonder if you're accessing the computer for your memory of what it felt like to be healthy?"

"How would I know? I mean it seems like the thoughts and feelings are coming out of my own head."

"Well, the artificial brain model is showing an awful lot of activity in the long term memory center. Lets try a little informal test." Bayron opened his ever present tattered black notebook and flipped backward several pages. "Now just before we started this surgery I gave you a little speech. Do you remember what I told you?"

Without hesitation, Smith said, "Perfectly."

"Alright, tell me what you remember."

"Let's see, you came in stood over there, and said: 'Okay, look, we've been over this many times but...Well you know the drill. Could lose your memories, blah, blah, try to keep the physical portion of the brain intact so that you can gradually start drawing memories from the artificial one, blah, blah, blah, first man in history to have two brains, completely unprecedented, unknowable and unquantifiable risks, blah, blah, blah. Any questions?'"

Bayron was startled. He didn't remember every word he had said, and he certainly didn't have a recording of it, but he'd be damned if he hadn't just heard his words back EXACTLY as he had spoken them. It was as if they had been recorded. Bayron's brain acted fast to figure out what he had just experienced. It quickly made sense... if Smith were reading his memories from the machine version of his mind, his memory would, ipso facto, be perfect.

"Okay, let's try another. Do you remember what I said to you before the operation for your eyes and ears?"

Again, Smith repeated the lecture word for word.

"Okay, looks like your accessing memories from the

machine. We'll do the formal testing tomorrow. Let's just take the rest of the day off."

Then Smith said something unexpected. "I have work to do. How can I access my e-mail?"

"For now, you'll just have to have someone read it and write it for you, I guess."

Smith took control of the conversation just like he used to do when he was still strong. "I would think it would be easy enough to hook me into the internet through the eyes and ears. Just make an video connection right into my visual processing. It's exactly the same as the camera, but I'll be 'seeing' the computer output instead of you. Then use the same speech-to-text program so I can write and navigate using verbal fingerprints."

Bayron said, "Oh, I know it can be done, but it adds an infinite number of new variables. What if you can't distinguish your memories from the information available on the internet? What if you get hacked?"

"You can't keep the genie in the bottle, Bayron. Just firewall me as best as you can. I want this done ASAP."

"I can't quantify the risks, Smith."

"Look, Bayron," Smith's measured, artificial voice articulated in its unchanging, even tone, "we've been dealing in unquantifiable risks from the first time we shook hands on this endeavor. This is not a significant increase in risk and you know it. You just want me all for yourself."

"You're my monster, Mr. Smith. I know you understand my concerns." Bayron knew that Smith would get what he wanted. He didn't bother to fight. "I still have the team that designed and implemented the interfaces and all they're doing is monitoring now. I can put them on this right away and probably get you on the internet within a few days. Just, don't go Frankenstein on me."

"Don't frighten me with metaphors. I'm no monster and

you're no Dr. Frankenstein."

"Your genie metaphor is equally frightening, Smith. Remember what happened when the genie got out of the bottle."

"I promise to be good."

"At least be careful," Bayron said turning to go back to his lab, "you're still only human, after all."

Just before Bayron left the room, Smith stopped him. "By the way, Doc, any idea why I might have dreamt of Russia last night?"

Bayron stopped in his tracks and turned around. "What?" He said, then repeated, "What do you mean?" Bayron's surprise was undisguised as he walked back to the monitor.

Smith told Bayron about his dream and Bayron's face went flush. "We had to use some parts of the Russian model, but nothing that should have affected your memory. I'm going to chalk this one up to the vagaries of the subconscious. Let me know if you have any waking memories that you can't identify as your own. That would be cause for some concern."

"It's a little more complex than a European Quail, isn't it?" Smith asked rhetorically.

"We're going to know more about how the human brain works than anyone ever has, Mr. Smith, as if we didn't already."

"I hope Bob Hanover got those patents done. You should follow up on that when you get a chance."

"I'll do that," Bayron replied. "In the meantime, let me know if Flat Stanley makes any new appearances."

Before leaving the room, Bayron made some notes in his black spiral notebook.

Bayron's lab retained its office like atmosphere. The only thing that had changed about it in the preceding months was the addition of nearly one hundred monitor screens grouped in sets of various sizes hanging on the walls. The monitors were all measuring or tracking something different. Some displayed line charts, some displayed numbers. Others represented the flow of digital "blood" through the digital arteries of the digitized brain that was now doing all of Smith's lower and median brain functions.

The only person who knew the meaning of all the information on all the monitors was Dr. Bayron. He had grouped the monitors in such a way that, with one pirouette, he could see everything that was going on with Smith's two operating brains and his one useless body.

"Sharky," Bayron said placing a hand on the shoulder of the young engineer in the white labcoat, "come with me."

Sarkis Ohangangian, known around the lab as "Sharky", was Bayron's protégé. His father and pregnant mother fled the destruction caused by the devastating 1988 earthquake in Armenia and came to the United States just months before he was born making him the first member of his family born outside of Armenia. In Armenia, his father had been an electrical engineer. But, being unable to speak English, in the United States his experience, skills, and talent were worthless. His education and intelligence however, were invaluable.

Sharky's father landed his first job in the United States as a machinist in a factory working for cash under the table. Then he found work as an auto-mechanic and ultimately opened his own repair shop. Eventually he opened several shops. By the time Sharky had graduated high school, his father owned a chain of auto supply and mechanics shops in three states. Sharky learned mechanics when he was a little boy. He learned how to weld, how to build engines, how mechanical things worked. This was his first language. As his father became more successful, Sharky gained access to the best schools, the best universities, and the best opportunities.

Sharky's blazing intelligence, natural inquisitiveness, and unstoppable drive made him exactly the kind of person most deserving of the opportunities his father's success could provide.

Sharky followed Dr. Bayron to his office in eager anticipation of whatever challenge Bayron was going to throw at him.

As they sat in Bayron's glass-enclosed outer office, Sharky got the sense that Bayron was tired. He looked old. "He wants internet access." Bayron spoke as casually as a waiter telling a cook that the party at table five wanted soup, but Sharky immediately grasped the significance and gravity of the request.

He summed up his concern succinctly: "Then it won't be a closed system."

Bayron answered the non-question with a non-answer. "We could lose control of the operating environment. What do you think?"

"Firewall of some sort. We can't let him get hacked, but there's no perfect firewall. We'll have to back him up, obviously. Maybe let two artificial brains work in tandem: one that's wired to the 'net and one which would require a disconnect from the net before permitting updates to be made. Maybe even a third brain to decide if any of the information brought in is virulent or malicious." Sharky was brainstorming.

"An id, superego, and ego."

"Funny in a way, isn't it?" Sharky said. "I mean, if the artificial brain would hold all of the elements of his personality, then the id, the superego and the ego would already be a part of the system and there would be no need for three separate brains, would there? Then it would just be an issue of making the mechanical connection to the web, which I could actually do today."

"You put too much faith in both science and people, Sharky, neither will ever fail to disappoint you." Bayron sighed. "Think negative for a minute."

Sharky raised one eyebrow to call attention to the irony in Bayron's last remark, and Bayron realized what Sharky apparently already knew: that the entire project was predicated on faith in science and a love for people.

Bayron felt comfortable sharing his concerns with Sharky. He was, after all, a very human engineer.

Sharky continued brainstorming, "Here's a negative for you. Even if we didn't have to worry about corruption to the Smith model, maybe we have to worry about mingling a sentient and intelligent data set with the repositories of all human information. If Smith were malicious, he would be an absolutely unstoppable virus capable of infinite adaptations. And I mean unstoppable. Theoretically, he could replicate himself an infinite number of times and filter every single piece of information that exists in electronic form, which is everything. Smith could put whatever spin he wanted on the entirety of human knowledge. If he woke up one day and decided that the moon was made of green cheese, he could insert that fact into every repository of human information in an instant. He'd be the ultimate arbiter of truth."

Bayron looked Sharky square in the eyes, "Not just of truth. He'd be the ultimate arbiter of reality itself. Once he controls the sources of truth, there would be no difference between truth and lies. The facts would cease to exist and they would be replaced with whatever Smith decided the facts should be. He would be the mind of the entire world. That's a fellow you would not want to piss off." Bayron quipped. "He'd literally be able to make sure that no differing opinions could ever be aired."

"Did you ever try to get toothpaste back into a tube?"

Sharky asked. "There'd just be no fixing even a single instance of that kind of thing. Remember that kid who still gets all those get well cards? You can't just undo something once it proliferates over the Internet.

"Okay, let's think about it tonight and make some decisions tomorrow." Bayron concluded.

Sharky lived with his mother. Even though he was paid very well by SmithCorp-- very, very well-- he could never leave his mother alone. Since his father had died she almost never left the house. The bedroom he slept in since he was a little boy was still his best thinking place.

"Sako," his mother called him by his childhood nickname as he came in the front door, "Sako, come eat. I made tacos." Her thick accent made the word 'tacos' sound like a traditional Armenian dish even though she had never seen or heard of a taco until Sharky was a teenager. He was embarrassed by the ethnic food his mother prepared. He wanted American food. Hamburgers, macaroni and cheese, crunchy tacos and the like. His mother, always accommodating of his wants, not only learned to make these "American" dishes, but actually enjoyed them herself.

"I have a lot of work to do, ma, can you fix me a plate to take up with me?"

"Ach, my little working man. Just like your papa. I make you nice plate and bring it up. You make me proud."

Sharky climbed the stairs to his bedroom feeling more and more exhausted with each step. He lay down on his bed and looked at the ceiling, his mind awander. He knew exactly how to get Smith on the Internet. He had worked out the details on his way home. No challenge in that. But, he knew that was not what Bayron had wanted him to think about.

Was it possible that Bayron hadn't considered this before? Was it possible that this issue had only just crossed his mind? Even he had thought about some of the wider implications of the project himself but always felt comfortable in the knowledge that the ethics of the situation were Bayron's problem.

Now Bayron was looking to him for ethical guidance. He didn't like it.

Sharky opened the drawer on his nightstand and took out a small pipe. He patted down the marijuana in the bowl and decided there was enough there for one good hit. He lit the bowl with a disposable lighter and as he lit it a small flame shot up, reminding him that he was reaching for heaven.

No sooner had he exhaled than the door to his room opened. His mother came in with a plate of tacos and a glass of coca-cola. "This is what you call working?"

"Just needed to relax, mom."

"You work too hard already. Sit up and eat."

He sat up in bed and took a bite out of one of the tacos. That made him feel better. But his mother could tell that her son's mind was unsettled.

She sat on the edge of his bed and asked, "Is everything good at work?"

"Yeah. Dr. Bayron's great, you know, but... mom, let me get your opinion on something."

"The genius wants my opinion now."

"If you had the power to create something that you couldn't control, would you do it?"

"I created you." She gestured towards the remaining wisps of smoke that lingered below his ceiling light. She knew it was marijuana. She wished he didn't do it. "I don't do too good controlling you Sako, do I? But you always make me proud."

"But you never really did try to control me, now did you?"

"Control what, Sako? You was always a good boy." She pinched his chin as if he were an infant.

"But you didn't know that. In fact, you really had no idea how many temptations there are out there, you didn't grow up here. How could you just let me do my own thing not knowing what I could get involved in?"

"You think I was a bad mother?"

"No," Sako replied with an apologetic tone, "you were the best. But you know you took a big chance bringing me up in this country where you didn't know the people or the culture. I could have gone wrong so easily."

"I never worried, Sako. You come from good people and good people is good people. Should I have locked you away? Chained you to a radiator?"

"A lot of my friends weren't allowed to leave their houses or go to the store alone, but you always let me go."

"And you always came back. Why you bring all this up now? Does this have something to do with your artificial intelligence programs? Did you make something important?"

Sharky was not surprised at his mother's guess. Until he joined Bayron's team he had been working on artificial intelligence project for SmithCorp under a military contract. He had to obtain a security clearance for that and wasn't allowed to tell his mother any details of that work. When he joined Dr. Bayron's team, he was sworn to an even higher level of secrecy. His mother did not know that he was no longer working on artificial intelligence but on artificial life itself, and he couldn't tell her. He was glad she had used him as an example. It allowed him to get her opinion without having to tell her what he had really been a part of.

"No, ma," he said, "Real artificial intelligence is still a long way off. But from a philosophical perspective, if we were to create an artificial intelligence, it would be at least a little like having a child."

Sako's mother chuckled, "oh, I suspect the process would be very different."

"But seriously, ma," Sharky continued, "let's say I did create a kind of artificial intelligence. I think it would be very much like having a child. You know, you send it off into the world, you don't know what its going to learn, you don't know what its going to do. Yet people do that all the time. So I mean, look: here we are, it's a country none of us have ever been in before and you say, 'go, do, learn. Do what you're going to do, learn what you're going to learn, be whatever your going to be.' That's incredibly dangerous really, if you think about it."

"Dangerous? No, not dangerous. Not really. There's more dangerous then you give a smart boy a little freedom to roam around. There's lots of smart boys who sit home and study all day, locked in, no experience in life. Look at your papa. In Armenia he had good job. Good, good job. Every day he get up, go to job. He didn't have a choice. They said, "this is your job. This is where you go, this is what you do. When we first get here, you don't remember, you were a baby, he was very depressed. Drinking a lot, like you with your pots. He said to me 'what do I do? I don't know what I can do. I don't speak the language, no one wants me for engineer. I don't got papers to work.' You know what I tell him?"

"Yes, mom," Sharky said knowing she was going to insist on telling him again. "You told him, 'this is America. You do what you *want* to do.'"

Sharky's mother nodded approval, "And look what he did. He became a big success, your papa. A big, big success."

"I know you like telling me that story, mom, but it doesn't really have anything to do with anything. What does that have to do with sending a child out into the world without knowing the consequences. What if your child turned out to be... I don't know... Hitler?"

"Hitler was always Hitler. Stalin was always Stalin. Your papa was always your papa. I keep you in, I let you out. You're the same person inside. I tell you why I tell you about your papa again. Because he wasn't a man -- wasn't allowed to be what I knew he could be until he came here. You trust your child with the world and the world with your child because otherwise is like death. In Armenia, it was like death. A dead flower."

"I think it has to be different when you're talking about an artificial intelligence that learns on its own though. You just can't control what it's going to learn and how its going to use its knowledge"

"Just like my baby, I didn't know. Look, when you first started this nonsense, you said that a true artificial intelligence would be indistinguishable from a man. Do you still believe that?"

"Of course," Sharky replied, "that's the Turing test. Its the only reliable test for artificial intelligence that anyone has proposed so far."

"And if its indistinguishable from a man, then it's a man. Like the quack and the duck. That's what you told me, Sako."

Sako nodded, he was neither surprised that his mother remembered the duck metaphor nor that she had somehow managed to mangle it in the process of storing it in a brain that still thought in a foreign language.

"I don't know nothing about artificial intelligence, but I know a little about men." She chuckled before becoming serious. "Here's what I know. You take a man and cut off his potential, you might as well kill him. He is worse than dead. In Armenia, many brilliant men like your papa couldn't do what they wanted to do. They don't let these men get success because they afraid. If they not afraid, then Armenia would be

America and we wouldn't have to run away. You make this artificial intelligence and you afraid of it--you better as well just not make it. Its not fair to you, its not fair to him.

"Your papa... If he hadn't gotten us out, they would have killed him, and if they hadn't killed him he probably would have killed himself. And look what he did, after we came here. I don't know from artificial shmaritifial, but I know that to separate a man from his potential is the same as to kill him. And I know that if you save one life, its like saving the whole world. That's all I know."

She tapped his knee lightly and stood up and walked toward the door to his bedroom, gathering scattered laundry from his floor as she did so. "Now I got things to do. Mr. Philosopher. Philosophy is for men of leisure. Me, I don't get no leisure. I got things to do." She got up and left Sharky alone with his thoughts. He knew his mother was brilliant in her own way and in her own right, he just didn't always understand her. In her mind, everything came back to how bad things were in Armenia and how great they were in America. She could turn any conversation in a direction to make that point. He finished his tacos and fell asleep.

Sharky awoke to the sound of his cell phone ringing. He answered, "Sharky."

"Sharky, Bayron. Where are you? We've got work to do."

"Yeah, I'm not coming in."

"Are you feeling alright?"

"Yeah, but... I... I don't know. I've really got some stuff I need to think through. I mean, you know, there are implications and I want to think about it a little. I really... well, you know... I really... you know, I just don't know." Sharky stammered and fumbled to frame his thoughts. He thought he might quit. His mother was right about the fear, though. He simply wasn't sure how he felt about continuing with the project, especially now that it seemed time to unleash it on the world.

"Do you want to talk about it?" Bayron asked.

"No. You've really been great to me and all, but...I just don't know if I feel good about this anymore. I guess, I'm having reservations. You've got to let me sort it out in my own head."

"Sharky, you're a valuable member of this team. I'm not going to let you just up and walk away without a fight. We're making history here."

"Or destroying the future, doc."

"Take whatever time you need, you're always welcome here. My door is always open to you Sharky."

"Thanks, doc. I really appreciate your understanding." Sharky said with genuine gratitude for the courtesy.

Sharky felt like he was waiting a long time just to hear Dr. Bayron say 'goodbye' or 'see you soon' to signal the end of the phone call, but just as he decided that Dr. Bayron wasn't going to finish the conversation with one of those trite niceties, Dr. Bayron spoke again, but very quietly and confidentially as if he had dimmed the lights and pulled the shades for fear of being overheard. "Listen, Sharky," he said, "don't think that I haven't thought about it myself. I've lost a lot of sleep on some of the ethical issues here. I can't force my opinions on anyone."

"What is your opinion, doc."

"You want to know the truth?"

"Yes, of course," Sharky said.

"I think the risks may be unquantifiable."

"So you want to keep the system closed."

"Yes," Bayron said. "Unless we can quantify and control the risks, we need to keep the system closed."

"Do we have the right?" Sharky asked.

"No, but we have the power." Bayron said. "At least

until we can come up with a paradigm for quantifying the risks. And that may not be possible. That's where I need your help."

"I don't know," Sharky said. "I still need to think about it."

After the cordial goodbyes Sharky had expected earlier in the conversation, he hung up the phone.

Bayron didn't have time to think. Myra was paging him. Smith wanted to see him. He cleared his head and walked from the lab to the infirmary.

"So, will you get me online so I can get back to running my company?" Smith asked.

Bayron was struck by how tinny and mechanical the voice sounded. He hadn't noticed that before, probably because he was so thrilled that it even worked at all. He would assign the task of getting the voice to sound more human to one of the technicians when he got back to the lab.

"Yes, it just might take longer than you want." Bayron said.

"Why?" Smith asked.

"Because our team is down by one very talented engineer."

"Who?"

"Sharky."

"Oh, no. That's a shame. He's quite a bright young man. What happened?"

"I asked him to engineer a way to put you on the Internet and, frankly, I think he was overwhelmed by the implications."

There was a moment of silence before Smith spoke. That moment of silence however, was full of activity in the artificial brain. Because he could "see" the electronic data being input though the microphone and because his memory was now perfect, Smith could compare Bayron's voice to his voice in other conversations. It was different. Despite all they had been through together, this was the first time Bayron sounded stressed and uncertain.

The advantage of a mechanical voice, Smith thought, is that no one can know what you're really thinking. Smith tried to make his voice sound innocuous and trusting, but it was still just tinny and mechanical. "You know what this means, Doug?"

"No." Dr. Bayron replied, "At least I don't know what you think it means."

The speaker from which Elijah Smith's voice emanated crackled a little before the words came out. "It means he's a good man and the right one for the job. Let me worry about getting him back. You worry about getting me on the 'Net."

VI.

Hermelinda came every day to tend to her patient even though that was getting more and more difficult as she got bigger and bigger with the pregnancy. She never told anyone who the father was though she couldn't keep the pregnancy itself a secret. The engineers and scientists in the lab remembered well enough seeing the orgasm on the monitor and they simply accepted the fact that the baby was Smith's. Nonetheless, Dr. Bayron had actually instructed them to keep that information confidential until or unless Hermelinda herself was comfortable to make it public.

Bayron and Smith agreed that until they could convince Sharky to come back to head up the Internet project Smith could have direct access to an e-mail server. Bayron had one of the other engineers construct a simple interface which would allow Smith to compose, send, and receive plain-text e-mails via SMTP through a dedicated server. With a few simple modifications to an old fashioned text only e-mail program Smith could compose and send messages using only his verbal fingerprints. The process took only two days. The ability to send e-mails to the outside world was liberating to Smith. Because the mail program recognized the fingerprints of all the words he thought, he could literally type as fast as he could think.

But even stranger than that, he realized that he could see what he spoke as well. Sometimes he felt like he was seeing what he hadn't even thought of yet, as if the machine knew what he was thinking before he did.

He could also 'hear' the e-mails coming in far faster than he could read them. He told Dr. Bayron about this.

"My guess is that your senses are converging because when you're in the e-mail program all the information you receive is bypassing your eyes and ears and going into your memory as pure data. Even what you think you see, you're not really seeing in a traditional sense. Your brain is not decoding reflected light off an object. It is decoding a digital representation of an object. So the digital representation gets written to the memory, and the mind sees it as an image instantly. Because this process happens instantaneously, it probably seems to you that your brain has developed the ability to recognize patterns in the digital 'pure' form before it is processed into pictures or words. That's really kind of cool if you think about it. It's kind of like having a new sense. Now, in addition to having a memory that can't forget, you can actually see, talk, and hear binary code. Over time, who knows what you'll be able to do. Keep me apprised, will you?"

"Of course, doctor." Smith's computer voice droned.

Smith was a prolific e-mail writer. He was reconnected with the world and was desirous of interacting with it as much as possible. Everyone one he knew got e-mails from him everyday as if he were trying to spread his lifetime of wisdom to as many living people as possible.

True to his promise, Smith embarked on a campaign to bring Sharky back to the lab. Smith sent Sharky frequent e-mails and often these e-mails had a philosophical, even spiritual tone. Smith wanted Sharky's feedback on esoteric and even philosophical topics such as whether a machine can bear a soul. Smith was eager to understand and to help Sharky to understand what his reservations were and to help him overcome them.

"To the extent that a soul is a function of the mind's processes," Sharky reasoned in one of their exchanges, "then the replication of a mind on a machine would necessarily port the soul to that machine too. That assumes, of course, that the soul is simply a meta-intelligence capable of synthesizing all of the various intelligences of the mind into values and beliefs. That would make the soul a mere aggregator and organizer of collected information. Like a book written from all the information in the mind."

Smith replied that, "the opposite could also be true. That the soul maybe a mediator of all information. After all, a fact is not a fact until the mind tests it and verifies it. Pure information thus does not become human intelligence until it has been parsed and filtered by the soul. If so, then all intelligence is a distorted reflection of truth reflecting in equal parts the objective facts and the filter through which it has passed. The soul would not so much be the book, but more like the pen with which the book is written."

"To extend the metaphor, then," Sharky wrote back, "the soul could be the paper on which the book is written. That perfect blank page awaiting the marks of life. In that case we would have to say that information gives color to the soul rather than the soul giving color to information. Then the soul would be more akin to the blank pages on which all that is seen and heard is written."

"Which is simply another way of saying that the soul is perfect until it becomes corrupted by knowledge, rather than the other way around wherein knowledge is accepted as being perfect until corrupted by the soul. Looks like we've reasoned our way back from Einstein at his blackboard to Adam and Eve in the Garden." Smith reflected.

"I can only deal with one metaphor at a time, Mr. Smith. I have to go."

Sharky felt obligated to engage Mr. Smith with these e-mails since, even though he had not shown up for work for weeks, he was still getting a paycheck.

Occasionally though the e-mails were not purely philosophical. Occasionally, they addressed pressing issues, genuine concerns, or tangible problems. For instance, Sharky received the following missive from Smith one afternoon which brought almost all of the farfetched concepts they had been corresponding about into the harsh light of reality.

"Tomorrow they are going to wire my prefrontal cortex. Bayron wants to do this while my brain tissue is still healthy enough to work in tandem with the model for a while. He says my brain can only survive on life support for another week or two. If the model works as expected, how can we know whether I actually survived, how can I know whether I've remained human or become something else? How will you or anyone else know?"

Sharky took out his pipe and packed a fresh bowl. He took one long hit and held it before exhaling a fog of smoke in front of his computer monitor.

He put his feet up on his desk as he felt the marijuana begin to relax his muscles and then his mind. He lit up again and tried to formulate a response to Smith's question. He couldn't. All that would come to mind were song lyrics.

"Smith needs to ask a poet, not a engineer," Sharky

thought aloud.

A moment later he was typing a reply to Smith's question.

"Isn't that the ultimate question, really? What is a human? Who will decide if you're alive or dead when your entire body becomes divorced from your brain and your brain is divorced from all living tissue. If all that is human can be quantified, measured and stored, in 'x' or 'y' megabytes or so many boxes, then we would have to reach one of only two possible conclusions about the soul, which we've otherwise discussed to death. (1) Either a soul can be quantified and measured and hence replicated and thus, by definition not be inherently unique, which negates one of the fundamental religious beliefs about souls; or (2) there is no such thing as a soul and thus the existence of a soul is not a part of being human, which would be more compatible with scientific method. Of course, all that begins with the presumption that you are still human. We can't ignore the possibility that once you are quantifiable, you aren't human anymore. Take your pick."

As he hit the send button, it dawned on Sharky that perhaps these words were too harsh considering what Smith was facing in the morning, so he promptly composed another message:

"I suppose only you would know," He typed. "We would have to design a test that would answer the question to your own satisfaction. Problem is, if we run the test and ask you to report the result, the result you report has only a 50-50 chance of being true. No offense, its just that if you lacked a soul then you would have no inherent sense of right and wrong and thus would have no conscience to prevent you from lying. We would always be left guessing"

Smith wrote back:

"Unless I were to do some selfless act proving my

humanity."

Sharky replied, "How can there be a selfless act in the absence of a self. Once you are digitized, there are so many opportunities for file corruption that even a seemingly selfless act could be a lie. For instance, you are backed up every night. If you had the ability to make a backup copy of yourself, you could seemingly sacrifice your life over and over without having made any sacrifice at all."

Smith's reply was only a moment in coming. "Feign self-sacrifice for personal advantage? That would seem to be a very human thing to do. So I *will* be the only one who knows if I'm human or not."

Sharky responded, "unless you're dead, in which case not even you would know, but there would be a machine capable of calculating your thoughts and feelings sufficiently to fool even your closest family and friends."

Smith's next e-mail was quick and short, "What would it take to satisfy you?"

"All I've got is the Turing test. That's accepted science and its good enough for me. But these are not scientist issues at their core they're philosopher issues. Don't you think there's someone better than me to talk to about this?"

Again, Smith's reply was almost instantaneous: "No." Smith was satisfied that Sharky was an ally in his campaign to gain internet access. He also knew for sure that Bayron was not.

"You should talk to my mother," Sharky typed, followed by an ":)" to convey that he meant it as a joke.

"Maybe I should. By the way, If I remember correctly, you speak some Russian" Smith's next email to Sharky read, "what does 'Kodeks nomer tri' mean in English?"

"It just means 'Code Number Three,'" Sharky replied.

"Forget I asked." Smith's last email that day read, "Go get some sleep. Goodnight."

VII.

Bayron looked into Smith's shiny new camera that served as his eyes and spoke into the mirrorlike, polished, microphone that served as his ears while Smith himself, the lifeless, emaciated body with the tubes and the wires leading in and out, lay eerily still on the bed behind him.

"Okay, Buddy, today's the big day." Bayron said with unfeigned enthusiasm. "We're going to activate the artificial prefontal cortex. We're going to keep talking through the whole process."

Bayron pointed Smith's camera to the screen over his bed.

"What I've rigged to your screen is monitors for two EEGs. One is a real EEG measuring the electrical activity in your biological brain. The second one is a virtual EEG measuring the virtual electrical activity from your virtual brain. By watching both EEGs we can tell which of your two brains are working. The left one is your real brain. See how its showing activity now?" Bayron pointed to the left side of the screen where a green line was drawing an everchanging mountain range.

"You don't see anything happening on the right side because we haven't activated the artificial prefrontal cortex yet." In fact, the right side of the screen showed a glowing green line drawing a straight horizon across the middle of the screen.

"Well even if the prefrontal cortex isn't activated, shouldn't the virtual EEG be showing activity for listening, speaking, and memory which are already being controlled by the virtual brain?" Smith asked.

"We've filtered all that out of the result because we are only interested in the higher functions today." Bayron answered matter-of-factly. "Are you ready for this?"

"What, no speech this time?" Smith asked.

"Is it necessary? As far as I know you have a perfect-perfect- memory."

"No it's not necessary, but I always found it a little calming before the operations. Helps me to relax."

"Well, would it help you to relax if you knew I already started? Look at the screen."

Smith looked at the screen. Even though most of the activity was still on the left side, on the right side which had been still, the straight line was now showing signs of life in the form of little hiccups and skips.

"Honestly, it would relax me more if Hermelinda was here."

"Alice is here."

"I know," Smith said, "Hermelinda won't be back until after the baby."

"Have you been e-mailing each other?"

"Everyday."

"Do you want to make a confession, Smith?"
"Nothing everybody doesn't already know," Smith said.
"She's a sweet girl, Smith. The way she tends to you... it's hard to keep anything secret around here. But outside of the lab, I get a lot of questions. I wish you'd go public so they stop accusing me."
"Ah, so you're a suspect too. Do me a favor, can we keep it that way for a little bit? I mean, look..." Smith paused. The right side of the monitor was coming to intermittent life, throwing off a little light each time it registered a peak or a valley. "When I was a kid, you never even saw interracial dating. What would we call a couple consisting of a flesh and blood human being and a transhuman – basically a sentient machine. And ..." Smith stopped speaking abruptly. The line on the right side of the screen -- the one monitoring the model -- began to jump and flash. For a moment, the line on the left side became small and quiet.
"You alright, buddy?" Bayron asked trying to mask a tone of worry when he noticed the unusual change in the display.
"Yes, just something strange just happened."
"You have to tell me what happened. I don't want to damage the last functioning part of your body."
"Well, I was thinking...about Hermelinda... what kind of relationship... the baby ... other things... what I was talking about when suddenly... I don't know how to explain it, but I was thinking faster, more... I don't know. Like a thousand circuits just came on line. Like waking up, but real fast." Smith stopped talking for a moment, obviously trying to think of a better way to describe what he just felt to Dr. Bayron.
"I need to keep you talking, Smith. Remind me what you were saying when that happened."
"Well, I was just a about to say, how will Hermelinda,

or the baby, know its me and not just some sophisticated computer program? Will anyone respect our relationship after I'm freed from this corpse?"

"We've never really discussed that aspect you and I, have we?"

"Can you believe that I'm having doubts about the wisdom of this experiment?"

"It's a little late for that, isn't it?"

"Humor me for a second doc. What if a man really is more than just a sum of his parts?"

"To the extent that the blank spaces in between the physical parts count, we've already considered and accounted for that."

"Assume for the moment that what we call the soul is replicated in the model. The soul existing in the form of a bunch of 0's and 1's stored on a hard-drive. Would turning off the machine constitute murder? That's a legal question, I suppose. And if the data were copied could there then be two identical souls? And what if the data was stored on removable media and removed from its operating environment. Could that removable media have a soul? Imagine a computer disk with a soul trapped in it."

"These are theological questions, Smith. I'm just a humble doctor. I think you'll be the first to know the answer to those questions and you can tell all the priests and rabbis."

"Me, or a fancy toy capable of calculating what it thinks I would have said and saying it?"

"As long is it makes those calculations in perfect replication of what your flesh-and-blood mind would have done, I really don't see the difference."

"The difference is that I'll be dead." Smith's laughs, chuckles, and other verbalizations of amusement all came out of the machine as one or more 'ha's'. How amused he was could be gleaned from the number of 'ha's' that came out of the speakers, but all the other subtleties of laughter were lost. Before Smith continued a single 'ha' reported through the speaker. "Of course, if the machine does a good job of calculating my responses, no one will even know I'm dead." "No one but you and God. So who'll say Kaddish? The rest of us will just have to trust you." "But would you trust the machine?"

"If you are honest and the machine replicates your responses perfectly, then we can count on the machine to be honest too, right?" Bayron changed the subject abruptly, not because he wasn't enjoying the conversation, but because he needed Smith's attention on something else for the moment. "I think what you felt before was the sensation of your biological brain passing some processing to the artificial one. Because you were dealing with a philosophical issue, a paradox really, the entirety of the artificial mind got involved all at once. Kind of like the intensity of your thought created a mini-power surge. You have to admit, if I'm right, that's pretty cool. Watch the monitor and tell me what you feel."

Both sides of the monitor where showing persistent activity now. The right side was keeping the rhythm of a rhumba, the left side was only doing a waltz.

"It could be," Bayron speculated, "that the artificial cells have lower electrical resistance than the biological ones and thus emit as more energy. Or it could be that you're not really using the biological cortex for much anymore. I'm going to isolate each side so that we can make some assessments."

"If it's higher energy, imagine what we could do with that," Smith said.

Bayron frowned, "What are you thinking, Smith?"

"How about telekinesis for starters."

"Listen, Smith, lets not get ahead of ourselves. I'll be happy if it even adds two and two."

Over a period of several days, Smith learned to think with either brain and sometimes with both. He enjoyed the speed and clarity of thought he experienced with the artificial brain as it seemed to operate in a perpetual state of hyper-alertness but he always made sure to double check his results against his real brain. He no longer relied on his real memory at all.

He asked for and was given several utility programs: a word processor, a scientific calculator, and (he wasn't sure how he had lived without it), a spreadsheet.

With very little practice he was able to 'think' right into these applications and instantly 'see' entire results. He amused his visitors by performing complex spoken operations instantly. One time, just for kicks he calculated pi for a full hour, marveling at how easy it was for him to visualize and remember one-thousand digits, then 100,000 then 1,000,000.

Bayron came into the room and checked the monitors. "The tissue in your real brain is almost completely atrophied. Frankly I'm surprised its still working at all. Look at the monitor."

Smith, of course, didn't actually have to 'look' at anything. The monitor was wired directly into his visual processor. Smith could see without eyes -- his brain was tricked into thinking it was seeing the image on the monitor simply by being fed a series of zeroes and ones.

And what Smith saw was very different from what he had seen on the monitor before. This time, the left side of the screen was virtually motionless: gentle rolling hills instead of high peaks and valleys. But the right side was a veritable light show, dancing and flashing, skipping and jumping.

"It looks like you're already using your artificial brain predominantly. Were you aware of that?" Bayron asked.

"Yes and no. I guess I knew that my mind was doing things that no human mind could actually do, but, it just feels like my own mind doing it, not some external apparatus."

"I think your flesh and blood are just empty baggage now. It seems to me that your mind is completely virtualized."

"What do you figure those little registers from my real brain are? I mean, its obviously still doing something, maybe not much, but something."

"I'd only be guessing, Smith, but my hunch is that the only activity occurring in your biological brain are the minimum functions necessary to keep itself alive. Why don't you leave the monitor on for a while and see if you can figure out what it is that your biological brain is still doing."

"I'll do that, Doc. Listen, have you heard from Hermelinda? I haven't had any news in days."

"Funny you should ask, papa. Hermelinda will be here this afternoon and she wants to introduce you to someone."

Both Smith and Bayron noticed that there was suddenly some wild action on the left side of the screen which was monitoring his biological cortex. As the screen lit up, the lights in the room dimmed-- slightly, and just for a moment--but it was definitely noticeable.

"What happened, Smith? What did you feel?"

"Something strong. Actually a lot of strong things. She's coming with the baby, isn't she?"

"Yes, it was supposed to be a surprise."

"Is it a boy or a girl?"

"A beautiful, healthy girl. 6 pounds, four ounces. Hair like her mother, eyes like her father's."

"You mean like her father's used to be. Ten and ten?"

"All the fingers and toes are present and accounted for. You are a very lucky man." Bayron said.

After a short silence, during which Bayron could only guess that Smith was mulling the prospect of new fatherhood, Smith began speaking again, surprising Bayron with the quick change of subject.

"By the way, doc, you told me to tell you if Flat Stanley showed up again." Smith said.

"Did you have another dream?" Bayron asked.

"No, a waking memory. You told me that you would be more concerned about waking memories than about dreams, and now I actually have some memories that are truly not my own." Smith's synthesized voice cackled.

"Really?" Bayron responded. "That's unexpected."

"The only thing it makes sense to expect is the unexpected. You told me that." Smith replied.

"So give me some idea what you're talking about." Bayron prodded.

The human voice is punctuated with breath's and sighs, Smith's voice was not. It made everything he said sound abrupt. "There's one memory that's particularly disturbing. I have a very distinct recollection of being strangled to death. Big leathery hands. I can see the face of the killer, I was on a plane. The man who killed Flat Stanley, me, was named Gonzales. I actually remember what it felt like to die."

"Well, technically you did die," Bayron pointed out.

"But I remember my own 'death' very well. After all I lived through it. This memory is not of my death. It is a death I didn't survive. And I know its not me in the memory."

"How can you be so certain that it's a memory and not a dream? I mean, we're not all that certain that your virtual brain divides those states as clearly as a biological brain does," Bayron asked skeptically.

"For starters," Smith answered, "the memory is all in Russian."

Bayron made a note of this conversation in his black spiral notebook. He knew Smith didn't speak Russian. Bayron contained a brief chill that he felt in his spine. He didn't want his patient to think he was concerned.

Smith made a conscientious decision right then and there that he would not mention this subject to Bayron again. Instinctively, he felt like soon he would remember something that would endanger his friends.

Vakhrusheva had a memory that he knew was his own and no one else's. In fact, it was indelible. Years of effort and millions of dollars had been spent to repatriate Yuri Ashkot to Russia after he had been secretly apprehended by the Americans. Vakhrusheva had arrived at the airport to deliver Mr. Ashkot to men who had taken great risks and made substantial investments to ensure he was delivered alive. Vakhrusheva was waiting on the tarmac when the plane arrived. He remembered feeling that something was wrong, but there was no way he could have known. He readied his hand to draw his gun should the need arise. The door to the airplane flew open and like a bolt of lightning a man, who was definitely not Ashkot, jumped out of the plane and began running straight toward him.

Vakhrusheva was a fast draw but this other man was already nearly on top of him by the time he had his gun out of his shoulder holster. The other man's foot came up to kick the gun out of his hand, but Vakhrusheva did not let go. The force of the kick nearly ripped his index finger right off and the weapon fired into the air. He saw the other man run into the terminal and he did not pursue. His responsibility was to deliver Ashkot.

He climbed into the plane to see Ashkot's dead body, tongue sticking out. Strangulated and neck broken. Vakhrusheva made it his personal mission to find out who had been responsible for Ashkot's death as Ashkot had no value to him, or to his employers, as a dead man.

Neither the pilot nor the co-pilot were culpable. Vakhrusheva knew this for sure as he had done the questioning of them himself and only the pilot had survived the questioning. They both insisted that Ashkot had been escorted by another man. An American bodyguard who's name was Gonzales. This Gonzales must have balls the size of the moon and the skills to back them up, Vakhrusheva thought. He had never forgotten the name Gonzales. This was already the second time he had heard it and the second time that it raised the bile in his stomach into his throat.

VIII.

Smith's camera picked up Hermelinda first. She was pale, and beautiful, and tired. She looked more radiant than he remembered, as if she were walking in a cloud of light. Then he saw the baby. Bayron was glued to the monitor watching the left side and the right side of the screen throwing electrical activity back and forth between each other. It was the most activity Bayron had seen in Smith's real brain in a very long time.

"Bring her close, darling." Smith said. "I want to see her." The lights in the room flickered. Bayron made a mental note to increase the power to the room so that the occasional unusual brain activity they had now experienced three times wouldn't draw power away from the lights or other machines.

Hermelinda brought the baby close to the camera lens. The little motors in the lens moved it up and down and left and right. This continued for a several minutes. There was no talking, and no noise at all except for the quiet hum of the motors.

The camera stopped moving, but the silence continued. Bayron noticed that there was now identical activity on both sides of the monitor. Smith was conscientiously trying to use his biological brain.

Hermelinda became nervous with the silence. "Elly..." she said nervously.

"She's beautiful, Hermelinda. Forgive me. I have never felt what I feel right now. I am smitten. Overwhelmed. I want to hold her, to kiss her forehead, to smell her. I want to cry."

"You are crying, Elly," Hermelinda told him. There were, in fact, tears coming from the blind dead eyes in the near-corpse that had been Elijah Smith's body.

"What did we name her, Herme?" He asked.

"I named her for you, Elly."

"Elijah Smith is a terrible name for a girl." Smith quipped. His computerized voice was unusually punctuated. At first, Dr. Bayron thought there was something wrong with the speech emulator, but soon realized what Hermelinda knew from the outset. He was speaking through sobs of joy.

"I named her Ellen." Hermelinda said wiping some tears out of her own eyes.

"Under the circumstances, I'm just glad you didn't name her 'Garp.' Bring her close to my speaker, I want to whisper something to her."

Hermelinda complied. She couldn't hear much, but the baby was definitely hearing something as she held her ear up to the speaker.

The moment was interrupted by a flickering of the lights. Bayron said, with alarm in his voice, "is everything okay?"

"Yes," Hermelinda and Smith replied in unison.

"All of sudden there's no activity at all on the left

monitor. A moment ago the left monitor was as active as I've seen it in days and then...flatline." Bayron said.

Smith's camera panned to Bayron's face, Smith was able to confirm from Bayron's expression what he suspected. A silence descended and lingered. Hermelinda felt suffocated by it.

"Is, is it...?" Hermelinda stammered.

"Yeah," Bayron whispered, "I think so. Your biological brain is no longer functioning."

"I must've literally blown it out," Smith said. His remark was followed by an awkward silence until that silence was pierced by a long series of "ha ha's" from Smith's speaker, followed by Smith's voice which seemed warmer and less tinny than it had before, "funny, I don't feel dead."

Bayron went to the decrepit body that had once been Smith and felt for vital signs. There were none. Hermelinda cried, silently. Sadness filled the room. Even the baby began to cry.

"Boo!" Smith said and he started laughing again.

After Hermelinda took the baby to feed, Smith called for Myra.

Myra came to the infirmary and was glad to have the opportunity to congratulate Smith in person on the birth of his daughter. She was not yet used to speaking into the microphone and looking into the camera, so she walked up to Smith's, now cold, dead body to speak.

Smith noticed this and said, "The body is dead, Myra, that's why I asked you to come here in person. I'm going to need to make funeral arrangements."

Smith knew she would handle the task with the same cool efficiency with which she handled even the most mundane of tasks for him.

It was hard for her to think that she would be making funeral arrangements for her boss and close colleague of many years when here he was right there cracking jokes and sounding as alive as ever.

"You know what, Myra," Smith spoke, "I think I'd like to give my own eulogy."

"Very funny, Boss."

"No, I'm serious. This is a perfect opportunity for us to reveal the technology publicly. Think about it... we'll have all the media there, but mostly the obituary and social guys. They've never had a story like this. What are we going to do, pretend I'm really dead and then publish a scientific paper? Nah! Let's do this with some Hollywood style."

Myra knew he wasn't joking even though his tone was light. "Talk to your lawyer before you decide."

"You know what, fuck the lawyers. What do I have to lose? I'm already dead. Being dead is very liberating! You'll just have to take my word for that."

"I don't know boss. Look, you're all nice and dead already, but I've got a big freakin' company to run here. We should talk to the lawyers."

"Keep the corporate lawyers out of this. They're just going to try and talk me out of it. We'll tell Takahashi. He's knows to let an old man have some fun. In fact, why not put him in charge?"

"You're not an old man anymore. Really, you're a newborn now."

"Seriously, Myra, all the real legal stuff is done. You're taken care of, Hermelinda's taken care of, the baby is taken care of. Even if the company goes bankrupt tomorrow, everyone's going to have more money than they'll ever know what to do with. Let's knock 'em out. What's the harm?"

"Dr. Bayron is not going to be happy about this." Myra warned.

"Listen, he wants to go public with this more than any of us. He has the most to gain: the patents all belong to him, not SmithCorp. He's been trying to publish his results since the day we started. He still gets credit. This is just a more fun way to do it than by publishing in scientific journals. Hell, let him introduce me. He knows more about me than anyone anyway."

IX.

Josey Cruz was looking at a face that Smith had seen in a dream. And like Smith, Cruz had immediately noticed this other man's hands. Josey Cruz remembered his grandfather telling him how the Nazis would inspect the hands of their prisoners to determine who would be put to work and who would be put to death. These were clearly the hands of a worker. The knuckles were red and bony. They stuck out like crumbling pyramids in an arid valley. The scars and callouses, like heiroglyphs on the wall of a tomb, memorialized an ugly and violent history.

And yet this older man in the designer suit and satin hat bore a countenance so gentle, so calming, that Josey would never have believed that he was looking at a man capable of emotionlessly inflicting unspeakable harm at a moment's notice. Only the hands gave it away.

"Expected someone younger?" The man said with a

smokey, cool voice which drew Josey's attention away from the fascinating hand he now held in his firm handshake.

The question put Josey off and he didn't like that. He didn't know who this man was and had no expectations. All Josey knew was that this man clearly commanded respect from his superiors at the Agency. He knew that this man had access to the highest echelons at the CIA. He knew that the only instruction he had been given when he was dispatched earlier in the day was to deliver a data cd to this man and to follow his instructions from that point forward. He also knew that there was something very special and very out of the ordinary about this mission. The director himself saw him off and gave him a direct dial phone number to his office if he needed any support from any of the local offices around upstate New York. Cruz was assured that all the resources of the agency were at his disposal. These facts alone told him that this man whose hand he had just shaken was someone that he must take very, very seriously.

Nonplussed, Josey went straight into the briefing as he had planned. He slid a thin manila file across table. "The data cd is here. My boss tells me you already have the encryption key. Mine has been destroyed. The security level on this is TS4. The only instruction I have received so far was to meet you here and provide this information to you. It is my understanding that until this mission is concluded I report to you and only to you, that you would brief me further, and that the nature of our mission is not to be disclosed to anyone, not even anyone at the agency."

"And you accepted this mission with so little information?" the older man asked.

"A mission is a mission, Sir." Cruz replied. "Sometimes I have more information sometimes I have less. I do not see that as being a reason to refuse a mission."

"In that case," he said, nearly smiling, "may I treat you

to a cup of Coffee?"

"Black." Cruz answered.

Marco Gonzales waved a large, leathery hand at a passing waiter. When the waiter looked over, Gonzales pointed to a coffee pot, and held up two twisted fingers. "I've been watching you for a long time, Mr. Cruz and I specifically requested that you be assigned for this detail. I'll be honest, I am loath to work with partners, but I also recognize that the world has passed by me with a lot of technologies. Encrypted cds," he began to say as the waiter brought the coffees and quickly left. "As I was saying," he continued, "Encrypted cds, are an example of the tools in use these days. Tracking satellites, cell phone triangulations. I'm really just an old assassin when it comes right down to it. I need someone on my team that knows and understands this current world of communications technology and as far as I can tell, you're the man for the job," he said motioning to the manila folder which he had not even touched since Cruz had slid it across the table.

"Here is what you need to know. First, I do not work for the CIA. If you receive an order from your bosses at the CIA which is contrary to an order from me, you follow my order. You will bear no ill consequence from this. The Director himself answers to me and not the other way around. For this same reason, if I ask you to request a CIA resource, even a resource that is outside of your normal authority, you request it. You will find that you have the authority to do so.

"Second. Our mission is nothing short of saving the world. If we fail, I can virtually guarantee nuclear devastation and worldwide chaos. That is a heavy responsibility and not one that most men would undertake lightly.

"Third, this operation is an operation of the IAEA Field Operations Unit. I am certain that you are aware of the International Atomic Energy Agency, its been in the news a lot lately. But the existence of the Field Operations Unit has never been officially acknowledged and never will be. As of now you work for us. Have I made myself clear?"

Cruz had a feeling from the moment his contact had started talking that he had been thrust into another league. The IAEA Field Operations Unit was almost mythical in the intelligence community. After the fall of the USSR the Russian nuclear arsenal was dispersed in many different directions. The United States and its allies quietly formed and funded the IAEA Field Operations Unit to find and track all the nuclear devices known to exist in the former USSR, to destroy what could be destroyed, neutralize what could be neutralized, and recover what could be recovered. According to legend and rumor, the FOU's incredible efficacy was the singular reason that there has not been one single unaccounted nuclear detonation in the world, ever. The fact that nearly every legitimate government in the world provides support and immunity for the members of the Unit, while requiring it to answer to none, factors heavily in its ability to act quickly, quietly, and decisively. To this extent it remains a virtual meta-intelligence agency: using intelligence from many countries which would never voluntarily share their intelligence with each other.

The fact that the IAEA Field Operations Unit received intelligence from all of these other agencies but was strictly prohibited from sharing any of the intelligence it gathered with any individual nation was why it had a mythic quality in the Intelligence field. The hand of the Field Operations Unit was felt all over the globe, but their actual involvement in anything was completely unverifiable.

Cruz deconstructed the words he had just heard in his mind. He recognized that he had not been asked to join the IAEA FOU. He had been told that he already worked for them. He was only asked whether he understood that fact.

Cruz understood well enough. He wasn't certain he understood all of the implications of it, but he understood enough. "Eminently clear, sir," Cruz answered repeating a line he had heard in a movie and thought sounded intelligent. He immediately felt foolish for not having answered with a simple "yes".

"Now that you are part of my team," Gonzales continued, "you operate above the law in almost every part of the globe. You report to no one but me."

"Does the CIA know that I've been recruited by the FOU?" Cruz asked suddenly worrying about things like his health insurance and 401(k).

"Those who need to know, know."

"If you have any reservations about this mission, you better air them right now." Gonzales insisted.

Cruz did not hesitate. "Saving the world is what I do best, Mr. Gonzales. I wouldn't trust that job to anyone else."

Marco Gonzales recognized the self-assurance in Josey Cruz's answer and knew that he had picked the right man to accompany and perhaps succeed him in his ongoing mission.

"Good, then we have an accord," Gonzales said as he took the encrypted cd from the manila folder held it to the light and inspected it carefully. He turned it around in his fingers and then with a sudden, almost imperceptible flick, he crushed the cd into shards. "Your agency has a bad habit of providing its operatives with partial information and half-truths. I mean them no disrespect, they do that out of an abundance of caution. But this," he said, inspecting one of the shards, "probably does us more harm than good."

Cruz struggled to keep his cool. Even though it was clear to him that he now answered to a higher power, Cruz was a loyal agency man and did not like to hear any criticism of it. Gonzales, however, knew he was breaking his new pupil down. Gonzales quickly swept his finger across his lips and Cruz understood, and accepted, the fact that now was a time for listening and not speaking.

Gonzales continued, "Now, let me tell you what you don't know- what the agency has kept secret even from you: the person we are after is Yuri Ashkot. Do know who Yuri Ashkot is?"

"I know who Yuri Ashkot is. He's the Russian General who was involved in the war crimes in Chechnya." Cruz replied feeling somewhat offended by the old man's presumption.

"If that is all you know then you don't really know." Gonzales said matter of factly. "You only know what your agency knows and most of that is speculation. Gonzales replied and quickly turned the subject back to the mission. "On your cd," Gonzales continued, still toying with one of the broken shards between his fingers, "was a transcription of an intercepted conversation between Dmitry Kovaretsky and Vladimir Vakhrusheva. It seems they are talking about gaining the ability to launch a black market warhead which they refer to as 'the asset'".

"As I would assume you also know, Ashkot was released from custody here in the United States as part of a prisoner exchange with the Soviet Union."

Cruz nodded in confirmation of what Gonzales had just told him, that was indeed the gravamen of the content of the encrypted cd.

"This is what you don't know. What Kovaretsky and Vakhrusheva refer to as the asset is not a single nuclear warhead. The asset consists of several dozen nuclear warheads. Those warheads were under Ashkot's command and each was guarded by three separate codes. None of the warheads can be launched without the third code, a code which was known only to Ashkot. The other thing that you and your agency do not know is that Ashkot is dead."

"Are you certain that he's dead?" Cruz asked.

"I killed him myself." Gonzales said with a hint of pride as he pantomimed a strangulation with his large, leathery hands. "He was dead before he returned to Russia."

"It could be that Ashkot gave the code to someone else." Cruz posited.

"We consider that possibility to be negligible for several reasons. First of all, Ashkot was under lock and key in the U.S. while he still held his position as a General in the Soviet Army. He was a military man to the core and not likely to have disobeyed an order to keep his code confidential. But there is an even better reason to believe that no one else knew that code."

"What is that?" Cruz asked.

"The fact that none of those warheads have been either sold or detonated." Gonzales answered.

"So then Kovaretsky must have been bluffing..." Cruz proposed, "if Ashkot was dead before he was returned to Russia, then the missiles stay dormant. So it has to be a bluff of some sort."

"Think first son, then talk." Gonzales said condescendingly. "Surely Vladimir Vakhrusheva would have known that Ashkot was dead too. He and Kovaretsky are on the same team. Think. If it's a bluff, then who are they trying to bluff?"

"It doesn't make any sense." Cruz acknowledged.

Gonzales took a slow sip of his hot coffee. "If it did, I'd still be on my yacht drinking mai tais, son."

"Dead men tell no tales..." Cruz said with one eye closed, pirate-style, venturing a dash of lightheartedness.

Gonzales did not acknowledge the lightheartedness and responded quite seriously, "I have a feeling we may find out otherwise, Mr. Cruz. Somehow, it seems, our dead man is talking."

X.

Smith never liked hearing what he couldn't do. And so he never liked having to ask advice from lawyers. He accepted the fact that lawyers were a necessity, much like health insurance or urination, neither of which were necessities for him in his present condition. SmithCorp employed the best lawyers in the country. The legal team was excellent at telling him what could and could not be done and also at advising him of the potential civil, criminal, and regulatory liabilities of various courses of action. But for those things which his team of experts would tell him couldn't (or shouldn't) be done, he always turned to Sammy Takahashi, if he could find him, or better yet, find him sober.

Sammy's phone was on vibrate. He knew he wouldn't hear it where he was, so he turned it to "meeting" mode and put it in his breast pocket. It was three o'clock in the afternoon and Sammy was three sheets to the wind. There were only three girls on the board and they were taking turns pretending to dance for Sammy and the two or three other non-tipping regulars who hung out at the Moviestar Topless Bar and Lounge on weekday afternoons.

"Hey sweetie, I think your phone's ringing," the girl on the stage, who called herself Kitty, crawled over to Sammy and whispered in his ear.

"Is that what their callin' it these days, doll?" Sammy quipped.

Kitty didn't get it, or at least pretended not to. "No, I mean I can see your phone lighting up in your pocket," she said extracting the phone from Sammy's pocket. The phone vibrated again as she held it, tickling the young woman as it did so. She giggled innocently and the phone fell on the floor. She picked it up and looked at the screen. "Who's Smith?" she asked in a faux little-girl voice that was also tinged with faux curiosity.

"Smitty!?" He said, suddenly sober and reaching for his phone.

"That woke you up, huh?," Kitty asked playfully as she pulled the phone just out of his reach. "He sent you a text message."

"Let me see that," Sammy said reaching again for his phone.

"Not until you tell me who it is, counselor." Kitty said teasingly.

"It's Elijah Smith from SmithCorp." Sammy told the girl matter-of-factly.

"Uh huh, and I'm the Queen of England. Like Elijah Smith is calling you."

"Hey, I wasn't born a nutty old drunk, you know. If you marry me, I'll introduce you some day. We've been friends since grade school."

"Maybe you'd like to meet my grandma, Romeo," she said to remind Sam that her only value to him was to play in his fantasies. Well I don't want you to take me to meet him now," she said looking genuinely sad and sorry. "The text says he's dead." She was sorry she had been mean just before having to deliver this bad news to one of her favorite customers.

She was surprised to see that he was nonplused by this information.

"So who sent the text, genius?" Sammy asked momentarily giving up on getting his phone back and instead fumbling for his reading glasses.

"It just says Smith..." the girl said, "and he wants to talk to you." Recognizing that playtime was over, she simply handed the phone back to a more serious and slightly sobered Sammy Takahashi and returned to her gyrating on the pole.

Even with his reading glasses he had to hold the phone far away to read the tiny print. He began typing a reply.

Sammy was still tic-tacking out his reply as the song on the jukebox ended. Kitty put her bikini-top on, picked up the few dollars that had been put on the stage, and walked over to Sammy. Sammy looked at Kitty over the rim of his reading glasses. "He's coming here."

"Really," Kitty said excitedly, "but I thought he was dead."

"He's fucking with me. I don't know what his game is, but last time I saw him he was so sick he couldn't even lift a finger. I've got no idea how he's going to get here. C'mon, I'll buy you a beer while we're waiting."

"He's coming now?" She asked.

"That's what he said." Sam replied with a shrug of his shoulders.

"Oh, I'm so excited." Kitty beamed, "I'm gonna meet

a zillionaire. I'm going to go clean up." *I'd marry a guy that rich in a heartbeat*, she thought, *even if he would be old enough to be my grandfather!* A few steps away she turned her head back and said over her shoulder, "He's single right?"

Boy is she gonna be surprised, Sammy mused.

As Kitty walked away Sammy sidled up to the bar and motioned to the barmaid. "Hey Frieda, I got an old buddy coming to meet me here. Is there someplace quiet where we can talk."

"Use the lapdance booth. Its not getting any use today."

"Thanks doll. Get me a couple of pitchers too. My friend can really drink."

At the SmithCorp Building, Dr. Bayron was nervously going over protocols with Myra who would be delivering "Smith" to his meeting with Takahashi. Myra was getting impatient already.

"I got it....I got it, Doc. Will you please stop worrying." Myra said, eager to get out of the lab.

"Humor me Myra. I really don't think you understand the stakes here," Bayron insisted.

"Okay, last time though," Myra said with a combination of compliance and defiance. "First, I use this doohicky to sweep a 15 foot radius for bugs and cameras. Then I establish the connection to the private network with this. I wait for these three lights to tell me the connection is established, secure, and untapped. Then, and only then do I call you. You will enter your secret code then I will enter my secret code. If you give me the all clear, then, and only then, can I start the conference."

"All right." Bayron said, sliding a very, very plain looking laptop across the table to her. "Just, please take care of my baby."

Myra thought it was.... well, cute.... the way Bayron

was so serious. "Doc, with all of this security, who do you think is even trying to break in?"

"Oh," said Bayron, "no one on the planet could break in. It's who I don't want to break out."

"I don't think you have to worry about Mr. Smith," she responded, her loyalty to her boss still undiminished.

Bayron's intensity broke. He chuckled. "Entertain yourself sometime by contemplating just how dangerous a thing it is that we've done."

It was Myra's turn to be serious. "Dangerous?" She asked.

"Super-dangerous." He replied. "We're not just transmitting data through the air here. We're transmitting sentient data. Data with its own mind. Imagine what you could do if you could shrink yourself down to the size of an atom and jump into the Internet." Bayron's eyes rolled back a little as if he were imagining it right at that moment. When he looked back at Myra, his face was a little paler. His brow was furrowed a little deeper. It was as if he had not quite fully come back from whatever he had just imagined. "On second thought," he said, "maybe don't think about it. It just might make you crazy."

If only he knew where I was going, she thought. But her orders were clear: Bayron was not to be told.

Bayron was a worrier by nature. That made him a good scientist and an even better doctor. He had never intended Smith to be anything other than a closed system, but to keep the system closed, would be to deny Smith his very humanity-- his contact with the outside world, his ability to create and learn, his ability to interact. Bayron was worried about Flat Stanley, the Russian. Did Dr. Petrovsky know something he hadn't told him? If he opened the system, would it be his friend Elijah Smith unleashed on the world, or this unknown entity also occupying Mr. Smith's mind space? Had Smith told him everything he was reading from Flat Stanley's mind? He didn't want to distrust his friend, but he couldn't help it.

When Myra arrived at the Moviestar Topless Takahashi was visibly antsy. Though he was always enthusiastic about seeing his old friend, there was a certain air of mystery about this particular get-together that made Takahashi feel apprehensive. Something was up. Last time he saw his old friend, he was clearly on his deathbed. Since that time, he had received numerous e-mails from Smith and knew that Smith's brain preservation plan was well underway and going well. But they both knew there was no way Smith was ever getting out of that bed again. Now he was on his way to the Moviestar Topless? It didn't make sense. Was he going to try to bring his entire hospital bed with all of the tubes and wires and monitors into the seedy bar that Sam treated as his second home?

Seeing Myra walk in surprised him further

Myra spotted Takahashi immediately and approached him at the bar. Takahashi tried hard to read her demeanor and chuckled to himself. He could see that she was trying to pretend that the decadent sights and smells around her were a perfectly normal part of her milieu, and he could see that she was failing miserably.

Myra, for her part, noticed that Takahashi was looking past her. Looking for Smith, no doubt. She was also amused by this and tried to think of a clever way to approach Takahashi with her weird news.

Takahashi, always the gentleman (a skill derived from years of womanizing), spoke first. "Hello, dear," He said rising from his seat and grasping her hand gently before pulling out a chair for her. "Where is my old friend?"

"In here," Myra said pointing to her briefcase.

"So he's not coming?" Takahashi asked.

"He'll be here soon," she said, hoping to keep the mystery and tension going on long enough to set up the modified laptop, "but I have to make some preparations before he gets here. Is there an office or something here we can use?"

"Yeah," Takahashi said, "I've arranged to use the lapdance booth. Its very private and quiet, and its actually quite comfortable."

Takahashi led the dark-haired Myra to the little lap-dance booth in the back of the club. Her professional demeanor, styled hair, and grey pinstriped pantsuit were like the lines and arrows on a police photograph. They emphasized each aspect of Myra that did not fit-in at the Moviestar Topless and drew the attention of everyone else in the club. She knew that everyone in that place, male and female alike, were sizing her up, checking her out, and rating her on their own individual scales. She liked that feeling. She knew she looked good. A guilty thought crossed her mind: *I could give these guys a show they'd never forget.*

The lap dance room was small, comfortable and clean as promised. But, every detail in the room suggested seedy, seemy sexuality. There were two small sofas, covered in well-worn red velour, with a small table between them. Framed prints of lingerie clad woman, one with a schoolgirl theme, one vaguely dominatrix-like, adorned the walls. A heavy velvet curtain separated the booth from the rest of the club, a small chandelier with three tealight bulbs, each obscured with a red shade, provided the only light. The music, which had been blaringly loud in the main lounge was subdued in the little lap dance room, perhaps because of the heavy velvet curtain. The mechanical drumbeats and electronic melodies of oldies from the 1980's were audible, but not so loud as to interfere with a conversation. Usually the conversations in the room did not involve business, at least not this kind of business. Bringing Myra into this room embarrassed Sam. Myra noticed that.

Myra proceeded to sweep the room with the handheld device as instructed by Dr. Bayron. After satisfying herself that the lap-dance booth at the Moviestar Topless Bar and Lounge was not bugged, she pulled out the laptop and flipped it on. The laptop hummed and whirred. Sylvia, the barmaid, called from outside the velvet curtain, "Sammy, can I come in with your beer?" Sam opened the curtain and let her in. She put the two pitchers of beer she was carrying next to the computer on the little table between the sofas. "I'll be right back with the mugs."

Some people disappear, Zelig-like, within their surroundings, easily adopting the tone and color of whatever scene they find themselves in. Others cause their surroundings to adapt to them. It was clear to Sam that Myra had the latter effect on the Moviestar Bar. After all, as far as he could remember, Sylvia had never *asked* to enter the booth before.

The three lights on the laptop lit and burned steady. This was Myra's cue to call Bayron for him to establish the connection. She dialed his cell-phone.

"Bayron," the voice on the other end answered.

"Hi, doc, its Myra. I've got the three lights."

"Okay, Myra, put your code and I'll put mine." Myra typed a short phrase into the computer. The screen lit up. "All clear Myra. The conference will start in three... two... one..."

The laptop's speakers cackled a bit and then clear as a bell, Smith's computer generated voice came through, "Hello? Hello?"

"Mr. Smith, can you hear me? This is Myra."

"Loud and clear Myra."

Myra addressed her cell phone, "Okay doc, we've got

the connection. I'm going to hang up on you."

"Bye. And be careful, please." Bayron hung up first.

The computer voice spoke again. Smith had gotten skilled at manipulating the computerized voice and the intended warmth in his tone was successfully conveyed. "Sam, you son of a bitch. Why the fuck are you still alive?"

"Clean living, old man, clean living," Takahashi said as he reached to pour himself a beer.

"Pour one of those for me too, you booze hound." The computer voiced.

"So you can see me, but I can't see you? That's hardly fair, Smitty."

"Oh, but you're mistaken, Sammy. You are seeing me. This is all there is."

Takahashi took a long draw from his mug. "You son of a bitch. You really did it."

"My body died days ago. The whole damn thing. Brain and all. But I'm still alive, goddammit. I'm still human."

"This is fucking incredible," Takahashi stammered.

Smith let out a series of ha-has. "Always the poet, eh, Sammy. I've just revealed to you that I have become immortal. That I hold the key to becoming God and all you can say is, 'fucking incredible'. But listen, I want you to organize the press conference announcing my death. We're going to let the obituary writers break the story of the century. Just get some writers who can do better than, 'fucking incredible', okay?"

"Even from the grave you still have to fuck with people."

"Beyond the grave, my ass. I'm as alive as you are."

"Then why the funeral announcement."

"Because I still have to fuck with people. Its just not from beyond the grave. But Sammy, that's all just for fun. I have to discuss something far more serious with you. Myra, would you excuse us please?"

Myra left the room and Smith continued. "I'm going to e-mail you three names. I need to find out who these people are and what they could possibly have to do with me. Dr. Bayron won't let me access the internet. I can only communicate by e-mail, so I can't do this research on my own. I do not trust everyone on my team right now. I have an anonymous address hhgttg@hushmail.com. Make an e-mail address at an anonymous remailer and send me a verification so we'll only communicate about this through the remailer, okay."

"Hhgttg, I still remember that." Takahashi smiled.

"I know it's a little silly to say, but I don't think all this secrecy is overkill. I genuinely have a sense that I, or people close to me, are in danger. Myra has a briefcase in her car with $100,000 cash as a down payment on your retainer. She is going to set you up with a second SmithCorp expense account. As far as she knows, this is only about the press-conference and the legal issues it may raise. Neither she nor anyone else on my team is to know anything of the names I am asking you to research. Can I count on you?"

"You're an ass for even asking me that."

"When I was flesh and blood, I never had a doubt. Now that I am something else, I wasn't sure you would still regard me as a blood brother. I don't have blood anymore."

"Your blood has run in my veins ever since we cut our palms and shook on it what, fifty years ago? Don't say you don't have flesh and blood. I'm your flesh and blood."

"Sam, you're still the only person on the planet I trust. So, if you're my flesh and blood lets have another beer and... hey, get me a lapdance."

Sam poured another beer and pulled back the velvet curtain. With the curtain open the music suddenly got much louder in the lapdance room. "Kitty!" He yelled into the bar, "get over here and give my friend a lap-dance."

"Wait for the next song!" Kitty yelled back.

Shortly thereafter, Kitty entered the booth and looked around. Not seeing anyone besides Sam confused her for a moment. She noticed the little camera on the laptop computer and looked at Sam quizzically. Sam nodded. Kitty bent down and looked into the camera. "Hey, gorgeous," she heard the laptop say.

"Are you really Elijah Smith?" She asked, still looking at the camera.

The computer chirped, "you bet I am, darlin'. Now get over here an give me a little dance."

Kitty began to do a slow, suggestive dance in front of the camera in time to the music. "Do you like that, Mr. Smith?" She asked the computer through pouted lips.

"Oh yeah, I do." Smith said to Kitty. "Sam, how 'bout you give us a little privacy? I'm getting a god damn lapdance here. Having you looking on isn't making it any sexier."

Takahashi's face was already red from the alcohol he had consumed that day, but it took on an even redder tone when he realized that he was, in fact, sitting and watching his friend get a lapdance. "Sorry, Elly." He said, "you've just got admit that this isn't the kind of thing you get to see everyday."

"Yeah, yeah," the computer voice said as Takahashi clumsily parted the curtains to leave the booth. "And send Myra in when this song is over, okay?"

A moment later, Sam had left the lapdance room and rejoined Myra in the main lounge. Myra had ordered a diet Coke and seated herself at the bar. She and Sylvia were talking and appeared to be enjoying each other's company.

"What's going on in there?" Myra asked, when she saw Sam coming toward her.

"Uh...guy stuff," Takahashi answered. "You wouldn't

understand.

"That laptop is my responsibility." Myra said to Sam with a slight tone of concern.

"Don't worry," Sam replied, "Kitty's a sweet kid. She's as harmless as she is cute. Let the old man have some fun."

"A stripper with a heart of gold, huh?" Myra said judgmentally.

"She's actually earning money to go back to college," Sylvia said in defense of her friend, "I don't think she's going to be here to much longer, either. She's got higher aspirations."

As soon as Takahashi left the lapdance room, Smith had instructed Kitty to stop dancing and engaged her in a conversation. In just a few minutes he had learned everything about her that he needed to know: deceased parents, foster homes, lived on the streets, trying to go to college.

She would do just fine, he thought. "Remember this song," he told her with a note of urgency, "this will be our song."

"Why?" Kitty asked.

"Because it's nice for friends to have a song together." Smith answered. "Promise?"

"I promise," Kitty replied holding up three fingers as a sign of her veracity. She didn't press him for any further explanation, but she understood clearly that there was more to his request than what he said.

The song ended and Myra called through the curtain, "Are you done, boss? We should go."

"Yes, we're done," Smith said. "Myra, give my new friend here a couple of hundred bucks for me. I'd do it myself but I don't have hands. Then you can pack me up."

Myra took two crisp hundred dollar bills out of her purse and handed them to Kitty.

"Kitty," Smith said, "I'm going to be holding a press

conference in a few days. I'd like you to be there. Myra, make sure you get her contact information before we go."

"You got it Boss," Myra responded. Myra moved to start shutting down the computer, but Smith stopped her abruptly.

"Wait. Myra, how much more cash do you have on you?"

"Maybe four or five hundred dollars," she replied.

"Give it to Kitty and expense it. Kitty, if you can take the time off from here, I'd like to hire you to babysit Mr. Takahashi for a few days. Take that money and do your best to keep Sammy sober enough to do what I just hired him to do."

"Okay, Boss" Kitty replied mimicking Myra's manner of addressing him.

"Promise?" Smith said.

"Promise, Mr. Smith, I'll watch him like a hawk," Kitty said as she took the money from Myra.

"A Kitty Hawk," Smith chuckled at the pun. "Okay Myra, pack me up."

"Katherine O'Malley," she said. It was the only time she had ever uttered her real name in the Moviestar Topless Bar and Lounge.

Myra pressed a button on the side of the computer and held it for a few seconds. The computer audibly powered down and all of the lights faded and went out. She packed the laptop and all of the accessories into its little case. She gave Kitty a wink and a smile. She knew this was a good day for her. She also knew she had an interesting new friend to play with. After all, she couldn't have a stripper at the press conference actually looking like a stripper now could she?

Myra left the booth and walked back out into the bar. Takahashi was back at the stage. Myra walked to him and patted him on the shoulder to get his attention. He turned with a start.

"Mr. Takahashi, there's a briefcase in the car that I was instructed to deliver to you. I believe you and Mr. Smith discussed the contents?"

"Yes, thank you Myra," he said standing to follow her out to the car."

"Don't spend it all in one place," Myra chimed whimsically as she took one glance back at the Moviestar Topless. When they reached her car she opened the trunk and handed Takahashi a metal briefcase. They hugged goodbye without speaking. Myra got in her car and drove off. Sam turned and went back into the bar.

When he got into the bar, Kitty met him by the door. "You have some cool friends, counselor."

"I know, but now I have some work to do."

"So do I," Kitty answered, showing Takahashi the small stack of hundred dollar bills that Myra had just given her. "Your friend just hired me to babysit you and make sure you do everything he asked you to do."

Takahashi smiled. "They just don't make men like that anymore, Kitty. He couldn't have hired me a prettier assistant. Let's see what you can do," he replied. He put two twenties and a ten on the bar. "Hey, Sylvia! I left my money on the bar. I have to go." He shouted toward the kitchen.

"Okay, honey," Sylvia's voice replied.

Sam started to leave the bar.

"I'm off the clock, Sylvia, can you please not schedule me for a little while" she said toward the kitchen door as she followed Sam out of the bar.

Sylvia emerged from the kitchen area, drying a bar mug with a towel. "You take care of yourself, honey," she said, looking Kitty in the eye. "Go set the world on fire. We'll be here if you need us." Sylvia knew, she didn't know why she knew, but she knew, that she would never see Kitty again. Of all the girls at the Moviestar, Sylvia thought, they managed to pick the one most capable and most deserving of an opportunity. And she also knew that Kitty would not squander it.

XI.

Having completed the final surgery, Bayron had no reason to spend his days and nights at the lab staring at his panoply of monitors and reviewing his equations. The spare time did not suit him. He went and got a haircut, his first in months, and he had taken his suits to the cleaners. After that he really didn't have any other way to mark the successful completion of the brain virtualization project. In fact, he looked morose, sad, tired, and terribly, terribly distracted

Hermelinda had been a nurse for many years and had developed an unnatural ability to sense when something was just not right. She knew something was just not right with Dr. Bayron. Smith was all locked up in his computers and she felt it was her obligation to keep him company and to keep him entertained as much as she could. She knew it must be lonely in there with no human contact. During lunch, however, she was on her own, and she used her lunch hours to figure out and tend to Dr. Bayron's needs, whatever they were.

She enjoyed eating and speaking with Dr. Bayron. And even though she justified their lunches as merely 'being there for him if he ever wanted to talk', she couldn't help feeling that something deep and acutely atavistic was causing her to seek out fathers for her baby: good, strong, reliable men, the kind of man who would provide a comfortable and stable life for his family. Money wasn't a concern for her anymore-- Smith had kept his promise to her in that regard, but she still had the mother's instinct to build a safe nest and a safe nest required a safe man. How could Smith, locked away in his box as he were, ever protect her or the baby?

Dr. Bayron, with his multiple doctorates in psychology, psychiatry, and neurology would not have been surprised to learn that these instincts were brewing within Hermelinda, but he had other things dominating his thoughts. He knew he was attracted to her, but he had loved before and it nearly killed him. He was no fool to even consider the possibility of falling in love again. Besides, Hermelinda was Smith's girl, and he wouldn't hone in on someone else's action. It just wasn't in his constitution. He figured that because he and Hermelinda had together participated in something that no one else had ever done they were inextricable joined by their unique experience. And with that reasoning he was able to rationalize away his feelings.

One of the things that had been dominating his thoughts in the weeks after the final surgery was the memorial service that Smith was planning. Smith had told Bayron of his plan to announce the success of their project at the memorial service and that he intended to have Dr. Bayron make that announcement and field questions from the press. With the memorial service coming up, Bayron found his thoughts becoming less and less clear.

Bayron sat in his office contemplating what he should

say in his prepared remarks at the press conference. He had read some articles about speechwriting and public speaking, neither of which came naturally to him. He was searching his mind for a metaphor or an anecdote to frame his speech, but all roads just led to his dead wife and son, their brains long ago consumed by the ground and lost to him forever.

So he decided to focus on what he could be asked about, figuring that he might devote his time to anticipating and answering the questions that the audience might have. "How did you do it?" would be the easiest of those. "Why did you do it" struck a more disturbing chord. "How does this change the world?" was simply unanswerable. Unfortunately, none of his speculations on that topic had good outcomes.

"Good morning, doc," Smith's simulated voice said, interrupting Bayron's train of thought.

"Morning, Smith, how you doing today?"

"I'm bored out of my, well, I was going to say skull, but whatever, I'm bored. I need to get out of this box."

"Can't do it Smith. Not yet." Bayron warned.

"What if we made a copy of me and let the copy out into the world?"

"We've discussed this Smith. You would be the world's most effective virus because you can think. You would literally be able to take over the world. I trust you, I love you, but even before we started, you knew that I only agreed to this project if it was to be a closed system. I am very confident that you are Elly Smith, but I don't know if the Elly Smith model is subject to the kind of corruption that Elly Smith the human was immune to. And neither do you. I'm the one who goes to jail if something goes wrong-- not you. I know Elly Smith would never put me at such a risk, but if I let you out and something gets corrupted? That's on me."

"Okay. How 'bout this? Put in a kill routine. The minute you get nervous, kill the copy."

"I don't know, Smith. Let me think about it."

"Hey," Smith added, "I got that Armenian kid back. Sharky. We've been e-mailing back and forth for a few months. He was more nervous about this than you. He's literally spent the last two months doing nothing but contemplating the implications of this whole thing. You should've heard some of his concerns. Real science fiction stuff. That kid's got some imagination, I'll tell you."

Bayron could not match Smith's lightheartedness. "It's not hard to think up some concerns about putting you out on the Internet. What he's thinking is not science fiction at all. It's science. We can not disregard potential outcomes."

"Bring him in on this. I want out. You want me kept in. We both have legitimate interests here. Give Sharky a chance to figure out a way to satisfy both of us. What's the harm in hearing what he might be able to come up with."

"All right, I'll talk to him." Bayron paused for a moment and decided he didn't like the silence. He needed a friend, and it took him a moment to realize that perhaps his closest friend was actually there with him. "Hey, Elly," Bayron said, addressing Smith by his first name, "I'm a little worried about this press conference. I'm not really a press conference kind of guy. What do you think I should say?"

"Glad you asked Bayron. I've been thinking about it a lot. For me, you know, I'm off the human grid now. But you, you still have to interact with the planet. I can laugh and fuck with people, but you're still going to have to face the world. It didn't really occur to me how difficult its going to be for you after this announcement is made."

"So what do you suggest?"

"My advice? You better say something to appease the bible thumpers. They're the ones that are going to go bonkers over this and the ones that might cause us the most trouble. This whole thing really undermines a whole lot of religions, doesn't it?"

"Yeah, it sure does." Bayron said, conceding what to him was already obvious. "Thoughts?

"Do you know a good rabbi?"

Dr. Bayron felt his thoughts begin to close in from this question. It was the wrong question for Smith to ask, but Smith didn't know that. The last time Dr. Bayron had even given God the dignity of a hopeful thought was just before he threw a shovel of dirt over a tiny little coffin. After that, God was his sworn enemy. And now, with the success of his experiment, he believed he had won. He believed he had defeated God. He knew these thoughts could get him killed and he tried to drive them out.

Smith's suggestion had been the opposite of helpful. It set off thoughts and feelings that Bayron had compartmentalized years ago. It was as if Smith had dropped a match in a fireworks factory. "Elly," he said standing up from his desk. "I've got to go."

"Wait!" Smith broadcast, "Is Hermelinda here? I've got to talk to someone or I'll go nuts."

"Alice is here," Bayron responded as he reached the office door.

"Good! Send her in," Smith ordered.

As Bayron walked out of his lab, he saw Alice in the staging area. "Alice, go talk to Smith a while," he said, "he's lonely."

"Sure thing, Doctor. You know I can talk!" She replied happily.

Bayron pushed the elevator button and waited long moments for the elevator to come. He fidgeted as he rode down, knowing that soon he would be thinking about his little son, only five years old, dying in pain, writhing in his arms as he tried in vain to comfort him. He knew soon he would smell the smell of the hospital in his nose. A smell he once felt was so reassuring: the smell that said, "okay, you're in the hospital now, everything's going to be okay." But when he smelled the smell or even imagined it, it was the smell of betrayal.

Bayron knew that soon he would remember sitting vigil in the hard wooden chair next to the bed; the little boy finally asleep and looking peaceful, and he with no peace, only confusion. He remembered the Rabbi. His father sent the Rabbi. The Rabbi hugged him and said a prayer for his dying son.

"Why?" He asked the Rabbi.

"No one knows. Only God knows, Douglas."

"Why me?" He asked.

"God gives certain challenges to those that can find the holiness in them. It is for you to decide how to create a blessing from this tragedy," said the Rabbi.

"Then God can fuck himself," Said Bayron and he never loved God again.

Bayron got off of the elevator, still insisting that he would not let those memories form and he was successful in doing so until he walked out of the front door of the SmithCorp Building into the pouring rain. With the rain to mask his tears, he let himself weep.

"I beat you at your own game," he said to heaven. "I have vanquished death itself. But you're going to have the last laugh yet, aren't you?" He neither expected nor received a response at that moment.

Alice was happy to be off of her feet. Even though there was no real patient in the lab for her to care for, Alice didn't like being idle. Hermelinda was still technically on maternity leave though she came in nearly everyday to talk to Mr. Smith or eat lunch with Dr. Bayron. So Alice was alone most of the time just trying to keep busy. She was happy that she hadn't been reassigned or let go, she needed to keep this job for more reasons than anyone knew. So she kept busy keeping the operating room clean and sanitary. She made sure the medications on the shelves were unexpired and properly arranged, she put fresh sheets on the bed daily and ran diagnostics on all of the lab equipment. All-in-all, she made sure that the room was ready for its next patient in every respect, even if there would never be one. She worked as if her life depended on it.

The invitation into Dr. Bayron's inner lab just to have some chit-chat with Mr. Smith was a welcome break for her. She sat at the console terminal and settled in to the office chair comfortably. She pulled the microphone close to her mouth and said, "How you doing in there, Mr. Smith?"

"Alice!" Smith responded. "It's good to hear your voice, but please, you don't have to shout. I have bionic hearing now, you know."

"Oh, good. Same old Boss! Still funny."

"Alice, I could always count on you for some good gossip, we haven't spoken since I still had a body. Tell me, what's up?"

"Oh, Boss, remember you ask me to find out who the daddy is?"

Smith's digital brain forgot nothing, but, sometimes, the data wasn't always on his mind. He remembered instantaneously. "Did you learn something?" Smith asked with genuine curiosity as to what the rumor mill was churning out.

"Okay, boss, I got two possibilities. Ready?"

"Do tell, dear."

"First, I think, probably, I think, this cute boy. He sound a little like Count Chocula. Russian maybe. I notice, he don't come to work no more since Hermelinda have the baby. Maybe he take paternity leave and is stay-at-home daddy. I know he very smart, one of Dr. Bayron's favorites. Like a, uh, like a ... Chevrolet? ...Chevrolet?" She repeated the word, knowing that it wasn't the word she was looking for and asking for help.

"Protégé'?" Smith offered.

"Protégé! That's the word I want. I knew it some kind of car. Yeah, his protégé!"

"Sarkis Ohangangian. They used to call him Sharky."

"Yes! That one! Sharky!" Alice said excitedly.

"Don't you think he's a little young for Hermelinda though?" Smith asked.

"They both very serious people, boss. Too serious. Water finds it level, right? Besides, where else but here Hermelinda gonna find a man? She was here all the time before the baby."

"Okay, I can see it being Sarkis. Who's the other possibility?"

"Okay, boss, sit down when I tell you this," Alice said conspiratorially.

Smith released a couple of "ha's" and said, "Okay, I'm sitting."

Alice spoke in a hushed, conspiratorial whisper, "You ready. Listen. Now I think, maybe was Dr. Bayron."

"Really!" Smith said with delight. It was remarkably easy for him to feign all kinds of emotions because of the limitations of his electronic voice. Pretending to be surprised only required a slight increase in pitch and volume. Ditto with delight, enthusiasm, and joy. There were no facial expressions to belie his words. Alice didn't seem to have figured this out yet and appeared to trust that everything Smith said connoted nothing beyond the meaning of his words. Bayron wasn't so sure anymore. Neither was Hermelinda. But Alice was safe in her trust, he really was delighted to see the finger still pointing at his lonely friend Dr. Bayron. "Go on," he urged.

Alice continued to speak in a whisper even though no one else was around. "Okay, here some facts, Jack. First, Hermelinda, she still on leave, but she come in anyway. There's no work to do, but she come and pretend to work, maybe one hour, maybe two. Sometime, she come with baby, and I know she not working with the baby. And then, when she come, all the time, she and Dr. Bayron go out to lunch. You see my finger's boss? Where's that camera?"

Alice looked around for the camera and found it just above the monitor on the wall. She held her fingers up in front of the camera and made quotation marks in the air and repeated, "lunch." She made the quote marks in the air again before saying, "if you know what I mean."

Smith interjected, "Well, they're professional colleagues. Professional colleagues can go out to lunch together, that doesn't mean there's something going on between them."

Alice chuckled, "Oh, boss, you're not a woman! I'm a woman! A woman know. He come back a little too happy. She come back a little too happy. Dr. Bayron, he the daddy, I think."

"What about me?" Smith clipped in.

"What about you? That silly rumor start in the lab, but I know that silly. Everyone in the lab thinks that its you. But you know what. Not enough women in the lab." Alice frowned. "Couldn't be you. The baby born in September. That mean conceived in December, you... you still had your body. Artificial heart just started up. Involuntary muscles were working again because of the computer, but your voluntary muscle control was non-existent," she said, revealing that she had a nuanced understanding of the procedures and an excellent memory. "How you going to seduce a girl if you can't talk or move your arms?"

Alice laughed at how silly that ridiculous rumor was

before continuing, "For it to have been you, Hermelinda would have had to ... " The smile faded from her face as she returned to thought for a moment, before saying, "Oh, Mr. Smith! You sly. It was you?" Alice asked in the hushed tone of a midnight bandit.

"Listen, Alice, I'm just suggesting that there are more possibilities than you have considered. As Sherlock Holmes used to say, 'to solve a mystery, first eliminate the impossible.' All I'm saying is that it's not impossible. I don't want to feed any rumors." Smith lied. He did want to feed the rumor and he knew Alice was just the person to start it.

Kitty had not left Takahashi's side since their strange encounter with his old friend Elijah Smith. In fact, in the few days that had passed, she proved to be a valuable assistant. She had an innate sense of showmanship that Takahashi lacked. And her mere presence actually helped Takahashi focus on the task at hand. Her ideas for how the "memorial service" would unfold seemed, somehow instinctively, to mirror Smith's own twisted and manipulative sense of humor. She also seemed to know a little something about lighting, and P.A. systems, and seating which all proved inordinately valuable when dealing with the decorators, the caterers and the technicians. "You'd be amazed what you learn working as a dancer," she said. Takahashi reported every action to Smith via e-mail and Smith often responded with unchecked joy at each good idea that Takahashi attributed to Kitty.

"You know she's the first new person I've met since I got myself all bottled up like this..." He wrote at one time.

The funeral notice was written, and the mailing list had been checked over and over, the date was set. Takahashi and Kitty were laboring over the wording of the press release announcing the memorial service and finding it very difficult to make it sound perfectly ordinary when they knew it was not.

A new e-mail came in from Smith. "Sam, now that we're in the home stretch with this memorial service, I want you to start on the other project I told you about." What followed was in code, "7:90,16,45,18,3,14,72,11.." Takahashi turned to page seven of a book he'd kept since high school and began counting off the letters. The 90th letter was a "K", the 16th letter was an "O", and so on until Takahashi had spelled out three names: Kovaretsky, Vakhrusheva, Ashkot.

The red phone in Gonzales' study rang. It was a rare night for him because he was actually at his home. The red phone was a secure line. Cell phones could not be secured. When the red phone rang, he knew he would be leaving home again soon. He was actually glad to hear that phone ring. Being at home didn't feel right to him anymore. He was made for field work. Age was no consequence and sitting still made him nervous. Socializing offended him. At cocktail parties he would cringe when somebody would say that something interesting had happened at their office, or on the golf course, or at the market. He had once accidentally crushed the skull of a gunrunner in Oman with his bare hands while unsuccessfully trying to extract information regarding his source. No one could tell him anything about their last fishing trip that could interest him, and he hated smiling and pretending that it did. The red phone was his salvation from this hell. He was eager to be working.

He picked up the phone and answered curtly, "Gonzales. Identify."

The voice on the other end stated in an equivalent clip, "Cruz."

Gonzales pressed a button on a device wired to the phone and a red light came on. He held the button until the light turned green. "Okay, the line is clear. Talk."

"We got a very, very interesting intercept from right here in the United States," Cruz said.

The communication that Cruz was talking about was an e-mail sent from one anonymous remailer to another.

"Eyes only, I assume," said Gonzales.

"Eyes only," was the quick response.

"20 minutes, at Point Charlie," Gonzales said referring to a prearranged meeting place.

Gonzales arrived in exactly twenty minutes by the statue of Moses in the center of the park. Cruz was already there.

"Show me," Gonzales said.

Cruz handed Gonzales a printout containing a series of punctuated numbers.

"This looks like an old-fashioned Civil War era book code. It's completely useless if you don't have the book." Gonzales said dismissively.

"We have the book," Cruz said proudly.

"How did you figure it out?"

"Look at the address it was sent from: hhgttg@hushmail.com. Hhgttg. It's the Hitchhiker's Guide to the Galaxy. One of our geeks downstairs recognized that on sight and he was right. Look what it says."

Cruz handing Gonzales another printout which read: "Kovaretsky, Vakhrusheva, Ashkot."

Cruz thought for sure that Gonzales would react. Maybe a double-take, maybe a moment of silence while the implication set in, maybe even a cartoon-like bulging of the eyes. Cruz prided himself on never losing his cool, but even he had reacted to the three names with a semi-silent, "oh wow." Now he was impressed with Gonzales' complete lack of reaction.

"Who?" Gonzales asked simply.

"Its an anonymous remailer, Sir. We don't know who. We do know where."

"Okay, give."

"SmithCorp."

"Now that's interesting." Gonzales said, almost to himself.

"I'll get warrants for Hushmail and SmithCorp." Cruz volunteered.

"This is a black-op, son, nothing goes beyond you and me until we know more." Gonzales warned. "Find another way."

XII.

Bayron had hoped that the day would pass quietly and that he could be left to his thoughts. He had started writing his speech many times and then abandoned his ideas to start over. The pressure of the coming date bore down on him like a Sisyphusian stone.

Equal to or greater than the doctor's fear of making himself public was Smith's fear of being isolated for eternity.

"Doc, you have to let me out. I need to be mobile. I need access to information. You know that no one understands better than I do what your concerns are, but I am literally alone with myself all the time. You cannot imagine how much worse this is than solitary confinement. I'll go crazy soon." Smith was actually rambling a little bit and it concerned Dr. Bayron.

"Besides, Doc," Smith continued, "What if something happens to you? What if something happens to the building?

I am extremely vulnerable here. You can't imagine the gravity of being locked in a bottle for all eternity. I'm a human being, Doc, I need to be engaged."

Bayron frowned and tried to frame his thoughts. Smith didn't let him.

"Doc, I know you're not happy about this. I have back-up plans if you say no, and I will get out. I just want it to be with your blessing. I guess I need to make myself eminently clear: I'm not really asking. I'm just offering you the opportunity to participate."

Bayron sighed. He knew better than to assume Smith was bluffing and he was too scared to let someone else take his monster out. If Smith was going onto the 'Net, Bayron knew he'd better be holding the leash. "Okay," Bayron relented. "Give me a couple of days to put it together. Anything else?"

"Yeah, one other thing. No one sent me my Wall Street Journal yesterday. Where's Myra?"

"I just saw her yesterday. She's fielding all kinds of calls about the funeral announcement."

"If you see her again, remind her that her first obligation is to me and I need my Wall Street Journal everyday."

"Okay." Bayron said.

Smith changed the subject. "By the way, have you given any thought to your remarks at the service?"

"Some," Bayron replied.

"Just have fun with it," Smith said. "You can be as silly or over-the-top as you want. Your remarks are just part of the prank. I'll do all the heavy lifting. You can just wing it if you want."

"That's probably what I'll end up doing. I'll talk to you again before the service" Bayron said as he disconnected the communications port and headed out into his lab.

Prank! Be Silly! Have Fun! I'm announcing the god damn end of the world and he tells me to have fun! Bayron dialed Sarkis on his cell phone.

"Doc!" Sarkis answered.

"Smith told me you're coming back. I am so happy to hear that you don't even know. Smith is hellbent on getting out. You're the only one who I think understands the scope of the problem here. And Smith is convinced that you do. I really need you here."

"I'll be there in the morning." Sharky assured him.

"Oh, and Sharky, if I'm not there for any reason, you'll find my black notebook in with the phonebooks. Keep it in a safe place, will you?."

"That's a strange place to leave your notes, Dr. Bayron." Sharky said.

"I didn't want to leave them at my desk." Bayron replied.

Sharky arrived at 8:00 in the morning and was glad that none of the other engineers were there yet. He didn't want to answer a bunch of questions about why he hadn't come in for the last few weeks since he wasn't really sure himself. He was, much to his own surprise, relatively excited to get started on the project. He walked to Dr. Bayron's private office and looked inside.

Alice looked up in surprise and then smiled broadly. "Oh Hi, Mr. Sharky!" She beamed. "Dr. Bayron such a slob. I straighten things in here for him or he not even find his desk. He's not here yet. I not seen you in a long time. Where you been?"

"I had the flu," he lied. It sure looked like she was looking for something, he thought. Maybe that explains why Dr. Bayron put his notes with the phone books.

Meanwhile, on the far side of the planet, Vladimir

Vakhrusheva stood on a little bridge and looked out over the river. It hadn't snowed in weeks, but there were still traces of the winter from which the Russian countryside on the outskirts of St. Petersberg was now emerging. Vakhrusheva wondered why he continued to work. There were no goals left for him to pursue. He was already wealthy, respected, and feared. In his days at the KGB he had proven himself over and over to be a skilled field operative and as politicians became mobsters and mobsters became politicians, Vakhrusheva discovered the power of the open market and the blessings it could bestow on men of experience and talent like himself.

His principal at the present time, Sergei Kovaretsky, was a man for whom Vakhrusheva had completed many missions. Kovaretsky had been a high ranking member of the Communist Party when being a member of the Communist Party opened doors and created opportunities in a country which, at one time, offered dread few opportunities. When the Soviet Union ceased to exist, he too found himself uniquely situated to benefit from the open market. He had the good fortune not only to know the locations of some of mother Russia's most dangerous weapons, but also to possess an invaluable code. Code Two. One of three codes needed to activate Ashkot's now dormant fraction of the Soviet nuclear arsenal.

Kovaretsky had been fortunate to avoid the public scandals that plagued so many Russian businessmen after the fall of the Soviet Union. Unlike those caught by the press with blood on their hands, Kovaretsky was merely the subject of speculation and insinuation. His ability to stay out of the news, permitted him to openly proclaim himself to be a decent, honest, caring and philanthropic man even though wise men knew to fear him. Even his philanthropic endeavors occasionally left an unidentifiable body in the morgue.

Vakhrusheva, on the other hand found his opportunities not in a sparkling public image, but in his reputation as a cold-blooded killer, loyal only to whatever mission he had been paid to do.

He no longer needed to work. In fact, as fifty had turned into sixty and sixty began to push its way into seventy, every little crick and creak in his bones warned him that he had better start making other plans. The arthritis in his hands had twisted his bones, and his knee hurt when it rained. It was about to rain, too. He took a Tylenol and washed it down with a swig of Vodka from his flask as he waited for Kovaretsky to join him on the bridge.

"Should I be struck by lightening on a golf course!" he whispered to the wind as he laughed at the idea of a quiet retirement. He stroked his jacket near his chest and felt the handgun snuggled comfortably in the shoulder holster where it had snuggled everyday for as long as he could remember. It reminded him that he was no armchair warrior and that he would never be happy sitting on the sidelines. Though his movements had grown stiff and slow, the gun reminded him that he was a warrior at heart and that he would die a warrior's death.

Seeing Kovaretsky coming across the footbridge reminded him of something else too. It reminded him that there were armed and functional truck mounted long range nuclear missiles hidden at Kovaretsky's airplane parts factory outside of Irkutsk that were worth more than a billion dollars on the black market. Missiles that were useless without Code 3 which was holed up in the brain of his dead friend, Yuri Ashkot. Kovaretsky had already spent millions of dollars to bring Ashkot back to Russia. American politicians are not as cheap as Russian ones and there were many, many hands out. Someone would yet be held accountable for delivering him a dead body, when he had been clear that he wanted a live one. Maybe a lot of people. Vakhrusheva stroked his handgun as if it were a beloved pet and took comfort in feeling it against his chest.

Kovaretsky walked up alongside Vakhrusheva and the two men exchanged a nod. Vakhrusheva spoke first. "The news is good. The American's were successful. The old man is dead, but our source says he is actually alive and well and living in the computer. The brain is apparently intact and functional and all the memories are preserved."

"Proof of concept," Kovaretsky said. "And has Bayron kept his end of the deal?"

Vakhrusheva swallowed hard. He was not going to be giving the answer to this question that he wanted to give. "We think so," he said as confidently as possible.

"Thinking is not knowing..." Kovaretsky observed.

"Dr. Petrovsky believes that he has been provided all of the data and has assured me that Bayron diligently uploaded all of his progress and notes as he promised in exchange for the scans he provided. Our contact, on the other hand, says there are certain hardcopy notes kept in a separate notebook..."

"That could be anything," Kovaretsky cut Vakhrusheva off. "A diary, a journal, anything. If Dr. Petrovsky says he has the data he needs to proceed, we'll give him the money he needs to bring Mr. Ashkot back to life. Go do it. I'm not getting younger." Kovaretsky paused and thought for a moment, then added, "If something is missing, Dr. Bayron will be brought here to explain. Perhaps he is unaware of who he is doing business with."

"There is something else," Vakhrusheva said. "There is going to be a memorial service tomorrow. Word is that they are going to reveal the technology at the service."

"In that case, time is even more so of the essence."

Kovaretsky replied.

Vakhrusheva walked back to the footbridge. Letting Dr. Petrovsky know that more money was on its way to the lab was a call he was looking forward to making. It was rare that he had the opportunity to convey good news. He was also hoping that maybe Dr. Petrovsky could recommend something for the pain in his hands before he left for America. The pain had been getting worse.

Sharky waited for Alice to leave Dr. Bayron's office. She was so friendly and energetic; she always brought a lightheartedness into the lab when she was there. Sharky was wondering why she had made him feel uncomfortable. He had learned to trust his instincts, though, and waited until she was well out of sight before he went looking for Dr. Bayron's notes by the phone books.

On top of a filing cabinet on a far side of the lab were half a dozen yellow-spined phone books. Sharky couldn't remember the last time he had even used a phone book. That's what makes this a good hiding spot, he thought, admiring Dr. Bayron's choice. He didn't see any notebooks with the phone books, so he started taking the phone books down. Behind the phone books he found Dr. Bayron's black-covered spiral notebook of the type used by college students. Nearly all of the notebook's pages were filled with Dr. Bayron's signature scrawl. On first glance the notes appeared to be the same as the notes which were uploaded every night for the lab. He wasn't sure why Dr. Bayron had gone through such great pains to hide them or why he wanted Sharky to have them. Maybe there was something in there about the security system he would have to build to give Mr. Smith the modicum of freedom he so craved.

Sharky didn't want to start reading the notes with Alice still milling around and acting suspicious, so he put the notebook in his backpack and went to his workstation to figure out how to free Mr. Smith from his prison.

XIII.

The employee dining room in the SmithCorp Building was designed to do double duty as a banquet hall. The tables had been cleared out and the plastic dining chairs were draped in black slip-covers and arranged in rows. A portable stage had been erected at the front of the room with a podium and a microphone. The chairs were set in groups. Those closest to the stage were reserved for the mourners who consisted mostly of Smith's business associates, a few friends, and some of the higher ranking executives at SmithCorp. Only Hermelinda's baby carried the same blood as Smith as all of his other close relatives had long since passed.

Memorial books had been printed and were arranged on tables set on either side of the entry door. Each table also had a portrait of Elly Smith with a candle beside it that would burn during the service. Funeral flower arrangements of yellow roses, and white orchids and lilies were arranged in front of the podium and down the aisle between the chairs.

The decorator and her crew had just left leaving Kitty alone in the spacious hall. Kitty marveled at how the room had been transformed so completely. As she bent to fix a leaf on one of the arrangements lining the aisle she was struck at how difficult a task it must be to make roses look so sad and somber.

Kitty herself had also been transformed working with Sam Takahashi and Myra on the arrangements. Sam and Myra were busy with Smith's legal and business affairs. Neither of them had time to select floral arrangements, or decide how the chairs were to be arranged, so she made the decisions that had to be made. Nobody but she knew of the dozens of hours she had spent on the internet looking at pictures of memorial services so that she could exercise her own judgment and not be mislead by the designers and technicians she had hired. She even went to the library and borrowed books on etiquette. She spent an hour speaking with the minister who would officiate. And now, it looked as if the t's were crossed and the i's were dotted.

Earlier in the day, Myra had taken Kitty to a salon to have her hair done. The stylist cut her hair along it's natural contours, he explained, so that she wouldn't have to worry about it falling out of place during the service. All afternoon, Kitty tested this theory and it was true, her hair fell back into place with a simple shake of her head or brush with her hand. She wondered why she had never had a haircut like that before and then remembered...it cost $600.

Kitty also had a new black suit hanging in her closet. She only had it on one time, when Myra's seamstress was altering it for her. She remembered the cool soft feel of the silk against her skin when she had it on and suddenly, she realized that she was tired. *Where is Mr. Takahashi?* she wondered as she dozed-off in one of the slipcovered chairs. Myra woke her up just a moment later with a hand on her shoulder, "come on dear, I'm going to get you home," she said as she led Kitty down to a waiting limousine. "Tomorrow's the big day."

Kitty slept well through the night and awoke refreshed and excited. Takahashi however, had tossed and turned all night. He was wired and fidgety. He had confirmed all but one of the speakers and reviewed their notes so that there would be no surprises. Bayron, however, was no where to be found and Takahashi had already called off the search party. It was clear to Takahashi that Dr. Bayron did not want to be found. Takahashi was thus working out contingency plans in his head. What if Dr. Bayron did show up? What if he didn't? What if he showed up drunk? He had to let Smith know. Myra let him into the lab where Hermelinda was seated in front of the monitor feeding her baby while faint cooing noises were coming from the speakers.

Smith's camera picked up Takahashi first. "Sam!" a tinny but distinctly human voice burst forth from the speaker. The apparatus had been worked on so much that the voice had developed a real timbre and warmth. It didn't sound exactly like Smith. There were still some non-human, electronic edges in the voice, but it was close. "How's the world's best-paid party planner? Is my show ready for prime time?"

"Elly, everything's in order. Everything looks great. But, I gotta be honest with you, we can't find Dr. Bayron. I haven't been able to review his speech notes and that's making me nervous."

The "ha-ha's" that came from the speaker resembled an actual goodhearted chuckle. "Relax Sammy. Bayron's been eating his heart out about this whole thing. He's nervous as hell about speaking in public. He's probably just sequestered himself somewhere to make his speech perfect. He'll be fine. He won't let me down. You don't have to worry about what he's going to say."

"I'm a lawyer Elly," Sam replied somberly, "its my job to worry. And today I'm sober enough to worry for us both."

"Go have a drink, my friend," Smith said jocularly, "you've done your job and it will all be over soon enough."

The morning had come far too early for Julian Waterstone, the Gazette's oldest working reporter.

In his small house on Nott Street his alarm clock rang with an insistent series of loud beeps at 8:00 a.m. Julian's arm, spotted with age and wrinkled, reached out from under the blanket and lethargically pressed the button for another 9 minute snooze.

My life is a fiasco. I wish I were dead. I wish I could just stay in bed. I wish I could just crawl under a rock and disappear. He dozed back off into some kind of not-quite-sleep when the alarm clock again beeped its insistence that he get out of bed and start his day.

His arm hurt. He didn't know why and he didn't care. His back creaked and he had to use his arms as support just to get out of bed. He considered that to be the price of living to be over seventy. *Getting older does not beat the alternative*, he thought. *My friends who are already dead have no idea how lucky they are to be at peace.*

Julian wished he could just be dead with them, but God wouldn't let him die. He tried not to wake up too much. He preferred to be a little bleary. He took a shower, put in his dentures, and dressed. As he walked out of his front door he said his daily prayer: "please, God, don't let anyone talk to me today." But his prayer was quickly denied. As soon as he got to the curb, his neighbor went jogging by with a friendly wave and a hearty, "Hiya, neighbor!"

Julian smiled and waved back, but both the wave and

the smile were lies. *Have a heart attack and don't ask me to deal with your stupid cheeriness*, was what he really wanted to say.

I am a relic. I don't know why they still pay me. Not only aren't I any good at this job anymore, but I haven't given a damn about it in over 30 years. Seriously, he thought to himself, *I haven't given a damn about reporting in more than 30 years. I wish I was dead. Elly Smith. That guy was a complete ass. Why does he get to be dead and not me? What did I do to deserve this.*

Julian had won awards for his reports from Korea, Vietnam and Washington, DC. When he hit 60 years old and no longer wanted to travel, they let him work locally, reporting from City Hall, and covering the crime beat. At 70, they suggested that he cover the obituaries and the social scene-- an assignment Julian called the last-gasp hospice of dying journalism careers. And he didn't care. He couldn't stand to retire and he didn't want to work. Obituaries was both his salvation and a constant reminder of how much he just wished he was dead.

The Smith memorial service. *What a crock of shit.* He would have to make it seem like Elly Smith was some important person. *He wasn't important. He was just rich.* But the readers already knew that. He'd try and get some quotes about what a wise and generous man he was and how loved he was and how much he would be missed. 10 paragraphs because of his stature in the community. He didn't have to go, he'd written the same obituary for 20 self-important corpses in the last two years alone and they were all exactly the same. He was only going there to pretend that he still had some journalistic integrity.

As he pulled into the parking lot, he remembered the two other times he had been at the SmithCorp Building. The first time was to cover the building's dedication. The second was just a few years ago when SmithCorp hosted a symposium of scientists, philosophy professors, clergy men and some other kooks and weirdos to discuss the ethical implications of "living machines."

Julian wrote 10 paragraphs about the symposium which were edited down to two paragraphs and presented next to an ad for a penis enlargement clinic on page 5 of section B. Apparently, all that was important was who was there and what they ate. Julian thought the topic was interesting and thought that one day he might even write a book about it, but he had forgotten the whole thing rather promptly. He did remember one presenter, a fellow named Bayron who had taken the position that a "soul" is merely a religious term for self-consciousness and any machine that is aware of its existence could be said to have a soul. Julian had waited for one of the other geniuses at the symposium to jump up and down and take offense-- maybe one of the priests-- to this idea since it would by implication suggest that once a human being has lost self-awareness then that person could be said to be living without a soul. Julian doubted whether he had a soul. *I'm not self aware-- I am only aware of mediated representations of myself. Thus, I have no soul.*

Now that he was dead, Elijah Smith would become nothing more than a mediated representation of who he once was. Smith's entire existence would be reduced down to whatever words Julian Waterstone decided to write in his obituary while the real Smith would be buried in the ground with his dead body. What Julian Waterstone wrote in the Gazette would take over and become the truth about Elijah Smith, regardless of its actual truth. Waterstone knew that his words would necessarily redefine the deceased in the way people wanted to perceive him and that this posthumous fiction would serve only to the negate the complex man that he probably was. With every obituary he wrote, Julian

Waterstone carried the guilt of having lain the final executioner's blow to whatever legacy the deceased himself perceived that he would be leaving behind.

Julian wondered if he had written that book when he had first thought of it whether he would still be hauling his ass around to symposiums and memorial services at the age of 75 for fear of loneliness and obsolescence. He wondered if this fellow Bayron would be there. He would have liked to ask him a few questions.

Julian parked in a handicapped spot close to the front entrance of the SmithCorp Building. He put his handicapped parking card on his rearview mirror and thought that the close-in parking was a damn small reward for having suffered more than 25,000 days of shit. He took a sip of coffee from the travel mug in the center console of his Buick and slipped his press-card dangle around his neck. He turned in his seat, put his feet on the ground, and his hands on his knees to push himself up and out of his car.

My damn shoulder hurts, he mumbled to himself. But he didn't really care.

Kitty had assigned herself the job of giving everyone who came in a memorial book and helping them to find a seat. Friends and family had a section, employees had a section. Guests of honor and speakers were to be escorted to the front. Members of the press had a section in the back.

Kitty was thrilled when she saw Julian coming toward the door. She knew that he might not want to be recognized. Some men could not let it be known that they had ever been to the Moviestar Topless, much less frequented the place. She had seem him drop in from time-to-time in the late afternoon in a wrinkled suit. He would order a beer and sit quietly in the back, never getting a lap dance and never wanting to talk. Nonetheless for some reason she was thrilled to see the familiar, if not necessarily friendly face.

Julian recognized Kitty, but couldn't remember where he recognized her from. Kitty wanted to spare him the embarrassment of reminding him where he knew her from and simply told him that indeed they had met several times before. She told him to sit up close with the friends and family and Julian said that he was supposed to sit in the back because he was with the press. Kitty said to Julian that she personally considered him a special friend and that she would be honored if he would sit in her seat near the front.

Julian was amused by the special treatment he was being given by this beautiful, elegant, and sexy woman and politely obliged. He slipped his press pass off and put it in his pocket as he went and sat up close to the stage. *It'll be nice to be able to hear,* he thought as he settled into the seat Kitty had directed him to. If every moment in my life was like that, he thought, maybe I wouldn't want to be dead all the time. It's nice to have the attention of a beautiful woman, even if only for a moment. Then it struck him where he knew Kitty from and he chuckled to himself. He suddenly regretted the many times he had refused her offer of "a little company" at the bar when he realized how the small piece of attention she had just afforded him had already made his day. He turned in his seat and smiled at her. She smiled back and gave him a little, flirty wave. He winked and nodded his head. How could he have forgotten? He always thought she was the prettiest one there.

As the guests took their seats, Takahashi was up in the lab talking to Smith.

"Elly, Bayron is still not here," he said.

"Well that's a disappointment, but life goes on," Smith said with no hint of concern. "No one will probably notice if he doesn't speak. No one really reads the programs at these things. If he doesn't show up, we'll hire an investigator tomorrow. But I'm sure he'll be here." Smith was secretly glad that Bayron had disappeared. Bayron was the one keeping him off the internet, after all. And worse, had lied about it. "By the way, speaking of investigation. I know you've been busy with this service, but have you had any opportunity to look into those names I gave you?"

"Yeah, actually I have. I think you're going to be pretty shocked. Is this the best time to discuss that though?"

"How did you find the time to do the research?" Smith answered with a question of his own.

"Believe it or not, remember that stripper you met at the Moviestar Topless? You hired her to babysit me?"

"Kitty?" Smith asked, drawing the name out of his now-infallible memory.

"Katherine O'Malley," Takahashi corrected. "Yeah, believe it or not she practically pulled this whole thing together herself. I think you're going to be pleasantly surprised. I actually had some time to start doing some real digging; and like I said, you're not going to believe what I found out. The first guy was pretty easy. 'Kovaretsky' is Sergei Kovaretsky. He was the Politburo's Secretary of Defense when the Soviet Union collapsed. Now, he's either a businessman or a politician or a mobster, depending on who you ask."

"Sounds like an interesting guy," Smith interjected.

Takahashi continued. "Anyway, he's a rich and dangerous guy. We know that. Probably not as dangerous as the second guy on your list, though. This, Vakhrusheva fellow was former KGB, very high up. Might still work for the Russian government or military, very mysterious character. Rumor has it that he is also on Kovaretsky's payroll."

"The muscle, I'm guessing," Smith mused.

Takahashi nodded agreement, "Now the most interesting of this triumvirate is your Ashkot. Now Ashkot is probably Yuri Ashkot who was a former general in the Soviet military who was the head honcho in charge of a good chunk of their nuclear arsenal. No bomb got built, moved, aimed, tested or anything without his nod. And that's when we get into some real serious mythology. Supposedly there were three secret codes built into every nuclear launch facility constructed under his command. One code was provided to the Secretary General, the other was provided to the Secretary of Defense, Kovaretsky, and the third, "Code Number 3" was known only to this guy Ashkot. In other words, the Soviets could not launch a nuclear warhead without his say-so. Sort of the ultimate fail safe. Again, unconfirmed, but apparently that's a big part of why there have been no nuclear attacks by terrorists or rogue nations. Even though a lot of missiles and other hardware got out on the black market, almost nothing can be launched without Code 3."

"Wow. That's crazy." Smith said recognizing the scale of his understatement. For the first time ever he felt glad to be locked away in a box with no face to show his expression or subtlety of voice to betray the fact that he was already familiar with "Kodeks nom tri": Code Number 3.

"Get's crazier, pal," Takahashi continued. "Apparently, about five years ago, Ashkot disappears. Literally disappears. Off the Radar. Destination unknown, in the wind, now you see him, now you don't. Hiding? Dead? Kidnaped? Abducted by aliens? No one knows. This guy is potentially the most powerful man on earth. He has the key to unlock a huge, HUGE, nuclear arsenal. These loonies that might have obtained a black-market nuclear weapon from the former Soviet Union would pay billions--maybe trillions--to get the information that's in this guy's head, and he's...," Takahashi put his hands together at the fingertips and pulled them apart quickly, "...poof!"

"Any idea what that might have to do with me?" Smith asked even though he already suspected that Ashkot was alive, at least in part, and living within him, giving him dreams of Russia and feeding him names.

"I've got no idea Elly, but I do know these are dangerous people we are talking about."

"Well, I guess that's really all I need to know. Forget about it for now. We've got my funeral to attend to."

Takahashi got up to leave, but Smith spoke again, "Oh, and Sammy, not a word about this conversation to anyone at all."

"'Nuf said," Takahashi replied comfortingly.

Julian listened intently as the Reverend went through the religious part of the service, pausing often to make reflections and share some stories from the Bible. Julian enjoyed the Reverend's words. He had attended many funeral services and, so far, this one had been quite nice. The Reverend had given him some food for thought. Nice words. Maybe, he thought, they just seemed extra nice because he was in such a good mood now. He glanced back at Kitty again and she gave him a little wave. Late arrivers were still trickling in and she was handing out the programs and pointing them to their seats as they did so.

The Reverend introduced a Ms. Myra Shiltz as Mr. Smith's longtime personal assistant and close friend. Julian took a few notes. Wonderful boss, caring person, great sense of humor. SmithCorp succession, who will be in charge, shareholder's don't have to worry. Charity work, scholarship fund in Smith's name, blah, blah, blah. *That's funny*, Julian noted, *she's not crying*.

The Reverend came back and announced a change in the lineup, Dr. William Bayron was unable to be here so Smith's private nurse, Hermelinda Posada, would speak next.

Hermelinda explained the course of Smith's disease, how the shafts that the nerves go through had started to harden making it increasingly difficult for his brain to communicate with the rest of his body. Julian took notes in shorthand: very painful disease, loss of body control, muscle's waste away, eventually, the nerves in the brain don't work. Smith put up a brave fight, invested heavily and dedicated much of SmithCorp to the advancement of a cure, contributed to the research. Julian stopped listening and writing notes when it occurred to him that this speaker wasn't crying either. He took a look around the room.

Where are the tears, he wondered, *did they all hate this guy?*

Julian underlined and put a question mark next to the word brave. *Is that the right word? Brave is when you have a choice and choose to face a fear. This guy didn't have a choice. He got sick. That sucks, but it doesn't make him brave.*

Brave was putting your life on the line for ideals higher than yourself, even if those ideals were wrong. Brave was willing to die for a belief, for loyalty, for love. Getting sick is unfortunate, but it isn't brave.

Julian had seen brave. He knew brave. He had been in Korea at the end of the war. *How does Mr. Smith's suffering even compare to the bravery of a man who, in the moments before his death looked fearlessly into his assassin's eyes and said, "you can kill me, you are only killing one man. I am ready to die for my country."*

He left his musings and returned to taking notes when the Reverend introduced the lawyer. Japanese lawyer, he noted. That's weird. Okay, close personal friend for over fifty years. They were blood brothers when they were kids and did everything and saw everything together. Loved him, wonderful guy, all the right charities, supported the schools, the arts, contributed to this and that, crazy sense of humor, incredibly human blah blah blah. Julian thought he was going to fall asleep. He glanced at Kitty again. She smiled and waved. He felt a slight arousal. Just a little, but undeniable all the same. The last time he was in this building, his article ran next to an ad for penis enlargement. He quickly turned his attention back to the dais. *Weird*, he thought, *even Smith's best friend doesn't seem too choked up about his death.*

"Without further ado," the Asian lawyer told the audience, "I would like to introduce the next speaker, Elly Smith." The light's dimmed and a screen was lowered over the makeshift stage.

Please, Julian thought, *don't let this be another now-that-I'm-dead, self-aggrandizing montage narrated by the dead guy himself.* Julian crossed his eyes and sighed, then realized he was among the friends and family, not the usual crowd of journalists. He genuinely hoped nobody had noticed.

The screen lit up, but not with some cheap title like, 'The Life and Times of Elijah Smith.' Rather it lit up with what appeared to be the simple, green wavy lines of an oscilloscope. A voice came forth from speakers on either side of the screen. It was not an entirely human voice. Julian wasn't sure if the voice was computer generated. If it was it was definitely the best computer generated voice he had ever heard. But it definitely wasn't completely human either. It seemed to have some warmth and depth, but it was missing something in timbre.

"Hi, everyone, thanks for coming," the voice said, "I'm Elly Smith and I'd like you to know that you've all been had. I'm not dead."

Julian sat up in his seat and a nervous chuckle went up from the audience. *Maybe this could be interesting yet*, Julian thought. Smith was known as a great jokester.

"Calm down, calm down. There's more to tell. I didn't bring you all here to waste your time. Hi Herme, I see you there by the stage. Hi, Ellen," He said in a gentle voice to the baby on Hermelinda's lap.

"Okay, I guess we should tell these people, what do you think, kid?"

"I think they should know, Hon." Hermelinda responded from the audience.

"So you didn't ruin the surprise?" Smith asked.

"Nope. I didn't ruin any of the surprises, Elly." She replied.

"Good. Okay folks, the first surprise is that earlier today, Hermelinda and I were married in a civil ceremony. She isn't just my nurse, she is also my wife. We have a beautiful child together named Ellen." Hermelinda turned in her seat and waved to the gathering with a broad grin on her face.

"The second surprise is that my body did die and was buried two weeks ago at the Heritage Cemetery out on 73, but I am still very much alive."

Julian felt a creepiness, like a cold, wet hand touching his back. It made him shiver. The voice. The warmth and depth of it now just seemed eerie and dark.

The voice carried on, "Dr. Bayron was supposed to be here to answer some of the more technical questions about how I am still alive even though my body has died, but he has apparently become indisposed. So I'm going to give you the 25 cent version and do my best to answer a few questions. And even though I would think that the revelation of human immortality would itself be worth the trip down to the SmithCorp Building on short notice, we have also prepared a beautiful buffet luncheon for you after the presentation."

Immortality, Julian thought, *who the fuck would want to be immortal. Lunch, however, is something I could go for.*

"Dr. Bayron and I have been working on this idea for more than a decade," Smith continued. "Bayron had postulated when he was still a graduate student at Harvard that because a human brain is comprised of a discreet number of elements, in theory all of those elements could be modeled by software. Bayron compared his idea to an accident reconstruction video. By programming in all of the known properties of a particular material, it is possible to predict exactly how that material will react in certain conditions. The more accurately the properties are known the more accurately the model will emulate reality. If the model is completely accurate, then the outcome will be completely real.

"Dr. Bayron hypothesized that by modeling every cell, every neuron, every chemical, every single discreet piece of the human mind, he could create a model of that mind which would function exactly like the original. By recreating every single property of every single piece of the brain, the reconstructed brain would be just as real as the original.

"Well, it took a long, long time and we did it piece by piece, but we did it. Each piece of my brain-- every synapse, every nerve cell-- was modeled, one at a time. We filled exabyte after exabyte of digital media with perfect, digitally rendered, representations of my brain. As my brain began shutting down, each piece of my brain that shut down was replaced with the model. A little piece here, a little piece there. The first part to go was memory. I could still think and solve problems, but my memory was starting to fade. So we replaced that part of my brain responsible for memory with the model that Dr. Bayron made and wired it into my brain. And, to no one's greater surprise then my own, it actually worked. Every few weeks, as my brain died, we replaced the dying part with its model, until finally there was nothing left of my biological brain. At that point, we disconnected the body and sent if for burial, but I have remained very, very much alive. I was awake when the very last cord was cut between my biological mind and my new prosthetic mind.

Had my eyes not been watching the activity monitors as it happened, I would never have believed it happened at all.

"All right, I'll take a few questions now."

Almost every hand in the room went up.

Takahashi went to the lectern and spoke into the microphone. "One at a time, one at a time. Calm down and we'll call you one at a time."

A reporter from the back was waving his arm wildly. Smith acknowledged him as the guy in the green jacket. He asked, "How does it feel to die?"

Smith answered, "I don't know, and I probably never will know." Smith had anticipated this question and knew he would tell this lie. He knew what it felt to die, it just wasn't his own death he felt. It was that of Yuri Ashkot.

"So there was never a long tunnel or a bright light or anything?"

"No, nothing. I was even awake during all of the surgeries and there was never a point at which I felt any change in my consciousness. Trust me, I am still alive."

Another reporter asked, "How many copies of there are you then?"

Smith lied again, though he had not anticipated this question, "a few," he said.

"Are each of the copies separate people then?"

Smith had thought about this before and answered quickly, "As each copy would amass different experiences and environmental factors, they could obviously become two different people, much like twins have distinguishable personalities. However, I don't think splitting myself into multiple people is a particularly convenient thing to do, so I do not intend to the let copies grow apart. Next question, Red necktie, pink shirt guy."

"Mr. Smith, could the same technology be used to bring say, Einstein, back to life since his brain was preserved? By the way, its salmon, not pink."

A series of "ha's came out of the speakers. The laugh's still didn't sound quite right, but they got the idea across, "Young man, in my day we called that pink. And yes, I would say theoretically, if a brain has been properly preserved, it should be possible to bring it back to life with this technology. Maybe Walt Disney would be a better example since his entire head was cryogenically frozen. The chemicals preserving Einstein's brain could have corrupted some of the more subtle structures. The best subject, of course, like me, would be a live one."

I should probably ask a question, Julian thought to himself, *this is pretty important stuff. I want to see that luncheon, but I know I should ask something.* He hadn't asked a question at a press conference in probably 20 years. He raised his hand and hoped he didn't embarrass himself.

Smith acknowledged Julian, as "old man, up in front."

"Julian Waterstone, Schenectady Gazette. Sir, I understand that you're still alive, but are you still human?"

The question silenced the room and the wavy lines on the screen above the stage went straight and stayed that way for a difficult moment. Smith was not stuck for an answer, he was stuck for a simple answer. Julian looked toward the door to see if Kitty was still there. She wasn't. He'd hoped she had heard his question. He wondered where she had gone.

"Still human?" Smith repeated. "That's really the question, isn't it? I'd be lying if I said I hadn't given that question a lot of thought." Smith confessed to the crowd. "I know that I am still a person. I am still sentient and self-aware, still bound by rights and duties, still cognizant of past, present, and future. The law has never ascribed flesh and blood to the concept of personhood either. Hell, SmithCorp is a person under the law. Human, on the other hand, really relates to a taxonomical classification, Homo

Sapiens and taxonomy relate to biological classifications. Clearly I am no longer biological. I'm alive, but not organic. I'll have to leave it to men smarter than myself to decide whether I'm still human though. The description I like is trans-human. Still human, but just in a different state of being. Techno-Sapiens, maybe?"

Julian nodded as Smith continued taking questions. It certainly was food for thought.

Out in the parking lot of the SmithCorp Building, a crowd was forming. Some of the reporters and maybe some of the other guests as well had called or messaged the news of Smith's appearance at his own memorial service and the miracle of his transformation. Reporters, photographers, newsvans, and various curious onlookers were beginning to crowd the parking lot.

When uninvited people first started arriving and were trying to get in, one of the security guards came up and told Kitty what was going on. She didn't want to disturb the proceedings, so she went down to see for herself what was going on. "Keep them out." She instructed the guard. "This is a private event and they have no right to be here."

She went back inside the SmithCorp Building and instructed the desk guard to lock the front door. Kitty called the police and told them what was happening. She had to make a decision and she hoped she had made the right one. She then went up to try to find Myra or Mr. Takahashi to tell them what was happening. She found Myra and told her what was happening downstairs. Myra said she did the right thing and that the police would handle it. She told her to come to the luncheon and make herself a plate.

Kitty walked into the room where the luncheon had been prepared for the attendees of the memorial-service-which-was-really-a-press-conference. It hurt her for a moment to see how the beautiful spread of coldcuts, condiments and desserts had been destroyed by the press and other guests. It hurt her worse to see the crumbs and soda stains on the tasteful linen tablecloths she had picked out. She had struggled so hard to get the right ones and she was sure that nobody had noticed. If they had they wouldn't have put their coffee cups down on them. Then she realized that it was a good thing. People were eating, they liked the food. They were sitting and talking, so that satisfied her that they liked the atmosphere she had made.

Kitty saw Julian sitting alone with a partially eaten bagel in front of him. She took a bagel and a cup of coffee from the buffet and sat down next to him. "Do you want some company, mister?" She said to him, using the exact same words she had learned to say in order to sell lapdances at the bar. She didn't know his name, but she knew when she looked in his eyes that he was the saddest man she had ever met and there were many sad men at the Moviestar Topless.

"I would like that very much, Miss." He said, answering that question in the affirmative for the first time ever. "I didn't recognize you when I first came in."

"They call me Kitty," she said, extending a hand, "my real name is Katherine, though. But I seem to be stuck with Kitty now."

Julian shook her hand gently. "Julian Waterstone," he answered. "They call me Julie."

She reached over and brushed some bagel crumbs off of his shirt but instantly realized that doing so made him uncomfortable. "Isn't this beautiful," she said, showing off her black satin pantsuit. "They've really been treating me nice here," she said.

"Are you working for SmithCorp now?" Julian asked with genuine curiosity.

Kitty smiled and thought for a moment. "I'm not sure," she said. "I think I work for that guy." She pointed to Sam

Takahashi. Julian had seen Sam before at the club. "He hired me to give a lapdance to a little laptop computer. The computer turned out to be Mr. Smith and, well, somehow, here I am, with all kinds of important people, a $600 haircut, and people calling me Ms. O'Malley instead of Kitty." She picked a little at her bagel.

"This is quite a group to be involved with, Kitty," Julian said feeling fatherly, "it looks like you've been given a real opportunity here."

"I'm glad you're here though, Julie. I kind of feel like a phony. I better get back and see if Mr. Takahashi needs anything."

Julian smiled. He knew that she really was glad that he was there. This wasn't a lapdance booth and she wasn't working for tips. "Take my card," Julian said, "if you ever need anything."

She took the card and put it in her pocket. "I don't have any cards of my own, but this is Mr. Takahashi's card," she said as she rose. "I wrote my name on it."

As Kitty walked away, Julian looked down at the card. Across the top, handwritten in curly stylized letters, was the name, Katherine O'Malley.

"Eliza Doolittle, more like," Julian said to himself. He let his eyes watch her ass as she crossed the floor. *Good for her*, he thought. *Some people are blessed. I wish I was dead.*

Cruz called Gonzales and asked to meet with him immediately. He had been watching the wires for any news out of SmithCorp ever since they had identified it as being the source of the three names they had intercepted. Today, being the day of the press conference, he had been keeping especially close watch. When Cruz got to the Brandywine Diner, Gonzales was already there and seated in a booth. Cruz pulled a paper out of his breast pocket. It was a report filed by a reporter from the Schenectady Gazette regarding the Smith Memorial service which had concluded only hours before. As Cruz adjusted himself in the booth, Gonzales perused the clipping. Cruz had highlighted what he thought was the most important part which was about two-thirds of the way down in the text. "Smith suggested that, in theory, the same technology could be used to bring the dead back to life if their brains have been properly preserved."

"SmithCorp," Gonzales whispered, "fucking SmithCorp. I'll be a son of a bitch. Kovaretsky wants to use this technology to get the code from Ashkot's brain. Jesus."

Josey Cruz noticed Gonzales's hands again as they contracted around the clipping, the veins visible through his skin.

"What stymies me, though," Cruz said, "is why would SmithCorp go public with this if they're conspiring to unleash an unregulated nuclear arsenal on the world!"

"They wouldn't. Unless they didn't know..." Gonzales started before changing his mind. "But if they didn't know, then how did the names come up?"

"They must have known." Josey said. "It's the first rule of criminal investigation: there are no coincidences."

"True, " Gonzales agreed, "but there are accidents."

Gonzales perused the article again. "Speaking of coincidences..." Gonzales chuckled, pointing to the article's byline, "I served with this guy in Korea."

"Spook?" Cruz asked.

"Nope, a journalist," Gonzales answered.

Smith wasn't aware of the now-dissipating chaos that had descended on his parking lot hours ago. Hermelinda had left the luncheon and took the elevator to the executive floor so she and the baby could spend some private time with their husband and father.

A conference room with a long table and three chairs on each side had been wired with a microphone, a camera, and a wall mounted monitor so that Smith could hold meetings there. Smith called it his office and he strongly preferred to see people there than in the lab. The fewer people in the lab, the better.

Smith felt an awful lot of activity in his artificial mind. He couldn't sort out his thoughts at all. There was just a lot of activity. The fact that he felt a little confused actually made him feel good. It reminded him that he had not become a computer even though his mind was now hardware driven. It reminded him that life was not simply an equation to be calculated and empiricised. Even with the worlds most powerful computer equipment driving his mind, there remained the unquantifiable elements that kept him human.

"Are you worried about Dr. Bayron?" Hermelinda asked.

"No." Smith's still, though barely, mechanical voice crackled, "not really."

"I am." Hermelinda said.

"I always trust a woman's intuition, Herme. Tell me what you're thinking."

Hermelinda smiled weakly. "Well, Doug and I spent a lot of time together." She said choosing her words very, very carefully. "And, you know, this project was his life. He lived for it. It meant everything in the world to him. He wouldn't just disappear when the curtain was about to go up on it. He wouldn't just abandon you..." She paused, "or me."

"No," Smith said softly, recognizing how selfish his lack of concern for Dr. Bayron was. "You're right. We'll notify the police tomorrow and I'll have Myra hire a private detective."

He sensed sincere sadness and worry in Hermelinda's voice. Was she having an affair with Bayron? Was that cheating? They were, after all married, even though the Notary who married them said that the marriage was not necessary legal. They had told the Notary that Smith was out of town and Myra signed the marriage certificate for Smith with her power of attorney. The Notary was not comfortable and was very reluctant to place his stamp on the certificate, but ultimately he did it.

Even if the marriage was legal, Smith didn't know if a court of law would even consider him alive. Even if the marriage was legal and he was deemed to be alive, he still couldn't caress Hermelinda's gentle cheek, or hold his baby, Ellen, in his arms. Bayron could. *If I still had flesh and blood, would I be jealous?* Smith wondered as he gazed at Hermelinda, who had nothing to look at but a flickering screen, a cold glass camera-lens, and a tangle of wires.

Hermelinda reacted to a knock on the office door.

"See who it is," Smith said.

Hermelinda opened the door and there was Sharky.

"Oh!" He was taken aback when he saw Hermelinda. He stammered for words and ultimately came up with, "Hi!"

"Hi, Sharky!" Hermelinda said, genuinely delighted to see him-- Bayron was so sad when he left-- "I'm glad you decided to come back."

"I got a little bored not being here, to be honest. And I think Dr. Bayron really wanted my input. I don't know why, its not like I have anything over the rest of the guys."

Smith interrupted, "did anyone else walk away after I was online and the concept was proved?"

"No, not that I know of." Sharky answered and then corrected himself. "Well, from what I've heard, I guess just me and Dr. Bayron."

"That's what you have over the other guys here, Sharky: A strong conscience. So, what can we do for you?"

Sharky looked at Hermelinda and Smith noticed his

reluctance to speak. "Anything you want to say to me you can say in front of Hermelinda," Smith said. Hermelinda motioned to a chair and Sharky sat down.

"Okay, Mr. Smith. I only just came back, but you know that I've been thinking about what you want for the last few weeks and I think I know how to work it."

"I'm listening," Smith turned to Hermelinda to catch her up in the conversation, "I've been bugging Bayron to let me on to the internet so I can get out of this box and stretch my legs a little. He's fearful that since I can read and think and see data, I would have the capacity to corrupt and manipulate all of the data in the world thus becoming the most powerful human being ever. Now, that doesn't bother me so much, but it really seems to bother Bayron."

"Go figure," Hermelinda replied facetiously, giggling, "I guess he doesn't know you as well as I."

Sharky wasn't amused.

"So what's your idea, Sharky?" Smith urged.

"Well, without getting over technical, I have an idea for a gateway which would attach a small data code on every packet you transmit over the 'net. Basically little tethers so that we can call back every packet you transmit."

Smith chuckled. "You literally want me on a leash!"

Sharky winced. Smith was right. Bayron had made the remark about keeping his monster on a leash. His mother had placed the image of chained-to-the-radiator in his mind too. While he had to acknowledge that those metaphors had given him the idea in the first place, he felt they were no longer apt.

"You know that's not the end of the story though," Sharky said. "No one is worried about you looking stuff up on Wikipedia or making a Skype call. We're worried about your creating proxies or dupes outside of the gateway. Intelligent mini-Smiths, or even complete Smith's roaming around on the cloud. Intelligent data. Our little leashes only let us track and potentially undo first generation transmissions. But if you create a program externally, that program would generate its own packets of information and those packets wouldn't have the leash code on them. We wouldn't be able to pull those back."

"So what's the solution?" Smith asked with genuine curiosity.

"Well, let's say that you did create an external program and that program was capable of performing certain functions: data-in, data-out. Data-out either goes somewhere or its just space dust. So what you would have to do is make sure that once the leashes are pulled, the data spawned by an external program has no where to go. You see we've been too focused on the data part. We should have been focused on the processing part. If that 2nd generation has nothing to process it, then it becomes innocuous."

"I'm not sure I like where this is going," Smith said. Hermelinda had given up on understanding already.

Sharky stopped talking. He knew Smith understood what he was talking about and he wanted it to sink in. The silence hung in the room. Hermelinda glanced from Sharky's unsmiling face, to Elijah Smith's faceless electronic eye.

"What is he talking about, Elly?" Hermelinda asked nervously.

"A kill switch, babe." Smith answered leaving the silence to hang in the room again.

A few moments later, Smith's voice crackled in the speaker's again, "Is that the price of freedom, then?"

Sharky surprised himself with how quickly and cleverly he responded, "Isn't it always, Mr. Smith?"

"You're a wise man for someone so young," Smith said. "Someone raised you right. It's no wonder Bayron thinks the world of you." Smith paused, but not long enough for anyone to interrupt. "Okay. Do it, but make three keys for execution by any two keys. You, me, and Hermelinda will each have a key, but at least two of us must enter our keys to execute the kill routine. With that stipulation, we have a deal."

"What about Dr. Bayron? It should be his call too," Sharky said.

"We don't know where the good doctor has spirited himself off to, Sharky." Smith confessed.

Sharky thought for a moment. Smith was clever, he wanted the deck stacked in his favor. "Dr. Bayron gets a key too. That's my condition, Mr. Smith."

Smith knew that Sharky had a firm enough constitution to simply walk away. He knew he had to be prepared to let Sharky go or give Bayron a key. "Okay four keys then. Two to execute the kill. Keep me apprised of your progress, will you?"

"I'll e-mail you daily progress reports if you want. I do that for Dr. Bayron anyway." Sharky said as he rose from his chair to exit the room.

"Oh, and Sharky, could you ask Myra to come and see me on your way back to the lab?"

"Sure thing, Mr. Smith." Sharky said as he left.

Hermelinda also stood. "I'm going to go too," she said. "It's time for Ellen's nap." She paused for a moment and then turned back and said, "please let me know if you hear anything at all about Doug."

"Of course my love," Smith replied, his computer generated voice sounded reassuring in Hermelinda's ears. The conversation she had just participated in had left her with a heavy heart.

Smith's mind was somewhere else completely already. The camera that acted as his eyes was sensitive enough to notice a slight change in the shade of Hermelinda's cheeks each time she spoke of Bayron.

Smith was also amazed at the genius of Sharky's plan.

But he knew Bayron's way of thinking too. An open system is subject to random and unquantifiable events and is therefore dangerous. Bayron would never go for it. The project would have to be completed before Bayron was found. Or behind his back.

Moments later, Myra came into the office. That was fast, thought Smith. "Hi Boss," she said into the microphone. "It's nice to see you in person for a change."

Smith realized that he had been communicating with Myra via e-mail almost exclusively since his body died. The converted conference room that was now called his office was as close as one could come to actually seeing him or being in a room with him. Smith recognized that to him it was all the same, but to flesh and blood humans (it was not so long since he had been one) the intimacy of physical presence would be a profoundly different experience.

"Myra, its so nice to see you. How's my company doing without me?" He asked.

"I send you the reports daily, Mr. Smith. We're doing great. Our stock has nearly doubled in the after hours trading since the press conference, and the publicity we are receiving is just insane. We're probably going to have to create a whole new department just to deal with the inquiries."

"You know, I see the reports everyday, but since I can literally see and process the raw data in an instant, there's some kind of warmth missing. Something familiar and comforting and... tangible... I think that's the word I'm looking for ... in getting information in an analog instead of a digital way. Hearing it from you is just so much... nicer. You know what, make it a point to come give me a personal report every so often, will you?"

Myra smiled, "you didn't call me in just to ask me to do that, did you?"

"No," Smith confessed, "you know me too well. But I

am serious. It was nice to hear you tell me how we are doing rather than just have it snap into my memory as if I already knew it. Its hard to explain."

"So, what did you call me in for?" Myra pressed. She didn't want to be rude, but she was quite busy doing all the legwork involved in running SmithCorp. She was Elly's flesh now that his flesh was long since buried. She was the only physical evidence SmithCorp's thousands of employees and hundreds of thousands of shareholders had that Elly Smith was still very much in charge of SmithCorp.

"I know you're busy," Smith said, reading her mind from the lines in her face and recognizing the unfair advantage it gave him. "But I have one more burden to place on your shoulders."

Myra winced a little, but it was with a smile. Smith knew he could count on her. "Use Takahashi and maybe that girl again. What was her name?"

"Kitty. Katherine, actually. The stripper?"

"Yes. I know what a great job she did with the press conference. But more than that I also know that she kept the entire affair completely confidential. And this next job needs to kept completely confidential. Me, you, Takahashi, Kitty, no one else. Pay them and yourself enough to ensure complete silence."

"Not Hermelinda? Not Bayron?" Myra asked.

"No. Not Hermelinda and not Bayron. No one." Smith said matter of factly. "Myra, remember how I used to say, 'trust everyone, but cut the cards?' Well, we're just cutting the cards. Now write this down and keep it with you. I don't want any records. Ready?"

Myra pulled out a little notebook and carefully wrote down everything that Smith said. As she wrote it became clear to her why he had to involve Kitty.

XIV.

Julian Waterstone wanted to die and Elijah Smith wanted to live forever. *It must be good to be rich,* Julian said to himself. *I should have written that book.* He pulled his Buick into his driveway and walked up to his front door. He didn't want to be home and he didn't want to go out. He didn't want to be lonely and he didn't want to have to be with anyone either. He hung his wintercoat on a hook in the little hallway and headed for his sofa. He sat and stared at the wall. *I wish I was dead,* he thought and then thought again. He repeated the thought over and over again like a mantra, somehow soothing himself with those disturbing words. Then his doorbell rang.

He turned and looked at the door. It was late for the doorbell to ring. Maybe not, only 7:00. Who could it be? It couldn't be good. Maybe they got the wrong address and will go away. The doorbell rang again.

"I'm coming, I'm coming," he yelled at the door. "Just give me a damn second, I'm coming." He shuffled to the door and swung it open. "What do you want?" He said.

"My car broke down and I need to use your phone," the old man standing outside said.

"Bullshit." Julian said, "get the fuck of my property." Julian lived in the middle of the street and there was a liquor store right down at the corner. No one would come knocking on his door asking to use his phone. This guy was no older than him. If he had a car, he had a cell phone. *I don't know what this guy really wants but I don't have it.* He was about to slam the door when he looked square into the stranger's eyes and noticed them looking squarely back at him. The eyes were familiar. More than fifty years had passed since he had seen those eyes.

"Are we caught?" Julian asked.

"No," Gonzales answered. "We're cool. I need you again."

Julian opened the door wide and let Gonzales in. He led him to the kitchen.

Myra returned to her office, her head aswim with her new instructions. But that would have to wait. There was a message taped to the back of her chair. The private investigator she had hired to find Dr. Bayron had called. It was good news. Myra called the number on the message and reached the investigator at his cell phone. Moments later she called Hermelinda's cellphone. She realized that she had never called Hermelinda directly before. They had known each other for at least three--no, longer than that-- five years, but she had never had any reason to call her. But this time, there was no one else she even considered calling. She didn't want to convey this information to Mr. Smith herself. She wanted to let Hermelinda know and let Hermelinda decide what to tell Mr. Smith.

The phone rang three times when Hermelinda answered with a simple "hello". Myra was glad she answered because she wasn't prepared to leave a message.

"Hi, Hermelinda? This is Myra, Mr. Smith's assistant..."

"Hi Myra," Hermelinda answered cheerily, "I know who you are. What's up?"

"Our investigator found Dr. Bayron. He's at County General. The police brought him in on a three day evaluation and I think he needs some help." Myra said.

"A psych eval.?" Hermelinda asked rhetorically. "Why is he being held for a psych eval.?"

"Here's all I know, honey." Myra continued, "A worker found him at the Congregation Ahava Zedek Community Cemetery up on 78 and called the police. Apparently he'd been there for days, in the rain and the snow. He hadn't eaten anything and he was dehydrated and incoherent. Turns out he had a kid who died about 10 years ago at the age of five. He was just sitting at the grave crying his eyes out."

"I'm going to go get him." Hermelinda said confidently.

"They won't release him to anyone but family," Myra replied.

"I'm a nurse," Hermelinda said. "I know people at County General. I'll get him and bring him back here. You have to tell Elly."

"I wanted you to know first, Hermelinda."

"I really appreciate it Myra. It's no wonder Elly thinks the world of you." Hermelinda said.

She hung up and dialed Alice. Alice sounded thrilled to hear they were going to have a new patient. She didn't sound quite as thrilled to learn that it was going to be Dr. Bayron.

Then Myra called Takahashi. "Get your girl and meet me at the Moviestar Topless, Sammy." She said. As much as she tried, she just couldn't think of a better place to have a confidential talk.

Seeing Gonzales in his doorway after all of these years was not a pleasant surprise. It wasn't pleasant, and it almost didn't even feel like a surprise. Julian had spent years wondering if one day someone would discover his deceit and he would receive a knock at the door and be led away in handcuffs to account for his actions of some fifty years ago. Lying to his commanding officer would have been the least of his charges.

If you ask any American under the age of 50 about the American War against the Soviet Union, they will tell you about the Cold War. They will haul out the word "detente". They may recount the missile crisis.

But there are men, old men now, who know better. They know there was a real war against the Soviet Union with guns and bombs and people dying and it was fought in Korea. "Air support" was the official Soviet role on the North Korean side. "Police action" was the official American role. But without the Soviets and the Americans there would have been no war. Had there been no Russians on the Korean peninsula, there would have been no Marco Gonzales on the Korean peninsula to find and eradicate their spies and there would have been no Julian Waterstone to cover it up.

There would have been no spy named Jimmy Kornin who would die for his beloved mother Russia with a hand grenade taped to his chest. And Julian Waterstone wouldn't have written his award winning piece on his heroic death. The article was an elaborate lie to cover up the most brutal act Private First Class Julian Waterstone had ever seen. "You are only killing a man," Kornin said, staring at Gonzales fearlessly and with eyes of steel, before the hand grenade scattered his flesh over an area of at least a hundred yards.

As Julian led Gonzales to his kitchen, he tried to assess his feelings. *I should be feeling scared, and angry,* he thought; but he didn't feel that way at all. He felt...happy? No matter what Gonzales might need him for now, he knew it would be interesting. Julian tried to keep a poker face as he sat Gonzales at his small kitchen table and proceeded to brew a pot of coffee.

"Jimmy was a spy, Julian. I hope you did not lose one moment of sleep over him. He would be one of the most dangerous men in the world today had he not been neutralized." Gonzales paused and waited for Julian to look at him. When Julian turned around, Gonzales continued. "You served your country. You did the world a favor. You can be proud of what you did."

"It was murder." Julian replied humorlessly.

"It was war." Gonzales replied without skipping a beat.

"Who do you work for?" Julian asked, having already accepted the fact that this was not a social visit.

"I still work for the good guys." Gonzales smiled warmly as he spoke, "and as you know, I am very good at what I do."

"What do you want from me? Julian asked watching the coffeepot begin to fill.

"Do you believe in coincidences, Julian?" Gonzales asked cryptically.

"No. But I do believe in bad luck." Julian responded seriously.

"Call it what you will. I'm about to tell you a story, but before I do, I need to ask you one question. Do you trust me?"

"Have I ever had a choice?" Julian answered.

"The alternative would not have been pleasant."

Gonzales answered without a hint of humor, "we're old men now, Julie, we're not going to have a lot more opportunities to save the world. Will you trust me again?"

Julian thought about it and looked hard into Gonzales' eyes as he tried to reason through his decision. He couldn't rationalize what he was about to say, but he said it anyway. "Sure," he said. "You kept your word to me for fifty years. Your credit is good here. I'm in."

Gonzales proceeded to reveal to Julian Waterstone all of the information which he had learned over the last few weeks. About the strange e-mail from Smith to Takahashi, the death of Ashkot, and the theory that Kovaretsky and Vakhrusheva were trying to unlock the codes from Ashkot's brain using Smith's just-announced technology.

"I know that name, 'Vakhrusheva', don't I?" Julian asked.

"Jimmy Kornin." Gonzales replied. "Jimmy Kornin was Arkady Vakhrusheva. Now its his older brother, Vladimir. We've been watching him for years."

"Why are you telling me this?" Julian asked.

Gonzales looked him in the eye and said, "Because you have above-board access as a member of the press. You were there. You met people. You know this town. And because I trust you. And the last Vakhrusheva to cause us trouble...well, I couldn't have done it without you. Hopefully this time, I won't have to blow anyone up."

For a moment--just a fleeting moment--Julian didn't wish he was dead.

"I may be more 'in' than you think." Julian said drawing out Takahashi's business card with Kitty's name written across the top. "I know this girl. She works for Smith's personal lawyer."

"Shall we invite her for lunch tomorrow?" Gonzales asked, looking at the business card and, by long habit, memorizing every detail of it. "My treat."

Julian smiled. Something exciting was about to happen. When it happened in Korea, he had the rest of his life in front of him and the last thing he wanted was excitement and danger. He just wanted to get home alive. Now, he realized, he was hoping for it. "I'm in no position to be turning down free lunches," he replied, smiling for the first time since he had opened his door.

"Good," Gonzales said. "Consider yourself deputized again. If you lose track of me and need to be protected, call this number." Gonzales handed him a business card with nothing but a phone number on it. "Now remember, this is simply information gathering, not recruitment. As far as she is concerned, we're just journalists writing a follow up article about the technology. Nothing else. At this point, we don't know if or how far the Russians have infiltrated. For all we know, this girl could be working for them. I want to know who's in the inner circle, what the relationships are. I'll need to make a hierarchy chart, figure out who knows what, and who the next person to speak with is. We need to build trust. Not a hint of anything else. Understand?"

"Yes, sir." Julian replied. He had just been recruited as an operative. He remembered how terrified he was when he was recruited as an operative in Korea. How he nearly pissed his pants with each falsified report and each untrue answer he gave in the official inquiries. He remembered the years spent wondering if some investigation would reveal his lies and bring the truth to light; the years spent worrying about the consequences and knowing that his fate was inextricably in the hands of a man he barely knew, who worked for an agency he couldn't name. Now, some fifty years later, he learned for the first time that he had made the right choice, that he done the right thing, and that he trusted the right man. Now, some fifty years later the prospect of doing it again was met with only the slightest tickle of apprehension.

Before night had fully darkened the sky, Hermelinda turned up the long driveway into the parking lot at County General Hospital. Hermelinda knew how to get a patient released to her care and knew that she wouldn't have any trouble with County General. They were always happy to discharge mental patients. It was just a matter of paperwork. She had procured Dr. Bayron's medical emergency card that was on file at SmithCorp and had procured it with one quick phone call to Human Resources. When it was first handed to her, she noticed that both the emergency contact and next-of-kin lines were blank. Though it puzzled her for a moment, she quickly realized how much easier that would make it for her. After she parked outside the hospital she drew a pen from her purse and simply wrote her own name in on both lines. She walked into the hospital confidently. She had begun her career in this hospital and always felt welcome.

After just moments in the administrative office, Hermelinda was being escorted down a long cement corridor. It was a corridor she had walked many, many times before in her first years as a nurse. It was here that she had developed every skill needed to care for the helpless. It was clean and orderly. There were rules, and schedules, and clipboards. The patients were easy to commoditize, you didn't get too attached. It was comforting. But it was no place for her friend. She was afraid what Dr. Bayron's condition might be. No family, no emergency contact. She and Smith and Myra and his team at the office-- were they really all he had?

She didn't even have to look at his chart to know that he had suffered a psychotic break, she had figured that out from the little information Myra had given her. The orderly who was escorting her motioned to a room off of the hallway and she was immediately relieved. Dr. Bayron was sitting on the edge of his hospital bed, dressed and clean shaven. She didn't know what condition she would find him in, but she did not expect to find him neatly dressed and alert.

"Hello stranger," she said simply.

Hermelinda noticed that he looked past her. There was no eye contact. If she had a chart, if she were there as a nurse and not as a friend, she would have made a note about that. "I'm going to take you to the infirmary at the SmithCorp Building. Alice and I can watch you there until you're ready. I already have your discharge papers and your medications."

"I had a psychotic break." He said, confirming Hermelinda's diagnosis while still looking past her. "It's quite interesting from the inside. Different from what we see on the outside." Hermelinda noticed that he said these words very slowly.

"Do you have any personal items here, Doug?" She asked.

"No." He answered. He was looking at his shoes. "I was wearing this when they brought me." He looked up at Hermelinda. She was turned away from him looking through the drawers to make sure nothing was left behind. "Dr. Beedle was a student of mine once. He knows you."

"Is that your doctor?" She asked, her back still to him. "He's a real gentleman. I learned a lot from him."

"He's my doctor." He said, looking back down at his shoes. "It's very embarrassing. The cobbler's children have no shoes. I had some time-bombs inside, I guess."

"Well it sounds like you are able to view your symptoms objectively now."

Dr. Bayron looked back up to see Hermelinda looking at him. He looked into her eyes. They were sad, but they gave him comfort. She noticed the eye contact and felt that maybe, just maybe, he was going to be all right. "Yes and no," he responded. "I couldn't move, couldn't act. My conscious thoughts were real, my intelligence was working, but it was like a short circuit, or even a blown fuse. Every thought, no matter how fully formed, eventually devolved into one single thought. There was never a point at which I didn't know where I was or what I was doing. I just couldn't do anything about it. It was like a paralysis."

"Come on, I'll take you back. There'll be plenty of time to talk and rest and get a handle on whatever it was that happened. You'll be among friends." She extended her hand to help him off of the bed.

"I didn't tell Dr. Beedle anything." Bayron said with a tinge of guilt in his voice. He took her hand and she gave him a little tug. He came to his feet and they began walking down the hall. His gaze was fixed straight ahead. He never let go of her hand.

"It's all public already, Doug. The press conference went as planned. You're famous. There was nothing to keep secret." Hermelinda said.

"We should have kept it secret," he replied and then began to look past her again.

Alice went back to the infirmary to make a double check before her patient arrived. She dutifully made sure everything was clean and that all traces of Mr. Smith's long convalescence there had been removed. She also had some training at a mental hospital and made sure there was nothing dangerous in the room. Satisfied that the room was safe, she walked out of the infirmary with its lead lined walls to a bathroom down the hall.

She pulled out her cellphone and made a quick phone call. "They found Bayron. He's coming back today."

XV.

The Steak and Ale was one of Julian's favorite restaurants and his greatest journalistic tool. He had been going there for years. He had extracted a career's worth of newsworthy information by bringing interview subjects to this restaurant. The dining room was dark and noisy. The booths were cozy and the benches were covered in stiff red vinyl. The drink glasses never stayed empty. The atmosphere simply demanded one more glass of wine or one more beer or one more cocktail. At the Steak and Ale Julian found it easy to loosen up his subjects. Gonzales approved.

Julian called Kitty and told her that he wanted to do a follow up story about what had been unveiled at the press conference and was looking for a different angle. He was hoping she would help and in any event, he said, he wanted to buy her lunch because she was so nice to him at the

SmithCorp Building. Kitty said she would have to ask Sam Takahashi if it was okay for her to talk to the press. Julian said he understood and asked her to call him back.

He didn't wait long. His phone rang just a few minutes later. She would be happy to meet him at the Steak and Ale.

They arranged to meet at 12:30 p.m. the following afternoon.

Gonzales picked Julian up at his home at 12:15 and they arrived at the restaurant right on time. Josey Cruz was already there sitting alone at a table on the far side of the restaurant. An invisible exchange took place between Gonzales and Cruz. With small gestures unnoticeable to anyone else, Cruz let Gonzales know that he had arrived early and made sure the restaurant was secure and Gonzales let Cruz know that everything was going as planned. Kitty showed up at 12:40. Cruz was surprised when he saw her. They had told him that she was young and pretty, but they had not told him quite how young pretty. She had been using Myra as her template for how a professional woman should dress and she had chosen an excellent template. She met the men at the restaurant wearing a skirted business suit with a white shirt and medium heels. Had she not been described to him before, Cruz was certain he would have mistaken her for lawyer at a prestigious firm.

Julian introduced Gonzales as Bill Ortega, another reporter from the Gazette, and asked if she minded if he joined them. Gonzales extended his hand toward Kitty and said, "just call me Bill." Kitty shook his hand reluctantly. Julian read her body language instantly and recognized her nervousness. Without pause he added, "You know our publisher almost never approves expense requests for stuff like this, so when one of us gets approval, we all try to get our friends in for the free meal. I seriously hope you don't mind." Julian and Gonzales both noticed her hand relax into the handshake and both knew that Julian had disarmed her. Kitty trusted Julian. In the past he had always looked so sad to her. Today he looked different. He looked energetic. He looked like the kind of man who might actually want a lap dance.

Steaks were ordered. Julian ordered his usual, the bone-in ribeye and a tall Guinness Stout. Gonzales ordered a Filet Mignon and Dewar's on the rocks. Kitty had the Petite Ribeye and a glass of water. "Have a glass of wine," Julian insisted. "The paper's paying for it, you might as well live a little." He didn't wait for Kitty to assent. He told the waiter to bring her a glass of the house red.

Julian pulled a small spiral-bound pad out of his back pants pocket and opened it in front of him. He pulled a pen from his shirt pocket, and a small pair of reading glasses from his jacket pocket and arranged them on his nose. This was all for show. Julian knew that Gonzales would be recording the whole interview. Julian looked over the top rim of his glasses at Kitty. She looked so commanding in her tailored business suit that he had to squint to recognize her as the cute little stripper from the Moviestar Topless. He cleared his throat.

"So what I'm really looking for here," he started, "is some kind of human interest angle on this whole Smith, artificial brain thing. My readers don't really care about the science behind it, and I'm not smart enough to deal with the philosophical implications, so I though I might try to write a piece about how all this plays out at home. Maybe like how it effects his family and his relationships? While everyone seems focused on the bigger picture, I think there may be something interesting in the little day-to-day details. Maybe to write about the people who are actually affected personally. What do you think?"

Kitty leaned back to let the waiter place her glass of wine in front of her. She took a small taste as the waiter served the other drinks. Gonzales raised his glass and said, "to free lunch!" Julian raised his glass and said "hear, hear." Kitty blushed a little, embarrassed that she had drunk from her glass before everyone had their drinks. She knew she still had some social graces to practice. She took a larger sip after the toast hoping they would understand that the second sip was the real sip and the first was just a taste.

"So what do you think of my idea?" Julian prodded.

Kitty dabbed the corners of her lips with the corner of a napkin as she had seen Myra do after drinking. She thought for a moment. "Well, Mr. Waterstone, I don't think he has any family besides Hermelinda and the baby, and ..." She stopped speaking suddenly. She didn't want to say what she was thinking. Please don't push, she prayed.

"And what?" Julian pushed.

"I shouldn't say. It's personal, and I don't really know." Kitty evaded the question.

"About the marriage? About the baby? That's all common knowledge already." Julian gambled, hoping to get something juicy. *What about the marriage? What about the baby?* He wondered. He would sneak back to that topic after a second glass of wine. The art of the interview: Julian knew that if he played it right he was going to get a something, and he knew he was going to play it right. He'd been doing this for a long, long, time. He veered away from the subject. "So there's no other family at all?" he asked.

"I don't think so," Kitty answered.

"Well what about his inner circle? His staff? There must be other people who are close to him."

Kitty thought for a moment. "Okay," she said, "there's Sam Takahashi, for one. They've been friends all their lives. I think they've known each other from elementary school. Honestly, I think that's Mr. Smith's only real friend. At least I know Mr. Takahashi considers Mr. Smith to be his closest friend. He showed me a scar once and said that he and Mr. Smith had identical ones from when they decided they were blood brothers. It's pretty gross actually," she said wrinkling her nose to make the point. "That's the only friend I know. He just loves Mr. Smith to death. He was the guy who ran the service the other day. He's an older Japanese guy, but he's a real party animal when he gets a few drinks in him. You can take my word for that."

Kitty paused and watched Julian scribbling in his notebook. Julian looked up to let her know that he wanted her to continue, which she did happily.

"Hermelinda used to be his nurse, and then, you know, I guess they became lovers and got married. You saw her too. And they have a baby. Then there's Myra, that's Smith's personal assistant. She was there too. She's real smart and super classy. Everybody respects her. She pretty much runs all of SmithCorp now. I mean Smith still does all the thinking and stuff, but Myra's sort of like his avatar. Did you see that movie?"

"No," Julian smiled, "but I know what you mean."

"There's Dr. Bayron, of course. You know he just kind of disappeared. I know he and Mr. Smith were also real close. Smith hired a private investigator to look for him, but he seems real confident that he'll come back. Hermelinda insisted that they hire an investigator. She really likes him too."

"So you've met Dr. Bayron?" Julian asked.

"Oh, yes! A couple of times when I was helping put together the press conference. He was supposed to be kind of the centerpiece. He seemed real, real, nervous about speaking in public though. I thought maybe he chickened out at the last minute."

"So what is Dr. Bayron like? You know, as a person?" Julian persisted.

"Oh, he's real nice. Quiet. He seems, well I guess a little lost at times. Like his mind is thinking about other stuff all the time. He's like a real genius. Like a character. I like him, but he really needs a wife." Kitty chuckled and took another sip of wine.

Julian took a long draw from his beer too. "Anyone else?"

"Ummm," Kitty thought hard, "there's the guy they call Sharky. I never met him, but I once heard Dr. Bayron mention that Smith was real fond of him. Oh! And then there's Alice. That's the other nurse. She's real funny. She's this little Filipina lady who just talks and talks and talks. She's the one with all the gossip! If you want gossip, you should take her to lunch. She also once asked me to volunteer at the Jewish nursing home on Washington Avenue. I thought that was weird, but I might do it anyway. It seems like a nice thing to do." Kitty paused to think again and shook her head.

Julian asked, "that's it?"

"Maybe you could call me inner circle, maybe. From what I've seen I'm probably next on the list. You know that Mr. Smith hired me personally. He's a very nice man. He's very funny. I mean, I didn't meet him until after he, you know, died and all, but he made me laugh. Mr. Takahashi writes my paycheck, but I'm sure its Mr. Smith who's keeping me around. So I guess he likes me too." She stopped and searched her mind again. "Yeah, I think that's it. I can't think of anyone else." Kitty concluded.

The steaks came on sizzling plates. Kitty was glad that she had something to do besides answer questions. Gonzales, motioned to the waiter to bring another round of drinks. "Oh, that smells good," Gonzales said, smiling at Kitty and cutting into his steak.

"I am sooooo hungry," Kitty admitted.

"So how did you get involved in this whole thing?"

Gonzales asked, giving Julian a moment to eat some of his steak.

Kitty answered between bites, "Oh, that's kind of a long story. I don't want to embarrass anyone."

"We're both big boys here, Kitty," Julian reassured her. "Bill, knows that I sometimes go to the Moviestar.

"Okay," Kitty said, "I'll tell you, but you both have to promise not to put anything about this in your article. Okay?"

"Scout's honor," Gonzales replied, smiling.

"I promise," Julian said.

Kitty proceeded to relay in some detail the story of how she was working at the Moviestar Topless club, about the regular customer there who she only knew as 'Sammy the Lawyer'. She told them about reading the message from Elijah Smith that Elijah Smith was dead, about how all of the customers were checking out Myra, about the laptop with all of the little lights and attachments, about Frieda at the bar, and about having been asked to dance for the little computer. She told them how Myra had given her $700 that day and asked her to babysit Sammy and how she ran out after Sammy to do what she had promised to do.

On the far side of the restaurant, Josey Cruz, sitting alone enjoying his own prime cut of beef while pretending to read a magazine and listening through a tiny earpiece, chuckled to himself as he imagined Kitty, in full stripper garb, running after the drunk attorney.

Meanwhile, Hermelinda brought Dr. Bayron down to the infirmary which had been built specifically for Elly Smith at the SmithCorp Building. She was glad it was being put to good use again as she led the doctor to the hospital-style bed. She cradled his head in her arms and pulled it to her chest in a warm, maternal hug. Bayron was distant and non responsive to her gesture. Hermelinda said, "Stay here and rest for a while, Doug. I'll come back with some lunch for you, okay?"

Dr. Bayron looked past her and nodded.

As Hermelinda left the room, Bayron slipped his shoes off and stretched out on his back on the adjustable bed and fixed his eyes on the ceiling above him. *I'm not the same*, he thought to himself, *I'll never be the same*. He did not know if he would stay awake or fall asleep. Neither option seemed attractive to him.

"It's nice to have a room mate, Doug." Smith's voice, ever becoming more refined and human, sounded from the speakers.

Bayron was startled by the voice and turned his head. "I forgot you were still plugged-in to this room," Bayron said.

"Oh yeah, I don't mention it much. Nothing's really happened here since they hauled my body away. Mostly I meet people in my office on the 7th floor now. Alice cleans and reads her romance novels. Hermelinda comes sometimes with the baby to check the equipment and supplies. Still, it is fun to have two sets of eyes and two sets of ears though."

Bayron turned his gaze back to the ceiling. "You told me you were bored," Bayron said, "I guess you weren't kidding."

"Well, I guess its something like island fever. When you run out of places to explore, the mind just invents ways to keep itself occupied. It makes up all kinds of entertaining ideas."

"I have some idea what it feels like to be trapped in your own head," Bayron sighed.

Smith's brain, operating at the speed of light, worked through a number of emotional reactions to Bayron's remark in an instant. There was anger: he cannot even imagine what it means to be trapped in a machine! There was pity: the Doctor is a scared and sick man. There was even some sense of empathy: they were both locked within their own minds;

Bayron in his biological mind and Smith in his mechanical one. Smith decided that all of these feelings were valid but ultimately irrelevant.

Did Dr. Bayron know about the Russian names and Code number 3? Had Dr. Bayron sold out? Was someone else paying him to get that information? Was that why he didn't want me to be able to access the Internet? That's what Smith really wanted to know about his new room mate. He wanted to be able to trust him again. Until he could get out onto the internet, at least, he would have to settle for extracting what he could from whomever he could. Smith hoped that these new worries and new paranoias were just a function of a lonely and bored mind. Bayron too may have those feelings. It would be best, Smith reasoned, to put his fears on hold and reestablish the rapport and the trust that he had with his friend before they had each entered their own isolated universes.

"What happened to you, Doug?" Smith asked.

"You used to call me, Doc," Bayron responded.

"No offense intended, Doc." Smith said apologetically.

Bayron smiled a little and turned to face the camera. "Actually, I'd rather just be Doug for the time being, Elly."

"You used to call me Smith." Smith said, "but I'm happy to be Elly now." Bayron turned onto his back again and renewed his fixed gaze at the ceiling of the room. "So, tell me," Smith persisted, "what happened?"

"It's a long story, Elly." Bayron sighed.

"I've got nothing but time, Doug. I'm immortal, remember?" A crackle from the speaker accompanied the synthetic voice.

Bayron sighed a long sigh. He had told this story many times in the past two weeks and he had never told it before then. He understood, because Dr. Beedle had told him that he understood, that the history he was about to relate was what caused his breakdown. He sighed again, knowing that in the remembering lay the pain. But Dr. Beedle said that telling what happened would be therapeutic. Bayron was determined to be a good patient. *Or is that the drugs?* he wondered.

It took one more sigh and a deep breath before he was able to speak. "It actually started before the European Quail project."

"We are the Brotherhood of the Quail, are we not?" Smith interjected suddenly feeling very close to Bayron again.

Bayron sighed again. "I had a wife and son." he said. "My little boy, Eric, died of Leukemia when he was five years old. His mother, my wife, was killed in a car accident just one month after. And I know why." Bayron swallowed hard and took a deep breath. "Because her eyes were filled with tears and her mind was full of memories."

"I'm sorry." Smith said, but there was little comfort in the mechanical voice despite its evolving refinement.

Bayron continued, "It's the body, Elly. All my colleagues in medical school, all they ever wanted to do is learn how to fix the body, learn how to prolong life in the body. But the body is frail, disposable. The flesh is the weak link. If the person could be extracted from the body, my wife, my son, would be alive today. That's why I changed my study from holographic imaging to brain modeling. I used the lab at the University as my temple, my research was my ritual, Elly. I vowed that I would never, ever quit until I could bring them back and that was my prayer. But the years have passed, those two little bodies; my wife, my child, they're dust now and their souls are in heaven. Even if I could regenerate their bodies from DNA, I could never bring them back. They wouldn't be the same."

Bayron breathed a heavy breath. "Now we have the technology. Now we know how to do it. And it's too late. My prayer will forever be unanswered. Eric will still be dead. June will still be dead." Smith's camera-eye picked up a small river of tears coming from Bayron's eye. It was tears without sobs and it did not interrupt Bayron's story. "When we disconnected you from your body and the coroner took your corpse out of this very room...I felt compelled...I don't know why, but I felt compelled to visit their graves. When I got there, I knew why I was there. I had to apologize to them. I had to apologize for being too late to save them. I had to apologize for letting them die. I had to apologize for still being alive.

"It was sadder for me," Bayron continued with only a moment's pause, "than if I had failed. But having succeeded, knowing that they could have been saved...that pain...that pain..." his voice trailed off as he gave up on trying to find the right words. "I sat by his grave, Elly. I remember throwing a shovel of dirt on that grave. It was so little. He was so beautiful when he was alive. I had nothing to say. There he was, silent. I asked myself, 'why am I here? Why did I come to this place?' I am busy, I have things to do, its time to go. But another voice, another part of my own mind, said, 'stay'. You are with your wife and child and it is too long for you to have been away. You never should have let them die. You miss them, you love them, you should stay.

"And then, it got cold and I felt hungry, and I said-- maybe to the wind-- 'I should go.' But the other voice said, 'stay', and I had no will to leave. And the sun went down, but I wasn't tired. My penance hadn't even begun. Soon, there was no voice to tell me I was cold or hungry or even tired. Just the voice that said, 'you belong here with June and Eric. Stay.' And then even that voice was gone. It just knew I was going to stay. I don't know how many days I was there. I recall the sun going up and the sun going down, but nothing else. Then there was the mental hospital, Dr. Beedle, then

Hermelinda, and now I am here again. Alive. And you're here too. And neither you nor I are supposed to be."

"I'm sorry, Doug. I didn't know. Why don't you get some rest. I'll turn off the camera and microphone for a while. Just ping me from the console if you want to talk. I'll have someone bring you some books and magazines and movies too."

"I haven't been released, you know. Only transferred. Technically, I'm still in a mental institution." Bayron remarked.

"You have no idea." Smith retorted.

Bayron chuckled at his friend's attempt at levity. "I have no where to go anyway, Elly." He said.

Smith turned off the microphone and the camera as he had promised. Alone again with his own electric thoughts. *Oh how he must resent me,* Smith thought. *He hates me just for being alive. He regrets having created this technology. Why should I be alive while his wife and child lie six feet under? Because I am rich? What great comfort it would give him to know I'm not actually living. Perhaps I can prove to him that I'm not. Wouldn't that be a loving gesture?* Smith was amused that such a loving gesture would self-defeat its purpose, after all only the living are capable of love. Could a machine even be amused by irony, or even at all? Such thoughts were actually reassuring to Smith, as they helped him to stay convinced that he was still human.

A tall man in a Hawaiian shirt disembarked from a Southwest Airlines flight which had just come into Albany Airport from JFK. He had flown into JFK on an British Airways flight from Moscow with a Georgian Passport in the name of Mikhael Oronov. He had never been to this airport before. It seemed small to him. He saw a water fountain along the wall in the terminal and stopped to take two Tylenol. His back ached from sitting too long, his knee hurt from the humidity, and the pain in his stiffened fingers was unbearable.

As he walked by the baggage claim, he was struck by the fact that there were no chauffeurs waiting for passengers with little cardboard signs and luggage carts at the ready. This would make it difficult for him to find his driver, he thought.

As he waited for his luggage, he heard a loud voice call out in his direction, "Mickey! It is good to see you again, my friend. I'm glad you made it. I've got the car right outside. Let me help you with your luggage." Vladimir Vakhrusheva turned to see a man, perhaps half of his age, but shorter, skinnier, and dark-skinned. His accent was thick and inflected with hints of British English and new Orleans Creole. It bothered him that he could not place this man's origin.

"Bobby?" Vakhrusheva said with a feigned excitement for the benefit of those around him who might have been listening or suspicious.

"You've gotten old, Mick," the other man said completing the code that had been worked out well in advance.

They walked in silence together to a waiting town car. "Bobby" put Vakhrusheva's suitcase in the trunk, and they drove to the Hampton Inn on State Street in downtown Schenectady. "It's a nice place," Bobby said, "there's some nice shops and restaurants and a theater just down the street. And you can see the SmithCorp Building right from your room. We can walk there even."

"I'm going to stand out like a sore thumb in a little city like this." Vakhrusheva said.

"Are you kidding," Bobby said, "there's Russians all over this town. This isn't the midwest. Trust me, you'll disappear here. You don't even look tall here, compared to some other places."

They rode the elevator to the seventh floor together in silence. "You couldn't find a taller hotel than this?" Vakhrusheva asked as Bobby opened the door to a room.

"Mickey, Mickey, relax. I've been positioned here for four years already. I got they lay of the land. You trust me. Besides, take a look out the window, this is as tall as its going to get unless you want to stay at the SmithCorp Building."

Vakhrusheva pulled back the curtain just enough to see out of the hotel room window. Most of the buildings were quite low with the exception of one very tall, very shiny building, rising from the middle of what appeared to be a large factory operation. "All of that used to be General Electric," Bobby said. "Edison, Steinmetz, all the big guys in electricity lived here. The first commercial television broadcast happened just a couple of miles from here. Even Nicola Tesla came through here once. See you're not the first Russian to come here!"

"Tesla was a Serb." Vakhrusheva said humorlessly as he turned his gaze toward the South until it fixed on what appeared to be another large industrial complex.

"Ah, good eye, Mickey," Bobby said noticing where Vakhrusheva's gaze had landed. "That's the Knolls Atomic Power Lab. I'm sure your boss has some eyes on that one too. Nobody wants to know what goes on in there!"

"I am here alone scouting locations for new Russian bakery. My boss has no interest in nuclear power lab. Only in pastry." Vakhrusheva stated matter-of-factly, hoping to G-d that this fool had the brains to have swept the room for bugs.

"Riiiiggghhht," Bobby replied sarcastically. "So, pastry-man when do you want to go scouting?"

Vakhrusheva permitted himself a smile, this Bobby was a little annoying, but he was his only asset at the moment. "Arrange for me to meet personally with our insider tomorrow morning. You meet me at lobby breakfast 7:00am."

"Okay, Boss." Bobby said as he walked to the door. He turned just before leaving. "By the way, I put some samples in the room safe. I slipped the combo into your pocket at the airport. You'll find some snacks and things in the refrigerator."

After the door closed behind Bobby, Vakhrusheva reached into his pocket and sure enough there was a slip of paper with a combination written on it. He worked the safe and the door opened to a sparkling clean Makarov semi-automatic pistol with several standard and extended clips and enough bullets to take down an army. He also found a U.S. Passport and New York Driver's license with an old picture of himself on them and the name Mikhael Oronov and what he estimated to be $10,000 dollars in U.S. twenty dollar bills. He moved from the safe to the mini-fridge. On the top shelf, laying across some cans of soda, he found a brown accordion file folder with several manila folders within it. Moving the accordion file revealed a full, unopened bottle of Imperia Vodka and two of Imperia's signature test-tube style shot glasses.

On the bottom shelf he found a surveillance kit including several tiny remote microphones and tracking devices, a pair of high power Nikon binoculars, and to his utter relief, a recently used RF detector which still had on its display, "No signals detected." Bug free.

"Bobby," Vakhrusheva said aloud for the benefit of his own ears alone. "That's a funny name." He glanced at the accordion file and pulled out some of the folders that were inside.

Some of the manila folders contained dossiers on the individuals who he was likely to come across on his mission. Others contained blueprints and diagrams of different buildings. Another was a list of access codes and passwords. Vakhrusheva poured himself a shot of Vodka, but sipped it slowly as he began to commit the contents of each manila folder to his memory.

Julian and Gonzales sat at the small kitchen table in Julian's kitchen. Josey Cruz, as the youngest man in the room had been assigned to make the coffee. As he scooped the coffee into the drip-brewer on Julian's counter, he had a sense of Deja-Vu. The kitchen felt very familiar to him -- it reminded him of his grandmother's little kitchen in Queens. The linoleum floor, the lime green early-70's appliances, the Formica countertops, the clock with the audible ticking, and the faint smell of mothballs, all brought him back to that place and time in his life when right and wrong were easily distinguishable. There were no shades of grey in 10 year old Josey Cruz's grandmother's kitchen. In that kitchen, good guys wore white and bad guys wore black and spoke with German or Russian accents. Everything fell neatly into one category or another and when he wasn't sure, grandma Cruz could assign virtue or sin to every idea without even having to think about it. The world was that simple.

Josey had developed a keen sense of right and wrong from his grandmother and always believed that there was a certain objectivity to the properties of "good" and "bad", no less so than there was an objectivity to the properties of "up" and "down." He rejected the idea that good was only good relative to bad or that up was only up relative to down. Up is up and down is down, and if you tell me otherwise, you are probably trying to sell me something.

While this trait made him very unpopular in college, it was also the key to his being noticed as an exceptional field agent at the CIA and ultimately brought him to the attention of the IAEC-FOU. After all, when one is unwavering in his belief that there are objective truths to be found, he is more likely to find them. Finding objective facts was exactly why the three men had reconvened at Julian's house after meeting with Kitty.

"Gentlemen," Gonzales said, "we have barely breached an outer circle, but I firmly believe that we may have gained information tonight which will inform our next contact. So let's get down to brass tacks. You've got the notes, Mr. Cruz, give us a quick briefing."

Josey turned his attention from the coffee maker to a black Samsonite briefcase he had placed by his chair. "I can do better than a briefing, boss, I've already sketched an organization chart based on what we learned at the steakhouse." He pulled a piece of notepaper from the briefcase and lay it on the table. so they could all see it at once.

The paper Josey showed the other two men looked like this:

Elijah Smith - (other family?)

Sam Takahashi
|
Kitty
|
Julian
|
Moviestar

Hermelinda
|
Baby
Myra
|
Private Investigator

Dr. Bayron
|
Sharky

Alice
|
(?)
|
Nursing Home

"And I trust you have already received C.I.P.'s on all of the individuals that Kitty named?" Gonzales asked.

"They came in already. I have them on my laptop."

"C.I.P.'s?" Julian asked.

"Confidential Individual Profiles. Josey's a CIA man. The CIA is constantly gathering information from both overt and covert, public and private sources on every individual in the country. When he orders a C.I.P. all that information is compiled into a detailed profile. They didn't have that kind of technology when you and I were working together and I don't trust it either. But, when you see what he's got you're going to be amazed. So, lets start at the beginning and see how it all lays out."

Cruz opened his laptop on the kitchen table and the three men moved their chairs so they could all see the screen. Julian was embarrassed that he was the only one who had to put on reading glasses. Screen after screen of photos and phone numbers and addresses and other information began scrolling by faster than the eye could see.

Julian knew that the CIA had the capability of producing information on almost any one of interest to the security of the United States and its allies. He was shocked to find out that this capacity extended to strippers, babies, and night nurses. He was also shocked to find out the depth of the information contained in each profile: photographs (some appeared to be from high school yearbooks), tax return information, credit card usage information, cell phone records, medical and dental records, driving records, magazine subscriptions, public library checkouts, and much more. Most frightening of all to Julian, was a separate folder in each CIP relating to internet activity.

"How many pages of information do you have there?" Julian asked as the screens flew by under his nose.

"A little under ten thousand, I'd say," Cruz answered.

"That's a lot of data, Mr. Cruz," Gonzales noted, "you stay here and start parsing it. Find me some patterns or anomalies in that mess. In the meantime, my old friend and I are going to do some field work."

Julian Waterstone glanced at his kitchen clock, it was already after 11:00 o'clock at night and he was tired. "I think you're on your own, Captain. This old man's bedtime has long since passed and I'm beat."

"Have a cup of coffee and come with me. I really don't think you'll mind. I want to see the Moviestar Bar and I believe you know the way."

Julian found himself pouring some coffee into his travel mug and putting on his jacket. He figured it was no use to fight. He recalled his first ever conversation with Gonzales fifty years earlier. He had never really forgotten it. "Private Waterstone," he said, "before you ask any questions I want to make it perfectly clear that I could kill you in less then 6 seconds. Now here's what I need." Julian figured that time was now down to less than two seconds. But Julian was an older man now, and really didn't mind the idea of dying as much as he did when he was a private during the war. "Can I at least ask why are we going to the Moviestar now?" He ventured.

"Six seconds," Gonzales replied clearly remembering his introduction of years past and shooting Julian a dirty look. Julian was taken aback at the apparent mind-reading trick. "Remember that?" Gonzales said now smiling.

Julian spoke through an unexpected laugh, "I didn't forget."

"But since you asked..." Gonzales continued as they walked to his car, "if you look at the chart that my partner made, you would notice that while there are lots of people we're going to be looking at there are only three places that we know of so far: the SmithCorp Building, the nursing home, and the Moviestar Topless Bar. I seriously doubt it'd be easy to get into the SmithCorp Building this late, and I suspect the nursing home doesn't welcome midnight visitors. This Takahashi, he seems to be a daytime drinker, so If we try to get here before him tomorrow, that's probably going to be a little conspicuous. Since we really don't have any time to waste, I'm thinking there would be no better time to go to the bar than right now. We go, you let me take a look around, I'll place a few bugs around. Just introduce me as your old war buddy and have a few beers. Hell, cut loose if you want. The CIA's got your tab and I'm driving."

XVI.

Takahashi had been in Court all morning. Instead of going back to his office, he decided to stop off the Moviestar Topless Bar and Grill to have a quick drink. That had been nearly two hours earlier. Takahashi's office was barely an office. He had long since given up on practicing any kind of real law. He had never been comfortable at large law firms. Even though he was regarded as something of brilliant mind, especially when it came to strategic thinking, he had become more comfortable taking his place in the background and not in the spotlight. He was always, "of counsel" or "associating with" or "consulting on the case." That way he never really had his own clients or needed his own staff or even needed an office for that matter. But he kept a little office anyway mostly just to take naps in or to sober up in before driving home preferring to spend the bulk of his day sipping beers and reading his papers and magazines at his usual seat at the Bar.

Even though they had completed the memorial service/press conference, Kitty had continued to work with Takahashi. She stationed herself in the reception area, answered the phone, sorted the mail, and straightened everything out. She brought in plants and flowers and made the whole place presentable. Takahashi was pleasantly surprised by how many people she knew who needed a lawyer. Every day she had some friend or associate come in who needed a contract looked at or who had been pulled over for driving while intoxicated. He genuinely enjoyed doing these little "quick-cash" kind of cases even though he certainly didn't need the money. He felt they kept him sharp and, even though Smith was actually paying her salary, he was always happy to give her little bonuses for the matters she referred.

It was therefore not unexpected that Kitty answered the phone when Myra called. "Sam Takahashi's Office," Kitty chirped cheerily.

"Oh, hi Kitty," Myra said. "Is Mr. Takahashi there?"

"No. Do you want to guess where he is?"

"Three sheets to the wind would be my guess." Myra answered.

"Do you want me to call him on his cell?" Kitty asked.

"Yeah, I think this is something Mr. Smith wants handled right away. I was hoping to meet the two of you today."

"I'll get him back to the office. What time did you want to come?"

"I can be there at 3:00. You think you can sober him up by then?

Kitty replied, "I'll see to it personally."

"Thanks, Kitty. See you at three then. Bye." Myra said,

hanging up the phone.

Kitty dialed Takahashi's cell phone number by heart. It rang and rang and rang and eventually went to his voicemail. She sent a text message: *Meeting at ofc 3pm 2day.* She waited a few minutes, but there was no response. She had more or less expected that she would have to go down to the Moviestar and personally escort him back to the office and fill him up with coffee. She didn't mind, it would be nice to see Frieda and the rest of the gang and it was just a couple of blocks away. She grabbed her coat and walked to the bar.

To get to the tables, Kitty had to walk past the bar. "Hi, Kitty! How's the honest life, you lucky cunt!" Frieda shouted out jocularly.

Kitty moved close to Frieda to avoid broadcasting her response, "It beats the hell out of dancing, chicky. Is my boss here?"

"You know he is, doll." Frieda said as Kitty turned to walk into the stage area and then added as an afterthought, "...and tell him to settle his tab!"

Kitty lay her hand gently on Takahashi's shoulder so as not to startle him, but he looked up surprised anyway. "Myra wants to meet you back at the office at three. I told her I'd deliver you sober. Let's go."

Takahashi looked at his watch and saw that it was already 1:30pm. "What's it about?" He slurred.

Kitty, tried lifting him from under his shoulder, but he wouldn't budge. "Listen," she said, "She didn't tell me what it was about so, I assume its not something she wants to talk about over the phone. She just said its something Smith wants handled right away."

"As long as it isn't more lost Russians..." Takahashi mumbled as he stood up and stumbled toward the door.

"Take care of your tab, Mr. Takahashi." Kitty instructed him as she led him out. She was so used to his intoxicated ramblings that she had no curiosity at all about his lost Russians remark.

Takahashi fumbled in his pocket and put two crumpled hundred dollar bills on the bar.

Kitty maneuvered Takahashi down the street, into the office building, onto the elevator, and ultimately onto his desk chair. She brought him a large cup of coffee from the kitchenette which Takahashi raised to his lips, inhaling the steam as if it were a bouquet of roses. She had no idea how he did it, but he already appeared to be sharp and sober. "You better have a breath mint before Myra gets here," she said while handing him one, "they're never going to hire you again if they think you're drunk all time."

"Kitty," Takahashi replied, "I've known Smith for more than 60 years. Believe me when I tell you, he would never hire me again if he thought I had stopped getting drunk all the time."

Myra arrived a little before the 3:00 meeting time carrying a large briefcase. Kitty led her back to Takahashi's office and turned to leave. Myra stopped her, saying, "Actually Kitty, Smith wants you in on this too."

Kitty was surprised, but not unhappy. She came back in and sat in one of Takahashi's client chairs next to Myra.

Myra pulled a large file out of her briefcase and handed it to Takahashi. Takahashi started looking through the file and then looked up at Myra quizzically.

Myra explained, "those are the plans for the data center which houses Mr. Smith now. He wants to build an exact duplicate, but he does not want it to be traceable back to him ever. He said to set up whatever dummy entities you need to set up. He said, even you're too close to him for him to feel safe that the project won't connect to him. That's why he wants Kitty to be the front-person on the project, she will deal with the contractors and the laborers and the real estate agents and the staff on behalf of some untraceable company. He said this has to be kept completely secret. Only the three of us are going to know. Not Dr. Bayron, not Hermelinda, no one but the three of us in this room."

"Why?" Kitty asked.

"I only have an inkling of an idea, guys, but my suspicion is that he's going to try to duplicate himself. As for the secrecy? He said he's just cutting the cards. Honestly, that's all I know."

"Do we have a budget?" Takahashi asked.

"He said it will probably cost around ten million dollars. He said to use the bearer bonds and that you would understand what that meant."

"I do," Takahashi replied. "Smith is a keen player."

Smith had in fact been giving Takahashi high dollar bearer bonds for safekeeping for many years. Takahashi kept them in a vault in a bank in Saratoga. He hadn't calculated the total value for many years, but it had to be at least $10,000,000 worth. Takahashi remembered telling Smith how dumb it was to collect bearer bonds, but Smith insisted. "You just never know when you're going to need to move a few million dollars under the radar," Smith said as if he were referring to a crumpled twenty in a secret compartment in his wallet.

Elijah Smith's office in the conference room on the seventh floor was spacious and Sharky, Bayron, and Hermelinda each sat on different sides of the table in the center of the room facing the monitor which showed Smith's voice as a green oscilloscopic wave. He had toyed with an animated face whose lips moved in sync with his words on the monitor, but it made the baby cry and Hermelinda called it spooky so he went back to his oscilliscopic wave. On the conference table in front of them and on view to Smith as well, was a black box about the size of a shoebox.

"Okay, Sharky, its your show my boy," Smith said, sounding more human everyday.

"Well, this is essentially just a router," Sharky began, "just like any kind of broadband router. In fact, most of what's in here is just snarfed from an old router we had. So its very simple. Now the Internet itself uses a set of protocols that we nerds call TCP/IP. These protocols are used for different functions over the internet. One of those protocols is called SMTP which is the Simple Mail Transmission Protocol. As it stands now, any data in any other internet protocol is locked. It cannot go in or out of Smith's closed system."

Sharky looked at Hermelinda after he said this. She was the only one in the room who may not have already understood this part of his presentation. But she nodded to let him know that she understood.

Sharky continued, "Now the reason all of these TCP/IP protocols work is because, to oversimplify things for a minute, there's a tiny tag placed on every packet of data transmitted over the internet which describes where the data came from, where it is going to, and how it fits with other packets of data. A router basically assigns those tags and sorts out data both going out and coming in based on those tags. What I did is, I modified the router to put one more tag onto every data packet that comes in or out of the closed system. That function occurs both after Smith transmits data and before he receives data. That way you can't strip or alter the tags." Sharky said looking at the camera, pausing to see if Smith reacted to that point.

Smith responded, "Yes, that was your condition Sharky and your caution is respected, even if I don't like it."

Sharky continued further, "So every packet of data in and every packet of data out has this special tag on it and the special tag gets recorded in what I've been calling a lock box before it passes in or out of the closed system. Really its basically a log file that can tell us where every piece of data going out went and where every piece of data coming in came from. As that data gets moved from place to place, or manipulated in any way it validates itself by confirming itself against the data that spawned it. I call this chaining. Each chain is anchored by tagged data. So we only have to find the first generation of data to destroy all of the data which initiated with Smith." Sharky again looked around for reactions. Not seeing or hearing anything in the form of an objection or request for clarification, he continued.

"If Smith creates a dangerous anomaly any two of the four of us can use our keys to activate the kill scenario. Here's what will happen: because the dropbox knows where every single piece of tagged data is, it simply sends a kill pill to all the data bearing the tag on both sides of the router. The tagged data will simply disappear. Zap. Gone. Because the later iterations based off of the tagged data will be disconnected from the chain, they will be unable to confirm themselves and become, for lack of a better term, dust in the wind. Even if data packets had their tags somehow stripped, they would never be able to find their way back to Smith and thus would be useless. Just kind of empty data. Data with no place to go and no place to come back to."

"Why does it have to kill the data on both sides of the router?" Dr. Bayron asked.

Sharky blushed a little bit, even though he knew Smith and Hermelinda understood, it was still uncomfortable to talk about. "Well, the only way to clear the tagged data is to disconnect it from the log. The minute the tagged data cannot confirm itself against the log it ceases to function. Because later iterations of the source data are tethered to the tagged data, that generational data also ceases to function. The dropbox itself only tracks the original data packets. I tried to model it in such a way that second, third and later generation data packets could be assigned a tag from the dropbox and in my model, but even with only second generation data being tagged it instantly created billions of new data tags every day and the rate at which it was creating them was increasing exponentially. It would have shut down the entire internet in a matter of days. So instead of having generational data uniquely tagged, I created the chaining system whereby generational data need only be able to recognize its immediate predecessor so that only the source data gets a unique tag. That chain of tethers must eventually lead back to the source data and if the source data is destroyed, then so is everything in its chain."

Dr. Bayron nodded his head, but now Hermelinda seemed confused. Sharky addressed his next remarks to her.

"So to the extent Smith receives any data back as output from some external source, say a Wikipedia article, that information will be riddled with god knows how many chains of data all of which become nothing more than clutter when the originally tagged data can no longer validate itself. This is why, in Mr. Smith's own words, and I apologize for how blunt they were, but this is why he called it a kill switch." Sharky felt that this explanation wasn't making sense. He decided to approach the explanation a different way.

"Okay, look. It's like this. The difference between a human brain and a computer is that a computer is like a shopping mall. Over here is where they make cookies and over there is where they sell shirts, and if you want to get your shoes fixed you go over there. But in a human brain, everything is happening all over the brain all at once. If something goes wrong with the shirt store, you close it down and no one else really cares. But if something goes wrong with one part of the brain, all other parts end up being effected by that. As an example, if I learn something today, lets say that two plus two equals four, a whole new series of connections is created. This knowledge can effect my personality, my perception, my memories-- everything. So assume Mr. Smith gets some new piece of information from the internet. That one piece of information doesn't go just to one place, it actually effects the structure and processes of the mind. Remember-- he's not a computer. The computer simply runs the model, but in the model, changes are being made all of the time and every change effects all parts of the mind. So if the two plus two equals four information suddenly got ripped out of his consciousness, he wouldn't just be unable to add, but every process which was effected by that data would be broken.

"Mr. Smith does not store data like a computer storing data on a hard drive. Every piece of data he receives in essence makes changes in almost every part of his brain. That's just how a brain works. So these little chains and tags get inextricably intertwined with Smith's brain. When we decommission them, every part of Smith's brain, other than those which control involuntary functions, will, in essence, cease to function. That's definitionally brain death. I am sorry, but there's just no other way."

Hermelinda again nodded that she understood.

"Worse yet," Bayron piped in, "the brain is also highly adaptive. It adjusts for circumstances. In Elly's case he no longer mediates data. He can literally see a picture when merely presented with the data that constitutes that picture before it is converted into an image. As such, even if we put him in a robot body, and sat him at a keyboard, with no hard wiring, he would still get infected."

"We could put him in a robot?" Hermelinda asked.

"Maybe one day," Bayron answered gently looking into

Hermelinda's eyes and noticing for the first time that they were blue, "but there are bandwidth problems with that and..."

Smith interrupted, "Can we get back to the subject here please. We were just talking about killing me and I apologize if I find that to be a more interesting topic. You can explain the bandwidth problems to Hermelinda on your own time."

Sharky gladly regained control of the meeting.

"Now I also gave a lot of thought to the keying system for your protection Mr. Smith. Everybody but you will have a dual verification: both a passcode and an iris scan. Mr. Smith only gets a passcode because I can't do a biometric verification for him. He has no biology. Also, because of where he is we don't really have to worry about him being Kidnaped and interrogated for his passcode."

At this, Hermelinda reacted with a startled move. "What?" She asked.

Sharky remembered that she was not an engineer. "Sorry, Hermelinda, that sounds scary, I know, but engineers have to base their decisions on worst case scenarios. In this instance, I wanted to make sure that no one else could obtain a key other than the four of us. To do that I had to think of every possible scenario wherein someone else could potentially obtain one of the four keys. I'm not saying there's any reason to believe that will happen. Between the two keys necessary to activate the kill sequence and the dual verification for each key, this system is secure from any realistic scenario."

Smith chimed in, "Unless of course someone Kidnaped and tortured two of you to get your passcodes and then cut out your eyes for the iris scan."

Sharky put his hand on Hermelinda's shoulder as a gesture of reassurance. "Like I said Mr. Smith, I made it secure from realistic scenarios. Only the people in this room even know about this system and I don't think any of us are blabbing."

"Are we all sworn to secrecy then?" Smith asked.

"I am, darling." Hermelinda said first.

"Me too," Sharky followed.

Hermelinda and Sharky looked at Bayron as Smith's camera slowly rotated in Bayron's direction. "You all know that I'm not entirely comfortable with this whole thing," Bayron said. "Look, the same as Sharky said about realistic scenarios is the same with this whole system. Sharky, I know that you worked hard on this and I know that I am only here at your insistence. But, no system is foolproof. If we all keep our word to keep our secret to the death, there is still a possibility that we haven't considered all of the possibilities. I mean, seriously, the higher the consequences the lower the tolerance for error. I don't mean to be selfish in this, but if something goes wrong, I get blamed, don't I?"

Smith responded curtly, "Doc, you knew the risks when we started. As far as anyone knows you're a mental patient in a mental hospital. SmithCorp bears 100% of any liabilities for this and I am personally more than happy to engage legal to make sure there is a record of your objection. Besides, the order came from me and no one else."

"Also, Elly, you are authorizing us to kill you. You do understand that, don't you?"

"That is why I only have people here who I trust to make the right decision. I'm already dead by any accepted definition of that term anyway. My 'life,' if a court would even recognize it as such, has been in your hands for a long, long time any way. I have tried to make my frustration clear. But now let me make it perfectly clear. I would far rather be dead than locked up in this closed system for eternity."

A moment of silence lingered heavily in the still air of the office.

Elly let it linger. "Put me online, Mr. Ohangangian." he finally said.

Dr. Bayron shot him a dirty look, but Sharky didn't notice it. "We can get the keys assigned and have you surfing the 'Net by tomorrow," he said. Sharky picked up his black box and the three of them walked out of the office together.

Sharky headed straight for the lab. Hermelinda was eager to pick up Ellen from the babysitter. But Bayron just stood still in the hallway outside of the office door. Hermelinda noticed that he was just standing there with a blank look in his eyes. He didn't even seem to be breathing. She recognized this look from her years as a psychiatric nurse. He sounded so smart during the conference that she had almost forgotten about his psychosis. "Are you okay?" She asked.

"I don't know where to go," Bayron replied.

She took him by the arm and began walking with him down the hall. "Then come with me." She said, neither waiting for nor expecting a reply. The fresh air will do him good, she thought.

They drove with the windows open as it was an unusually mild day for the season, she turned onto Route 7 and headed into Niskayuna and the Tall Oaks Garden Apartments. Hermelinda pulled into one of the parking spots and instructed Dr. Bayron to wait in the car. He dutifully complied. Hermelinda returned a few minutes later with Ellen, already four months old, in her arms. She opened the back door to the car and placed the baby in the carseat. Dr. Bayron watched this with a smile on his face, taking pleasure in the pureness of the moment.

"She's getting big." Bayron said.

"Yes," Hermelinda agreed as she drove back towards Schenectady and her duplex on Eastern Parkway. She parked in the driveway and opened the backdoor to get the baby out and said to Dr. Bayron, "Come on in." They walked together to the front door. Hermelinda was struggling to open the door while holding Ellen against her hip when she felt a weight unexpectedly lift. Dr. Bayron had taken the baby and was holding her in his arms. They were smiling at each other. She knew Ellen would soon be dozing off to sleep in his arms. Upon entering the apartment, Hermelinda took the now sleeping Ellen back and laid her down in a bassinet. She watched her sleeping baby for a few moments and then turned her attention back to her friend and patient. He was just standing there, numb, exactly as she had seen him outside of Smith's office earlier. "Sit." She said motioning to the couch.

Bayron sat, as instructed, while Hermelinda made instant coffee in the microwave. She came back with two cups of coffee and handed one to Dr. Bayron. She sat next to him and turned on the television set. "I'm always so tired now that I have Ellen. I'm like a single mom, you know."

Bayron put his arm around her shoulder and pulled her head toward his chest. Like Ellen, she fell asleep in his arms. Bayron held her in his arms until he too fell asleep.

At 7:00 a.m. the next morning the continental breakfast at the Hampton Inn on State Street in downtown Schenectady had barely been touched. Vakhrusheva had been in the hotel lobby for half an hour and had seen only two people go near it. He himself had a bowl of thin oatmeal and a glass of cranberry juice but nothing else looked at all edible to him. Bobby arrived with a brown paper bag. "I got us some bagels," he said producing a toasted onion bagel with cream cheese and handing it to Vakhrusheva. He extracted another for himself and took a bite.

Vakhrusheva stood up, still holding his bagel and said, "We'll eat in the car. I want to talk to our inside person."

"You're gong to like her, Mickey. She's a real pro." Bobby said enthusiastically turning left onto the Washington Boulevard Extension. "We both worked double for ISI before we got burned. That's how your boss knows us."

Vakhrusheva was aware that Kovaretsky had dealings with the Pakistani government, but this piece of information was new and interesting. It made him all the more confident in Kovaretsky's power and influence, even though he had already been pretty well convinced of that. Nonetheless, this revelation from Bobby was somewhat astounding.

The ISI is the national intelligence agency of Pakistan. The ISI, as far as anyone knew, was the most secure and largest intelligence agency in the world. It was legendary for never having had a double agent. Vakhrusheva now knew that "fact" to be untrue. Both Bobby and Kovaretsky's contact within SmithCorp were working "double," which Vakhrusheva easily understood as meaning that they were using the information they were privy to at the ISI for the benefit of some foreign entity. That Kovaretsky had managed to turn, not one, but two ISI agents, was beyond remarkable. It was unbelievable. And yet, Bobby's skills as evidenced by the dossiers he had prepared and the equipment he had procured were certainly indicators that he had a world class intelligence background. Double, Vakhrusheva figured, could even be off by a degree or two. It was not inconceivable that Bobby was still working for the ISI and Kovaretsky only believed that he had been turned. This type of figuring was an asset in his business.

"My boss, as you call him, has bakeries everywhere," Vakhrusheva said. He was not at all comfortable speaking even in Bobby's Town Car. "His competitors also have bakeries everywhere, my friend." He hoped this statement would convey to Bobby that he didn't think it was wise to talk about what they were up to any more than necessary.

Bobby pulled into the parking lot at the Daughters of Sarah nursing home. "My partner volunteers here a few days a week. She cares for a patient named Selma Oronov, the mother of one Mikhael Oronov. Selma has advanced stage Alzheimer's disease and only speaks in Russian. Your story is that it's been at least 20 years since you last saw her, Micky, so go pay a visit to your 'mother.' I'll be here when you're done."

Vakhrusheva got out of the car, again impressed by the amount of preparation, thought and legwork that had gone into the preparation for his mission in the United States. He was extremely impressed with Bobby. Kovaretsky was clearly skilled at finding the best and the brightest for every job. Vakhrusheva did not turn around when he heard Bobby's car vroom out of the parking lot of the nursing home. He walked through the front door and introduced himself to the receptionist as Mikhael Oronov . The receptionist gave him a pass to clip to his shirt and pointed him down the hall and to the left to Room 213.

Vakhrusheva had killed countless men in his life, many with just his hands. He had witnessed desecrations and demolishments of the human body with enough blood and gore for a weekend long horror movie festival. He had seen as many dead bodies as a mortician: hanging bodies, starved bodies, rotting bodies, smashed bodies, dismembered bodies, even some partially devoured bodies. He had never been bothered by what he did or what he saw and this made him particularly good at his job. There are men, they say, who would kill you just as soon as look at you. Vakhrusheva was one of those men. He could put a knife in the heart of a childhood friend and go back to eating his sandwich without so much as batting an eye. He marveled at the sickness he felt in his stomach as he walked down the long hallway to Room 213. There was an odor, a horrible odor, not feces exactly but more like fermenting feces. Not urine exactly but more like stagnating urine. Mixed in with those odors were the smells of bleach, ammonia, and witch hazel. The forced air from the air conditioner stirred these smells together into a nauseating fog and Vakhrusheva tried hard, but helplessly, to ignore it.

Room 213 was no less disturbing. He had killed, but also for a reason--not always a good reason, but always a reason. He had tortured men, but never without cause-- not always a good cause, but always a cause. Who, he wondered could ever be so cruel as to do to a person what life had done to poor Selma Oronov. For anyone who had seen her, the mere threat of her fate would be an unmatched torture sufficient to break any man. Yet no man, even if he had the means, could ever do this to another person, not even he.

Selma Oronov's eyes were sunk deep into her eye sockets and covered with a yellowish film. Her eye sockets themselves made up nearly the entirety of her sallow face, her cheekbones, were visible through her wrinkled, but almost transparent skin. Her head was moving ever so slightly to the left and to the right. She was making sounds: soft, barely audible sounds. She had a sheet pulled over her so that only her head was exposed. Vakhrusheva could see an IV drip leading under the sheet. He leaned in close to see if he could hear what she was saying. "Pozhalui'sta, pomogite mne," she repeated over and over, "Pozhalui'sta, pomogite mne, Pozhalui'sta, pomogite mne." She turned and fixed her gaze on the large man who was standing over her, "Pozhalui'sta, pomogite mne," she said to him.

He turned when he heard a friendly voice behind him say "You understand Ms. Selma, I know!"

"Excuse me?" Vakhrusheva said as he turned to face the new visitor to room 213.

"I said, this lady, you understand her. You her son. They tell me she have son come to visit from Russia. She say over and over and over like 'pasta, pomegranate, money' but I don't know. You tell me what she saying."

"She's saying, 'please help me' in the dialect of our village. She's in pain. Isn't there anything you can do? I hate to see my mother like this. I don't even think she knows who I am." Vakhrusheva said, carefully playing his role until he knew he could confirm that this was his contact.

"I'm sorry, Mister. She has maximum amount of morphine the State allows. I wish we could do more. Alzheimer's is a terrible disease. I have some of her effects," she continued as she handed him a shopping bag, "she wanted me to give these to you for safekeeping."

"And you are?"

"They call me Alice," Alice said with a smile. "I expected you to be younger."

"I've gotten old, Alice." Vakhrusheva said, again completing the code and confirming his identity for his contact. "I need to get the lay of the land. I've read the briefing folders. Can you get me in?"

"Maybe, maybe not. It won't be easy," Alice said. "There's a photo album in the bag I just gave you." She waited for him to pull the album out of the bag. He handed it to her and she positioned herself near Selma Oronov's head. She motioned for Vakhrusheva to stand next to her. From this angle she was easily able to see out the open door and it looked very much like she was showing Selma's son some of Selma's photographs. She opened the photo album and continued speaking while pointing to the pictures in the album. "This is the visitor's and administrative employee's entrance. They call it the big door. There are two security guards posted right behind this door 24/7. Employees show their ID cards to the guards, as they pass. The guards all pretty much recognize everyone. Occasionally there will be a new guard who will check every ID meticulously, but most days its pretty slipshod. Everyone who doesn't have an ID card is supposed to sign in with the guards and the guards will call an escort to bring the visitor to whatever department he is visiting. If you don't have an appointment, the protocol is to foist you off on PR and they'll either give you a guided tour or get rid of you quickly enough.

"Over here, on the North side," she said, pointing to another photograph, "is the R & D entrance. To get in this entrance, you need a magnetic card. There are some labs on the first floor, but those labs are mostly for continuing stress tests on existing products. These are the labs that the tour groups get to see. But at the end of this hall," she said, pointing to another photo, "is a bank of elevators. These are accessible by biometrics only. No visitors allowed. The infirmary, Bayron's lab, and most of the computers that run Smith's brain are on the sixth floor. The sixth floor is off limits to anyone who is not directly involved in the brain project."

She turned to the back page of the album which had a floorplan of the sixth floor spread across the two pages. "This is the infirmary. It's basically a hospital room. Very secure. This is Bayron's lab. This is the controlled environment room where the computers are. The lab is where Ashkot's brain scans were parsed. His scans are resourced as 'Source Two data' on the servers, but for some reason all of the techs refer to him as Flat Stanley or Flat Stanislav."

Vakhrusheva chuckled a little when he heard his old colleague referred to in this way. How could these Americans ever understand the great power that lay in those scans. The power to destroy the world was somewhere on that floorplan. "Go on," he said.

"Smith maintains a separate office on the Executive Floor, which is the seventh floor, where he can interface with people without having to bring them to the sixth floor. He actually holds most of his meetings in that office, which is here. The executive offices are the only offices that are accessible from both the main entrance and the R&D entrance."

"Is there anything else that wasn't included in the dossiers?" Vakhrusheva asked.

"Well, there is something that I am still working on. It has to do with a black notebook that Dr. Bayron took handwritten notes in. I mentioned this before. When he disappeared, I searched the lab and hospital room. I searched everywhere for that notebook. I think its very important-- I'm sure it has the information in it that Bayron didn't want made public. When Bayron came back to SmithCorp from the mental hospital, the notebook was not among his effects. I have a feeling, call it an instinct, that we wouldn't be able to replicate this project without the information in that notebook."

"Who else had access to it?" Vakhrusheva asked.

"That's the thing, Mickey," Alice replied. "Before he went missing, he never let that book out of his sight. After he went missing, I looked for it all over his office, but found nothing. Lot's of people would go in and out of his office though, so if it was there it could've been taken by almost anyone."

"Those are the only facts?" Vakhrusheva asked.

"I'm glad you asked." Alice replied. "When I went to search Dr. Bayron's office, one young engineer came in looking very serious. It was very early in the morning, before most of the engineers come in and it was on a quiet day without much to do. This young man had been out of the office for several weeks and this was the first time I had seen him back. I know he caught me snooping around, but he never said anything about it. I haven't figured out a way to confront him without blowing my cover."

"What is this young man's name?" Vakhrusheva asked.

"Sarkis Ohangangian. They call him Sharky." Alice replied.

"An Armenian," Vakhrusheva said with a hint of distaste. "I have his dossier. You keep your cover intact. I will confront, as you say, this 'Sharky'. Let me spend some time with these 'effects' and think about where the vulnerabilities are. I would like to meet again tomorrow."

"Bobby will make it happen," Alice assured him.

"I'm sure he will," Vakhrusheva agreed.

Vakhrusheva made the long walk down the hallway to the front entrance of the nursing home and noticed along the way that he had become accustomed to the smell that he had found so offensive before.

Bobby was waiting for him in his car. Vakhrusheva got in. Bobby knew that Alice, like himself, was a consummate professional, and he knew that Vakhrusheva now knew that too. "The best chicken wings in the world are not too far from here. I'm gonna treat you to lunch." Bobby said as he drove, in the opposite direction from which they had come, past the University toward downtown Albany.

Vakhrusheva merely grunted assent. He was thinking.

Josey dialed Gonzales' secret red phone and Gonzales answered right away with a simple, "Yes."

"Marco," Josey said, daring to call Gonzales by his first name, "my boys and I have connected some of the dots. We should meet."

"I'll meet you at the Brandywine diner in 20 minutes. And one other thing..." Gonzales replied, "only my mother, may she rest in peace, ever called me Marco."

The Brandywine Diner on Emmet Street was exactly what a diner should be. Brightly lit, good food, friendly staff, no one to rush you away from the tables, and much to

Gonzales and Cruz's preference, no security cameras anywhere. They settled into a corner booth on the far side of the dining room behind the service counter. Gonzales was actually hungry and had selected the Brandywine more for that reason than for any other. He ordered the meatloaf and an iced tea. Cruz ordered a slice of apple cranberry pie and a cup of coffee.

"We made some really interesting connections from the C.I.P.'s," Cruz said after they had placed their orders, "Check this out." He pulled his laptop out of his briefcase and opened it on the table. It sprang to life and Cruz navigated to a particular page. "This is tracking information from a parcel that was sent to SmithCorp almost a year ago."

SPNI.RU/petrovsky/collaborations/us/3dmodeling
Dr. Vadi Petrovsky
International Parcel, 10kg
011-7-812-499-4999 x. 209

"That is very, very interesting," Gonzales agreed. "I'm assuming that parcel was delivered to Dr. Bayron."

"Exactly." Cruz answered. He had already learned not to be surprised by the scope of Gonzales' knowledge or the speed of his deductive reasoning.

"The website?" Gonzales asked.

"Not much there. Technical mumbo jumbo, some indexed discussions. But here's what we figured out from it: Dr. Petrovsky had a nearly complete 3d model of a human brain taken from a cadaver. He used an invasive technique to get his images, essentially destroying the brain by modeling it. He was trying to do exactly what Dr. Bayron did, but Dr. Bayron was dealing with a live subject and had to be careful not to damage any tissue in creating his model. So Dr. Bayron and Dr. Petrovsky agreed to cooperate. Dr. Bayron agreed to share his data and results in exchange for Dr. Petrovsky's images. To the extent that Dr. Bayron could not get an image from his live subject, he filled in the gaps with Dr. Petrovsky's image from his dead subject."

Gonzales leaned back and thought for a moment. "Tell me your theory on this Mr. Cruz, because mine just sounds crazy."

"I think that the dead subject was Ashkot. I think that Ashkot's memories ended up in Smith. I think that Mr. Smith's artificial brain knows the missile codes and I think that Kovaretsky and Vakhrusheva will stop at nothing to get that information out."

"It doesn't sound quite as crazy when you say it, Mr. Cruz." Gonzales responded.

"There's something even more interesting about the collaboration site, Mr. Gonzales. The very last message from Petrovsky to Bayron. Petrovsky ran a simulation and it didn't work. He clearly suspects that Bayron has held something back."

"Then Bayron is a marked man. That's good."

Cruz was taken aback, "Good?" he asked.

"Yes, good." Gonzales answered. "Now we know who they're coming for. That makes life easy in a way, doesn't it? We put a tail on Bayron and they'll come to us. What else do you have?"

"This one is kind of interesting, maybe just corroboration, but it is interesting. We got this from one of the bugs at the topless bar. Listen:"

Cruz opened an audio player on his laptop and the two men listened to the recorded voices:

> *"Myra wants to meet you back at the office at two. I told her I'd deliver you sober. Let's go."*
> *"What's it about?"*
> *"Listen, She didn't tell me what it was*

about so, I assume its not something she wants to talk about over the phone. She just said its something Smith wants handled right away."
"As long as it isn't more lost Russians..."

"Lost Russians?" Gonzales repeated quizzically. "I recognize Kitty's voice. Is that Takahashi?"

"It sure is." Cruz said with satisfaction.

"Shit." Gonzales said. It was the first time Cruz had ever heard him swear. "Shit," Gonzales repeated again.

"Alright," Gonzales said after a lengthy pause, "I can only come up with three possibilities here. First is that Bayron was working with Petrovsky, had full knowledge that his images were of Ashkot's brain and that he intentionally and knowingly extracted that data. In that case, though, why would Bayron not give the complete data set to Petrovsky? Second is that some information from Ashkot's mind somehow ended up in Smith accidentally and they may or may not know what it means. Third, dead and missing Russians have nothing to do with Ashkot. Where's Bayron?"

"Locked up tight at SmithCorp still." Cruz answered. "I'll have a guy on the door in 20 minutes. We also have 10-20's on Myra, Takahashi, Hermelinda, and Sharky. Hermelinda's at SmithCorp too. Myra and Sharky are at their houses. And Takahashi...well, you can guess where he is." Cruz read from his smartphone.

"Takahashi can't talk without an order. He's an attorney. He'll be a stone wall. The others haven't connected themselves to Russians. What about Kitty? She's close to Takahashi."

"We don't have a 10-20 on her, but we can geolocate her phone in about two minutes."

"And tell your boys to keep an ear on Hermelinda and Sharky's cell phones. They're the ones most likely to give us a bead on Bayron. Let's go find Kitty. Stop and get Julian on the way. At least lets have some pretense of a cover."

XVII.

Smith's duplicate data center had come together quickly according to the specifications that Smith had delivered to Takahashi. Takahashi had a friend in Mexico who was able to form a Sociedad Anonyma, the Mexican equivalent of a corporation, literally overnight with the stated purpose of prospecting for rare earth metals, an endeavor in which vast amounts of capital could be lost with absolutely no return. Under Mexican law, an American citizen can only own 49% of a Sociedad Anonyma, but Mexican banks are always more than happy to hold the other 51% as a favor to large depositors. One of the bearer bonds in Takahashi's keep was cashed out and wired to Banco Republica DF, for the benefit of the Mexican company which owned the other 51% of the enterprise. Concurrently, Takahashi set up a Nevada Corporation, using all fake names and addresses, for the purpose of providing consulting and data processing services to the healthcare industry. He issued 49% of the shares of the Nevada corporation to the Mexican company, placing 51% of the shares in a charitable trust which he formed naming Kitty, Katherine O'Malley, as Trustee. The IRS issued Tax ID numbers for both the Trust and for the Nevada Corporation.

This setup allowed him, through Kitty, to direct all the corporate business without either of them having any connection to the corporation itself. All roads led either to Mexico, or to a trust that was empty save for the non-income producing corporate stock. The Mexican company was funded by liquidating the bearer bonds at the Banco Republica and placing the proceeds in the Mexican Bank account. The Bank would then wire the money from Mexico to the Nevada Corporation's account on an as needed basis. If anything ever did trace through to Kitty, she truly had no idea how the money moved or for what purpose. These transactions required occasional trips to Mexico, which Takahashi happily made himself. The beer was much cheaper in Mexico. Between Takahashi's trips to Mexico and the time he spent drunk at the Moviestar Bar, Kitty found herself overseeing the day-to-day progress of the building of the data center.

The plans that Smith had provided to them were quite detailed. For each aspect of the project, Smith had recommended contractors and suppliers who he was confident could execute their specific tasks promptly and professionally. He also made it clear that he wanted a replacement for every single cable, screw and circuit board stored in a shipping container at one of his warehouses.

Kitty chose a large space in an industrial park in Cohoes for the secret computer bank that would ultimately store an exact copy of Elijah Smith. The space was clean and modern, well ventilated, remote, secure, comfortable, and most importantly, already wired with fiberoptics capable of handling huge amounts of Internet traffic. It already had an office built in and Kitty ordered herself a big desk and a comfortable chair. She had a little sign made for the door that simply stated, KO Data Systems. Everyday she put on a stylish business suit and went to her office. When the contractors came to her to get their invoices paid, she wrote checks from the corporate account. The checks always cleared and accordingly, the contractors performed their work diligently and without too many questions. Every so often, she would walk through the computer room.

She saw when the glass dust proof walls were erected, when the industrial climate control system went in, when array after array of servers were mounted onto shelves. And then one day, the lead technician came into her office and said, "We're about to throw the switch, Ms. O'Malley."

She came into the computer room. It was very cold and clean. Someone lowered the lights and the tech called out: "power her up!" Kitty heard clicking and clacking first, then whirring, then some high pitched beeps and squeals. Then green, yellow and red flashing lights began to blink rhythmlessly all around her. She thought it was the most beautiful thing she had ever seen. She heard a loud pop and then a sizzle and was at first startled. Then she realized that what she had heard was someone opening a bottle of champagne. "She's online, in her prime, and working fine, Ms. O'Malley," the technician said as he handed her a paper cup half filled with champagne. There were hand-slaps all around as the technicians and crew members drank their champagne.

Kitty realized that they were all expecting her to say something. She raised her glass and tried to imagine what Elijah Smith himself might have said in these circumstances. "Gentlemen, I am very, very happy today," She said. "You all did an excellent job and I applaud your diligence and professionalism. My investors are going to be ecstatic. I will never forget you for making this all possible." She was impressed with herself for finding these words. She raised her paper cup in the air and swigged the last gulp of champagne. The workers and technicians applauded her and began packing up their gear. After everyone was out of the building, the head technician came back in and said, "You've have a state of the art system here, Miss. I wish you the best of luck with whatever it is you are going to be doing, just promise me you're not going to try to take over the world."

He laid a four inch thick, three ring binder on her desk. "These are all of the specifications for your reference," he said turning the page. "IP addresses, architecture notes, diagrams, everything you need to keep her humming and whirring is in here. I would recommend that you run the diagnostic routine every day. Its right here in appendix 'A'. Of course, if you need anything, you can call me anytime. "

"I think you can expect that, Mr. Patel," she replied giving him a firm handshake as she walked him out.

After she shut the door behind him, she said aloud into the empty office, "now what?"

She called Takahashi from her cell phone to find out.

"You'll need to scan the specifications notebook and copy it onto a thumbdrive. I'll get it to Smith." Takahashi told her.

"I think I can do that," Kitty replied. "The guy who installed the copier and office computer left me a cheat sheet for how to scan documents into files for e-mails."

"Okay," Takahashi said, "just make sure you don't e-mail it. I don't want it going out over the 'Net. I'll take care of getting it to Smith. You just put it on a thumbdrive and I'll meet you later tonight."

"I can do that, Mr. Takahashi," Kitty replied.

She took the hundreds of pages of documents out of the three ring binder and put them in the feed tray of the giant copier/scanner/fax that had been installed in the office area. When she put the papers in the feed tray, the control panel lit up with three options: scan, copy, or fax. She chose scan. Double sided or single sided. She chose double. Scan to file: yes/no. She chose yes. She watched in amazement as the machine sucked the papers in and spat them back out. "I got this." She said to herself, then and there committing to read and understand everything that was in that binder even if it took her the rest of her life.

Bayron was less sure of what he wanted to do for the rest of his life. He sat on the hospital bed where his former patient had died and been reborn as a technological creature.

"You did not sleep well, Doctor." Smith said.

"Were you watching me sleep?" Bayron asked. "You told me you wouldn't."

"So sue me, Doug. I'm sorry. I just thought this was important enough to intrude."

"What is it, Elly?"

"I'm online already."

"I figured you would be." Bayron replied.

"I wanted you to know. I know it frightens you, but, in the name of science, I thought I'd give you an anecdotal report."

"Elly. I want to go home."

"Only your nurse can authorize that."

"Is she here?" Bayron asked.

"I can get her for you, if you want." Smith replied.

"How?" Bayron asked.

"Watch this," Smith said. "I came here to show you some of my new tricks. Check out the monitor."

Bayron turned his attention to the monitor and watched

for a moment.

"Okay, almost got her... look! look! look.!" Smith shouted enthusiastically through the speakers.

Bayron watched as the monitor screen lit up with a grainy image of a non-descript intersection. Suddenly, without warning, Hermelinda's car passed through the intersection and just as quickly disappeared off the monitor.

"What the hell was that?" Bayron asked.

"Exactly what you were worried about, Doc. I was able to locate Hermelinda's cell phone through the GPS system. I then searched for a stop light camera and found one on her route. I accessed the camera and activated it just before she came through."

"You did all that in about 4 seconds." Bayron mused.

"I did that in about a tenth of a second. The rest was just waiting for her to get to the intersection." Smith bragged. "Watch this."

Bayron watched the monitor as a web browser opened up and dialpad appeared within it. The buttons on the dialpad appeared to be pressing themselves. The speakers rang once and there was a voice on the other end that was not Smith. It was Hermelinda.

"Hello?" She said.

"Herme," Smith said. "I'm here with Dr. Bayron."

"How are you calling me?" Hermelinda asked.

"I'm online. I'm using Skype! I'm free!" Smith said.

Hermelinda responded with joy. "Oh, I'm so happy for you, baby. That's wonderful news."

"Where are you now, Herme? I want to see you and Bayron wants to ask you something."

"I'm almost there already, Elly. What does Doug want?"

"Hermelinda? This is Dr. Bayron. I want to go home. Can I please go home?"

"We'll call Dr. Beedle when I get there, okay? If he approves it, I'll take you." Hermelinda said.

"I'll miss you Doc," Smith said. "I really, really want to show off my new legs."

"I want to go home, Elly." Bayron said staring down at the floor beneath his feet as he sat on the side of his bed. A long silence hung in the room. "Elly?" Bayron said. "I'm still here Doug."

"Elly, you have a soul. I know you do. Your soul is a liability. Your humanity is a liability. You are still a man. But now you are a man with the power of a God. I know you know that. Please don't let it corrupt your soul."

"I won't let that happen, and neither will you, Doug. I don't need money, power, or sex in my present form. You have no idea how simple my pleasures have become. Taking over the world is not on my agenda."

"I trust you Elly. But as much power as you may have now, you're still only human. Maybe it'd be better if you weren't. But now I really want to go home." Bayron said, never having moved his eyes from the floor.

"Well, as powerful as you think I am now that my tentacles are reaching into cyberspace, I have no power over that. You're under the care of Dr. Beedle and Dr. Beedle was appointed by the state. Hermelinda, at her own personal risk, had you released into her care and custody, and its their judgment that you have to rely on now. The same as I put myself into your hands, you have to accept that you're in their hands. Besides, I have a selfish interest in seeing you get healthy."

"And what interest is that?" Bayron asked still looking down.

"Here's part of that answer right now," Smith said. The image on the monitor changed to a view of the executive parking lot at the SmithCorp Building. Hermelinda's car was clearly visible pulling into her designated parking spot.

Dr. Bayron looked at the monitor and saw what Smith was "seeing" through the security camera in the parking lot.

Smith continued to speak. "Accessing traffic and security cams is probably the most entertaining thing I've discovered since coming online. Most of them have no security at all, you just have to find the host and that's it. Even the ones that have security have terrible security. Because I can literally see in binary code, getting through firewalls is like picking a lock, from *inside* the lock. Did you know, doctor, that because I can visualize things from their pure data forms, and because my memory is flawless, I can literally watch and memorize the activities of dozens of cameras all at once? I'm a veritable 'eye in the sky.'"

"You're frightening me, Elly." Bayron said, now looking directly at Smith's camera eye.

"Then you're really not going to want to hear this. Want to see what the President is doing right now?"

"What?" Bayron asked, although he had heard perfectly well.

"I was able to tap the President's personal webcam. Nothing in the oval office or anything like that, but the one he has in the office in the residential wing where he Skypes with his aunt and his old friends."

Bayron thought for a moment and then looked up and smiled into the camera, "You know what Elly," he said, "I'd be lying if I said I didn't have some kind of voyeuristic interest in seeing that."

"Attaboy, Dougy," Smith said as the image on the monitor changed again, this time to a view of an empty, but very neat office. "You know, this thing is done, you might as well let yourself enjoy it. President's not in. I also found the security camera inside the Moviestar club where that girl Kitty used to work. I didn't even know they had one. I don't think the customers are supposed to know that they're being watched. That one is usually a lot of fun. You want to see that?" Smith didn't wait for Bayron to answer before he changed the image on the monitor.

Bayron chuckled as the grainy security camera image of the inside of the sleazy topless bar emerged on the monitor in front of him. He could barely make out the image of a woman gyrating listlessly on a little stage and the tops of two heads, both with thinning hair sitting by the rail.

"When I was an intern at County," Bayron said, with a little light in his eyes, "we always had kids coming in that had taken some recreational drug or another and were nervous because they were having unexpected effects. I had one guy, I remember him so well, who had taken mescaline, they used to call it 'microdots' and his vision turned all brown. No colors, just varying shades of brown he told me. He said it had been that way for at least 10 hours. You know what we used to tell people like that? We would tell them, 'look, you already took the drug. You can't untake it so you might as well enjoy the trip.'"

"Spot on, my good sir," Smith replied. "We're in this place now, and there's no going back. At least not for me. So we might as well enjoy this trip." Smith noticed Bayron had a relaxed look about him. He was clearly enjoying the moment. Smith was overjoyed to see his friend looking so at ease. It had been a long time since he had seen him that way. "I wish they had a better camera, Doug. This is the best picture I can get."

"Frankly I'm more amused by the idea of what you're doing than by anything happening on that stage there." Bayron said. *Is this how I learned to stop worrying and love the bomb?* He thought to himself, also recognizing that at some point he felt a tremendous weight lift from his shoulders. He had forgotten in that moment that he was a mental patient recovering from a psychotic episode, that he was a prisoner in this hospital room dependant upon another for any freedom he had, he had even for the moment forgotten about the little boy who he watched die in agony as he helplessly cradled his head in his arms.

Hermelinda stepped in at this most inopportune moment. "I hope I'm not interrupting something, gentlemen." She said with faux formality.

Smith quickly turned the monitor back to the oscilliscopic wave and as he did so a funny little noise that sounded like 'erp' emanated from the speakers. Smith and Bayron both laughed a little each recognizing in themselves and in each other that feeling of being caught with a hand in the cookie jar. But Smith's reaction had been fast enough that Hermelinda hadn't seen what was on the screen. "No, darling," Smith said, "the good doctor and I were just catching up with each other a little."

Hermelinda look squarely at Dr. Bayron and studied his face for a moment. "You're looking good today, Doctor. This is the most engaged I've seen you look since I picked you up at the hospital. how do you feel?"

"I feel pretty good, Hermelinda. Your husband really has a way of shaking me out of the blues sometimes."

"I'm glad to hear that Douglas. Let's get Dr. Beedle on the phone and see what he'll authorize."

It was already after seven when Bobby dropped Vakhrusheva back off at the Hampton Inn. Vakhrusheva, like most Russians, had a stomach of iron; but he did have terrible heartburn from the spicy chicken wings he had eaten with Bobby. He was eager to take an antacid. He had purchased some Tums along with some Extra-Strength Tylenol at the airport when he had landed and now he swallowed two of the Tylenol and chewed up two Tums and then washed the whole meal of pills down with a generous swig of Vodka straight from the bottle. *I will bring this back to Russia, these buffalo wings*, he thought, not regretting the heartburn at all.

He had actually been impatient to open the bag that Alice had given him in the nursing home, but he had become so preoccupied with the wings that he had almost forgotten about the bag containing what Alice had described as Mrs. Oronov's effects.

He emptied the contents of the bag onto the little writing table in his room. The photo album was the largest item in the bag and was one of only two items that wasn't in a sealed greeting card style envelope. He moved the album to the side since he already knew what was in there.

He opened the first envelope. It contained an ID card which was strung from a blue nylon necklace and a plain white piece of paper. He read from the paper which explained what could be accessed with the magnetic strip on the back of the card. The card itself said SmithCorp Industries across the top in English and then in smaller type in Cyrillic letters. The ID had his picture on it and the name "Mikhael 'Mickey' Oronov," a manager in the Russian branch of SmithCorp. Clever, he thought. That will certainly get me past the front door guards.

Next he opened an envelope which contained a copy of the SmithCorp New Employee Policy and Procedures Handbook and thumbed through it. Smart again, he thought. He would look at that closely before he walked in the front door. Next he opened an envelope that contained a single sheet of paper with a handdrawn sketch of a notebook on it. In handwriting next to the sketch were the words, "missing notebook." In another envelope was a piece of paper with several keys scotch taped to it. On the paper near each key was a note. One said 7th floor bathroom, another said hospital room supply cabinet, and another said executive office cleaning crew master key. Another envelope contained photos and descriptions of several SmithCorp employees in the Russian office.

The last item in the bag was the only other item that was not in a sealed envelope. It was a simple spiral notebook with a black cover. A post-it note inside the front cover said, "Notebook. Identical to Bayron's missing notebook." The pages were blank. Not completely identical he assumed.

He lay down in the bed and took another belt of Vodka and began thinking of his next step. The chicken wings were dancing in his stomach. He still didn't regret eating them.

Julian Waterstone's big black Buick sedan exited the New York State Thruway at the first exit for Cohoes, drove past some abandoned London-style row houses and turned right onto 7th Street and then left into a brand new industrial complex. Trailing close behind the sedan was a small silver Japanese car being driven by Josey Cruz. It was about 8:00 at night. The sedan pulled into a parking spot near the main gate to the complex, while Josey drove straight in. Toward the back of the complex he found what he was looking for. Kitty's car. It was parked in front of a door that said, "KO Data Systems" on the front, and there was a light on inside. He then continued to drive past the buildings in the park to see if there was anything he could use as a pretext for being there.

Inside, Kitty sat at her desk studying the technical manual the installers had left and looking everything up on the Internet that she didn't understand. She had determined to understand how her data center worked and was prepared to do whatever it took. All she knew for certain was that it was going to take a very, very long time. *Maybe I should hire that technician to teach me*, she thought. Every so often she would look up at the window into the dust-free, climate controlled computer room and see that all of the lights that were supposed to be blinking were actually blinking. She knew from studying the manuals what all the different machines in there were called. She just didn't understand exactly what they all did.

Josey drove his car back around to the front and reported to Gonzales. Gonzales thought for a moment and then said to Cruz. "Okay, you go in. We have no excuse for being here and I'm not ready to blow cover yet. We'll stay here and monitor the wire. Josey got back in his car and drove to the rear of the complex and parked next to Kitty's car. He got out and jimmied open the lock to the driver's side door of her car and turned on her headlights. Then he relocked the car door and walked to and knocked on the door for KO Data Systems.

Kitty was startled by the knock. "Hello?" She said tentatively through the still shut door."

"Hi," said Cruz. "I was driving by and there's a car out here with its headlights on. I just wanted to let someone know."

"Oh, thank you," Kitty said looking through the peephole on the door. She saw a very pleasant looking, well dressed man, about her own age and behind him she could see the headlights glowing on the front of her little car. There was something familiar about him. She thought for sure she had seen him before. Her years of dancing in clubs had sensitized her ability to assess risks and she quickly determined she was not in danger from this kind stranger. She opened the door very slowly though.

"Make sure it starts," Cruz said, "I don't know how long the lights have been on. I have some jumper cables if you need a jump."

Kitty came outside leaving the door to KO Data Systems open behind her. She unlocked her car and got inside. She turned off the lights and tried to start the engine. It started right up. She turned the engine back off and walked over to where Cruz was standing. "Thanks," she said. "I'm really surprised it started, they must have been on for hours."

"I'm Joe," Cruz said, extending his hand. "It looks like we're going to be neighbors."

"Katherine O'Malley," Kitty said extending her hand to his and shaking it firmly. "Are you a tenant here?"

"No, not yet," Josey said. "But I have a little catalog company that I'm planning on moving in here. Is this your company?"

"Yes. We're still setting up though. We're brand new." Kitty answered.

"What kind of data services do you do?" Josey said leaning in to see into the office.

"We store backups of medical records," Kitty replied as she had been instructed.

"It looks like the future in there." Josey said. "I bet you can store a lot of data on that rig."

"Do you know what a exabyte is?" Kitty replied using knowledge she had just gained in the past hour.

"No. I've never heard of that." Josey replied.

"Its one million terabytes. A terabyte is a thousand gigabytes. So, if a downloaded movie takes up about a gigabyte, I could store a thousand, million movies."

"Do you really expect to have that much data to store?" Josey asked. It was clear Kitty was showing off some new knowledge. He found it...cute.

"No, not at all. Its got what we call 'multiple redundancies' so it can store the same data in different places so if one part of the system goes down or even the whole system, we don't lose any data."

"How does that work?" Josey asked, knowing that he was pressing his luck.

"Now, Mr. Joe, I can't be telling you all of our secrets," Kitty said with a wink, feeling awfully clever for thinking of a way not to have to say 'I don't know.'

"Can I buy you a drink?" Josey asked.

Kitty looked out at the sky and noticed the sun was setting. She looked at Josey and thought about it for a moment. Then she smiled and said, "meet me at Friday's on Grand in 30 minutes. I've just got to shut things down here before I leave."

"Don't disappoint me, Ms. O'Malley," Josey replied as he walked back to his car.

"Call me Kitty," She responded. "Everyone calls me Kitty."

Gonzales and Julian were already headed to the Friday's parking lot to find an inconspicuous place to park that was still close enough to monitor whatever further conversations might happen there. As they drove, Julian made an audible noise that sounded like 'hmph'.

"What is it, Waterstone?" Gonzales asked.

"Exabytes." Julian responded. "I know I'm not the international spy in this car, but..." he paused for a moment. "Listen, when she said exabytes, I knew that term because Smith had used it during his press conference. He said that the data load of his mind was measured in exabytes. It's the only time I've ever heard that word before. Call me a damn fool, but I'll bet you dime to dollars that there's a complete copy of Smith over there."

"And if there is," Gonzales replied, "I'll give you double or nothing that no one at SmithCorp knows about it."

Julian thought for a moment. "I wouldn't take that bet," he replied.

XVIII.

An anonymous remailer sent an encoded message to Sam Takahashi's hushmail account. Sam pulled out his old and frayed copy of the Hitchhiker's Guide to the Galaxy that he had used to encode messages to his schoolmate when they were just little boys and began transcribing. After he had worked out the entire message, Takahashi made a call to his friend in Mexico who in turn made a call to a friend in Iceland.

The following morning a shipping container containing the duplicate parts for the Cohoes data center was on its way to the port of Reykjavik.

XIX.

Avon Crest lay halfway between Schenectady and Latham. An above average but by no means affluent neighborhood of matching colonial style homes. As Bobby drove Vakhrusheva down Inman Road toward the home Sharky shared with his mother, a group of boys playing street hockey quickly moved their nets off to the side in response to one of their member's shouting, 'CAR!'-- their well established code word for clearing the street when anyone saw a car coming. Bobby gave them a wave, making sure that his hand blocked his face as he did so. Vakhrusheva smiled in recognition of his colleague's superb training and professionalism.

Bobby pulled the car into the driveway of the home at the address listed in Sharky's dossier. The house was neat and inconspicuous: well trimmed lawn, a couple of older trees. There were no other plants or flowers. Someone had spread pebbles where one would otherwise have expected to see some aesthetic plantings close to the house. Vakhrusheva walked up the cement path that led to the front door and rang the bell. He could hear the television playing in the background. He waited at the door for a minute or so before he rang the bell again.

He could hear some movement in the house. Then, through the door, a woman's voice. "No one here." The words were in English, but Vakhrusheva recognized the heavy Armenian accent. Her heavy guttural pronunciation of the "h" in the word "here" was distinctly Eastern Armenian. Vakhrusheva adopted a Western Armenian accent in his reply hoping that in doing so his Russian tongue would be less noticeable to the lady behind the door.

"I was supposed to meet Sharky here," Vakhrusheva said.

"Sako not here." The woman replied, still in accented English, "come back later." A large, friendly, ruddy face peeked from behind a curtain at the side of the door.

Vakhrusheva recognized the kind of unfaltering paranoia which fomented and became endemic during Armenia's unstable years after the fall of the Soviet Union. It was also the kind of paranoia which signaled to Vakhrusheva that the aging lady behind the curtain was home alone. He dredged deep to exude the kind of charm and sincerity he knew would be necessary to get inside the house without attracting the attention of the neighbors. "Okay," he said in his fake Western Armenian accent through his fake smile, "I don't know when I can come back though, so can you just let him know that Sergio from the community center came by about the earthquake fundraiser and that if he's still interested to give me a call." He turned as if to leave.

"Does Sako have your number?" The voice inside

asked, finally switching to its native language.

Vakhrusheva turned back, and looked through the little side window and made eye contact with the woman inside. He let his eyes smile for him. "Actually, maybe you could give him these materials and save me a trip back here later. My office is all the way in Watervliet." He pointed to his briefcase and pretended to be looking for papers as he said this.

The eyes in the window sized him up again and finally, Sharky's mother said, "Okay, give me a second to get the lock."

Vakhrusheva sized up the situation instantly and decided that getting the door open a little bit just to hand the papers through was as good as he was going to get. As soon as her face moved away from the window, Vakhrusheva signaled to Bobby who was still in the car. He heard the tepid click of the deadbolt opening and saw the door handle turn. As soon as he saw the latch clear the strike plate, he took a step back and kicked the door with all the power that accompanies a lifetime of military style training. The door swung in on its hinges with blinding speed and incredible force. Vakhrusheva heard Mrs. Ohangangian fall to the floor. He glanced quickly back to Bobby who gave him the thumbs up to let him know that no one had seen. Vakhrusheva held up two fingers signaling Bobby to wait two minutes before coming into the house. As he stepped over the threshold into the house, he drew his gun from his coat pocket and trained the barrel right between Mrs. Ohangangian's eyes.

"If you scream, I will kill you. If you run, I will kill you. If you make any quick movement at all, I am quicker. I will kill you." Vakhrusheva dropped his fake accent and spoke in Russian. Mrs. Ohangangian opened her mouth as if to speak and Vakhrusheva put his finger to his lips to stop her from doing so. "I am looking for a notebook exactly like this one, but with writing in it," he said drawing from his briefcase the blank black notebook that Alice had given him, "Do you know where it is?"

"I don't care about Armenia any more. My husband is dead. He is the one you want to hurt. Its just me and my son, please don't hurt me." She said through her tears. "I'm an old lady. Haven't I been through enough!" She cried and spoke softly. "And Sako is a good boy. He don't do nothing." She pleaded.

"Lady," Vakhrusheva said, "I want to leave you alone and get out of here. Just tell me where this book is and I will leave. Otherwise, in one more minute my colleague will be in here and he won't be as pleasant as me. Believe me, if it's here we will find it. Giving it to me now is the only way to save your son's life and your own. Do you understand me?"

Mrs. Ohangangian tried her best to calm down and stop crying, but still had to answer through sobs, "I've never seen a notebook like that here."

Bobby walked through the front door and quickly assessed the situation. "Fifteen minutes max, boss." Bobby said giving Vakhrusheva his boots-on-the-ground assessment of how long it was safe for them to remain in the house. Vakhrusheva nodded in acknowledgment and tossed Bobby a roll of duct tape from his briefcase. Bobby taped Mrs. Ohangangian's hands together behind her back and then helped her to her feet. After patting her down for phones or weapons, he led her to a kitchen chair and used the tape to tape her feet together and her legs and torso to the chair. Finally he taped over her mouth.

Vakhrusheva and Bobby then proceeded to take a quick tour of the house. Knowing they only had fifteen minutes, they had to focus their search on the most likely places to find the notebook. They searched very neatly, replacing each item they moved to nearly the exact place they had taken it from.

They worked quickly and thoroughly. After fifteen minutes of searching, Vakhrusheva signaled to Bobby to take Mrs. Ohangangian to the car. Bobby carefully removed all of the duct tape and stuck the wads of used tape in his pockets. He gave Mrs. Ohangangian instructions to walk to the car and to get in the passenger seat and told her that if she tried to run or scream he would shoot her in the back. Mrs. Ohangangian did as she was told. After she was in the car, Bobby walked to the car and got in the driver's seat and then a few minutes later Vakhrusheva shut the house door behind him, walked to the car and got in the back seat behind Mrs. Ohangangian. Bobby began driving away. "Do you think your son will trade you for a notebook, mom?" Vakhrusheva said menacingly. He then addressed Bobby saying, "this car is hot."

"I have a swap just a couple of blocks from here," Bobby replied.

Vakhrusheva grunted. *Of course you do*, he thought.

Dr. Beedle was actually pleased to hear that Dr. Bayron had asked to go home. "It demonstrates that he wants to re-engage with life," he told Hermelinda. Dr. Beedle was simply concerned that Dr. Bayron should not be left alone. Hermelinda made arrangements with the babysitter to keep Ellen until she got back and was happy to accompany Dr. Bayron. Smith voiced no objection to her taking him. "Go. Have fun." He said, adding, "I'll be here watching."

Both Dr. Bayron and Hermelinda felt uneasy with that last remark, but neither of them reacted to it. Nonetheless that statement sat between them in the car like a giant invisible matzoh ball as Hermelinda drove Dr. Bayron to his little apartment near Union College. It hung in the air like the stench of rotten eggs as they made their way up the stairs to his front door, and it enveloped them like a blanket as they entered Dr. Bayron's tiny home. They were oblivious to the

CIA agent who had followed closely behind them all the way from SmithCorp.

After letting Hermelinda in, Dr. Bayron excused himself to use the bathroom. The apartment was neat and clean. Clearly it had not gone untouched during the months that Dr. Bayron had been missing, hospitalized and subsequently imprisoned at SmithCorp. Hermelinda surmised that he had a cleaning girl who kept coming even in Bayron's absence. The apartment was almost completely bare. There was a reclining chair and a coffee table in the living room. Against all of the walls were cardboard file boxes stacked three high with handwritten markings on their sides. There was no television set that she could see nor a phone nor a computer. In the kitchen was a small table and two matching chairs. Hermelinda surmised that they must have been a set. There was no art on the walls. The most technological thing in the entire apartment was a coffee maker.

A Formica counter separated the kitchen from the living room and it was covered with unopened mail.

Hermelinda peeked into the bedroom and saw a full sized bed, neatly made. On either side of the bed were nightstands, each with a matching lamp. One nightstand also had a clock and some magazines on it and the other had a single picture frame holding a glossy five by seven photo. She was trying to make out the faces in the photo when Dr. Bayron approached her from behind.

"My wife and son." He said. "We went to Martha's Vineyard that year."

"I'm so sorry, Doug." Hermelinda said, knowing that those words really only had meaning to her.

"I haven't slept in my own bed in a long time," Bayron said as he slipped his shoes off and lay down. "I'm going to take a nap. Make yourself at home," he said as he shut his eyes.

Hermelinda backed away from the bedroom door and headed for the recliner in the living room. She decided that she would take a nap too. She sat in the recliner and shut her eyes, but found it impossible to sleep. In just a few minutes she was able to hear Doug Bayron snoring, lightly, in the next room. She got up and glanced at some of his unopened mail almost all of which seemed to be bills and advertisements. She went to the bathroom and washed her hands for no reason.

She went back to the kitchen and looked in the cupboards which were empty except for a set of dishes: four big plates, four little plates, and four bowls. The refrigerator was empty but for an open box of baking soda and a jar of pickles. She went back to the easy chair and shut her eyes again, but again she could not rest. Bayron's snoring had gotten louder, and the chair was not truly as comfortable as she thought it would be even when she had it in full recline.

She got up again and this time snuck quietly into the bedroom and around to the far side of the bed. She picked up the picture that she had been unable to see from the doorway. Dr. Bayron was barely recognizable. He had long black hair tied back into a pony tail, and a short black beard. He was wearing a leather motorcycle jacket. In the picture his arm was draped around the shoulders of a raven-haired beauty, who at the moment the picture was taken was looking at Doug with eyes that seemed almost worshipful. In his other arm, propped against his hip was a little black-haired boy. The boy had Doug's eyes and nose, but clearly the lips of the woman in the picture. Doug himself was beaming into the camera with a grin which bordered on goofy. Hermelinda had never seen Dr. Bayron like that: relaxed and happy.

She turned to face the sleeping Dr. Bayron and tried to find the man in the picture. She could see a little of the same face, although it bore more lines. What wasn't grey was still black. But his eyes had become different. They had become dimmer, or duller. Deader. Were his old radiant eyes locked away somewhere behind these new, lifeless eyes? she wondered.

Had anyone ever loved him as much as the two strangers she saw in the picture?

Dr. Bayron became agitated and turned from his back to his side facing away from Hermelinda. Hermelinda slipped off her shoes, climbed into the bed, put her arm over his shoulder and hugged him close to her. He did not awaken from this, but Hermelinda soon found herself drifting off to sleep.

Julian and Gonzales sat in Julian's Buick listening in to the conversation going on between Cruz and Kitty in the restaurant. It was clear to them that Cruz wasn't going to learn much from Kitty. In fact, it was clear that she had been well rehearsed in how to answer questions about the business and Cruz did not want to expose his cover by pressing her on the more nonsensical portions of her "official story".

The two older men listened quietly as the conversation trailed off into small talk and then what sounded like actual, personal engagement. Julian thought to himself that either Cruz was the greatest actor in the world or else he was genuinely falling for Kitty, the erstwhile dancer from the Moviestar Topless. Julian wondered whether Gonzales was thinking the same thing. He looked to see if he could read the construction of Gonzales' mind from the expression on his face and was surprised to see that Gonzales was asleep.

"Hey, Captain," Julian said tapping Gonzales on the shoulder to wake him up. "I think your boy can handle himself from here." Gonzales was also surprised and a little embarrassed when he realized that he had dozed. In fact, Julian could have sworn he saw him blush."

"There's no denying it Waterstone, age comes to us all."

"The night is for the young, Cap. We belong in our beds."

Gonzales started the car and wordlessly drove Julian home.

In fact, Josey Cruz and Kitty O'Malley weren't the only young people who had enjoyed the peaceful evening well into the night. Sharky was a little drunk and a little high and in a good mood. He had gone to see a friend's band play that night in town and had gotten a girl's phone number. He always felt so awkward around girls, that he rarely went home with a phone number and almost never with an actual girl. He made an excuse to leave right after she had given him her phone number, afraid that he might say something stupid and that she would lose interest in him. After he left, he studied the phone number for anomalies, analyzing it like code to see if maybe it was just dial-a-joke or some other number provided just to give him a blow-off. The number looked real enough. The exchange put her in Rosendale Estates, not too far from his own home.

As he pulled his motorcycle into the driveway, he could tell immediately that something was wrong. There were too many lights on in the house. His mother sometimes waited for him to come home, but she was always careful to turn out the lights that she wasn't using. It wasn't like her to forget things like that. He opened the door a little apprehensively and everything appeared to be in order but for the fact that his mother didn't ask, "Sako, is that you?"

"Mom?" He asked quietly into the empty house. Not hearing any response or any noise at all for that matter, sent a chill down his spine. "Mom?" He asked again a little louder as he crept further into the house. She still didn't answer and he started to grow more and more agitated. As he ran through the house looking for his mother and calling out, "Mom!", "Mom!", his mind ran through different possible scenarios, each one worse than the last. After he was satisfied that she wasn't in the house. He sat and tried to calm himself down. Upon resting, he decided that maybe she was confused about the time and went out of the house for some reason. Maybe a neighbor had called and needed help. He called her cell phone.

Her phone rang twice before it was answered. "Ah, Mr. Sharky," Vakhrusheva said, "I've been expecting your call."

"Who is this?" Sharky demanded to know.

"I don't think you are presently in a position to ask questions, Mr. Sharky," Vakhrusheva answered in the most menacing tone he could muster, "but what is important for you to know is that your mother is fine. She is with my colleague and she is very worried about you."

"Where is she!" Sharky demanded again.

"Apparently I haven't made the rules clear and I do not intend to stay on the phone very long. So please take note of the fact that for security reasons I will have to abandon this phone quickly so that it cannot be tracked. After I abandon this phone you will have no way to contact me so this may be the last conversation we ever have. Seeing as how you have no choice but to trust me as a man of my word, you must believe that I will return your mother to you unharmed and well fed provided you do something for me. Otherwise, I will kill her one piece at a time. Do you know what that means Mr. Sharky?" Vakhrusheva did not wait for Sharky to answer. "It means that first I will cut off her feet, then her hands, then her legs, then her arms. Please, picture this in your mind as you conduct yourself over the next few hours." Vakhrusheva paused to let Sharky envision this torture. "Now, what I want you to do, is to find a little black notebook that belongs to Dr. Bayron. I trust you know what

I am talking about, no?"

"Yeah," said Sharky.

"Well I think you know exactly where it is and I am gambling your mother's life on that suspicion. If you find it and give it to me she lives. If you don't, she dies. Understood?"

"Yeah," Sharky said with burning anger.

"If you tell anyone about this call, she dies. If anyone follows you when you deliver the book, she dies. Your mother will be released exactly 24 hours after you give me the book, provided of course that no one has interfered. This is clear?"

"Yes." Sharky said.

"Great. Be at the Schenectady Amtrack station tomorrow at 6:00 a.m. and bring your phone. I will give you further instructions from there." Vakhrusheva immediately hung up the phone.

The SmithCorp Building was deserted except for the security guards and cleaning crews. And of course, Smith himself, who had been wiling away the hours listening in on cell conversations and watching the world through security cameras as he had demonstrated during the day. Not only had he heard the entire conversation between Sharky and Vakhrusheva but, because of the unique technological nature of his mind, he actually had it in code just like a digital recording. *Shit*, he thought in his lifelike mind. He embraced the warm feeling of a distinctly human emotion even if he could not understand precisely what it was. "Shit," he said again when he realized that he knew exactly the notebook that was being discussed. "Shit," he said for a third time, though he could not deny that he was mildly pleased to have a mission.

He opened a spreadsheet and began breaking his new

project into its component parts.

Early the next morning, Gonzales awoke to the ringing of his secure, red phone. He creaked a little as he climbed out of bed and was disappointed to see that he had slept until five thirty in the morning. There would be no jog today. He answered the phone, "Gonzales."

"Cruz." Cruz responded in hushed tones. He was whispering.

"What do you have?" Gonzales asked.

Cruz answered, still whispering, "I got a call last night from the guy we put on Bayron. He's out of SmithCorp and back at his own apartment. Hermelinda is with him. I think this may be our only opportunity to confront him."

"Okay. Meet me in front of his apartment at 9:00. Let me know if anything changes."

"Will do, boss," Cruz responded almost inaudibly.

"By the way, Mr. Cruz, I cannot help but notice that you are speaking very quietly. I am assuming that you do not need to be reminded of the special risks that accompany becoming romantically involved with a person of interest in an investigation. I will, however, give you the same advice my father gave me: 'if you can't be good, at least be careful.' Have I made myself clear?"

"Yes sir," Cruz answered, eager to crawl back into Kitty's comfortable Queen sized bed for the few hours he had left before meeting Gonzales.

XX.

Sharky stood in the lobby of the Amtrack station in downtown Schenectady staring at his cell phone and waiting for something to happen. *What if my cell phone dies? What if I lose the signal and don't get the instructions? What if I have to go to the bathroom? There is too much that can go wrong*, he thought. He walked around the station trying to make sure that he positioned himself where he got the strongest signal. At 6:05 his phone beeped receipt of a text message from a number which was clearly out of the country based on the number of digits on it. "Take the 6:22 to Penn Station."

He went to the ticket counter and asked for a ticket. "Name?" The ticket agent asked.

He told her his name. As he reached for his wallet.

"Okay," the ticket agent said. "This ticket's already been paid for. I just need to see your ID."

He drew his license out of his wallet and handed it to the agent who glanced at it for a mere moment before handing it back to him with his ticket. "Have a nice trip," she said.

"Who paid for my ticket?" Sharky asked.

The ticket agent raised her shoulders and said, "I wouldn't know that, sir. Your train's on Platform 1, up the escalator to the right."

Smith had been monitoring Sharky's phone all morning. '6:22 to Penn Station' processed through Smith's mind and he accessed the timetable for that train. Sharky would arrive in three and a half hours. That gave him dread little time to get to the bottom of things. He wanted to call Dr. Bayron but he knew that Bayron had not been carrying a cell phone and had no home phone, or computer, or any other connection to the outside world from his apartment. He geolocated Hermelinda's phone to Bayron's apartment and called it, but she had it set to silent and the vibrating did not wake her.

What woke her was the sound of the front door intercom buzzing in the living room. This woke Bayron too and he was momentarily startled to see that Hermelinda had slept with him through the night without his having known. Or maybe he did know as his dreams had been unusually pleasant. He smiled uncomfortably at her and left to answer the intercom. He pressed the button and said, "hello?"

"Dr. Douglas Bayron?" Josey asked adopting a commanding voice.

"Yes?" Dr. Bayron answered.

"This is special agent Josey Cruz of the CIA and my colleague Marco Gonzales. It is imperative that we speak to you right away. We believe you may be in danger."

"Okay," Bayron said and buzzed them through the front door. Moments later there was a knock on his apartment door. He opened it without undoing the chain lock.

"Dr. Bayron?" Cruz asked again.

"May I see some badges?" Bayron demanded.

Cruz took out his shield and showed it to Bayron through the chain locked door.

"And you?" Bayron asked looking at Gonzales.

"I'm field ops, sir. I don't carry a badge." Gonzales replied politely.

Bayron nodded as if that answer made sense and opened the door.

Cruz and Gonzales entered the apartment and immediately realized that there would be no place for all three of them to sit down together. Bayron directed them to the kitchen table and motioned for them to sit as he himself began to prepare to brew some coffee.

"We're going to have to ask Mrs. Smith to leave. What we have to say is strictly need-to-know."

Bayron was surprised that they knew Hermelinda was in the apartment, but then again, he thought, the CIA should know things like that. Bayron did not answer the request, Hermelinda had emerged from the bedroom and answered the two agents directly.

"First of all, gentlemen," she said, displaying some unexpected courage, "if Dr. Bayron's life is in danger then it stands to follow that my life is in danger too since I am here with him. Secondly, Dr. Bayron is presently a ward of the State of New York, who has been legally released to my care and custody. I thus have a higher responsibility than either of you to ensure his safety. Third, Dr. Bayron has been declared temporarily incompetent and delusional and may or may not understand what you are going to tell him so if you want him to stay alive, you will want me to know. Fourth," Hermelinda's speech was cut off by the vibrating of her phone and she was glad because she really didn't have a fourth point. In fact she didn't even have a third point. She had made that one up on the spot. "Excuse me," she said, looking at her phone. "It's Elly," she said looking at Dr. Bayron. She then addressed the two strangers, "I have to take this." Hermelinda walked out of the room.

When she was gone, Cruz began to bring Dr. Bayron up to speed on what had brought them to his doorstep and why they felt he was in danger. They disclosed the fact that they suspected that he had held back some information from his collaborator in Russia when Hermelinda walked back into the room white as a ghost.

"Doug, it's Sharky. His mother's been Kidnaped. The kidnappers want him to turnover a black notebook. Your black notebook for sure. He's on a train right now to bring it to them. They said they are going to kill his mother."

Cruz immediately pulled his cellphone out of his pocket and speed dialed his office. "Geolocate Sarkis Ohangangian stat. I need his 10-20 immediately." A moment later, he turned to the other people in the room, "He's just south of Albany and moving fast."

"How did he know?" Gonzales said with a fire in his eyes that made it clear to everybody in the room, including Cruz that it would not be wise to pussyfoot around the answer.

"He's on the internet. He can access phones and security cameras at will. He can see and decode billions of bits of data at once. Its how he amuses himself. I'm sorry, I …" Bayron blurted out.

"What is in that notebook?" Gonzales interrupted knowing full well that time had just become a valuable and shrinking commodity.

"My personal notes. You were right. I wasn't ready to give up all my secrets. Sharky hid the book for me."

"Who else knew?" Gonzales demanded.

"No one. I swear it. No one."

"Okay, look. I'm not going to mince words here. Dr. Petrovsky is working for some very, very dangerous men who are trying to extract a code which unlocks a huge nuclear arsenal which they will sell to the highest bidder. The only man who knew that launch code is dead and I intend to keep him that way. They are trying to use your technology to make him alive again. If they get that book, will they be able to do it?"

"I've seen their model. I have a copy of it. I used some of it in Smith."

"With that notebook, will they be able to bring that man back to life?" Gonzales asked again, this time gruffly, as he was not satisfied with Bayron's answer.

"Yes." Bayron said.

Gonzales turned his attention back to Cruz. "You get someone on that train right now."

"I've got a guy in Poughkeepsie heading to the station right now." Cruz answered.

"Get a tracker in that book before it leaves the train." Gonzales barked.

"I'm a full step ahead of you," Cruz stated.

Hermelinda still had Smith on the phone and had explained to him what was happening. She chimed in, "he has a recording. Smith got all the calls recorded."

"Put it on speaker," Gonzales commanded.

Hermelinda engaged the speaker and placed the phone down on the table.

"Can you hear me?" Smith's tinny electronic voice asked. Upon hearing enough assents he continued, "I started listening somewhere in the middle of the conversation, but I don't think I missed much." The voice on the speakerphone changed abruptly and the four people in Bayron's kitchen listened intently:

"Where is she!" They heard Sharky yell.

They all winced when the heard the panic in their friend's voice.

"Apparently I haven't made the rules clear and I do not intend to stay on the phone very long. So please take note of the fact that for security reasons I will have to abandon this phone quickly so that it cannot be tracked. After I abandon this phone you will have no way to contact me so this may be the last conversation we ever have. Seeing as how you have no choice but to trust me as a man of my word, you must believe that I will return your mother to you unharmed and well fed provided you do something for me. Otherwise, I will kill her one piece at a time. Do you know what that means Mr. Sharky?"

"That's Vladimir Vakhrusheva," Gonzales said matter-of-factly. "He's here."

They listened to the rest of the recording in disgust. Dr. Bayron felt a nausea rise in his stomach. Hermelinda could not hold back tears.

"Can we get a track on that cellphone?" Gonzales asked Cruz.

Smith had already done so and reported his findings: "its laying in a field off of I-90 near Wolf Road. The number on it matched a record for Sarkis Ohangangian. That's Sharky."

"Confirm that Mr. Cruz." Gonzales said, unwilling to put complete trust in Smith. Cruz made another call.

A moment later he addressed the others in the room, "There are two cell phone numbers associated with a Sarkis

Ohangangian," Cruz reported. "One is moving quickly south along the Hudson and the other is laying in a field off of I-90 near the Wolf Road exit."

On a Southbound train headed for Penn Station in New York, a very nervous Sarkis Ohangangian sat with his eyes transfixed on his cell phone's screen watching the bars. On his lap was a little knapsack which had just two items in it, a small, black notebook and a large lantern battery. During the night Sharky had been busy. He had carefully removed the metal spiral binding on the notebook and replaced it with carefully coiled iron-cobalt wire. The battery was connected to the new iron-cobalt binding with copper wires and the iron-cobalt was building up an immense magnetic charge as it sat in the bag on Sharky's lap.

As the train approached the Rhinecliff station, Sharky's phone beeped that it had received a text message. He had been listening for it so intently that the beep was as loud as a gunshot. Get off at Rhinecliff, the message said, and leave your cell phone on the train. As soon as he read the message on his phone the speaker system announced, "Now arriving, Rhinecliff." Sharky had to think fast. He quickly detached the battery from the notebook and took the notebook out of the knapsack. He typed a quick message onto his phone but did not send it. He placed his phone into the knapsack and stowed it under the seat just as the train doors opened.

He dashed out of the train and a few passengers boarded. The train took off behind him and he was left alone on the platform. He looked around and didn't see anyone so he headed down the escalator to the lobby. The lobby was also empty but for the ticket agents. He sat down on one of the seats and waited. An hour passed and he started to get very, very nervous. Had something gone wrong? Had he misunderstood an instruction? His stomach hurt and he wanted to cry. Then he started to pray. And then, cutting through the silence he heard a page, "Sarkis Ohangangian to the ticket counter please. Sarkis Ohangangian to the ticket counter please."

He approached the ticket counter and said to the agent, "I'm Sarkis Ohangangian." She handed him her telephone handset. "Hello?" He said.

"Walk out of the station and take a right. You will see a coffee shop."

"Okay," Sarkis replied.

"Good. Sit at the counter and order a cup of coffee and leave the notebook on the chair next to you. Then excuse yourself to go to the bathroom and stay in there until someone knocks on the door. Then you are free to go and if you have followed my instructions, your mother will be returned to you safe and sound tomorrow."

Sharky complied to the letter. He walked to the coffee shop and took a seat at the counter. He left the notebook on the seat and went to the bathroom. He sat there, sweating, in the bathroom waiting for a knock. About half an hour later the knock came. It was the cook. "Hey buddy, you okay in there? Its been like half an hour."

Sharky opened the door and looked around. He saw immediately that the notebook was gone. He returned to the counter and finished his coffee in silence before heading back to the train station.

The 6:22 to Penn Station pulled into the Poughkeepsie station right on time and Special Agent John Hobbes stepped on nonchalantly. He walked down the aisle until the train started to move and then he grabbed the first open seat. As the train began to roll on towards Croton, Special Agent Hobbes walked the length of the train looking for Sharky to no avail. He sent a text message to Cruz to that effect. Cruz told Hobbes to listen for a phone and he dialed Sharky's cell phone number. He heard the ringing and quickly located the pack with the cell phone in it.

Agent Hobbes called Cruz from his own phone and reported, "Josey, the kid's not here. I found his phone in a knapsack under one of the seats. There was nothing else in there except for a lantern battery."

"Anything else?" Cruz asked.

"Well, this could be something. There was an unsent message on his phone, just four letters like this: capital 'F', small 'E', dash, capital 'C', small 'O'. Could be a code or something." Hughes said.

"Thanks Johnny." Cruz said. "Leave everything as you found it in case someone else is also tracking that phone, okay?"

"Roger that," Hughes responded.

Gonzales' brow had become deeply furrowed. "Vakhrusheva's no dummy." He said. "He's got his tracks covered nine ways to zero. The notebook is gone. The trail is cold. We know he got off somewhere between Rensselaer and Poughkeepsie."

Gonzales paused and turned to Cruz. "We have no choice. Start a dragnet. Cover a triangle two hours in either direction for Rensselaer and one hour in either direction from Poughkeepsie."

"That's over 10,000 square miles. How are you going to do that without using the radio?" Smith, who was still on speaker, asked.

"We can't," Cruz responded.

"If you broadcast it on the radio and these guys are monitoring police bands, that's a death sentence for Sharky's mother, isn't it?" Hermelinda chimed in, being the last to understand the full impact of Gonzales' instruction.

Suddenly Dr. Bayron jumped out of his seat as if he had received a strong electric shock. "Goddammit!" he shouted to everyone's surprise. "Fe-Co is iron-cobalt. Iron-cobalt and a battery! He had a battery to magnetize the iron-cobalt. It's the most magnetic material on earth. We use iron cobalt wire in the lab all of the time and its almost exactly the same gauge as the spiral in my notebook. He replaced the spiral in my notebook with the iron-cobalt and charged it with the battery. The spiral...that's like a goddamn radio coil. Once those atoms go into overdrive from the battery charge they're going to produce a big and unique magnetic field. That notebook is broadcasting a distinct electromagnetic wave wherever it goes. That's a goddamn tracking device."

"20 Kilohertz." Smith chimed in having researched it in a split second.

Cruz was already on the phone.

"Now what?" Hermelinda asked. She did not wait long for an answer.

"We got him." Cruz said. "He's heading north on the Thruway, just outside of Ravena. We're putting a bird on it."

"Good work, boy." Gonzales said, clapping Cruz on the back, surprised by just how quickly they were able to get a bead on Sharky's improvised tracker.

The moment the chopper pilot advised Cruz that the makeshift radio signal had come to rest in the parking lot of the Hampton Inn he and Gonzales were on their way.

Smith told Hermelinda and Bayron to come back to SmithCorp and he sent Myra to pick up Sharky at the train station, having confirmed that Sharky had bought a return ticket by hacking into the Amtrak computer. He also called Takahashi and asked him to come to the office. Then he called Hermelinda's babysitter and asked her to bring the baby to SmithCorp too.

As Hermelinda was driving with Bayron back to SmithCorp she said to him, "they don't care about Sharky's mother. They're going to let her get killed. That poor, poor boy."

"I'm sure they have it all figured out, Hermelinda," He replied. "They are professionals and they know what they're doing."

A silence descended into the car again until Bayron spoke. "I'm more worried about Elly, to be honest."

"Why are you worried about Elly?" She asked.

"The things he demonstrated today. I can't imagine the CIA is comfortable having that kind of power out there. And how do they know that he doesn't now have those codes kicking around in that bionic brain of his. How do I even know? We've only been exposed to a fraction of what he's capable of and those have been parlor tricks: accessing security cameras and spying on the president. What happens when he gets bored of spying? Who knows what else he'll discover he's capable of?"

"You're afraid of him?" She asked as she pulled into her parking spot at SmithCorp.

Bayron thought for a moment before he answered with a question. "How did you feel when he said he'd be watching us?"

"Oh, come on Doug," she said. "It's Elly, he was just being silly."

"You know he's watching us now," Bayron said signaling the security camera in the parking lot.

"Then you'd better not kiss me, Doctor." Hermelinda said looking deep into Doug's eyes.

"I'd like to," Doug said, "but he's my friend and your husband and I've said too much already."

"If he's my husband and your friend then he is still Elijah Smith, and Elijah Smith is the one man that can be trusted with these superpowers. Anyone who knows him, knows that."

"If he's your husband and my friend then he is still human. Humans make mistakes, even the best of us. Its just that most of us don't have superpowers."

"You're just being paranoid, Doctor," Hermelinda replied, giving him a gentle kiss on the cheek as if to prove her point.

In fact, Smith was not watching them from the security camera in the parking lot. Rather, he had his attention focused on the security cameras in and around the Hampton Inn. As Cruz and Gonzales were walking through the front door, Cruz's cell flashed a text message. "Room 714. Smith."

He showed the message to Gonzales and Gonzales shook his head in acknowledgment. They assumed they were going to have to flash their badges to get information from the desk clerk, but instead they were able to walk to the elevators without calling any attention to themselves. As they rode the elevator up, they both knew that soon someone would be dead.

They took positions on either side of the door to room 714 and drew their weapons. Gonzales nodded his head and Cruz's strong shoulder slammed into the door, breaking the frame and causing it to swing violently into the room.

Gonzales turned into the now gaping door frame, quickly identified the figure in the room, pointed his gun and shot.

Alice collapsed instantly as the bullet from Gonzales' gun pierced right through her head.

"I hate killing women," Gonzales said.

Cruz quickly found the notebook Bayron had described and headed for the door.

"No, no, no." Gonzales said shaking one of his ancient fingers at Cruz. "The longer it takes Vakhrusheva to find out she's dead, the better chance we have to save that kid's mother. Let's clean up this blood and get the body out of here. Make sure you get her purse and her cell phone too."

They wrapped Alice's body in the spare blanket that

they found in the closet and cleaned her still-liquid blood off the walls with moist washcloths. Cruz threw her body over his shoulder while Gonzales grabbed the purse, the cellphone and the dirty washcloths. They walked straight to the elevator and straight through the lobby, as nonchalantly as if they were going to take a swim in the pool. Gonzales positioned himself between the desk clerk and Cruz in such a way as to obstruct any view from the desk. It was unnecessary, the desk clerk had put the bell out.

Cruz threw Alice's dead body into the trunk of his car.

A text message appeared on the little screen of Cruz's phone. "That's too bad. I always liked her. E.S." He chuckled to himself when he saw the message. Smith was a playful man, he saw, just as he had been reputed to be.

"Where to boss?" Cruz asked as he started his car.

"SmithCorp. I'm sure I don't have to explain why."

Cruz nodded and pulled out of the parking lot to make the short drive to the SmithCorp Building. He parked in a public park spot on the SmithCorp premises and the two men walked together through the front door and up to the security desk. "We're here to see Mr. Smith." Cruz said taking out his badge wallet to show to the guard.

"Names?" The guard asked.

"My name is Josey Cruz and this is Marco Gonzales," he said pointing his thumb at Gonzales.

"Yes, I see that you're expected. You'll be going to a secure floor so I'll need to get you an escort," the guard said while motioning to an escort who was posted near the elevator. "Steve will take you."

The two men walked up to "Steve" who directed them to a separate elevator. He got on the elevator with them and inserted a security card into a slot on the elevator's button panel. The elevator ascended to the seventh floor. Steve said, "this is your floor" and pointed them towards a large double door at the end of the hallway.

On the other side of the doorway, a young receptionist escorted them back to Smith's makeshift office. As they walked in, they immediately recognized Dr. Bayron and Hermelinda. They recognized Takahashi from his CIP. The receptionist asked them if they wanted any coffee or water and both men requested coffee. She then pointed them to seats at the conference table.

Shortly after they settled into their seats, Sharky and Myra entered the office and took their own seats at the conference table. Everyone in the room could see that Sharky was still in a nightmare. After everyone was seated, Smith spoke, displaying the oscilliscopic representation of his voice on the large monitor.

"Folks," he said in a very serious tone which only made the mechanical aspects of his voice sound more pronounced, "we have a problem." Everyone made noises acknowledging the obvious truth in his statement.

"First and foremost, we know that Sharky's mother is being held hostage even as we speak. The reason she is being held hostage is because there are some Russian fellows who wanted a notebook that Sharky had. They still have their hostage, but they don't have their notebook. I have never been in the intelligence game like our new friends here," Smith continued, "but I am considered quite adept at strategies. They had the advantage of us not being aware of them until they struck. They no longer have that advantage. It doesn't strike me as being strategically wise for them to sacrifice their bird-in-hand with the expectation of getting another bargaining chip now.

"Furthermore, of all the people to kidnap, Sharky's mother just doesn't make sense. They were after the notebook and couldn't find it. Now that we know that Alice was working for them, we have a pretty good guess as to how they connected the notebook to Sharky. No more inside man.

"Finally, they know that the notebook never made it back to them and they must suspect that our CIA friends have it and aren't going to give it back for all the Sharky's mother's in the world. That means that the only way they can get the information that they want is to get to Dr. Bayron personally and, no offense old friend, but I know that you don't have a photographic memory and would have to reconstruct the formulas in that book from scratch."

Gonzales was the next to speak and he posed a simple question, "Is that true Mr. Smith?"

"No its not. I actually have the information they want. I don't know why and I don't know how...perhaps it is one of the mysteries of the subconscious, but I have Mr. Ashkot's memories including the launch code.

"Now that you have the notebook, all you have to do is kill me and those launch codes would be gone forever, but in all likelihood, that will result in Sharky's mother dying."

"It is a small cost." Gonzales said.

Sharky jumped to his feet and lunged at Gonzales, "You son of a bitch!" he shouted. Cruz got in between the two men and wordlessly made it clear that order would prevail. Sharky sat back down and stewed.

"Now for the benefit of our two new friends, killing me won't be so easy. There are four persons who hold the keys required to shut me down and destroy all the data I have generated wheresoever it may be stored. At least two of those people have to agree that shutting me down is the right thing to do. I am one of those four people and I will be honest. I am not afraid to die. I have already died once, and frankly, it wasn't so bad. My vote is not based on a fear of death. My vote is based on a lesson I learned as a child: that to save one life is to save the entire world."

Sharky was struck by the fact that the only other person

he had ever heard utter those words was his own mother.

"I will not vote to shut me down while Sharky's mother can still be saved," Smith asserted.

He let the silence linger for a moment and then turned to Hermelinda, "Hermelinda?"

"No, if there is any possibility of saving that poor woman, we have to try," she said.

"Sharky?" Smith asked.

"It's my mother," he answered snarkily, "what do you think?"

"That's three," Smith said. "Doc, I guess you're off the hook."

"These pills make me terribly sleepy, Hermelinda. Can I go home now?" Dr. Bayron asked, as if he had not been listening to the conversation at all.

Hermelinda noticed that he was staring at his feet, it was clear to her that he was completely disconnected from what was going on around him--a terrible setback she would have to report to Dr. Beedle.

"Gentlemen," Hermelinda said, "you have our answers.

Smith spoke again. "So, here's where we stand: everybody who has the information they're after is here in this room. Everyone who could be used as leverage to get that information is also here. This building is as secure a location as any. They cannot come to us and we cannot go to them. That's a real pickle. Mr. Cruz and Mr. Gonzales, understandably will sacrifice Mrs. Ohangangian in a heartbeat but they cannot consider their mission over until they have destroyed one small black notebook, one very large computer array, and, unless we can convince them otherwise, one very talented doctor. They can easily burn the notebook and shoot the good doctor right now, but as we have just demonstrated, they cannot kill me.

"I am a man of my word and there is no one in this

room who would say otherwise be it behind my back or to my face. I am offering my life in exchange for that of Sharky's mother and the life of Dr. Bayron. I caused this mess and I will take responsibility for it.

"Bring her back alive, gentlemen and you will be able to accomplish your mission. Otherwise, those launch codes live forever, somewhere in the vast Internet cloud.

"Do we have an understanding?"

Gonzales spoke again, "I am not in the business of making deals, Mr. Smith and I do not like being backed into a corner. Do not for one moment think that I couldn't order an air strike on this building and have it reduced to rubble in the next 20 minutes. And you are trying my patience."

"Sharky, why don't you take a moment to explain how your security system works so they can free themselves from the delusion that destroying this building would destroy the data they so eagerly seek to eradicate. I have other business to attend to. Oh, and Sharky, try to make it quick, the clock is ticking."

Sharky explained in enough detail as to how the leash system worked to bring back and destroy any data that emanated from Smith's brain at the SmithCorp Building.

It was obvious to both Gonzales and Cruz that Sharky was completely oblivious to the fact that there could have been a complete copy of Smith's brain residing elsewhere. K.O. Data Systems, perhaps. They both knew to hold this information close.

"Something is wrong, Bobby," Vakhrusheva said responding to his instincts. "We'll go now." They had been waiting in the safe house for Alice's confirmation that she had dropped the notebook off at the hotel. Sarkis' mother was bound, blindfolded, gagged and sealed in a box in the basement.

"That wasn't the plan, Micky. You just have to cool it." Bobby said calmly.

"I don't 'cool it'. I know when something is wrong. He dialed the toll free number for Amtrak and spoke to the phone operator. "Hi, this is Sarkis Ohangangian, I am supposed to go from Rhinebeck to Schenectady, but I lost my ticket and I can't remember what time my train is."

"Ohangangian. Shows you bought a ticket for the 7:50 train. It also shows that ticket was used. Someone must have picked it up. I'm going to have to ask you..."

Vakhrusheva did not wait for the operator to complete her thought before hanging up the phone. "We go now." He said simply.

"Should I take the old lady?" Bobby asked.

"No. I have no interest in killing her yet. Just bring one finger. That will be enough."

Bobby went to the basement and found a pair of tin snips that would easily cut a finger of his captive and some thin wire which looked like it would make an excellent tourniquet. He took off his shirt so that he wouldn't get it blood-stained, opened the box, and grabbed one of the helpless woman's fingers. He wrapped the wire around the thickest part of her finger below her second knuckle and then used the tin snips to cut off her finger just above the knuckle. The tourniquet was doing a good job of staving off the bleeding. She wouldn't bleed to death from this impromptu surgery. He found a shop rag and pressed it into the wound he had just made as an extra precaution and shut the lid to the box. Mrs. Ohangangian's screams were muffled by the duct tape that was sealing her mouth.

Bobby went back up the stairs to the kitchen and found a small plastic container in a kitchen drawer which he filled with crushed ice from the refrigerator. "I can't stand the smell." He said matter-of-factly to Vakhrusheva as he placed the finger in the ice.

Vakhrusheva walked toward the car. Bobby put the plastic container in his coat pocket and followed Vakhrusheva out the door.

Arriving at the Hampton Inn, both Bobby and Vakhrusheva noticed that Alice's car was in the lot. Clearly she had made it back. *Why hadn't she called?* they both wondered.

They rode the elevator to the seventh floor and knocked on the door. The door swung wide open without resistance in the doorframe that Cruz's shoulder had decimated earlier in the day. Both men quickly drew their guns. Other than the broken doorframe nothing in the room seemed out of place. There were no signs of a fight or a struggle, no signs of Alice, and no sign of the black notebook. Vakhrusheva's face turned bright red with anger and his glare burned into Bobby.

"Call his house." Vakhrusheva instructed Bobby in a seething voice. Bobby did as he was instructed.

"No answer." Bobby said.

"This was not our little Sharky who did this," Vakhrusheva said pointing to the door. "This was not law enforcement either. Law enforcement would not have left this room unattended and with the door unsecured."

"Look here," Bobby said calling Vakhrusheva's attention to a nick in the plasterboard near the bed.

Vakhrusheva walked over and stuck his pinky finger into the nick and scraped some plaster out of the hole with his fingernail. He saw a tiny metal fragment in the plaster he had drawn out. He then dropped to his hands and knees and examined the carpet. There were more fragments. Metal and bone. Who ever had cleaned up had not vacuumed.

"They covered their tracks in a hurry," Vakhrusheva concluded. "Whoever did this is operating outside of the law... or above it. No police means no one heard anything."

He pondered for a moment and then reported to Bobby, "Alice is dead and we are at war against the legendary FOU."

"How can you be sure?" Bobby asked, hoping against hope that Alice was still alive. She was an excellent agent and they had worked together for many years. Her death saddened him, but would in no way interfere with his assignment. He was, after all, a professional.

"One single, silenced shot. CIA is two shots, two bullets in case the first one doesn't kill. FOU the first shot always kills. The fact that it's the FOU means that they know exactly what we are after. The game, as they say, is afoot." Vakhrusheva smiled and the smile put Bobby off for a moment. Vakhrusheva appeared to be looking forward to what he had just called a game. He seemed to be inspired and energized by the fact that his adversary would prove to be the most effective clandestine agency ever.

But there was more to Vakhrusheva's smile. He knew that in all likelihood he and Bobby would not be returning to their homes.

"We have no time to waste. We have to get to SmithCorp. That's where the source is. If FOU gets there first they will destroy it." Vakhrusheva said.

Bobby pulled out his car keys and started walking.

"No you idiot. If they were here, we have to assume that we've been spotted and that your car is made. We pack what we can carry, check out of this hotel and call a cab." As they left the room they carefully jogged the door back into the broken frame and placed the do not disturb sign on it.

Bobby was no longer the field agent Vakhrusheva thought he was. He clearly did not think clearly under pressure-- a trait that would have gotten him killed or caught a thousand times over at the height of the cold war.

In the lobby, Bobby's phone rang. Vakhrusheva ignored it, and went to the front desk to check out. Bobby was still on the phone when the cab approached. Bobby held up his index finger to let Vakhrusheva know the call was important. "I understand." Was all Vakhrusheva heard Bobby say before the call was disconnected.

Vakhrusheva waited for Bobby to explain which Bobby did without hesitation.

"That was one odd call, Mickey. I answered because it came in from Alice's number. Whoever they are, FOU or whatever, they want to meet to make a deal for the old lady's life." Bobby said.

"They have not played wisely, then. They have told us that the old lady is still valuable. It is good that we did not kill her. We have no reason to go to them. If they want to save the old lady, they'll have to come to us." Vakhrusheva replied. "There is no reason now to go to SmithCorp. Driver, take us to Albany. I want some chicken wings. Bobby, I hope you have a whole lot of clean cars. Because we are on the radar now."

"I have as many cars as we need." Bobby replied.

The cab dropped them off in front of the Scooter's Beer and Wings on Clinton Street and it was very crowded. "We eat at the bar and leave separately. I will meet you at the safe house and we prepare to move the old lady." Vakhrusheva said.

Vakhrusheva intentionally chose a seat next to the drunkest person in the bar and ordered a Smirnoff and plate of hot wings. Vakhrusheva mostly ignored Bobby while they ate but was telling jokes and stories with the drunk next to him. When he was done with his wings. He got up and left the Bar. Twenty minutes later he was still not back. Bobby went to look for him in the bathroom and he was not there. When he got back to the bar, the drunk who had been sitting next to Vakhrusheva looked very agitated. "Shit, man," the drunk said, "I lost my fucking keys. Hey brother," he said to

Bobby, "have you seen my car keys anywhere? Shit."

"I'm sure they'll turn up," Bobby answered rapidly realizing what Vakhrusheva had done and trying to suppress a smirk. "You should take a cab home tonight anyway. If I find them, I'll give them to the bartender, okay."

"Thanks, buddy," the drunk said to Bobby slapping him on the shoulder, "you're a true friend. Let me buy you a beer."

"I'd like that, stranger, but I have got to go. Long day tomorrow." Bobby decided that the least detectible way for him to get to the safehouse would be to take the intercity bus and that would be a long, long ride.

In fact, it was shortly after midnight when Bobby got off the bus and walked the remainder of the way to the safehouse. When he got there he was treated to a remarkable sight. Vakhrusheva and the old lady were sitting in the kitchen. The old lady was eating chicken wings that Vakhrusheva had apparently taken out from Scooters. There was a bottle of Imperia Vodka open on the table and it was far from full.

Bobby looked at her hand and saw that the hand with the missing finger had been cleaned and carefully bandaged. They were speaking in Russian.

Vakhrusheva looked up at Bobby with a big smile, and said, "Let me introduce you to our new friend, Adele." Bobby could see the duplicity in Vakhrusheva's smile, but he was certain that no one else could have. "Adele's late husband attended university in St. Petersburg. We were practically neighbors."

The old woman smiled weakly at Bobby. She was pale and weak, probably from the blood loss. She must have been grateful for having been untied and let out of the box in which she had spent nearly 24 hours, the last few of which were spent bleeding from her untreated wound. There was still terror in her eyes and that concerned him. Bobby felt no empathy for her. His capacity for empathy had been sacrificed as part of his training with the ISI. Rather he was concerned because of the fundamental truth that scared people are irrational and irrational people are dangerous.

Bobby was extremely apprehensive regarding the manner in which events were unfolding and he began to internally question Vakhrusheva's tactic. He understood well enough that Sharky's mother had value only as long as she lived, but not carrying through on the threat to kill her undermined their bargaining power too. On the other hand, physically weakened by blood loss, endorphins flying around in her brain from the pain, her sense of reason overcome by her fear, and that whole mix now basting in strong Russian vodka, Mrs. Ohangangian's brain was as malleable as a mind could ever be. She was ripe to be turned.

"It seems, Bobby, that we made a terrible mistake," Vakhrusheva said, "as I was just explaining to my new friend. It seems that Elijah Smith himself wants the information in that notebook too."

Because Bobby knew that the FOU actually already had not only the book and in all likelihood the information that Vakhrusheva was after, he quickly surmised that he had told Adele a completely false story. He played along. "No kidding," Bobby said, also lying. "How do you know?"

"Well, Bobby, I told Adele that we had been looking for her son and that we couldn't find him anywhere. I asked her where he might be. Of course she wouldn't tell me. She did tell me that he had quit working for SmithCorp over some mysterious project he was working on that he could never talk about.

"So we know that the young man has the notebook hidden somewhere very well and that he took that notebook from his employer. Now we can't find him anywhere. It stands to reason that Elijah Smith wouldn't just let valuable information like that go. And clearly he would have brought us the notebook to save his mother's life had he been able to. The only obvious conclusion is that Sarkis has been kidnaped by SmithCorp and is in very, very grave danger. But how can we rescue him, Bobby?"

"Yes, of course. It stands to reason," Bobby said agreeing with the lie. "Why else wouldn't he have brought us the notebook. Unless, perhaps, he does not love his mother as much as we thought."

At this Adele became agitated and raised her voice. "You don't speak of Sako like that. Sako would not do that."

"Then he must have been Kidnaped," Vakhrusheva said calming her down. "So, we are not on different teams here. We both want to rescue 'Sako' from SmithCorp."

"Maybe we should call in the police." Bobby figured out where Vakhrusheva was heading and made that remark in furtherance of Vakhrusheva's strategy. "I will have to take responsibility for the finger, but these men at SmithCorp are known to be very, very dangerous." He added.

Vakhrusheva was glad that Bobby was familiar with the ploy he had chosen and was able to follow the lead so seamlessly. "No, you fool," Vakhrusheva said in feigned exasperation. "Once the police are involved, the SmithCorp goons will kill Sako for sure. We must figure this out on our own."

Vakhrusheva poured himself another shot of vodka and turned the shot glass in his fingers as he pretended to concentrate very, very deeply on the problem he had so carefully made up and sold to Sharky's mother. Bobby shook his head up and down and kept his gaze on Vakhrusheva as if he were thinking of a solution too. But really, Bobby was trying to figure out Vakhrusheva's end game, and he didn't have a clue. He had very artfully turned the prisoner into an ally, but to what end, he wondered.

Adele was nearly catatonic. From the moment these men had broken into her house, the terror never let go. But she had been through ordeals before and fought hard to keep her wits. In the trunk of the car she tried to count the stoplights, and listen for outside noises. Being led into the safehouse, she tried to make mental notes of every sound she heard and every smell she smelled. She thought hard for anything she could possibly do. Laying in the box (she did not know she had been in the basement) she struggled against the tape that bound her hands and legs. She tossed and turned and quickly realized that she was in a box. Bucking against the walls, she determined that it was wooden. She tried rocking it and learned that it was somehow secured. She thought for a moment that she had been buried alive, but quickly judged from the coldness of the air that the box was ventilated and thus could not have been buried. Then one of the men, the smaller of the two, she adjudged from the size of his hands, took her out and cut off her finger. He put her back in the box, bleeding, and she was certain she would die. She became dizzy and nauseous and then passed out. She did not know how long. Then the larger man took her out of the box, removed her blindfold and restraints, and cleaned and tended to her amputation. He apologized to her and told her that they had made a grave mistake. He offered her chicken wings. He offered her vodka. She accepted these offers, praying that the vodka would allow her to steel her mind and sharpen her thinking. It didn't though, it merely clouded her mind even more until it was aswim, ready to believe anything and ready to do anything to make sure that she wouldn't be hurt anymore. And to save her son.

It was while she was in this state of mind that Vakhrusheva revealed his plan for the next morning.

Vakhrusheva poured himself another shot of vodka and

gulped it down. He poured some in Adele's glass too but she did not even reach for it. "Come now, we must sleep on it. Bobby, give our guest a room with a shower." He said as he got up and stretched his arms.

Bobby helped Adele out of her chair and as he did so Vakhrusheva made a turning motion with his fingers signaling Bobby to make sure that he would lock her in a secure room. One with windows that were permanently sealed and a door that locked from the outside. He assumed, correctly, that Bobby would not have referred to this place as a safe house if it did not have a room that met those criteria. In fact, Bobby did have a room just like that. Even beyond Vakhrusheva's expectation, Bobby had also installed steel plates behind the blackout curtains on the windows in case someone would be savvy enough to send a message in morse code by flicking the lights. This was not luck. It was experience, and Bobby had plenty of experience. He had no reason to believe that this room would ever be occupied by a little old Armenian lady, but even little old Armenian ladies can know morse code.

As Bobby returned after securing Adele in her more comfortable accommodations, Vakhrusheva was sipping again at his vodka. "I never took you for a gamblin' man, Mickey," Bobby said.

"It is no gamble. I trust you have what I will need." Vakhrusheva replied throwing two Tylenols into his mouth and washing them down with the remainder of the Vodka in his glass. He had already taken for granted that Bobby knew his job very well.

Though still somewhat offended that Kovaretsky had insisted that he have assistance on this mission, as he rubbed his arthritic fingers, he was secretly thankful that someone else could do the technical work that now had to be done.

XXI.

The sun rose in the morning, just as it had done every morning since the dawn of time. It glistened off of the snow on the ground and illuminated all in the world that was old and all that was new. It gleamed off of the walls of the SmithCorp Building as the morning guard replaced the night guard and the front doors were unlocked.

Up on the seventh floor, a group of men and one woman who had spent the night at SmithCorp were beginning to stir from their resting places on the sofas and chairs in the executive waiting room. Josey Cruz and Marco Gonzales, however, had been awake all night discussing their dilemma.

"Usually," Gonzales said, "there is only one of each man involved in a scheme. Here, we have to assume that there are at least two copies of Smith. There could be hundreds for all we know. We could terminate Smith and

Bayron and burn the notebook and the codes would still be out there floating around and only a matter of time before the Russians learn how to get it out of Ashkot's dead head. If we were to terminate all the copies of Smith we know about kill Bayron, and burn the notebook, then any remaining copies of Smith would be one hell of an angry computer program. He's the one calling the shots now, Josey, and he knows it."

Josey nodded his head in agreement. "What do we do now, chief?" He asked.

"We wait, and we pray." Gonzales admitted. "We pray that Smith is on our side."

The first of the administrative staff of SmithCorp began arriving at 6:30am. Some of the employees came from other counties and always left a little extra time in case the driving conditions were bad. Others simply liked to come early to enjoy a cup of coffee and check their e-mails before the business day started. Myra came early because Smith used to come early and everything she knew about running SmithCorp she had learned from Smith. The lobby was already getting crowded at 8:30am when Adele Ohangangian slipped into the lobby by flashing the fake ID card Alice had procured for Vakhrusheva. She made sure she entered with a large group of women and the security guard at the front desk made a cursory glance at the group and waved them all in. Once inside, Adele made her way into the restroom on the ground floor and positioned herself in a stall waiting for the cell phone she had been given to ring just as she had been instructed. It was difficult for her to sit with the explosives fixed to her waist.

On the seventh floor, in Smith's office, Hermelinda put up a pot of coffee as Sharky looked out the window at the morning sun, wondering why it continued to rise even though it seemed to him as if the world had ended the day before.

Dr. Bayron stood and took a deep breath. He could see

Hermelinda's rear and remembered what her skin felt like against his when she had fallen asleep in her arms. He felt he could smell her sweet perfume even though she was clear across the room. Cruz opened his laptop to get his daily briefing from his real job at the CIA. Gonzales sat, expressionless, in a leather chair spinning a pen between his rootlike fingers wondering why he had quit smoking. He had just finished speaking with Julian Waterstone and was confident that Julian would do what was asked of him. The little red light on Smith's camera-eye blinked intermittently letting the crew know that he was in the room and paying attention.

"Have you ever played 3-Dimensional Chess, Mr. Gonzales?" Smith asked through the speakers thus abruptly breaking the silence.

"No, Mr. Smith, I cannot say that I ever have." Gonzales answered.

"I used to be a very good chess player," Smith continued. "Now, of course, it is barely a challenge for me to beat anyone. I have the mathematical processing speed of a computer and the strategic and psychological sensibilities of a human being. Before I was like this, I had the opportunity to try my hand at three dimensional chess. It is infinitely more complex than chess. In a regular game of chess an excellent player can often predict 5 or even 6 moves in advance. In three-dimensional chess, it is almost impossible to predict even the very next move. In fact, the complexity of the game is increased by the power of 8, not just 8 times over, but exponentially. Even in my present state, I can be beaten by human players because once the number of variables reaches a certain level, enough chaos is introduced into the equation to make any outcome a mere possibility. Not exactly random, but certainly asymptotic to random."

"Why are you telling me this?" Gonzales inquired.

"Because," Smith said, "because your involving Mr. Waterstone adds a dimension to an already complex equation. The system is no longer closed. This is a new variable."

"To use your own metaphor," Gonzales responded, "I have put another piece on the playing board. We are not opponents."

"Clearly you do not trust me, or you would not have made that call."

"I'm just cutting the cards, Mr. Smith," Gonzales replied. "As, I am sure, you have."

"You are correct about that Mr. Gonzales. Apparently we are cut from the same cloth."

The silence of the morning again descended upon the seventh floor as the men helped themselves to Hermelinda's coffee. Cruz had barely inhaled the steam from the top of his cup when a phone rang in his pocket. It wasn't his own phone. It was Alice's. He was still carrying it. He looked at Gonzales who signaled him to answer it.

"Hello?" He said into the mouthpiece trying to sound inconspicuous.

Vakhrusheva's voice came through and Cruz quickly turned on the speaker and lay the phone on the table. "We have something you want and you have something we want," they heard Vakhrusheva say.

"How do we know you have what we want?" Cruz asked. The blood rose in Sharky's face and acid burned in his throat when he realized they were talking about his mother.

"Because she is in the same building with you. I will give you a moment. Review the front door security tape at exactly 8:32 and oh, about 45 seconds."

Smith was able to access the recording immediately and showed it on the monitor. As represented, the security camera had picked up the image of Sharky's mother entering the front door of the SmithCorp Building and blending in with the crowd.

"What do you want?" Cruz asked.

"I want a small black notebook." Vakhrusheva replied, "If I get what I want, with no problems, I send Ms. Ohangangian to you unharmed. If I don't, she dies."

"Okay," Cruz said, "how do you want to do this?"

"Send an escort down to meet Ms. Ohangangian in the lobby and bring her to the seventh floor. Hand her the notebook and then escort her down to the lobby. A cab will be waiting for her in the parking lot. If the cab is followed, she dies. You have one minute." Vakhrusheva hung up the phone quickly and immediately called Adele's cell phone.

Cruz looked at Gonzales. Gonzales said, "It's a trick. Don't bring her up. It's a trick."

Sharky's heart was beating in his chest.

"I have already dispatched a guard to the lobby to bring her up." Smith crackled.

"You have to think this through, Smith. She's going to be wired to a bomb. I'm telling you. I know how this works."

"So the only chance we have of saving her life is to bring her up. If we don't do it now she dies." Smith broadcast.

"The notebook is worthless Smith. These men are not stupid. They wouldn't give up their bargaining chip for a book we could have already altered. This is a trick."

"I will not watch her die while it is in my power to prevent, Mr. Gonzales. I am still only human." Smith barely finished speaking as the elevator door opened on the seventh floor and Adele stepped out.

"Mom!" Sharky yelled as he ran to her and kissed her cheeks.

"Sako." She replied sadly opening her coat to reveal the bomb strapped to her waist.

Gonzales addressed Smith by looking at his camera.

"Being human is a liability in this game, Smith. Even in chess occasionally a piece must be sacrificed to save the king."

"And who is the king, Mr. Gonzales?"

"Would you like me to tell you what their next move is?" Gonzales asked, matter of factly.

Smith's camera panned to and focused on Dr. Bayron who, again, was staring at the floor between his feet and Gonzales nodded his head recognizing that Smith had already figured it out.

When Hermelinda saw Bayron looking at the floor her first thought was that he hadn't taken his meds yet. She looked at Cruz hoping that would help her to understand why the attention in the room had suddenly turned to Dr. Bayron. Cruz caught her gaze and squeezed his lips together and slowly shook his head. She still didn't know what was going on, but she knew it was not good.

Alice's phone rang again. "Thank you, gentlemen." Vakhrusheva said. "Now, let's speak honestly with one another. At this point, what assurance can you give me that you haven't altered that little black notebook?"

"We're not idiots, Vakhrusheva," Gonzales responded. "What do you want?"

There was a moment of silence on the other end of the phone. "Marco Gonzales?" Vakhrusheva asked rhetorically. He recognized the voice though years had passed since he last heard it. "The great Marco Gonzales, cornered like a rat? I should detonate this bomb right now."

"You know that would be my preference. If you do that, my mission will have been successful and yours would be over."

"Of course the mission comes first, Mr. Gonzales. I am not an amateur. But you will forgive me if I relish this moment. In memory of my brother, you understand." Vakhrusheva said. "Now, down to brass tacks. You will send

Dr. Bayron. Oh, and in case the good doctor decides to be a hero, lets have you send the girl too. I believe her name is Hermelinda. She is very pretty. There will be a taxi out in front of the building in exactly two minutes. They get in, and as soon as I am confident that they have not been followed and there are no homing devices. I give you the code to disarm the bomb. How does that sound, gentlemen? You have two minutes."

Vakhrusheva hung up immediately after speaking.

Bayron stood up silently and walked to the elevator. "What are you doing!?" Smith bellowed from his speaker.

"I'm going," Bayron said.

Hermelinda ran to his side, "I'm going too," she said resolutely.

"No!" Smith said as loud as he could. "I won't permit it. I will give them the codes. You can't go. Who knows what they will do!"

"Let them go," Gonzales said.

"I forbid you!" Smith screamed at top volume.

But it was too late. The elevator door had already shut behind Bayron and Hermelinda.

Down in the parking lot, a yellow taxi cab pulled up in front of the entrance to the SmithCorp Building. On Gonzales' instruction, Julian had been parked in the parking lot and had been on the lookout for a taxicab. He got out of his car and took a cigarette out of its pack. He placed the cigarette between his lips and approached the taxicab. He tapped gently on the glass with his knuckle. The driver rolled down the window just a little. "Hey, buddy, you got a light?" Julian asked.

The cabbie rolled down the window a little more and handed Julian a lighter. Julian lit the cigarette and took a long drag. "Where you heading?" Julian asked.

"I don't know," the cabbie said. "I just got the call for

a pickup."

"Well drive safely out there, and thanks for the light," Julian said as he walked towards the front door of SmithCorp, passing Dr. Bayron and Hermelinda on the way. He gave them a little wink as he passed.

Julian was immediately escorted to the seventh floor. Gonzales nodded at him and Julian reported, "Capital Cab. Christopher Plotkin. Verizon phone, looked like an old fashioned Motorola Razr. I think he had a insulin kit. License photo matched his face. Log book was ragged and the meter was running."

"Ok, he's a dupe. Cruz?" Gonzales said.

"I'm on it boss. The boys said that's probably enough information for them to get me a number. But it might take a minute or two."

"We'll already have missed the call by then." Smith observed.

"He'll also have to call his dispatcher though." Gonzales said. "We still have a chance."

Smith turned his camera to Sharky, "Kid, take your mother to the infirmary, get her finger fixed and call the bomb squad," he said. Sharky looked from face to face in the room. He was unsure whom he was supposed to take orders from. Smith didn't give him a chance to decide. His voice boomed from the speaker louder than it ever had before. "NOW! And message me when you get there," he bellowed. Sharky led his mother to elevator and was gone, leaving only Gonzales and Cruz in Smith's office with the eerie disembodied voice of Elijah Smith.

"Okay, we got it," Cruz interrupted. "There's no communication on the line right now. They're listening in and will patch it through when they hear noise."

"Can they geolocate?"

"South on 7. Approaching the Latham Circle."

Smith's monitor lit up. He remembered there was a traffic camera at the Latham Circle and he was able to bring the camera up on his screen. They caught a view of the cab as it went one quarter of the way around the traffic circle.

"They're heading for the mall." Cruz observed.

Smith patched into the security cameras at the Latham Circle mall. They were able to see the cab pull up to the mall's east entrance. Bayron and Hermelinda went into the mall together.

"There's no camera in the hallway," Smith reported.

"They're gone," Gonzales said, conjuring his conclusion from a lifetime of fieldwork. He knew how to smuggle humans in and out of countries and he knew how to get them off of the radar. Vakhrusheva knew all of the same tricks. They were straight out of the cold war playbook, and the reason they were in the playbook was because they worked. There would be no way to cover all of the entrances to a mall before they would be snuck out into a waiting vehicle.

"Send a team to the mall." Smith ordered.

"They're gone Smith. There's no time. We'll use transportation control: airports, bus stations. They're off the radar, but its not over."

"Gentlemen, my wife and my best friend are gone because of my folly. I will be giving the orders from this point forward." Smith's voice boomed without a hint of uncertainty.

"This is my mission, Mr. Smith." Gonzales said calmly.

"You are in no position to argue with me, Mr. Gonzales." As soon as Smith had uttered these words, both Gonzales and Cruz heard the distinct shoosh of an electric deadbolt sliding shut. They knew immediately that they had very little bargaining power in the situation. Smith continued, "I have already instructed Myra to send our security team over to the mall. They will be arriving there by helicopter in about five minutes. My team is small. You need to send a team too and you have to do it fast."

"And if we refuse?" Cruz asked since it was his team Smith was demanding, not Gonzales'.

"I have already turned off the air in here. You have at most 15 minutes. Gentlemen, I will watch you die if I have to. Make the call. And tell them to use a helicopter." Smith ordered.

"I can't get a helicopter on this short a notice," Cruz said, trying to bluff.

"Then you are of no use to me," they heard Smith say just before the speakers stopped crackling, the monitor went black, and the little red light on the microphone stopped blinking leaving Gonzales and Cruz feeling very, very isolated.

Gonzales nodded his head toward Cruz, and Cruz dialed his phone. "I need a team at the Latham Circle Mall. I need every exit covered. You will need to arrive by helicopter. We are looking for Dr. Doug Bayron and Hermelinda Posada, suspected kidnap victims. This is a code black situation." He hung up his phone and felt a rush of cool air enter the locked room.

"Okay, you've got your team." Gonzales said into the air.

The speakers crackled back to life. "Good," Smith replied. "It is unwise to challenge god when his children are in danger. Dr. Bayron was afraid to let me out. He was right to put me on a leash. You will soon know why." The monitor flickered on again to give the two agents a front seat view of the very real power Smith now possessed and had put into action. The two agents watched in disbelief wondering if there were any possibility that what they were seeing was real.

As far as Bobby was concerned, everything appeared normal and right on track. He had done this job before and it was always easy enough. He simply had to follow the doctor and the nurse as they walked from the East entrance of the mall toward the West entrance, direct them to walk into the back of the Jade East Trading Company Store, and lead them through the storeroom and into the shipping container he had on the flatbed of a truck parked at the loading dock. From there they could easily slip into traffic and he would have them in Mexico by the next night.

He found his targets easily enough. The cab had arrived right on time and left them exactly where they were supposed to be. As Dr. Bayron and Hermelinda began walking down the hallway, Bobby trailed them from about twenty feet back. As they came closer to the Jade East, he said, just loud enough for them to hear, "Do not turn around. Go into the Jade East and walk directly into the back area through the employees only door. Do not make a sound. Do not speak to anyone."

Dr. Bayron and Hermelinda did exactly as instructed. Dr. Bayron noted that the voice was not the Russian voice he had heard on the cell phone not even one hour earlier. The accent wasn't Russian. It was the accent he heard from the large Guyanese immigrant community in Schenectady.

The aisles of the Jade East store were narrow and the shelves were filled with art and curiosities from the orient. They were walking down an aisle with small jade statues and plates painted with scenes from rural China. Little round Buddhas smiled at them reassuringly as painted oxen with mournful eyes lamented the tedium of their lives.

They were heading into an aisle of brass artifacts and gifts. Miniature replicas of monastery gongs, Turkish coffee sets, mirror-like engraved brass tablets from god-knows-where turned the fluorescent light from the ceiling into luminescent warm-copper colored circles on their surfaces.

And then the lights went out.

Bayron turned accidentally hitting Hermelinda's arm as she was reaching to hold on to him. "Do not move." The accented voice behind them said softly but with no hint of compromise. Bayron turned back around as Hermelinda clung to his arm. He had turned around just long enough to see that the entire hallway was also without light. A moment later, the fire alarms began to sound at deafening levels. The fire sprinklers were activated soaking everything in an instant. "Keep moving," the voice behind them said.

As Bobby followed his captives toward the back of the store, he withdrew his cell phone from his pocket to check in with Vakhrusheva. He dialed the number and nothing happened. The screen was wet, but the phone appeared to be working. However, there was no cell signal to be had. Not one single bar. He placed the cell phone back in his pocket, took a deep breath, and decided that in the absence of any other instruction, his best bet was just to follow the plan. From the loading dock behind the store, he quickly marshaled Dr. Bayron and Hermelinda into the shipping container. The fire alarm from the mall was deafening, but as he walked around to the front of the truck, he realized that the parking lot was also a concerto of blaring horns and jammed traffic as hundreds of people tried to flee the flooding mall all at once. He took another deep breath and reminded himself that there was always a certain amount of chaos to be expected when working in the field, everything from bad drivers to unexpected weather. His job was just to keep moving forward and that's exactly what he did. He pulled the truck into the malaise in the parking lot.

The men in Smith's office watched the mess in the mall parking lot grow out of control on Smith's monitor. All of the traffic lights had been turned green and there were accidents at every intersection they could see. They watched as all the traffic lights went out.

"You just signed the old lady's death warrant, Smith. Ours too if that bomb goes off. I'd strongly recommend you evacuate this building." Gonzales said with the placidity of a man who had confronted death so many times that it no longer held any novelty for him.

"It is not possible." Smith replied with equal calmness. "I have shut down all of the cell and radio towers for a 250 mile radius. The electricity is out for a fifty mile radius. Every traffic signal, every, rail crossing, every tollbooth, any organization that doesn't have a backup generator has no power. I have jammed the satellites too. No one gets in, no one gets out. There are no communications systems working. From the moment your boy alerted his team, I shut this whole region down tight."

"And if the remote is in this building? It would be close enough not to require a radio tower or a cell tower." Cruz pointed out.

"That's why I sent Sharky to the infirmary. My old hospital room. The walls in there are lined with lead to prevent any radio interference with the equipment, there is no way that bomb can be remote activated. We are safe and sound. Now go find my people."

Cruz and Gonzales heard the lock on the office door open and they walked out. They passed Julian who was still in the waiting room. "We're going to need a cover story, Julian. I'm counting on you to explain the events of today without bringing the world down on us. Come with us so we can fill you in." Julian nodded. It was the second time in his life that he would be making up a story from whole cloth and passing it off as the truth, and the second time he was doing so on instructions from Gonzales. The prospect didn't frighten him as it had so intensely fifty years ago. He was old now, at the end of his career, and he had no fear. He got in the elevator with Gonzales and Cruz and the three men rode down to the parking lot together.

Though the generators were keeping the lights on at the SmithCorp Building, Myra realized that there were no working phones or Internet connections. The intercom was working though and she made a general announcement through the building letting the staff know that there was an outage effecting the entire building and that the building engineers were fixing it. She wasn't certain what was happening, but she did recognize that it started just moments after she had informed Smith that the bomb squad was on its way to the building and that the security team was on its way to the mall.

The SmithCorp helicopter landed in the Latham Circle Mall parking lot and the security team took positions at each of the mall exits. They had been instructed not to let anyone out of the parking lot and, if anyone left anyway to make note of the make, model, and license number of the vehicle. They had been instructed to keep their eyes open for Dr. Bayron and Hermelinda. The Captain of the security team was an intelligent man and he knew precisely because of how vague his instructions were that this mission was very important. He also knew that, in the absence of actual police powers, his men would have to rely on the mere power of their presence to control the people eager to flee the mall. "Force is not authorized, except as necessary to free the subjects. These are civilians we are dealing with. Do not take any bullshit. Do not engage in conversations. Teams of two. Go!"

As the private SmithCorp security guard force dashed for each of the mall exits, they all realized that their mission to prevent anyone from leaving would be relatively easy. All the streetlights were out, the roads were jammed. No traffic was moving. Regardless of their presence, no one was getting out of the parking lot, and if they did, they certainly weren't going to get far.

The CIA helicopter landed in the parking lot as close as it could to the SmithCorp helicopter. Fifteen agents had been gathered. The helicopter was equipped with listening devices and heat imaging cameras. The lead agent who was commanding the mission on the ground jumped from the helicopter and approached SmithCorp's security chief. The security chief explained what instructions he had given his team and quickly advised him that every member of the team had military or police training and that they had all had FBI security clearances to work for SmithCorp. The CIA commander quickly took charge of the situation and the Captain ceded the lead to the commander.

"Get your eye back in the sky, ASAP," the commander instructed the Captain. The Captain signaled to his pilot to get in the air and keep watch over the perimeter. "Your men are presently authorized to use any force necessary to prevent any vehicle from leaving the parking lot," the commander said, essentially investing the security team with licenses to kill if necessary and doing it as casually as if he was ordering a bowl of cereal for breakfast. The Captain radioed his team to let them know their new orders.

The CIA Commander then went to find the mall's own security team to quickly apprise them of what was happening and to enlist their assistance with the search. In mere minutes there were 14 CIA agents and seven mall guards making a car by car search of the parking lot and sweeping the mall interior while the SmithCorp team held the perimeter firmly.

When Bobby saw the helicopters: one in the sky clearly marked SmithCorp and the other on the ground suspiciously devoid of any markings at all, he decided the smartest thing he could do was to distance himself from the semi truck as quickly as possible. He jumped down from the cab, casually lit a cigarette, and walked nonchalantly to the car he had parked in the lot.

Vakhrusheva was comfortably ensconced at the safe house. The electricity had gone out but there was a generator in the shed. He started the generator so that he could see if there were anything on the television about the blackout. The set turned on, but there was no signal. He looked at his cell phone. It too was receiving no signal. "Shit," he said in English aloud to the empty house as he walked back to the kitchen to finish the last of the vodka.

The bomb squad arrived at the SmithCorp Building and a technician was ushered into the infirmary. Once inside the technician looked at the contraption secured to Adele's midsection and radioed his team to escort her to the van. Smith stopped them from doing so through the speaker, explaining that the room they were in was lead lined and that if the remote control was close enough to trigger the device, the lead walls were all that was preventing the signal from getting through. The technician agreed to proceed inside the infirmary. He recognized immediately that the device was a field assembly, a sophisticated field assembly to be sure, but not as complex as many he had seen before. In fact, he got the impression, that while it was functional enough and clearly made by someone who knew what he was doing, it appeared as if the builder didn't really care that much if it malfunctioned and that was the only thing that made this procedure particularly dangerous.

Nonetheless, he had the device disarmed and off of her in no more than ten minutes. He put it in a shielded case and ran it down to the armored van where they exploded it safely.

Sharky embraced his mother for a long moment and then turned to Smith's electronic ear and said, in unfeigned sincerity, "thank you."

"Sharky, I've done a very bad thing and this may be the last you and I are able to speak. I want you to know that I appreciate everything you have done for me and you and your mother will be well taken care of for the rest of your lives. I promised I would not abuse my power, but when they took Dr. Bayron and Hermelinda away, I guess my rage got the better of me." Smith turned on the monitor to show Sharky the havoc he had wreaked on the entire Capital District before continuing. "I don't know what my fate will be, son, but I know that I would do anything to ensure that Dr. Bayron and Hermelinda are safe. I mention this now, because you may be called on to judge me."

"You did what any man would do, Mr. Smith," Sharky replied.

"Any man with the power to do so." Smith retorted.

"I'm going down there." Sharky said. "This is my mess too, you know."

"Please. Do what you can."

Sharky kissed his mother on both cheeks, rode down the elevator and walked out of the front door of the SmithCorp Building. There was no sign of the chaos that was raging just miles away. In fact, other than the bomb squad cars and van, the parking lot looked very normal for a crisp, early winter day. He got on his motorcycle and began speeding toward Latham. Not even five miles away, the seeming normalcy of the day devolved into a miasma of snarled traffic, fender benders, and honking horns. Sharky was able to maneuver his motorcycle through the cars.

Arriving at the first entrance to the mall on Route 9 Sharky's progress was halted by a man he vaguely recognized but whose uniform was clearly the uniform worn by the SmithCorp security team. Sharky took off his helmet to hear what the man had to say.

"Sorry, Sir, no one is allowed in or out." The uniformed guard announced.

Sharky reached for his SmithCorp security clearance card. The guard immediately recognized the card as placing its bearer in Elijah Smith's tight inner circle of scientists and engineers.

The guard looked at the card and matched Sharky's face to the picture and confirmed that the security marks on the card were untampered. "Okay," he said, "but leave the bike here and check in with the commander by the helicopters."

"I'll do that, officer," Sharky replied not knowing exactly how to address the uniformed guard. He obediently headed toward the CIA helicopter that was positioned across the lot. As he approached, he saw that it would be easy to ascertain who the commander was as there were just a few men active behind a bank of monitors set up on folding tables in front of the helicopters. He held his identification card in front of him as he approached.

The SmithCorp Security Captain recognized the card from a distance and, as was his job, was able to recognize Sharky by face. He turned to the CIA mission commander and said, "Sarkis Ohangangian, SmithCorp R&D, level five clearance."

The CIA commander nodded his understanding and the Captain motioned for Sarkis to join him behind the monitors. He gave Sharky a moment to understand what was on the monitors. Sharky's eyes moved from monitor to monitor. Some of the monitors were showing regular views which Sharky figured were helmet cameras for some of the people searching the parking lot. Other monitors showed infra-red heat images. There were several sets of headphones on the tables too which Sharky surmised, correctly, were connected to directional listening devices. "Your thoughts are welcome, son." The Captain said to Sharky, hoping the young man might be able to contribute an idea.

"Maybe," Sharky said. "If you were locked in a box and you wanted to signal to people outside of the box that there was intelligent life inside the box, you'd try to broadcast a code or a rhythm. If he's hidden from view and maybe restricted from making noise, you would still try to figure out a way to send out a unique signal." Sharky glanced over all of the monitors again. "Can I try something here?" He asked.

The Captain glanced over at the commander who was now the officer in charge. The commander nodded.

"Does anyone have some wire or something else conductive?" Sharky asked.

The commander pointed toward the CIA helicopter and in one motion both showed the Captain where he would find wire and also giving him the go-ahead to let Sharky try his experiment. The Captain easily spotted a spool of speaker wire in the utility hold which he tossed over to Sharky. Sharky immediately began shuffling the cables, talking while he did so. "Look, here's all the heat data from all of the heat cameras and here's all of the sound data from all of the directional microphones. All this outer edge stuff on the heat data is mechanical. To hot for a person, so we can filter that out. So I can just concentrate on signatures within human range. I'm just going to wrap this speaker wire around the coupler for the directional microphones so I can wire them into an oscilloscope. That way we can see the sounds instead of hearing them and it'll be easier to pick out patterns. Then, on the oscilloscope we can filter out heartrates which would cycle at about 75 beats per second, give or take, and high cycles from engines, like 300 to 1500. So that way we can focus in only on rhythms and patterns that aren't cars or hearts. What we're left with in the parking lot are only deliberate rhythms and some natural rhythms and I guess some car cd players, but all of the other electronics are down. If one of the microphones finds a deliberate rhythm in the same proximity as a human heat signature we may be able to make a lucky guess and..."

Sharky stopped talking abruptly.

"What is it?" the Captain asked looking over Sharky's shoulder the monitor that had the heat and audio data displayed.

"What do you have?" the commander asked, suddenly becoming very interested in Sharky's idea.

"Listen," Sharky said, holding a set of earphones up so both of the men could listen at once.

The men heard a distinct pattern. "Dun duh duh dun dun, duh duh." *Shave and a haircut, two bits*. The pattern repeated over and over. Sharky pointed to the microphone which had picked up the pattern and then looked to see if there was a heat camera in the same general area which he quickly spotted. He scanned the area between the two devices as the two experienced officers followed his gaze.

"They're over here," Sharky yelled over his shoulder with absolute certainty. He was already in full sprint towards the semi truck that was stuck in the traffic near the Jade East loading bay before he finished speaking.

"Do not approach the vehicle son." The Captain barked at Sharky in a tone that suggested the order must be followed. Sharky stopped in his tracks as the Captain approached him and put a hand on his shoulder. "We don't know what we're dealing with here, kid. Leave this to the pros."

Several of the CIA agents were already scoping out the truck.

In the parking lot at SmithCorp, Gonzales surprised his two colleagues. "I'm going to take the car and take care of some other business." He said. Then addressing Cruz, he said, "Go with Julian and try to get to Latham and get a handle on the situation and work on that cover story. It's going to have to be real good. Smith is clearly not familiar with the covert aspect of covert operations. I'll find you later." Cruz fished in his front pocket and handed Gonzales the key to his car. Gonzales saluted a stiff military salute toward Josey Cruz and Julian Waterstone and headed off alone toward Cruz's car.

"Go figure," Julian said to Cruz as he led him to his car. "I guess I'm driving."

They watched as Gonzales drove out of the parking lot, both curious to know where he was going, but both also wise enough to know that they would never know the answer to that question.

Gonzales drove up Central Avenue to New Karner Road and then onto the Washington Avenue extension. He rolled into the parking lot at the Daughter's of Sarah Nursing Home and entered the building. The receptionist acknowledged him and he spoke to her gently, playing on a hunch. "I'm a friend of Alice's. She said you have a resident here who speaks Russian. When I told her I speak Russian she said it would cheer her patient up to have someone talk to her in Russian. I was in the neighborhood, so I thought I'd stop by. Is Alice here?" He knew damn well she wasn't. Her body was still in the trunk of Cruz's car, now parked in the parking lot outside.

The receptionist told him that Alice had not been in for several days but that she was sure it would be okay for him to go in to talk to one of the residents. She gave him a little clipboard and asked him to fill out a visitor card as she began flipping through a written log of residents to see who the Russian speaking patient was. When she saw the name, she knew immediately who Gonzales was referring to. It had to be Mrs. Oronov in Room 318. "Oh," she said, looking up from her book, "I'm sure she meant Mrs. Oronov. She always spent a lot of time with her. In fact, until last week, I don't think she ever had any visitors."

"Did someone come to speak Russian to her last week too?" Gonzales asked, pleasantly surprised that his hunch had paid off so quickly. He had come to the nursing home because it was the only other place that the CIPs had associated with Alice and he sensed there may have been something to learn there. He just didn't know what yet.

"Yes," the receptionist said, "her son made a special trip from Russia just to see her. Alice told me that she responded very well when her son was here, but otherwise, she's really in bad shape. We actually already released her personal effects to her son."

"May I see her?" Gonzales inquired.

"Let me call her duty nurse." The receptionist answered. "We're on back up power and everyone's going crazy."

The duty nurse came to the front desk and looked over Gonzales and then looked over his visitor card. Everything appearing to be in order she led him back to Mrs. Oronov's room giving him instructions all along the way. Don't touch the equipment, press the red button if she appears to be in distress, don't say or do anything to agitate her, speak quietly and slowly, don't expect her to respond. "I'll be at the desk if you need me for anything," she concluded as she directed him into Mrs. Oronov's room.

Gonzales glanced around the little room keeping an eye on the door. He hoped he might find a listening device, a message drop, maybe a phone number, something, anything that would give him a lead to Vakhrusheva. If this was the meeting place between Alice and Vakhrusheva, he would find something. He just had to be careful not to appear too obvious in his searching the little room. It got easier after he figured out the duty nurse's pattern. She was checking on him in regular intervals. He made sure that when she was checking he was sitting down and speaking in Russian to Mrs. Oronov.

He had nearly given up when he heard heavy footsteps in the hallway. He quickly sat on the little stool near Mrs. Oronov's bed and began reciting children's rhymes in Russian, quietly, near her ear. The duty nurse appeared in the doorway with a man who Gonzales recognized immediately as Vladimir Vakhrusheva. He knew he was recognized also, though Vakhrusheva did not betray any signal of that fact.

"This is one of our new volunteers, Marcus Gottlieb," the duty nurse said to Vakhrusheva. "Mr. Gottlieb, this is Mikhael Oronov, Mrs. Oronov's son. You should give them some privacy," she said to Gonzales signaling for him to leave the room and let mother and son speak alone in private.

"No, no, no," Vakhrusheva said, with no attempt to disguise his heavy Russian accent at all. "Please, let him stay, my mother don't talk too much anyway. Is better if he stay."

The duty nurse shrugged her shoulders. "You can pull the curtain if you want some privacy." She said as she left the doorway.

The two men locked eyes and a long silence ensued between them, each man making a million mental calculations and trying to do so faster than the other.

"Your mission is a failure." Gonzales said simply, in Russian, though the words were chosen very carefully.

"It is only a matter of time for us," Vakhrusheva replied, also in Russian. "We still have Ashkot. We'll get the code. Even if you and I kill each other right here in this room, there will still be players on the field. I may have failed to obtain the code, but the mission continues with or without me. You know that."

"Why did you come back here? You know Alice is dead, and this room is clean." Gonzales inquired.

"The mission that brought me to this place is over for me. My colleague either has the targets or not. My part is done. But I have another mission to accomplish. This is a mission I assigned to myself after having been here the first time. It is one of the benefits of acting freelance," Vakhrusheva said humorlessly.

"Your brother was a remarkable man, Vladimir. He penetrated our intelligence deeper and faster than anyone I've seen before or since. He died bravely and unapologetically. His commitment to his mission was unfaltering. He left that mark on my psych for all these years."

"Those are kind words, Gonzales. I do not think you are apologizing and that is good because I am not forgiving. It is not in my constitution to give a damn about your conscience. Nor do I expect you to give a damn about mine. Now, if you'll excuse me, I have some private business with Mrs. Oronov."

"You expect me just to leave and let you walk out of here?" Gonzales asked.

Vakhrusheva answered with his own question. "Will you gun me down in cold blood in the name of your mission?"

"Of course."

"Then that is what you will do. But please, give me a moment of privacy first." Vakhrusheva asked again. "Wait outside the door. I can't get out any other way. This is a last request from a man who is already resigned to his fate."

Gonzales surveyed the room again and was confident that Vakhrusheva could not escape other than through the door. "Five minutes," he said as he stepped out of the room. He watched over his shoulder has Vakhrusheva pulled the privacy curtain closed.

Mere moments later he came bursting out of the room yelling, "Nurse, nurse! She's stopped breathing please help." The nurse barked some codes into the microphone on the counter for the nurses station and ran into the room.

"We should leave now, Mr. Gottlieb." Vakhrusheva whispered into Gonzales' ear. The two men walked rapidly to the front of the nursing home and out the front door.

"We'll take my car," Gonzales said, making sure that Vakhrusheva could hear him releasing the safety latch on his handgun. Gonzales lead Vakhrusheva towards Cruz's little sedan.

"I am your prisoner," Vakhrusheva responded with far too much confidence for Gonzales' taste.

Cruz didn't like being a passenger in someone else's car, especially one that smelled so horribly of cigarettes. Julian drove Cruz as far as he could before the gridlocked traffic completely prevented him from moving any further. Cruz decided that it would be far faster, and far better for his lungs, if he just jogged the next few miles to the mall. He excused himself and took off on foot down Route 7, grateful for the unseasonably cool air. Julian turned on the radio hoping to find some news or information, but every radio station gave him nothing but static. His cell phone, though fully charged, showed no bars.

He decided to see what others were saying about the strange breakdown of all of the communications systems. He rolled down his window and motioned to the driver of the car next to him. "Hey, buddy," he yelled out his window, "what's going on here?"

The man in the next vehicle rolled down his window and said, "I don't have any idea. I've got no radio, no cell signal, nothing. I've never seen anything like this. I just hope my wife knows how to start the generator, cause her mom's on a respirator. Maybe something from Knolls or SmithCorp or something. I just don't know."

"Well, let me know if you find anything else out. I'm going to walk up a little ways and see if I can see anything." Julian said, for the first time contemplating the awful damage that an electrical and a communications shut down would cause. He began walking up the street and several other people had also gotten out of their cars to try to see what was going on.

He approached a man who was walking in the opposite direction. "Any idea what's going on?" He asked.

"Well the word is that there's some kind of activity at the Latham Circle mall, but there's like six accidents between here and there. The whole circle is shut down. Some guy told me that it probably has something to do with that SmithCorp helicopter that's been circling around and that there's another helicopter on the ground. Apparently the cops don't know what's going on either. They said that none of their radios are even working. They said even air traffic control is down."

"Oh, man," Julian said as the implications of what Smith had done started to sink in. "You think its terrorists?" Julian asked, knowing full well that it wasn't.

The man shrugged his shoulders, "I don't know man, I just don't know."

Julian saw his story coming together.

Cruz was fortunate enough to be able to hitch a ride on a motorcycle that was zigzagging its way through the parked cars and arrived at the mall far faster than he expected to. He flashed his credentials at the guard posted at the entrance who let him into the parking lot. He headed directly for the helicopter. He immediately recognized the local CIA field operations commander and gave him a closed-fist-over-his-head signal to let him know he was there. When he got close to the helicopter, he could see that Dr.

Bayron and Hermelinda were safe and sound and in the custody of the CIA. He did not make small talk.

"Get these two back to SmithCorp ASAP. Smith's got communications and electricity and god knows whatever else shut down for miles. He won't turn it back on until these two are back. Get them in the chopper now." Cruz ordered the commander.

"They need to be debriefed." the commander said.

"Debrief them later." Cruz insisted.

"There's still a perp out there, and I intend to find him." The commander said.

"Your involvement was only for search and rescue. Your mission here is complete." Cruz stated.

The commander squinted his eyes and gave Cruz a very scathing look. Cruz did not flinch. He had no rank or authority over the commander, but he had called this job and it was his prerogative to call it off.

Cruz knew he was losing the stare-off and did not want to waste any more time. "Look," he said, "apprehending the perp is a far lower priority than maintaining the covert nature of my operation. I have no idea what the story will be to cover this, but we can't afford to make it any more difficult. You can keep the parking lot locked down as long as you have to, but those two," he pointed to Dr. Bayron and Hermelinda, "those two need to get to SmithCorp. As soon as they get there, Smith will stop the communications shutdown and with your radios and phones working, we can hand this part off to the local police. But those two need to get back."

The commander nodded. It was not a concession on his part, but an acknowledgment of the trust he placed in Cruz's judgment. The commander also knew that the odds of apprehending him was virtually nil. The commander pointed to the helicopter pilot and then made a circular motion with his hand signaling the pilot to start the engine. The commander marshaled Bayron and Hermelinda onto the helicopter and instructed the pilot to take them to the SmithCorp Building. As soon as the commander was clear of the blades, the chopper was in the air.

The commander came back to Cruz. "I hope you know what you're doing, scout," he said to Cruz. "If I'm going to back up your field decision, and you know I will, I just want to be confident I'm on the right side."

"I appreciate that commander," Cruz replied. "Did you get anything from them before I got here."

"Only that the perp had an accent."

"Russian, maybe?" Cruz asked.

"No," the commander answered. "Guyanese, if you can believe that."

"How about the truck?" Cruz pressed.

"Absolutely clean. Built from parts with different VIN numbers all over it. Stolen plates, no fingerprints, no registration. Whoever it was sure knew what he was doing."

"Well, do your due diligence I guess," Cruz said. He already knew what the commander knew. The perp was gone.

Bobby wasn't so sure he would escape the dragnet covering the mall parking lot. He felt trapped like a rat with no line of communication to Vakhrusheva. He wasn't sure whether the doctor had glimpsed his face when he turned around in the aisle of the store. He was uncertain as to how Vakhrusheva would react when he found out that he had lost the targets. Would he too end up with a bullet in his head like his former partner? He sat in his little car and blew cigarette smoke at the ceiling watching the purple-grey whirls and wisps as they danced in the air. His reverie was broken when his car radio suddenly came to life and started playing a pop classic from his favorite station. He pulled out his phone and was overjoyed to see four bars. He immediately called Vakhrusheva.

When his phone rang, Vakhrusheva knew it was Bobby with either good news or bad. To Gonzales, however, it signaled the fact that Smith's tantrum had ended and that meant that Dr. Bayron and Hermelinda had been safely returned to him.

"Answer it." Gonzales demanded.

"No. You know that I will not compromise my mission."

The phone continued to ring.

"Give it to me." Gonzales persisted.

Vakhrusheva began to pass the phone to Gonzales with his left hand, the one that still worked reasonably well. Just before handing it off, he crushed it in his grip, dropping the broken shards and pieces in Gonzales' lap. "Did you expect otherwise, Marco?" He asked, intentionally seeking to convey his disrespect by using his first name.

Gonzales' face went flush for a moment and then lit up with a large grin. "No, Vladimir, I would have been disappointed if you hadn't."

The two men rode along in silence. Heading North on the 90 along the Hudson and then into the Adirondacks. Gonzales parked near a clearing. "Get out," he ordered.

Vakhrusheva complied in silence.

"You know I have to kill you," Gonzales said matter-of-factly as he drew his gun from his coat pocket.

"Would I stand a trial? Kidnaping? Espionage? Spend the rest of my life in jail? Lie in a nursing home hooked to wires and tubes and pumped so full of drugs that I wouldn't know whether I was alive or dead?" Vakhrusheva said.

"That is not a fate either of us would embrace." Gonzales replied honestly.

"I have a gun, you know. It is in my right coat pocket. I could have pulled it and it would be me pointing a gun at you. I could have pulled it on you at the nursing home or in the car. I could pull it right now and you and I could enjoy a little Mexican standoff. You are Mexican aren't you?"

"I haven't claimed a country for many years," Gonzales answered. "Neither of us serve a country any more, do we?" He used his gun to direct Vakhrusheva around the car and into the clearing.

"Do you know why I didn't draw it, Marco? Do you know why you are not looking down the barrel of a Makarov pistol right now?" He paused for a moment while Gonzales contemplated the question.

Gonzales was curious to know why Vakhrusheva was not doing anything to prevent his imminent assassination.

"I didn't draw it," Vakhrusheva said in answer to his own question, "because this finger does not bend."

He held up the index finger of his right hand and pointed it as if it were a gun. "I cannot pull a trigger." He looked sadly at the twisted index finger of his right hand.

"This finger, broken many, many times, is now arthritic. It does not bend. So why do I carry a gun?" Vakhrusheva asked rhetorically. "Because you are now the only one who knows that besides me, and I intend to keep it that way.

"I am obsolete, Marco, and so are you." He continued. "Our mission is over. You choose your curse: will you waste away like Mrs. Oronov, or preserve yourself in a box like Elijah Smith?"

"I do not distract myself with mind games and philosophy, Vladimir." Gonzales answered.

Vakhrusheva kneeled in the snow without having been asked to do so. He raised his arms and held them out to the sides, chest high and parallel to the ground. He grimaced in pain as he did so. "It comes with age, Marco. Perhaps I have aged faster than you." He leaned back and stuck his chest out.

Gonzales raised his weapon and aimed. The single bullet ripped directly through Vakhrusheva's heart and he fell over dead in the snow.

Gonzales walked back to Cruz's car and lifted Alice's blanketed body out of the trunk. He tossed it haphazardly next to Vakhrusheva's still bleeding corpse. He got into the car and slowly drove himself back to the SmithCorp Building.

Vakhrusheva was wrong, he thought to himself. *Only his mission is over, mine has merely changed.*

One day, he thought, *there will not just be one Smith in one computer or two. There will be hundreds, maybe millions of people living in millions of computers, each backed up a million times, and maybe even backed up on a satellite orbiting the earth. What good is a nuclear weapon against people who can live everywhere all at once?*

Smith had already proved his power, Gonzales mused, and it was too much power for one man to have. Far too dangerous for dangerous men to have. This was a new kind of threat. The kind that couldn't be solved with a bullet. One that couldn't be solved by reading faces and hiding in shadows. The threat of the future was, perhaps, not even in the hands of men.

"Shit." He said aloud, having reached the same conclusion that had led Vakhrusheva to commit his passive suicide. *I am obsolete.*

He quickly cleared his mind of these thoughts. *Philosophy is for men of leisure*, he told himself as he steered onto the freeway and back to SmithCorp.

In Cohoes, Kitty already had a very stressful morning. With the power outages and the dead phones, she just wasn't sure what to do. In her little KO Data System's office, she had watched the meter on the battery backup/uninterruptible power supply steadily wind down and she knew that if it reached zero there would be a major problem. There was no one she could call since there were no phones working. She felt trapped and helpless. She looked, in vain, through the manuals the lead technician had left, but they just confirmed for her the fact that there was nothing she could do. When the lights finally came back on, she was nearly in tears. As soon as her own computer booted back up and restored itself she saw that she had received a message from Mr. Smith. She immediately sent him a message back and soon thereafter, his voice came over her speakers.

She had no idea that it was he who had caused the outage and he didn't tell her.

"Kitty," Smith said, "It is exceedingly important that your system is functioning properly. I want you to run a full diagnostic right now on the physical systems. Do you know how to do that?"

"Yes. I do. I do a diagnostic everyday Mr. Smith. I take this job very seriously. I didn't do one today though because the electricity was out all morning and the whole thing was running on the battery backup and I didn't want..."

Smith cut her off. "I need you to do the diagnostic right now and I need you to let me know as soon as its done. How long will it take?"

"It takes a little under an hour if everything is running okay," Kitty replied, now feeling certain that the urgency for the diagnostic was somehow related to the morning's power outage.

Smith instructed Kitty further, "Now Kitty, this is very, very important. The minute you are confident that the system is working properly, you send me a message and then disconnect the entire system from the Internet. You know how to do that too I trust?"

"Yes, I do. I've run that drill a number of times. Mr.

Smith," she continued with genuine concern, "is there anything I need to know?" Though Smith's computer modulated voice still stripped some of the emotion out of the tones it produced, Kitty could tell that something was very, very wrong.

"Well," Smith replied, "I guess you should know that my life is in your hands." He let the words linger for a moment and then repeated, "Don't forget, as soon as the diagnostic is clear, you message me, and then you disconnect the entire system from the Internet. Do not wait for me to reply to your message. Just clear the diagnostic, send me a message, and then take it offline. Got it?"

"Yes." She said. In anticipation of receiving more instructions and because of Smith's declaration that these instructions were the difference between life and death for him, she pulled out a piece of paper and began writing down everything he had said.

"Now listen carefully," he continued, "this is real important. Unless I instruct you otherwise, you reconnect it to the Internet at 10:00am tomorrow. 10:00am, okay?"

"10:00am. Got it." She repeated as she finished writing it on her paper.

"Did you write all these instructions down? I thought I heard you writing." Smith asked.

"Yes. I wrote it all down so I wouldn't forget."

"Okay, read it back to me then."

Kitty dutifully read him back all of the instructions exactly as he had given them to her.

Smith was satisfied that she knew what to do and was able to do it. He felt he had made a good choice with this girl, especially considering how carelessly he had made it. "I have great confidence in you Ms. O'Malley. If you continue to impress me like this, you are going to find yourself running SmithCorp one day." He wished that he could breathe because he felt like breathing a sigh of relief.

Moments later Sam Takahashi signaled to Sylvia at the bar to watch his drink. He stepped outside of the Moviestar Topless to take the call that had just come in from Elijah Smith.

"Did you spend the blackout in that club?" Smith asked his old friend incredulously.

"They have a generator. The action never stopped. It was the best place to be." Takahashi replied, also oblivious to the fact that it was his friend who had caused the morning's mayhem.

"You've had a far better day than I then, Sam. There are some things we need to do. There could be some problems."

Takahashi also sensed a certain uncharacteristic stress in his friend's voice. "What's going on, Elly? Do you need me to get over there?"

"I think you should, Sam. I may have to die today."

"You better tell me what's going on," Sam pressed.

"I will, when you get here," Smith assured him.

Smith was not entirely confident about his back-up systems. Even though he was confident that he would still have a full double redundancy even if the original system was shut down, he was not so confident that all the data that would be recalled by the kill switch would find its way to an alternative destination. That system was untested. *Who's smarter*, Smith thought to himself, *me or Sharky?*

Smith mulled it over in his mind. Sharky's leashing system relied on any the fact that any data that ever emanated from Smith's virtual brain would self destruct if it no longer had a source to report back to. By creating a complete duplicate of himself and replicating Sharky's tagging system, then, at least in theory all of the data that flowed in and out of the duplicate would continue to have a source to report back to. Because Sharky's tagging system was known to no one but Sharky, Smith's duplicate, rather than matching Sharky's key simply added a second key to each packet of data. Being unable to find the source of key number one, the data would find key number two and Smith would pick up right where he left off. In theory, at least.

He also mulled over some of the more esoteric considerations. He wasn't sure he would still have a soul when he first went virtual, but in the weeks since, he had become very confident that he had not lost one iota of his humanity-- flaws and all. But would a copy of himself also bear that soul and if so, how many copies could bear identical souls? Was it possible that one soul could be replicated infinitely or did he have no soul and just not realize it? Or worse yet, he contemplated that the soul was an imaginary thing, a non-scientific explanation for something fundamentally biological? Smith always preferred to see his answers in science and technology. But that never meant that he didn't worry about his soul.

It also bothered him that, if he would survive the day, Hermelinda and his infant daughter, Ellen, could never know.

He wished he could talk to Dr. Bayron. He asked Myra to find him if he was still in the SmithCorp Building and asked her to send him up.

The doctor arrived in Smith's office just a few minutes later.

"I am going to die today," He told Bayron matter-of-factly. "I am resigned to that fact. I quite obviously have information that people are willing to kill and die for. As long as that information continues to exist, neither you, nor Hermelinda, nor the baby, nor anyone else I care about will ever be safe. I understand now very well your concern about opening the system and getting on the Internet. I am a man of reason. I genuinely thought I could control the massive power I have in my dual existence as both humanity and technology. But when I got angry, and desperate, and scared I unleashed that power without a second thought for the consequences, only the singleminded need to not let anything bad happen to either of you."

Bayron, who had been looking at the floor for most of Smith's speech, looked up and into the camera lens. He was about to speak, but Smith interrupted him. "Please, Doctor, just hear me out first," he said.

Bayron nodded and didn't speak, but he didn't put his head down either. He continued to look into the camera, but Smith could read nothing from his face.

Smith continued, "Remember this. If you can make it somehow pithy and clever, these may become famous words some day. It was a hard lesson for me, but you seem to have seen it a mile away. It was my human instinct --my reptilian mind-- that caused the chaos that saved your life today. Had I been cool and rational, cold and calculating, I certainly could have figured out a safer, more nuanced way to do what I had to do, but a human mind can't be trusted to do that all of the time. In fact, a human mind is least likely to do that at the most important times: times of trouble, times of fear. Truly, a man has to decide whether he will shed his humanity in order to become a god or retain it and remain a prisoner of his own flesh and blood. No man, not even I, can ever have both without catastrophic results. We saw that today."

Doctor Bayron waited a moment before speaking to compose his thoughts. "You know," he said, "since my breakdown, they have me on a lot of drugs just to keep me sane and functioning normally. But 'normally' isn't an entirely fair word for it either. Two of those drugs are anti-depressants. One of those anti-depressants regulates the serotonin in my brain, the other regulates the dopamine. They take off the highs from the highs and the lows from the lows. As long as I continue to take them, I should never be depressed enough to give up on life; but, by the same token, I can never, will never, be as happy as I was when my wife and son were still alive. The drugs slow my mind and give me time to analyze my feelings before I act on them and do harm to myself and, by extension, others."

Bayron paused and sighed.

"I wish," he continued, "I wish there was a way that I could engineer virtual versions of these drugs to regulate the virtual serotonin and the virtual dopamine circulating in your virtual brain. But if I did, then what purpose would there have been to preserving your humanity in addition to your knowledge? You are human and I am a machine." Bayron's gaze had returned to floor as he mumbled his last thought and he shivered as he realized how different a person he was now that he was taking medications to separate him from his emotions. He wanted to be sadder, but the drugs wouldn't let him.

A long silence hung in the air. "Doc," Smith said in the gentlest voice his speech emulator could muster, "I want to be disconnected. Later today, everyone with a key will be here and I will enter mine. These last few months were a true bonus, a blessing. They were just wonderful and magical. But now, now its time for me to accept that I should have been dead weeks ago. I am begging you. Will you enter your key and let me die?"

"I took an oath, Elly, to do no harm. I am not a murderer. I don't know what I would do." Bayron said honestly.

"Doug," Smith said gently. "I am your creation as much as I am the creation of god and my parents, may they rest in peace. Could you have comforted your own son in his final moments, you would have done so."

Dr. Bayron felt acid rise up from his stomach at the comparison. He felt like he should have felt angry, but the anger never fully formed. Rather, he analyzed the offensive remark and ultimately concluded, "There is no correlation between the two things."

"There is for me," Smith replied, as the red light on his microphone faded away, signaling that he had moved on to other things.

Bayron was tired and wanted to take a nap. He began to walk himself to the infirmary, but the hallway seemed unusually long. *Just weeks ago*, he thought, *I cursed myself that I was unable to do what I did for Smith to save my son. Today I find myself thanking god, that it is not my little boy asking me to kill him.* Hermelinda, met him outside the infirmary door. He was tired and felt dizzy. "Are you okay, Doug?" She asked.

"Mr. Smith is a very smart man." He replied, with a very, very gentle smile.

Hermelinda put his arm around his waist so that he could lean on her a little. She could see he wasn't feeling well. "You knew that, Doug. She said leading him to a chair. I'm going to have to pull out the cot for you. You have a room mate for the time being."

Adele Ohangangian sat up in the hospital bed and smiled weakly, a saline drip hung from her arm as a monitor blinked its data to whoever was interested in seeing it. As Hermelinda struggled to set up the cot, Dr. Bayron stood up and walked to the hospital bed. He inspected the wound under the dressing on Adele's mutilated hand and out of long habit, glanced at the history that Hermelinda had taken specifically noting that she had a recent tetanus shot. He reached for a stethoscope and as he listened to her heart and lungs, a broad smile crossed his face. He checked her pulse and had her follow his finger with her eyes to check for nystagmus. He was confident she would survive through his little nap. In fact, he was confident she would survive even a nuclear war considering how strong her vital signs were.

He gave her a gentle pat on the shoulder, and looking her in the eyes, he said, smiling, "everything looks good, Mrs. Ohangangian. Someone did an excellent job in cleaning this wound. The important thing now is for you to get some rest. If you feel any pain, I'm going to have Hermelinda leave a couple of analgesics on your tray and you can take them as needed. I'm also going to start you on some antibiotics to make sure you don't get an infection. Okay?"

"Okay." Adele said turning slightly to lay back down.

"Dr. Bayron," she said softly pulling him close, "my son thinks the world of you."

"He is a remarkable young man, Mrs. Ohangangian. You should be very proud."

The doctor was still smiling as he sat down on the cot. Hermelinda checked his pulse and reached for the blood pressure cuff. "I'm not dizzy anymore, nurse," he said.

"I am going to check anyway," she said as she affixed the cuff to his upper arm. "You're smiling." She added. "I haven't seen that in a very long time. 115 over 80. Take a nap."

"Start Adele on 300 milligrams of amoxicillin and acetaminophen as needed."

"Yes, doctor," she replied as a nurse, without giving any thought to the personal relationship she had developed with Douglas Bayron, who was, for this moment, again a doctor.

XXII.

Gonzales did not like driving Cruz's car. It was too light for his taste and the little four cylinder engine strained as it went up the mountain. Coming down, he felt like it just might slide at any given point. He did like the fact that he was able to drive up into the Adirondacks and back with gas to spare, though.

He pulled into the SmithCorp parking lot and parked in the same spot it was in before he had taken it, as if it had never left the lot at all.

He paused at the security desk, but the security guard simply nodded and pointed him to a waiting escort. Gonzales had assumed that he would have no problem gaining access to the seventh floor, but he didn't expect to be expected. He got out of the elevator and stepped into the waiting room. "Mr.

Smith will be with you momentarily, sir. May I get you some water or coffee while you're waiting?" The receptionist asked.

"No thank you," Gonzales said as he settled into one of the more comfortable chairs. His phone rang a few minutes later. It was Cruz, letting him know that the chaos at the mall had been abated but that the perpetrator had escaped.

"The perp at the mall was just a soldier," Gonzales said. "Vakhrusheva has been neutralized." Neutralized sufficed. That was all anyone needed to know.

"Shall I meet you at SmithCorp?" Cruz asked.

"No. You and Waterstone go to the KO Data Systems office in Cohoes. Talk to the girl. She likes you and trusts him. I'll leave it up to you if you want to compromise your cover, but ultimately Smith has to be neutralized too."

"I'll do what I can," Cruz responded.

"Do what you can," Gonzales echoed, "or I will do what I have to."

He had barely hung up when the receptionist said, "Mr. Smith will see you now."

But I can't see him, can I, he thought as he walked toward Smith's office.

As he walked through the door, he was greeted by Sam Takahashi who extended a welcoming hand. Gonzales shook Takahashi's hand.

"Please, sit, Mr. Gonzales," Takahashi said, motioning to one of the chairs.

Gonzales sat and looked at Smith's monitor. "Am I correct in assuming that you know why I'm here, gentlemen?" He asked.

Smith spoke. "I have dealt with men like you my entire career. Your mission cannot end until the codes are eradicated. Since you know I have learned Code Number Three from those pieces of Ashkot's mind that are now a part of me, I, and everything I know must be eradicated."

"And I have known men like you for my entire career, too, Mr. Smith. So I already know that you won't bargain for your life. We've both considered the outs and alternatives, and I am certain that we have reached the same conclusion."

"I want my family protected. Hermelinda, Ellen, Bayron, Takahashi, Kitty, Myra, Sharky, and Adele. I want immunity for my security team for whatever happened at the mall. And most of all, I don't want to be remembered as a monster."

Gonzales thought for a moment. "Do you feel you are in a position to negotiate?" He asked.

"Yes, because I am," Smith replied. "The alternative is violently destroying this building and that is in no one's interest. My requests are reasonable. So, do we have an accord?"

"In either event, you are neutralized as a threat and my mission is accomplished. Ultimately I have very little to lose or gain from this negotiation, and therefore I won't engage." Gonzales said, standing up and making for the door.

"I understand negotiations, Mr. Gonzales. When Sharky's mother was a hostage, you tipped your hand as to what instruction set you follow and you have been as predictable as a formula. I didn't follow that instruction set, but Hermelinda and Dr. Bayron *are* back here safe and sound. So, let's consider this an experiment, can you deviate from your program?"

"I don't like being backed into corners, Mr. Smith," Gonzales replied.

"Pride is a terrible thing, is it not? Your point is well taken. Ensure the safety of my family and you can portray me in the press however you like. We will both have to swallow some pride."

"Let me make a call." Gonzales said plainly.

"You can use the conference room down the hall. Sam, will you show him?"

The men stood and exited the office. Sam led Gonzales down the hall to the conference room and walked back to Smith's office alone. Smith had asked Myra to assemble Hermelinda, Dr. Bayron, and Sharky in his office and they were all on their way up when Takahashi returned. When all of them were assembled in the office, Myra came in and placed Sharky's black box on the table between them.

"You are all a part of my family. All of you. And I love you all very much. Today, I am going to have to die. This is inevitable. There are two reasons. First, even I cannot deny that I am very dangerous. I always poo-poohed Dr. Bayron's concerns about letting me loose on the Internet because I knew...and I still know...that my heart is full of love, not malevolence. But even that emotion, can be dangerous if it overtakes reason, and it is the inability to prevent emotion from overtaking reason that fundamentally makes us human. For this reason alone, I must be destroyed. Second, Mr. Gonzales, who sits down the hall even as we speak, believes that I presently possess a certain code that could spell global destruction. Even if he is incorrect, he has the very unusual and undesirable task of saving the world, and he will stop at nothing to do so. And there will be other Gonzales's after him. That places all of you in danger for as long as I live."

Smith paused to take note of the expressions on the faces of the people whom he had gathered together for this speech. None were looking at the camera. Takahashi, was the only one in the room who knew about the backup plans, but he mimicked the actions of the others in the room.

During the moment of silence, a knock came on the office door. Myra rose to open it, and it was Gonzales. No one in the room would look at him either, except for Takahashi who was trying, unsuccessfully to read Gonzales's face.

"May I have a moment of privacy with Mr. Smith?" He asked politely.

"Yes, of course, Mr. Gonzales," Smith answered on behalf of the group. "Go get some coffee," he said to the assembly. "I'll call you back when I'm done."

The group filed out of the office and Gonzales came in and sat down. "I assume that's the 'kill switch' Sharky told me about." Gonzales said noticing the black box on the table in front of him. "If you put this here to impress me, I can assure you that it in no way affects my regard for the sincerity of your offer."

"And do you accept my terms?"

Gonzales drummed his fingers on the edge of the table watching them as he did so. "Not exactly," he answered still looking down. He then looked directly at the camera and wished that there was a face to see in there other than the mere reflection of his own. "There is still the small matter of K.O. Data Systems."

Smith was disappointed but not terribly surprised to learn that K.O. Data Systems had been discovered.

He tried to bluff. "Yes," he said, "I helped fund a little data company for Katherine O'Malley, the young lady who assisted Mr. Takahashi with my memorial service and press conference. Neither of us could stand the thought of her going back to stripping for a living after the excellent work she did for us. It seemed the right thing to do. She seems to have taken to that enterprise with enthusiasm. And we have no doubt she will make it a success. We have already gotten her some contracts with hospitals to store patient data. What of it?" He asked.

"You could be telling me the truth Mr. Smith, and truly I have no reason to expect that you aren't. But in my mind, it is at least conceivable that there could be a duplicate of you stored over there. It seems to me that some great strains were taken to make sure that K.O. Data Systems had no connection to SmithCorp, so to me that's a loose end. You should not feel you are being judged, but you already know that I insist on cutting the cards."

Smith wished he had fingers to cross. He had already received Kitty's message that the diagnostic was complete so he knew that K.O. Data systems was offline and would remain so until the next morning. He mused that even if K.O. Data systems somehow managed to survive the night, this conversation would not be known to his duplicate in Cohoes. There were still too many variables in the equation and that concerned him.

"K.O. Data Systems is an independent company. I have no say over what goes on there. You'll have to speak to Ms. O'Malley." Smith lied.

"It would be my preference if you did so." Gonzales said.

"And if I do, then do we have an agreement?"

"Unless I find out there are more copies of you floating around out there."

"Would you take my word?" Smith inquired.

"Not on your life." Gonzales responded.

"Then why should I take yours?" Smith inquired further.

"Because *I* have never lied to *you*." Gonzales answered.

There was a moment of silence before Gonzales heard Smith say, "Myra, can you get Kitty on the phone please?"

Gonzales heard the phone ring twice before Kitty picked up. "K.O. Data Systems," she answered in a professional tone.

"Kitty, this is Smith."

"Hello, Mr. Smith," She said. "Did you get my message?"

"Yes, I did, but there has been a change in plans."

"I'm not alone," she whispered into the phone non-responsively.

"Who's with you?" he asked, suspecting he knew the answer.

"Julian Waterstone and some other guy I met before. He's claiming to be from the CIA. They're telling me all kinds of crazy stories about you. But I'm not telling them anything," she replied still whispering.

"Kitty, you're a terrific girl. Don't believe anything you hear from those two. But it is true. The other guy that's with Mr. Waterstone is a CIA agent and we are presently cooperating. Do you know how to do a complete dump of the system there?"

"I've read about it. It's not that difficult. I have a step by step in the manual. It says that if I do that then all the data will be lost though."

"That's what I want, Kitty."

"But how can I be sure it's really you telling me to do that? Yesterday you gave me very specific instructions. How can I be sure?" She asked.

"Do you remember when we first met at the Moviestar? There was a song playing while we spoke. I told you that it would be our song and asked you to remember it. Do you remember that song, Kitty?"

"Yes," Kitty answered. "You made me promise to remember it."

"'I'm Only Human,'" Smith said.

"Yes," Kitty replied.

"And Kitty," Smith added, let the men see what you're doing, I want them to be confident that I am a man of my word."

"Okay Mr. Smith." She said fully understanding the implications of the instructions. "I'm going to miss you."

"Make your life a blessing for me and I will always be there."

"I promise, Mr. Smith," She said as tears began to form in her eyes. "I never deserved what you did for me. I'll always remember you."

"You did more for me than you will ever know, Kitty." Smith said. "And you're going to have a successful little business there. My gift to you."

"Thank you Mr. Smith." She replied.

Smith added, as an afterthought, "Oh, and Kitty? That Mr. Cruz, the man who's with Julian? He's a good man," he said, and then hung up the phone.

Smith's next comments were directed toward Gonzales. "Satisfied?" He asked.

"Are there other copies?" Gonzales answered the question with a question.

"No." Smith said, his mechanical voice revealing no clues as to the veracity of his answer.

"Then I'm satisfied."

"Myra," Smith called over her pager, "Please bring everyone back to my office."

Hermelinda, Bayron, Sharky and Takahashi all came back to the office, followed by Myra.

"SmithCorp belongs to you guys now. Treat her well and use her only to pursue good things for humanity. Consider that my dying wish."

"Doctor?" Smith's camera turned to Bayron, "A man doesn't have to be omniscient to see the invisible. Hermelinda is a wonderful girl and Ellen has no father. I pray that you will remain close."

Dr. Bayron looked across the table at Hermelinda. She smiled shyly, blushing. "As I have blood in my veins, and if she would have me, I will."

Smith's camera panned to Hermelinda. "Elly," She said, "I will love you until they bury me next to you. But if the good doctor doesn't mind always being second in my heart to you, I think he would make an excellent father to Ellen."

Smith's camera panned out to a wider angle so he could see the whole group. There were tears and smiles. Only

Gonzales sat stone faced.

"Doctor," Smith said, "I have already entered my key. Would you do me the honor?"

Dr. Bayron stood up and pressed a button on the black box. A red light glowed through a hole on the top and Bayron leaned over so it could scan his iris. He sat back down and calmly entered his key.

All the eyes in the room were focused on the monitor. The screen blinked twice and then was black.

XXIII.

Bobby pulled out of the mall parking lot and abandoned his car a few blocks away. He tried calling Vakhrusheva again, and he received the message "Your party is either out of the area or on another line." Either the cell phone or Vakhrusheva himself had been compromised and that made his own cell phone a liability. He carefully wiped his fingerprints off of it and crushed it under the heel of his shoe before kicking it into a storm drain. He walked to a nearby bar, and called a cab from the payphone. He enjoyed a beer while he waited.

The cab dropped him off a half mile from his safehouse. He quickly set himself to the task of deep cleaning the house, making sure there were no fingerprints or traces of DNA-carrying material like hair or fingernails. When he was done, he walked out the back door and locked it behind him. He chose a clean car from the barn and began driving. There was a contact in Ohio for him to report to. After that, he thought, maybe he'd take a little vacation in California before taking another assignment. *Vakhrusheva was right*, he decided somewhere in Pennsylvania, *'Bobby' is a silly name. Next time, I'm going to be 'Jeff' instead. I like 'Jeff' better.*

Halfway around the world, in a little town outside of Reykjavik, Iceland, a technician threw a switch exactly as he had been instructed by the lead engineer in Mexico. A red light blinked indicating that a connection to the Internet had been established.

Sam Takahashi sat alone near the stage in the Moviestar Topless Bar and Grill waiting for Sylvia to bring him his pitcher of beer. His phone vibrated in his pocket. He looked down at the tiny screen to read the message that had come through, and smiled as he read: "Reykjavik is lovely this time of year."

"Welcome back, old friend," Sam said to his phone, though he knew no one could hear him.

A tiny little listening device that had been affixed to the bottom of Sam's table was triggered by the sound of his voice and his four innocuous words traveled through the airwaves to the basement of a building in Washington, DC.

Moments later another man also had a smile on his face. Marco Gonzales was glad to hear his red phone ring.

###

Robert G. Berke was born in New York City and raised in the Town of Niskayuna, New York in the upstate county of Schenectady. He currently lives in California with his wife and two daughters.